MARVEL-VERSE
MORBIUS

MARVEL-VERSE
MORBIUS

MARVEL TWO-IN-ONE #15

WRITER: **BILL MANTLO**

PENCILER: **ARVELL JONES**

INKER: **DICK GIORDANO**

COLORIST: **PHIL RACHELSON**

LETTERER: **KAREN MANTLO**

EDITOR: **MARV WOLFMAN**

AMAZING SPIDER-MAN #101-102

WRITER: **ROY THOMAS**

PENCILER: **GIL KANE**

INKER: **FRANK GIACOIA**

LETTERER: **ART SIMEK**

EDITOR: **STAN LEE**

MARVEL-VERSE: MORBIUS. Contains material originally published in magazine form as AMAZING SPIDER-MAN (1963) #101-102, MARVEL TWO-IN-ONE (1974) #15, MORBIUS: BOND OF BLOOD (2021) #1 and SPIDER-MAN FAMILY (2007) #5. First printing 2021. ISBN 978-1-302-93367-8. Published by MARVEL WORLDWIDE, INC., a subsidiary of MARVEL ENTERTAINMENT, LLC. OFFICE OF PUBLICATION: 1290 Avenue of the Americas, New York, NY 10104. © 2021 MARVEL No similarity between any of the names, characters, persons, and/or institutions in this book with those of any living or dead person or institution is intended, and any such similarity which may exist is purely coincidental. **Printed in Canada.** KEVIN FEIGE, Chief Creative Officer; DAN BUCKLEY, President, Marvel Entertainment; JOE QUESADA, EVP & Creative Director; DAVID BOGART, Associate Publisher & SVP of Talent Affairs; TOM BREVOORT, VP, Executive Editor; NICK LOWE, Executive Editor, VP of Content, Digital Publishing; DAVID GABRIEL, VP of Print & Digital Publishing; JEFF YOUNGQUIST, VP of Production & Special Projects; ALEX MORALES, Director of Publishing Operations; DAN EDINGTON, Managing Editor; RICKEY PURDIN, Director of Talent Relations; JENNIFER GRÜNWALD, Senior Editor, Special Projects; SUSAN CRESPI, Production Manager; STAN LEE, Chairman Emeritus. For information regarding advertising in Marvel Comics or on Marvel.com, please contact Vit DeBellis, Custom Solutions & Integrated Advertising Manager, at vdebellis@marvel.com. For Marvel subscription inquiries, please call 888-511-5480. **Manufactured between 10/22/2021 and 11/23/2021 by SOLISCO PRINTERS, SCOTT, QC, CANADA.**

10 9 8 7 6 5 4 3 2 1

SPIDER-MAN FAMILY #5

WRITER: **KEVIN GREVIOUX**
ARTIST: **CLAYTON HENRY**
COLORIST: **LEE LOUGHRIDGE**
LETTERER: **BLAMBOT's NATE PIEKOS**
COVER ART: **TAKESHI MIYAZAWA**
CONSULTING EDITOR: **MARK PANICCIA**
EDITOR: **NATHAN COSBY**

MORBIUS: BOND OF BLOOD

WRITER: **RALPH MACCHIO**
ARTIST: **TOM REILLY**
COLORIST: **CHRIS O'HALLORAN**
LETTERER: **VC's ARIANA MAHER**
COVER ART: **GIUSEPPE CAMUNCOLI &
ERICK ARCINIEGA**
EDITOR: **DANNY KHAZEM**
SUPERVISING EDITOR: **DEVIN LEWIS**
EXECUTIVE EDITOR: **NICK LOWE**

COLLECTION EDITOR: **JENNIFER GRÜNWALD** ASSISTANT EDITOR: **DANIEL KIRCHHOFFER**
ASSISTANT MANAGING EDITOR: **MAIA LOY** ASSISTANT MANAGING EDITOR: **LISA MONTALBANO**
ASSOCIATE MANAGER, DIGITAL ASSETS: **JOE HOCHSTEIN** MASTERWORKS EDITOR: **CORY SEDLMEIER**
VP PRODUCTION & SPECIAL PROJECTS: **JEFF YOUNGQUIST** RESEARCH: **JESS HARROLD**
PRODUCTION: **JOE FRONTIRRE** BOOK DESIGNERS: **STACIE ZUCKER & ADAM DEL RE** WITH **JAY BOWEN**
SVP PRINT, SALES & MARKETING: **DAVID GABRIEL** EDITOR IN CHIEF: **C.B. CEBULSKI**

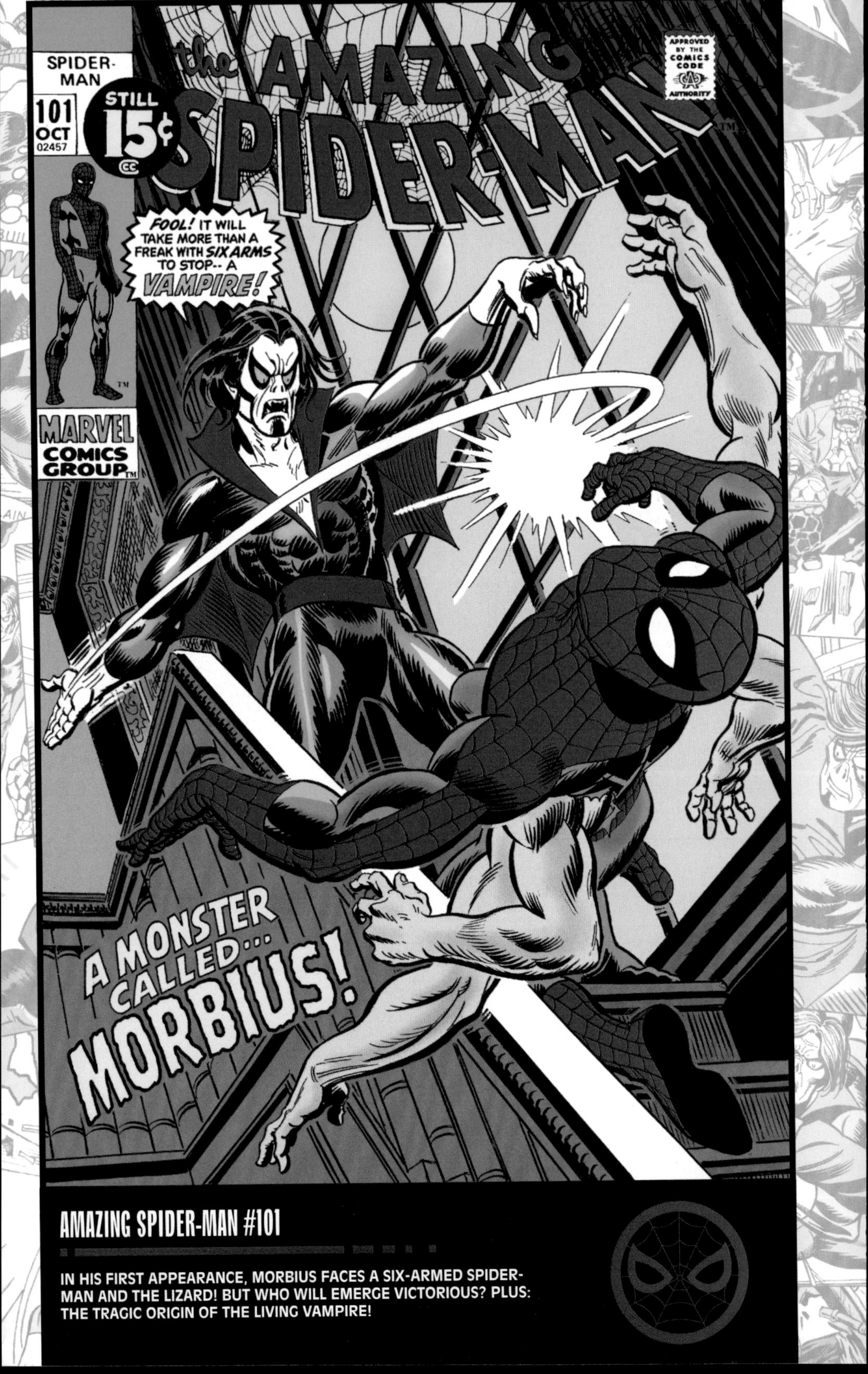

SPIDER-MAN
101
OCT
02457
STILL
15¢
the AMAZING SPIDER-MAN
APPROVED BY THE COMICS CODE AUTHORITY
FOOL! IT WILL TAKE MORE THAN A FREAK WITH SIX ARMS TO STOP-- A VAMPIRE!
MARVEL COMICS GROUP
A MONSTER CALLED... MORBIUS!

AMAZING SPIDER-MAN #101

IN HIS FIRST APPEARANCE, MORBIUS FACES A SIX-ARMED SPIDER-MAN AND THE LIZARD! BUT WHO WILL EMERGE VICTORIOUS? PLUS: THE TRAGIC ORIGIN OF THE LIVING VAMPIRE!

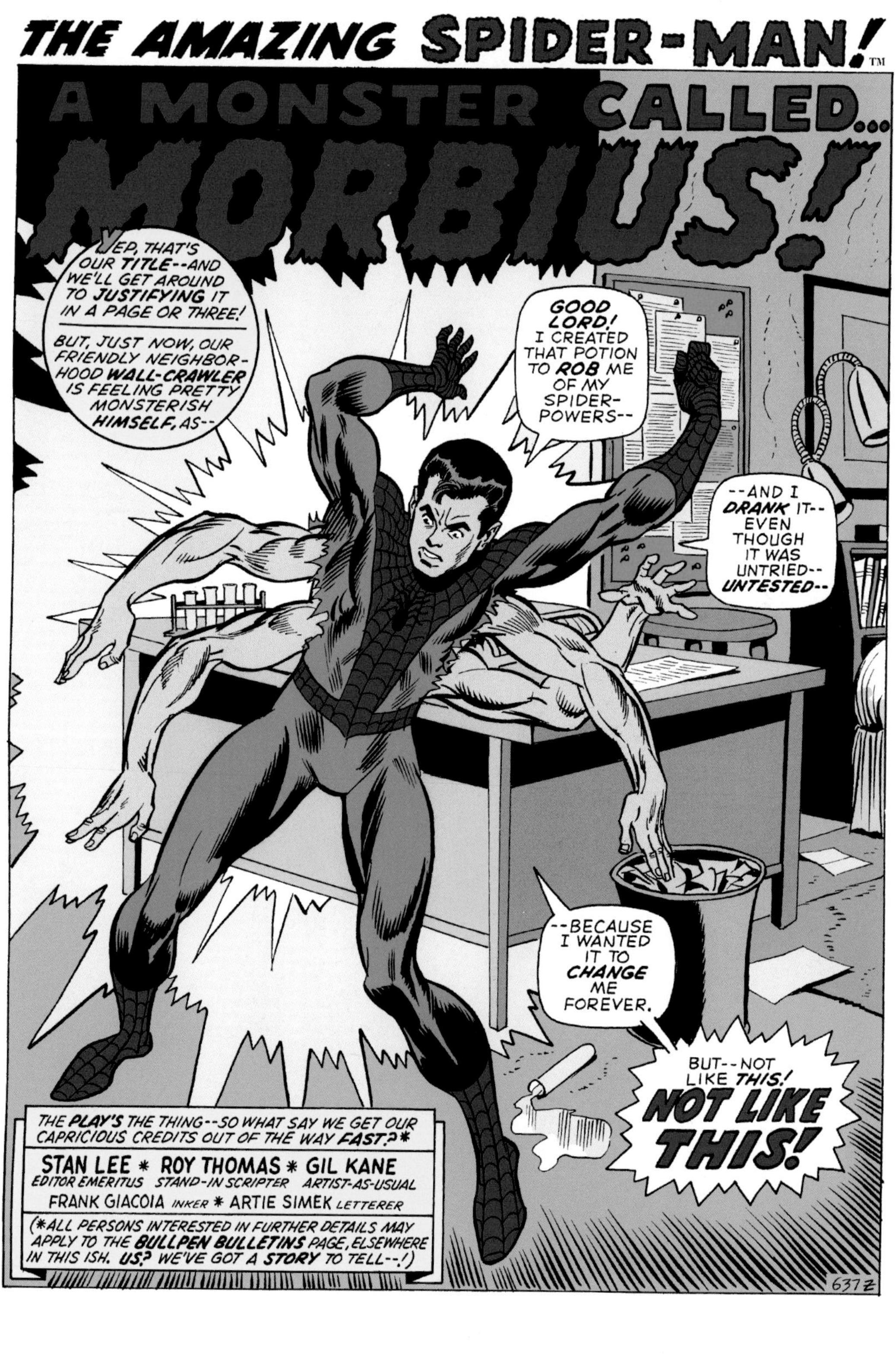

THE AMAZING SPIDER-MAN!
A MONSTER CALLED... MORBIUS!
YEP, THAT'S OUR TITLE--AND WE'LL GET AROUND TO JUSTIFYING IT IN A PAGE OR THREE!
BUT, JUST NOW, OUR FRIENDLY NEIGHBOR-HOOD WALL-CRAWLER IS FEELING PRETTY MONSTERISH HIMSELF, AS--
GOOD LORD! I CREATED THAT POTION TO ROB ME OF MY SPIDER-POWERS--
--AND I DRANK IT--EVEN THOUGH IT WAS UNTRIED--UNTESTED--
--BECAUSE I WANTED IT TO CHANGE ME FOREVER.
BUT--NOT LIKE THIS! NOT LIKE THIS!
THE PLAY'S THE THING--SO WHAT SAY WE GET OUR CAPRICIOUS CREDITS OUT OF THE WAY FAST?*
STAN LEE * ROY THOMAS * GIL KANE
EDITOR EMERITUS STAND-IN SCRIPTER ARTIST-AS-USUAL
FRANK GIACOIA INKER * ARTIE SIMEK LETTERER
(*ALL PERSONS INTERESTED IN FURTHER DETAILS MAY APPLY TO THE BULLPEN BULLETINS PAGE, ELSEWHERE IN THIS ISH. US? WE'VE GOT A STORY TO TELL--!)
637 Z

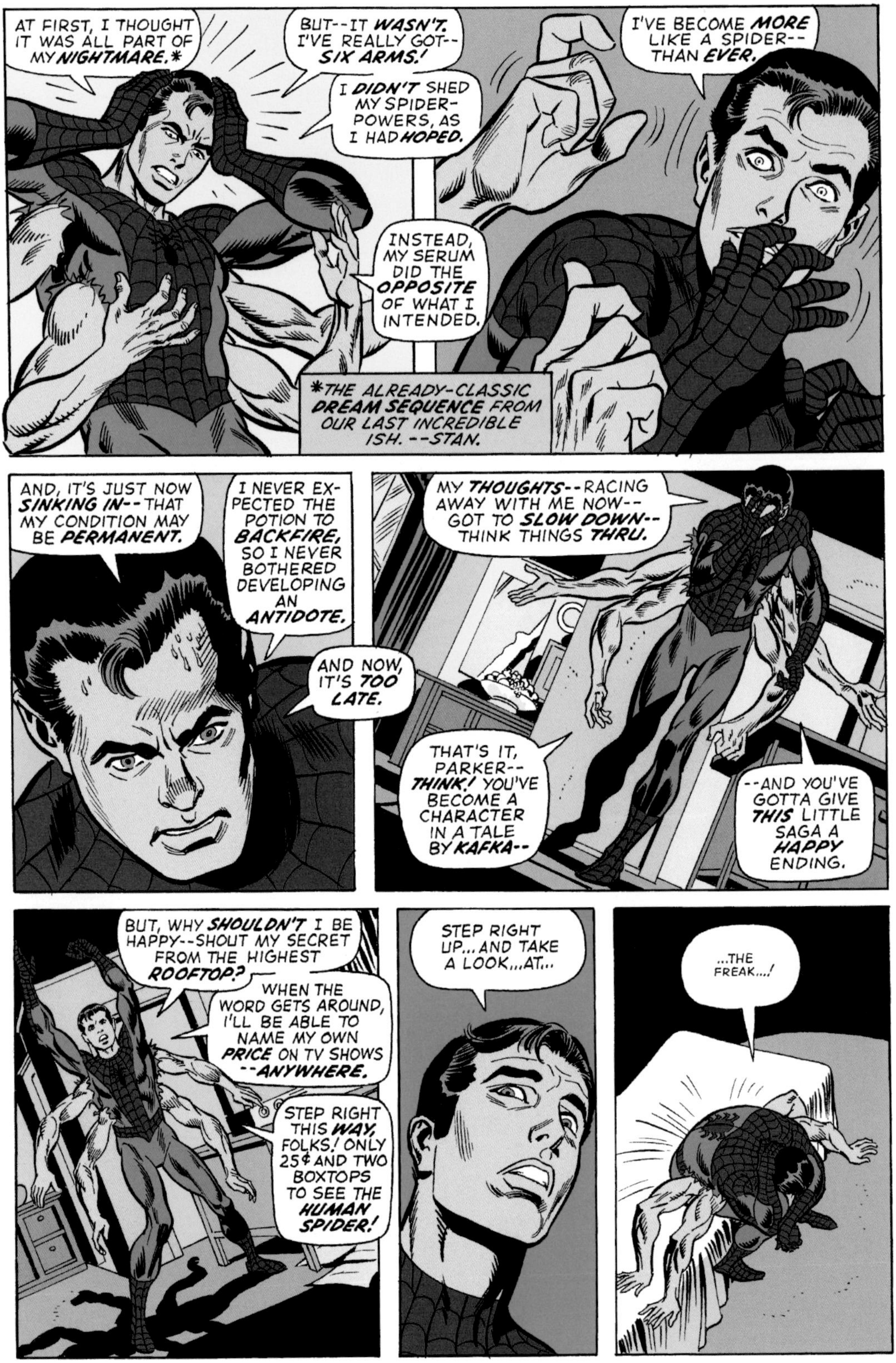
AT FIRST, I THOUGHT IT WAS ALL PART OF MY NIGHTMARE.*
BUT--IT WASN'T. I'VE REALLY GOT-- SIX ARMS!
I DIDN'T SHED MY SPIDER-POWERS, AS I HAD HOPED.
INSTEAD, MY SERUM DID THE OPPOSITE OF WHAT I INTENDED.
I'VE BECOME MORE LIKE A SPIDER-- THAN EVER.
*THE ALREADY-CLASSIC DREAM SEQUENCE FROM OUR LAST INCREDIBLE ISH. --STAN.
AND, IT'S JUST NOW SINKING IN--THAT MY CONDITION MAY BE PERMANENT.
I NEVER EXPECTED THE POTION TO BACKFIRE, SO I NEVER BOTHERED DEVELOPING AN ANTIDOTE.
AND NOW, IT'S TOO LATE.
MY THOUGHTS--RACING AWAY WITH ME NOW-- GOT TO SLOW DOWN-- THINK THINGS THRU.
THAT'S IT, PARKER-- THINK! YOU'VE BECOME A CHARACTER IN A TALE BY KAFKA--
--AND YOU'VE GOTTA GIVE THIS LITTLE SAGA A HAPPY ENDING.
BUT, WHY SHOULDN'T I BE HAPPY--SHOUT MY SECRET FROM THE HIGHEST ROOFTOP?
WHEN THE WORD GETS AROUND, I'LL BE ABLE TO NAME MY OWN PRICE ON TV SHOWS --ANYWHERE.
STEP RIGHT THIS WAY, FOLKS! ONLY 25¢ AND TWO BOXTOPS TO SEE THE HUMAN SPIDER!
STEP RIGHT UP... AND TAKE A LOOK... AT...
...THE FREAK...!

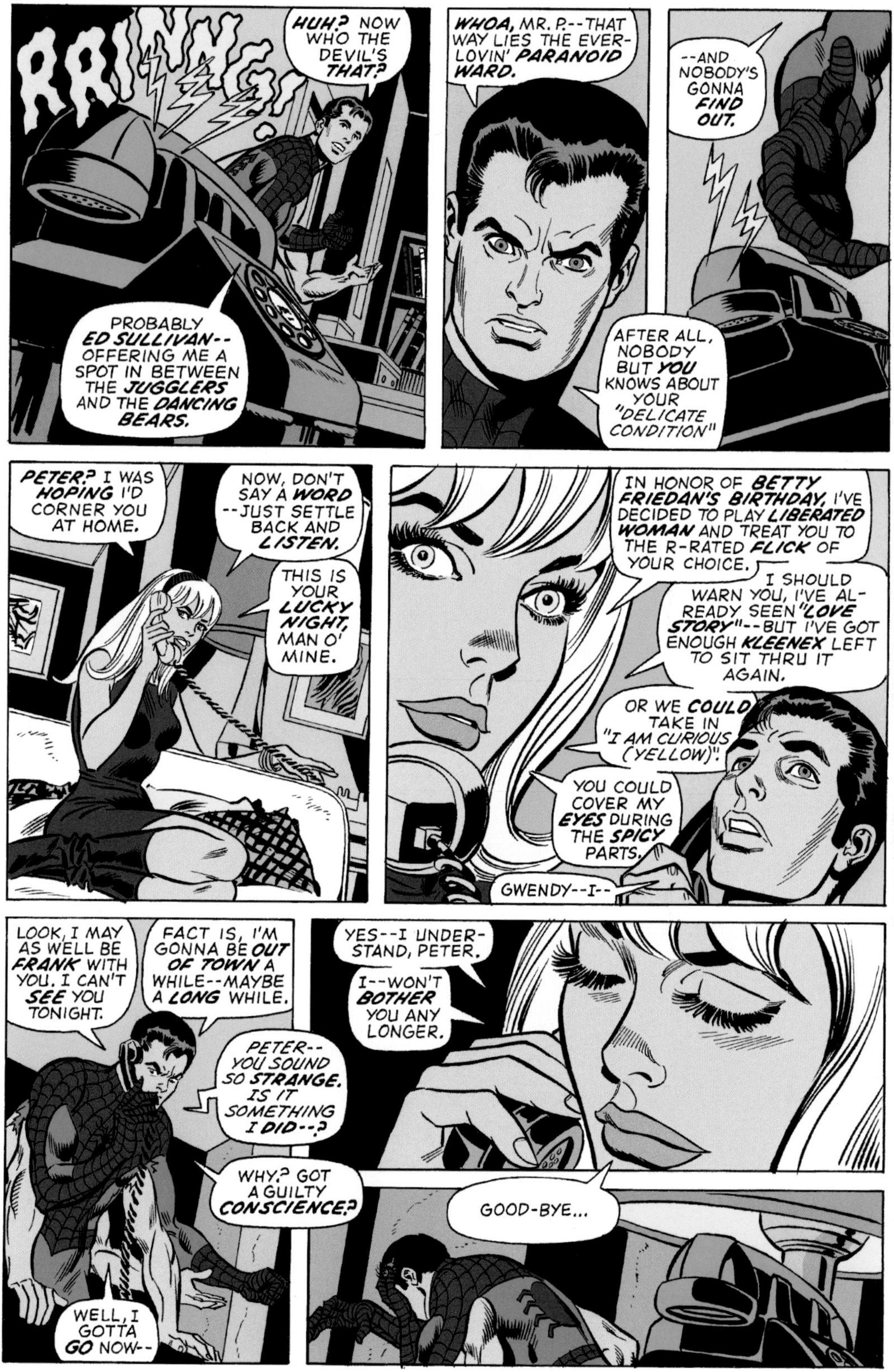
RRINNG!
HUH? NOW WHO THE DEVIL'S THAT?
PROBABLY ED SULLIVAN--OFFERING ME A SPOT IN BETWEEN THE JUGGLERS AND THE DANCING BEARS.
WHOA, MR. P.--THAT WAY LIES THE EVER-LOVIN' PARANOID WARD.
AFTER ALL, NOBODY BUT YOU KNOWS ABOUT YOUR "DELICATE CONDITION"
--AND NOBODY'S GONNA FIND OUT.
PETER? I WAS HOPING I'D CORNER YOU AT HOME.
NOW, DON'T SAY A WORD--JUST SETTLE BACK AND LISTEN.
THIS IS YOUR LUCKY NIGHT, MAN O' MINE.
IN HONOR OF BETTY FRIEDAN'S BIRTHDAY, I'VE DECIDED TO PLAY LIBERATED WOMAN AND TREAT YOU TO THE R-RATED FLICK OF YOUR CHOICE.
I SHOULD WARN YOU, I'VE AL-READY SEEN "LOVE STORY"--BUT I'VE GOT ENOUGH KLEENEX LEFT TO SIT THRU IT AGAIN.
OR WE COULD TAKE IN "I AM CURIOUS (YELLOW)".
YOU COULD COVER MY EYES DURING THE SPICY PARTS.
GWENDY--I--
LOOK, I MAY AS WELL BE FRANK WITH YOU. I CAN'T SEE YOU TONIGHT.
FACT IS, I'M GONNA BE OUT OF TOWN A WHILE--MAYBE A LONG WHILE.
PETER--YOU SOUND SO STRANGE. IS IT SOMETHING I DID--?
WHY? GOT A GUILTY CONSCIENCE?
WELL, I GOTTA GO NOW--
YES--I UNDER-STAND, PETER.
I--WON'T BOTHER YOU ANY LONGER.
GOOD-BYE...

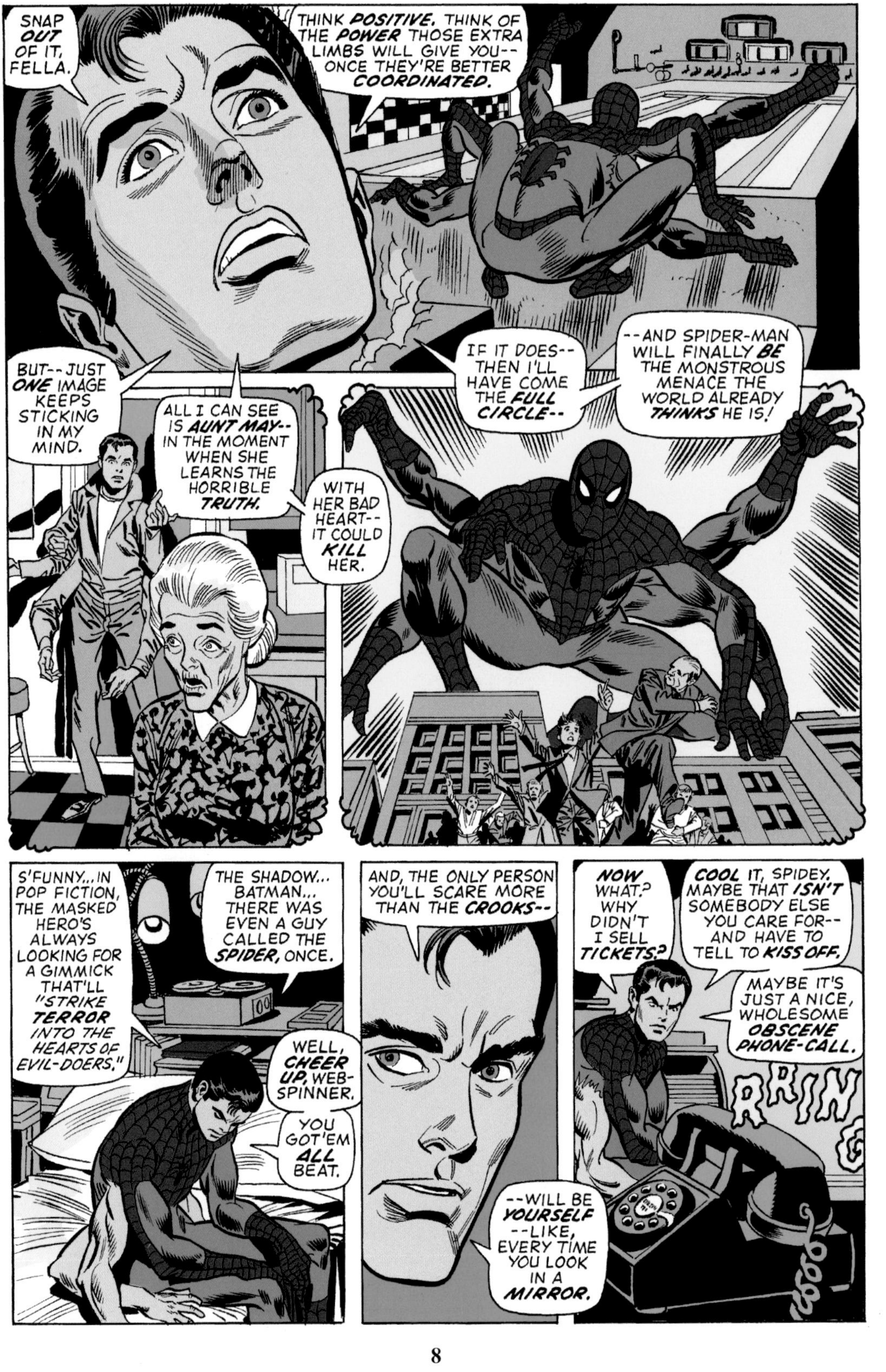
SNAP OUT OF IT, FELLA.
THINK POSITIVE. THINK OF THE POWER THOSE EXTRA LIMBS WILL GIVE YOU-- ONCE THEY'RE BETTER COORDINATED.
BUT--JUST ONE IMAGE KEEPS STICKING IN MY MIND.
ALL I CAN SEE IS AUNT MAY-- IN THE MOMENT WHEN SHE LEARNS THE HORRIBLE TRUTH.
WITH HER BAD HEART-- IT COULD KILL HER.
IF IT DOES-- THEN I'LL HAVE COME THE FULL CIRCLE--
--AND SPIDER-MAN WILL FINALLY BE THE MONSTROUS MENACE THE WORLD ALREADY THINKS HE IS!
S'FUNNY... IN POP FICTION, THE MASKED HERO'S ALWAYS LOOKING FOR A GIMMICK THAT'LL "STRIKE TERROR INTO THE HEARTS OF EVIL-DOERS."
THE SHADOW... BATMAN... THERE WAS EVEN A GUY CALLED THE SPIDER, ONCE.
WELL, CHEER UP, WEB-SPINNER.
YOU GOT'EM ALL BEAT.
AND, THE ONLY PERSON YOU'LL SCARE MORE THAN THE CROOKS--
--WILL BE YOURSELF --LIKE, EVERY TIME YOU LOOK IN A MIRROR.
NOW WHAT? WHY DIDN'T I SELL TICKETS?
COOL IT, SPIDEY. MAYBE THAT ISN'T SOMEBODY ELSE YOU CARE FOR-- AND HAVE TO TELL TO KISS OFF.
MAYBE IT'S JUST A NICE, WHOLESOME OBSCENE PHONE-CALL.
RRING

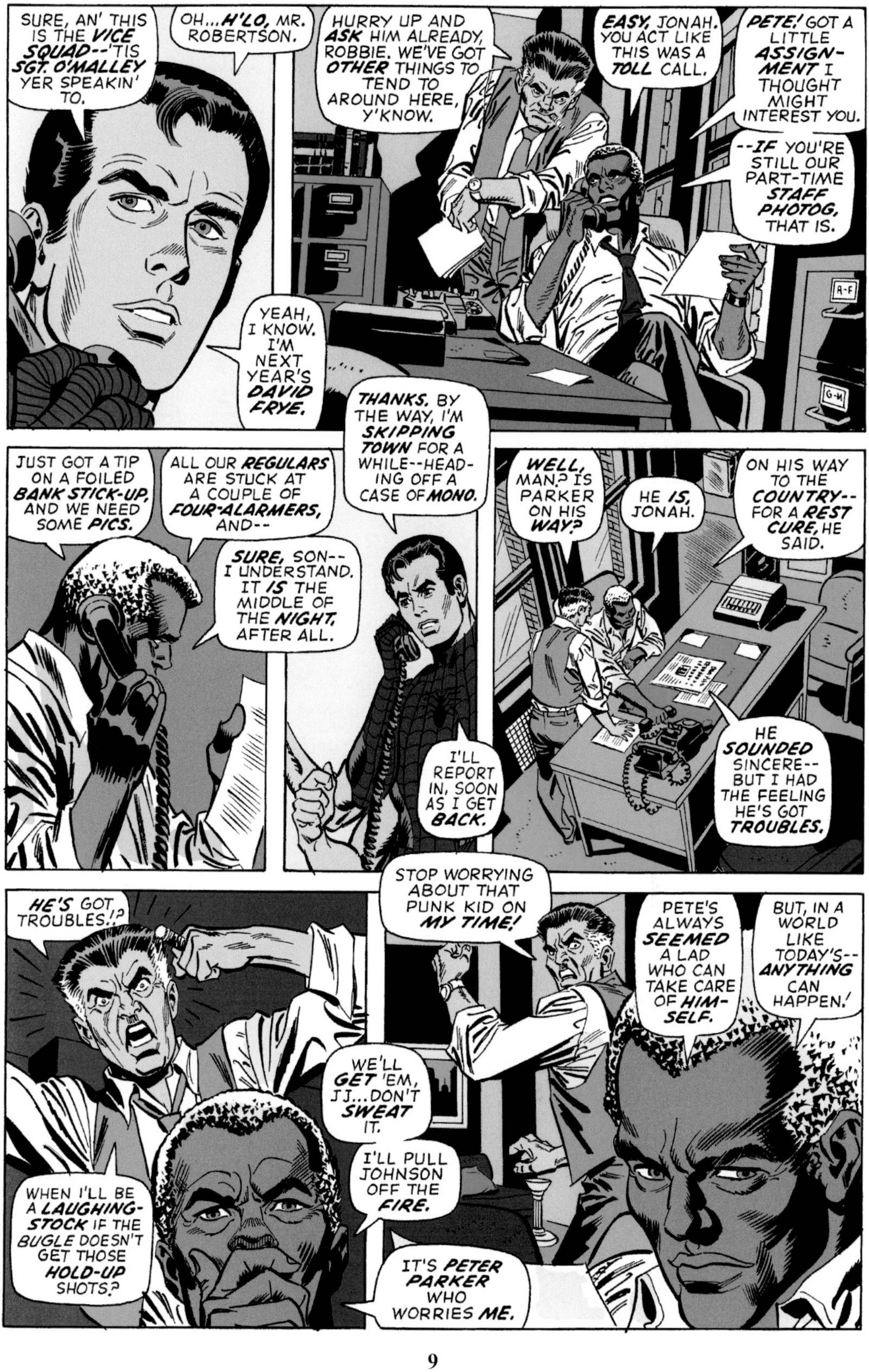
SURE, AN' THIS IS THE VICE SQUAD--'TIS SGT. O'MALLEY YER SPEAKIN' TO.
OH...H'LO, MR. ROBERTSON.
HURRY UP AND ASK HIM ALREADY, ROBBIE. WE'VE GOT OTHER THINGS TO TEND TO AROUND HERE, Y'KNOW.
EASY, JONAH. YOU ACT LIKE THIS WAS A TOLL CALL.
PETE! GOT A LITTLE ASSIGNMENT I THOUGHT MIGHT INTEREST YOU.
--IF YOU'RE STILL OUR PART-TIME STAFF PHOTOG, THAT IS.
YEAH, I KNOW. I'M NEXT YEAR'S DAVID FRYE.
A-F
G-H
JUST GOT A TIP ON A FOILED BANK STICK-UP, AND WE NEED SOME PICS.
ALL OUR REGULARS ARE STUCK AT A COUPLE OF FOUR-ALARMERS, AND--
THANKS. BY THE WAY, I'M SKIPPING TOWN FOR A WHILE--HEADING OFF A CASE OF MONO.
SURE, SON--I UNDERSTAND. IT IS THE MIDDLE OF THE NIGHT, AFTER ALL.
I'LL REPORT IN, SOON AS I GET BACK.
WELL, MAN? IS PARKER ON HIS WAY?
HE IS, JONAH.
ON HIS WAY TO THE COUNTRY--FOR A REST CURE, HE SAID.
HE SOUNDED SINCERE--BUT I HAD THE FEELING HE'S GOT TROUBLES.
HE'S GOT TROUBLES!?
WHEN I'LL BE A LAUGHING-STOCK IF THE BUGLE DOESN'T GET THOSE HOLD-UP SHOTS?
WE'LL GET 'EM, JJ...DON'T SWEAT IT.
I'LL PULL JOHNSON OFF THE FIRE.
STOP WORRYING ABOUT THAT PUNK KID ON MY TIME!
PETE'S ALWAYS SEEMED A LAD WHO CAN TAKE CARE OF HIMSELF.
BUT, IN A WORLD LIKE TODAY'S--ANYTHING CAN HAPPEN!
IT'S PETER PARKER WHO WORRIES ME.

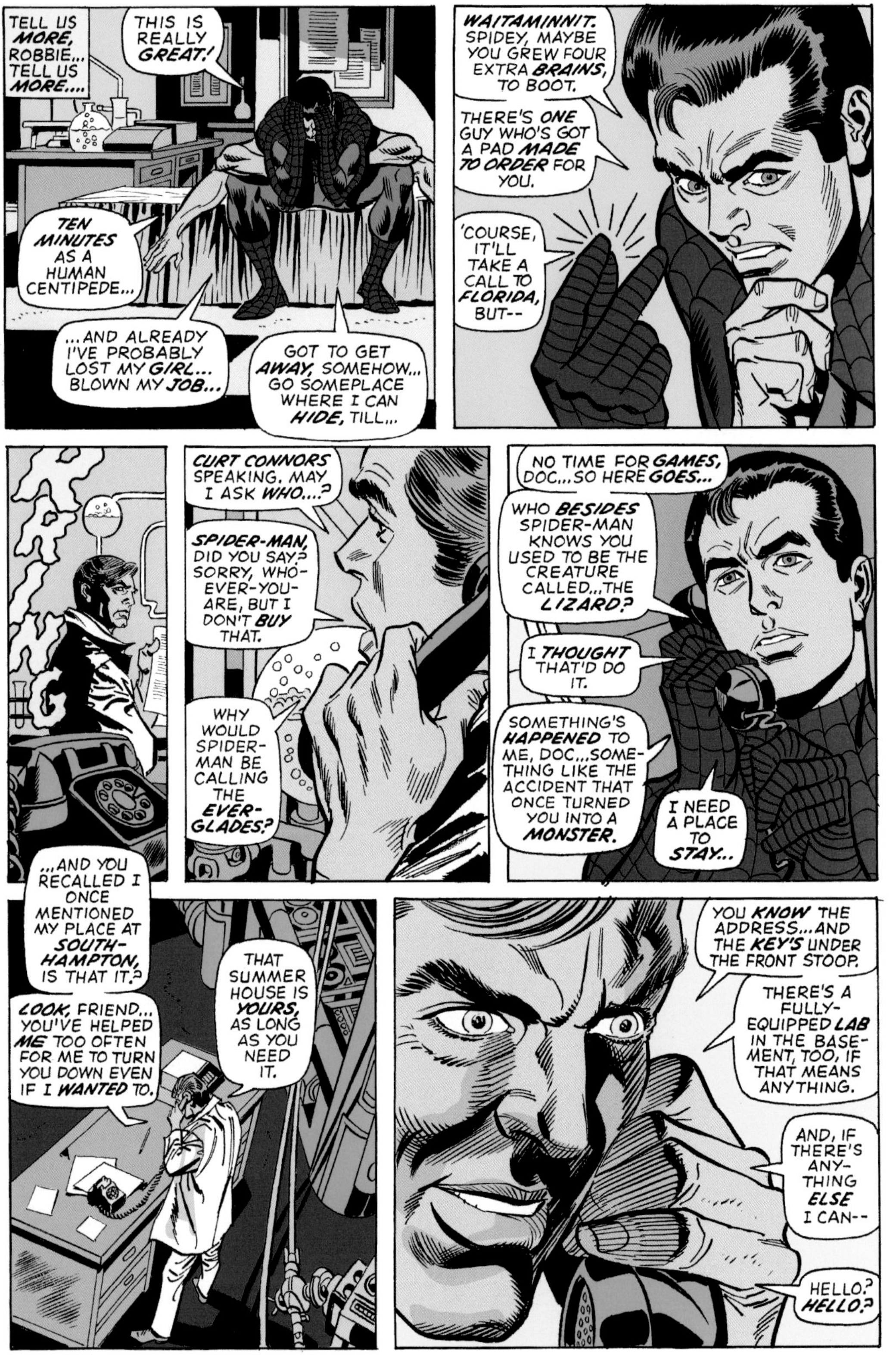

TELL US MORE, ROBBIE... TELL US MORE....
THIS IS REALLY GREAT!
TEN MINUTES AS A HUMAN CENTIPEDE...
...AND ALREADY I'VE PROBABLY LOST MY GIRL... BLOWN MY JOB...
GOT TO GET AWAY, SOMEHOW... GO SOMEPLACE WHERE I CAN HIDE, TILL...
WAITAMINNIT. SPIDEY, MAYBE YOU GREW FOUR EXTRA BRAINS, TO BOOT.
THERE'S ONE GUY WHO'S GOT A PAD MADE TO ORDER FOR YOU.
'COURSE, IT'LL TAKE A CALL TO FLORIDA, BUT--
CURT CONNORS SPEAKING. MAY I ASK WHO...?
SPIDER-MAN, DID YOU SAY? SORRY, WHO-EVER-YOU-ARE, BUT I DON'T BUY THAT.
WHY WOULD SPIDER-MAN BE CALLING THE EVER-GLADES?
NO TIME FOR GAMES, DOC...SO HERE GOES...
WHO BESIDES SPIDER-MAN KNOWS YOU USED TO BE THE CREATURE CALLED...THE LIZARD?
I THOUGHT THAT'D DO IT.
SOMETHING'S HAPPENED TO ME, DOC...SOME-THING LIKE THE ACCIDENT THAT ONCE TURNED YOU INTO A MONSTER.
I NEED A PLACE TO STAY...
...AND YOU RECALLED I ONCE MENTIONED MY PLACE AT SOUTH-HAMPTON, IS THAT IT?
LOOK, FRIEND... YOU'VE HELPED ME TOO OFTEN FOR ME TO TURN YOU DOWN EVEN IF I WANTED TO.
THAT SUMMER HOUSE IS YOURS, AS LONG AS YOU NEED IT.
YOU KNOW THE ADDRESS...AND THE KEY'S UNDER THE FRONT STOOP.
THERE'S A FULLY-EQUIPPED LAB IN THE BASE-MENT, TOO, IF THAT MEANS ANYTHING.
AND, IF THERE'S ANY-THING ELSE I CAN--
HELLO? HELLO?

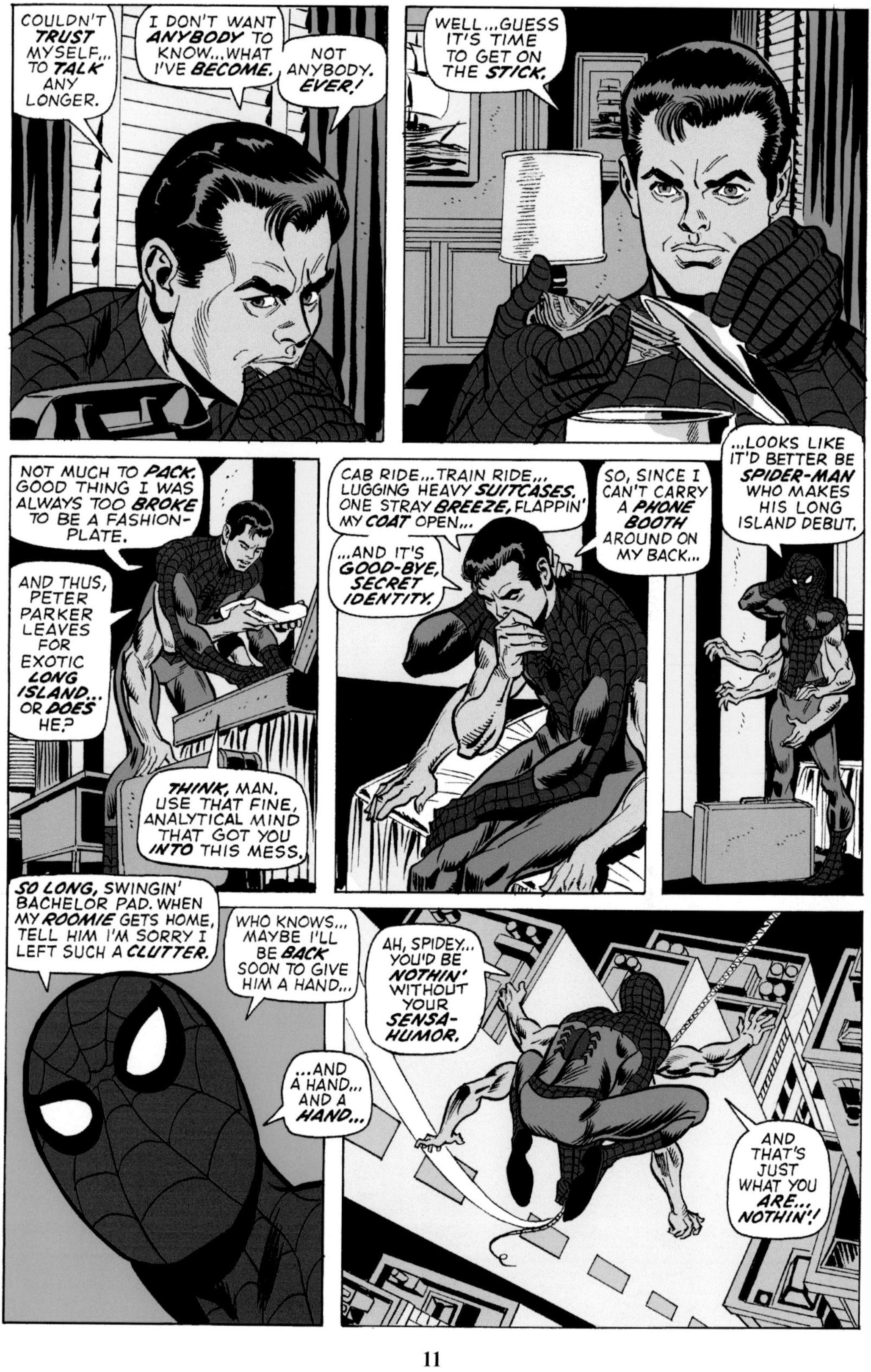
COULDN'T TRUST MYSELF... TO TALK ANY LONGER.
I DON'T WANT ANYBODY TO KNOW... WHAT I'VE BECOME.
NOT ANYBODY. EVER!
WELL... GUESS IT'S TIME TO GET ON THE STICK.
NOT MUCH TO PACK. GOOD THING I WAS ALWAYS TOO BROKE TO BE A FASHION-PLATE.
AND THUS, PETER PARKER LEAVES FOR EXOTIC LONG ISLAND... OR DOES HE?
THINK, MAN. USE THAT FINE, ANALYTICAL MIND THAT GOT YOU INTO THIS MESS.
CAB RIDE... TRAIN RIDE... LUGGING HEAVY SUITCASES. ONE STRAY BREEZE, FLAPPIN' MY COAT OPEN...
...AND IT'S GOOD-BYE, SECRET IDENTITY.
SO, SINCE I CAN'T CARRY A PHONE BOOTH AROUND ON MY BACK...
...LOOKS LIKE IT'D BETTER BE SPIDER-MAN WHO MAKES HIS LONG ISLAND DEBUT.
SO LONG, SWINGIN' BACHELOR PAD. WHEN MY ROOMIE GETS HOME, TELL HIM I'M SORRY I LEFT SUCH A CLUTTER.
WHO KNOWS... MAYBE I'LL BE BACK SOON TO GIVE HIM A HAND...
...AND A HAND... AND A HAND...
AH, SPIDEY... YOU'D BE NOTHIN' WITHOUT YOUR SENSA-HUMOR.
AND THAT'S JUST WHAT YOU ARE... NOTHIN'!

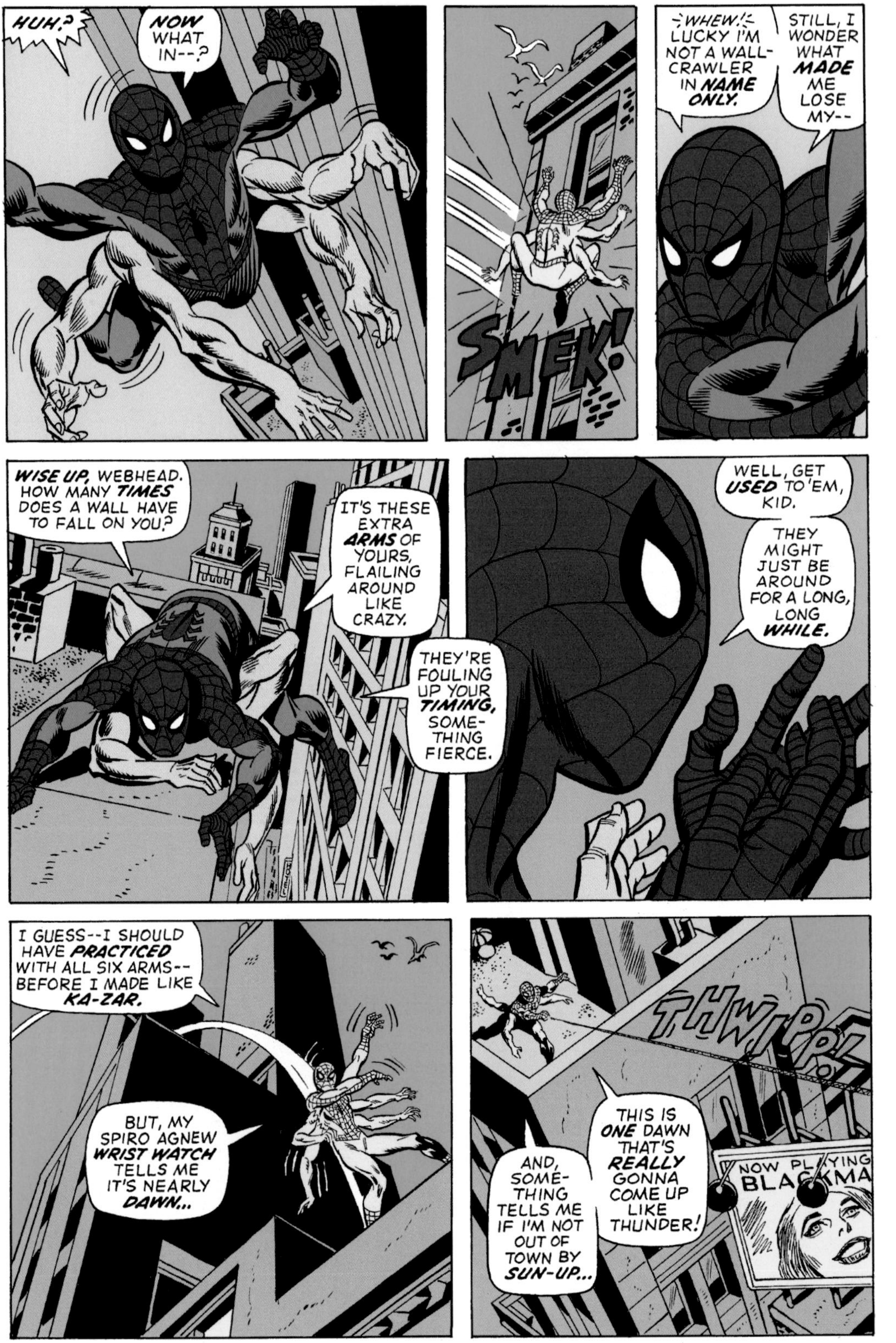
HUH?
NOW WHAT IN--?
SMEK!
WHEW! LUCKY I'M NOT A WALL-CRAWLER IN NAME ONLY.
STILL, I WONDER WHAT MADE ME LOSE MY--
WISE UP, WEBHEAD. HOW MANY TIMES DOES A WALL HAVE TO FALL ON YOU?
IT'S THESE EXTRA ARMS OF YOURS, FLAILING AROUND LIKE CRAZY.
THEY'RE FOULING UP YOUR TIMING, SOMETHING FIERCE.
WELL, GET USED TO 'EM, KID.
THEY MIGHT JUST BE AROUND FOR A LONG, LONG WHILE.
I GUESS--I SHOULD HAVE PRACTICED WITH ALL SIX ARMS--BEFORE I MADE LIKE KA-ZAR.
BUT, MY SPIRO AGNEW WRIST WATCH TELLS ME IT'S NEARLY DAWN...
THWIPP!
NOW PLAYING BLACKMA
AND, SOMETHING TELLS ME IF I'M NOT OUT OF TOWN BY SUN-UP...
THIS IS ONE DAWN THAT'S REALLY GONNA COME UP LIKE THUNDER!

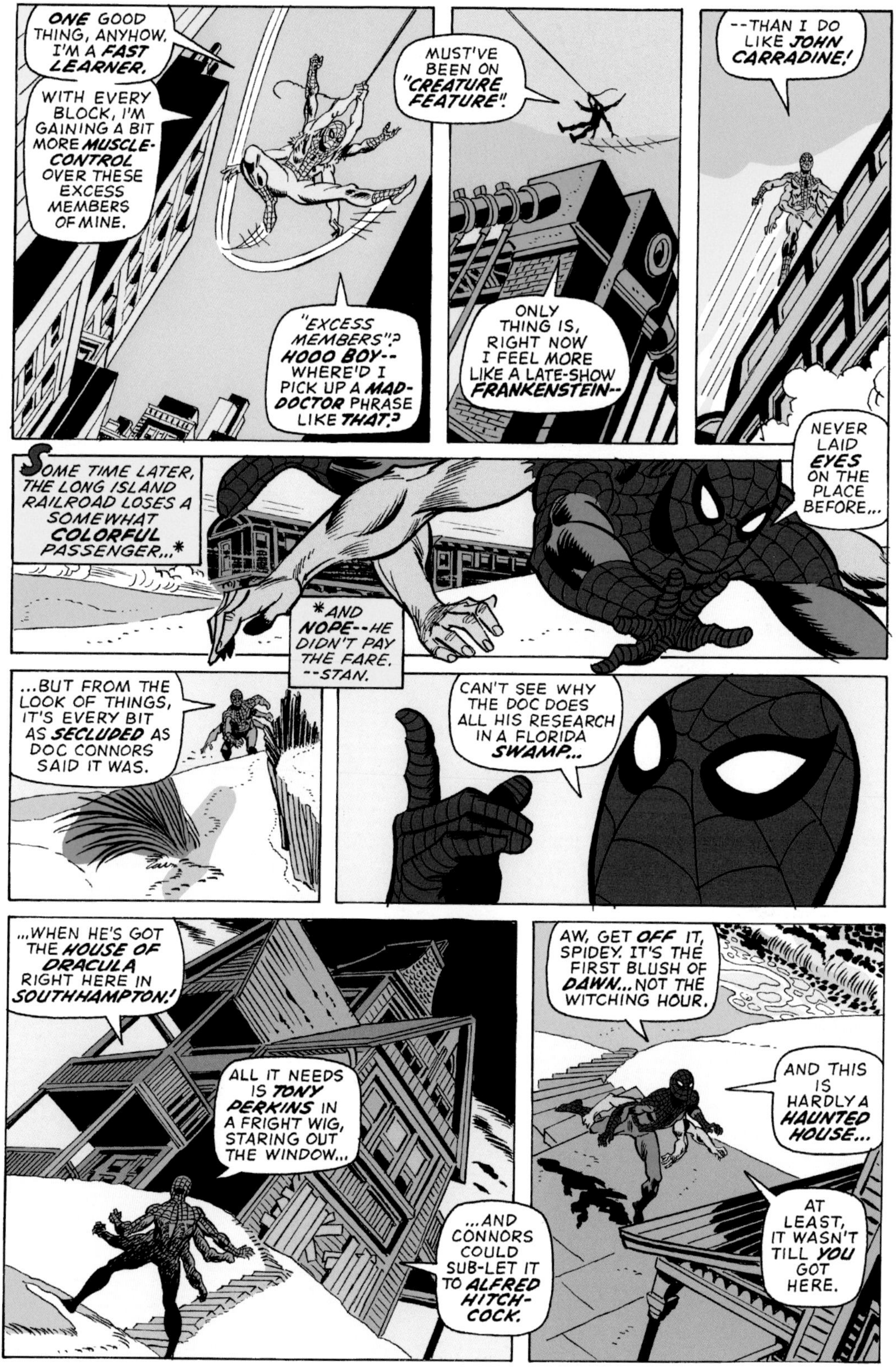

ONE GOOD THING, ANYHOW, I'M A FAST LEARNER.
WITH EVERY BLOCK, I'M GAINING A BIT MORE MUSCLE-CONTROL OVER THESE EXCESS MEMBERS OF MINE.
"EXCESS MEMBERS"? HOOO BOY-- WHERE'D I PICK UP A MAD-DOCTOR PHRASE LIKE THAT?
MUST'VE BEEN ON "CREATURE FEATURE".
ONLY THING IS, RIGHT NOW I FEEL MORE LIKE A LATE-SHOW FRANKENSTEIN--
--THAN I DO LIKE JOHN CARRADINE!
SOME TIME LATER, THE LONG ISLAND RAILROAD LOSES A SOMEWHAT COLORFUL PASSENGER...*
NEVER LAID EYES ON THE PLACE BEFORE...
*AND NOPE--HE DIDN'T PAY THE FARE. --STAN.
...BUT FROM THE LOOK OF THINGS, IT'S EVERY BIT AS SECLUDED AS DOC CONNORS SAID IT WAS.
CAN'T SEE WHY THE DOC DOES ALL HIS RESEARCH IN A FLORIDA SWAMP...
...WHEN HE'S GOT THE HOUSE OF DRACULA RIGHT HERE IN SOUTHHAMPTON!
ALL IT NEEDS IS TONY PERKINS IN A FRIGHT WIG, STARING OUT THE WINDOW...
...AND CONNORS COULD SUB-LET IT TO ALFRED HITCH-COCK.
AW, GET OFF IT, SPIDEY. IT'S THE FIRST BLUSH OF DAWN... NOT THE WITCHING HOUR.
AND THIS IS HARDLY A HAUNTED HOUSE...
AT LEAST, IT WASN'T TILL YOU GOT HERE.

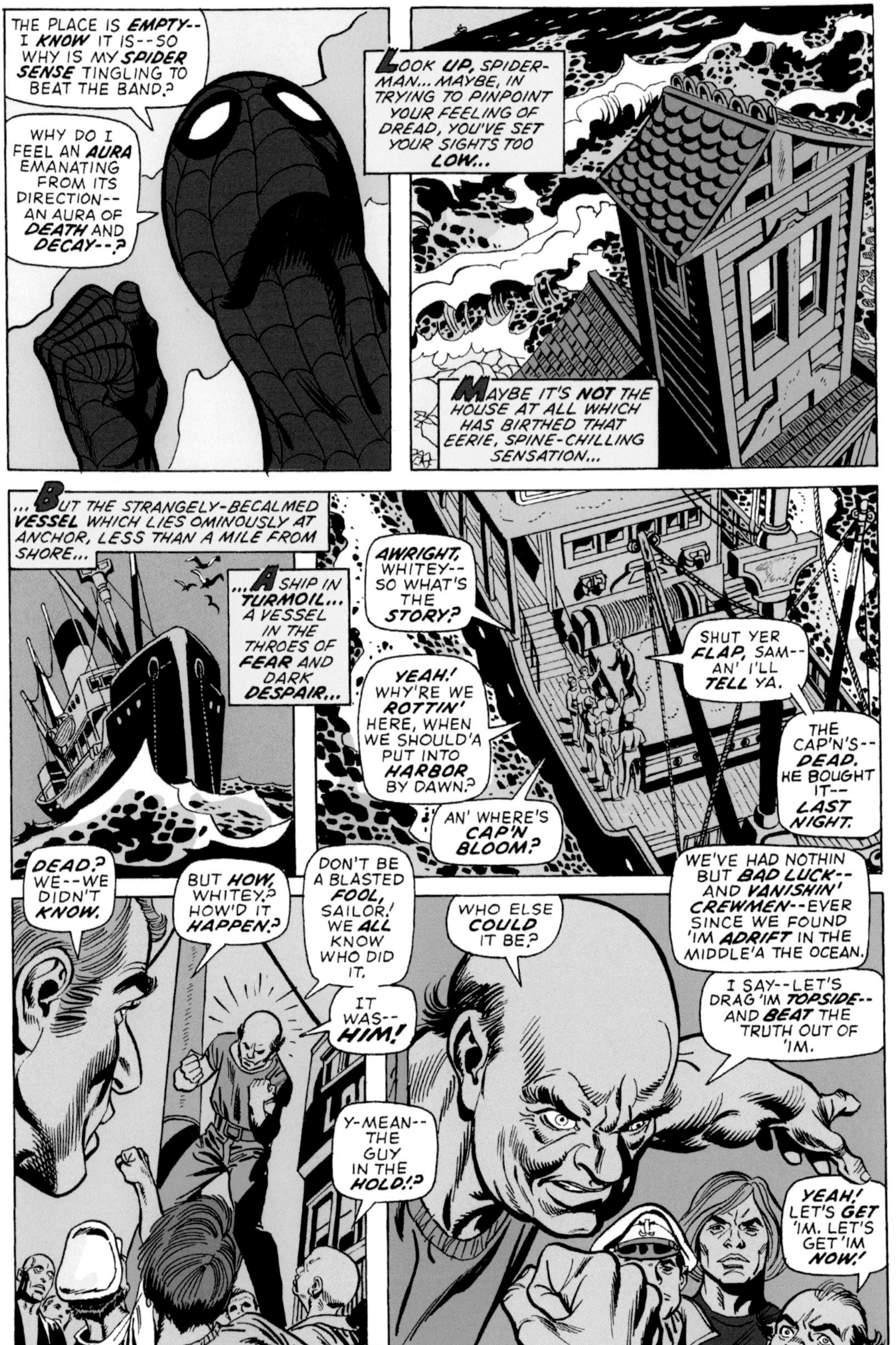

THE PLACE IS EMPTY-- I KNOW IT IS--SO WHY IS MY SPIDER SENSE TINGLING TO BEAT THE BAND?
WHY DO I FEEL AN AURA EMANATING FROM ITS DIRECTION-- AN AURA OF DEATH AND DECAY--?
LOOK UP, SPIDER-MAN... MAYBE, IN TRYING TO PINPOINT YOUR FEELING OF DREAD, YOU'VE SET YOUR SIGHTS TOO LOW...
MAYBE IT'S NOT THE HOUSE AT ALL WHICH HAS BIRTHED THAT EERIE, SPINE-CHILLING SENSATION...
...BUT THE STRANGELY-BECALMED VESSEL WHICH LIES OMINOUSLY AT ANCHOR, LESS THAN A MILE FROM SHORE...
...A SHIP IN TURMOIL... A VESSEL IN THE THROES OF FEAR AND DARK DESPAIR...
AWRIGHT, WHITEY-- SO WHAT'S THE STORY?
YEAH! WHY'RE WE ROTTIN' HERE, WHEN WE SHOULD'A PUT INTO HARBOR BY DAWN?
AN' WHERE'S CAP'N BLOOM?
SHUT YER FLAP, SAM-- AN' I'LL TELL YA.
THE CAP'N'S-- DEAD. HE BOUGHT IT-- LAST NIGHT.
DEAD? WE--WE DIDN'T KNOW.
BUT HOW, WHITEY? HOW'D IT HAPPEN?
DON'T BE A BLASTED FOOL, SAILOR! WE ALL KNOW WHO DID IT.
IT WAS-- HIM!
Y-MEAN-- THE GUY IN THE HOLD!?
WHO ELSE COULD IT BE?
WE'VE HAD NOTHIN BUT BAD LUCK-- AND VANISHIN' CREWMEN--EVER SINCE WE FOUND 'IM ADRIFT IN THE MIDDLE'A THE OCEAN.
I SAY--LET'S DRAG 'IM TOPSIDE-- AND BEAT THE TRUTH OUT OF 'IM.
YEAH! LET'S GET 'IM. LET'S GET 'IM NOW!

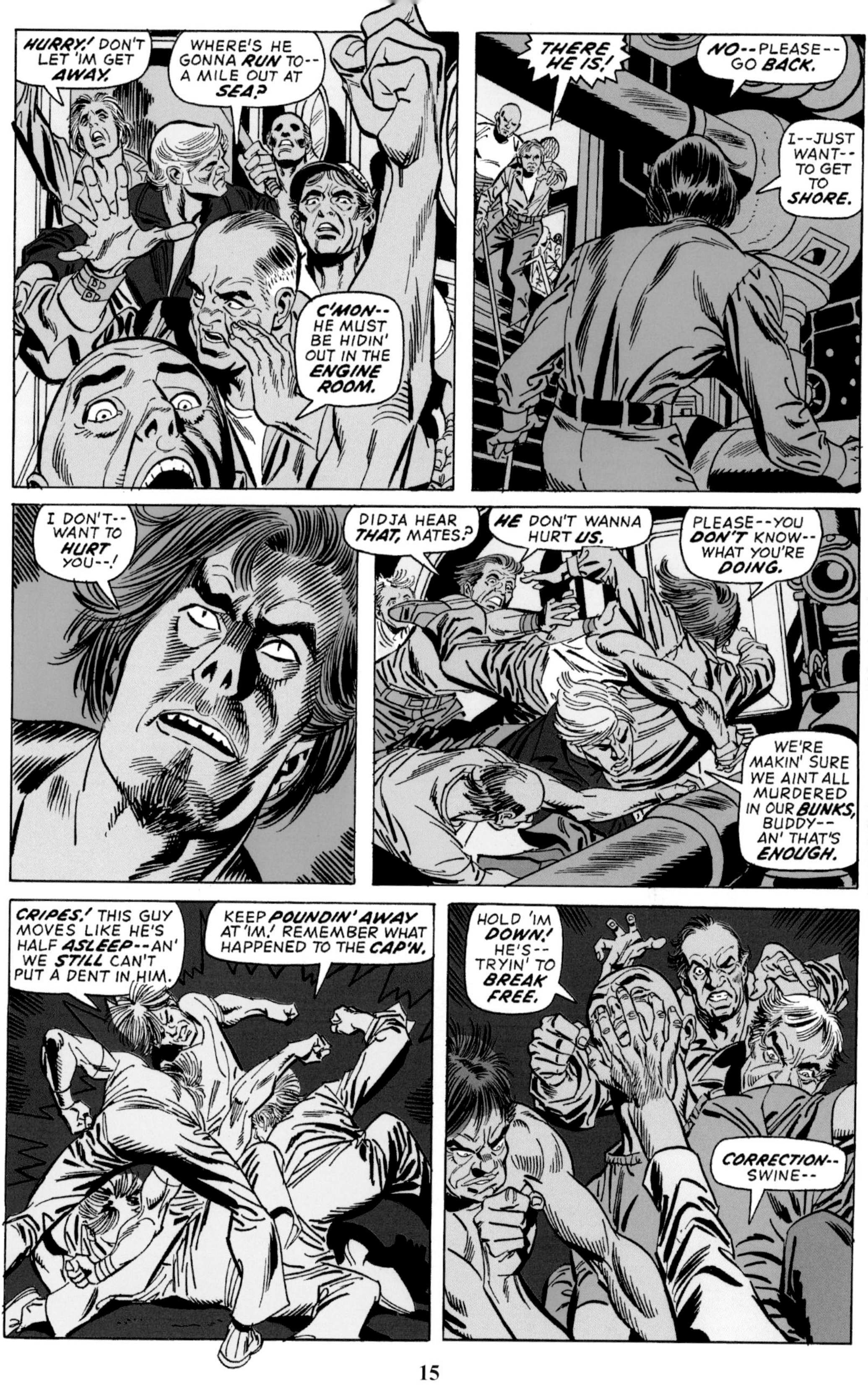
HURRY! DON'T LET 'IM GET AWAY.
WHERE'S HE GONNA RUN TO-- A MILE OUT AT SEA?
C'MON-- HE MUST BE HIDIN' OUT IN THE ENGINE ROOM.
THERE HE IS!
NO--PLEASE-- GO BACK.
I--JUST WANT-- TO GET TO SHORE.
I DON'T-- WANT TO HURT YOU--!
DIDJA HEAR THAT, MATES?
HE DON'T WANNA HURT US.
PLEASE--YOU DON'T KNOW-- WHAT YOU'RE DOING.
WE'RE MAKIN' SURE WE AINT ALL MURDERED IN OUR BUNKS, BUDDY-- AN' THAT'S ENOUGH.
CRIPES! THIS GUY MOVES LIKE HE'S HALF ASLEEP--AN' WE STILL CAN'T PUT A DENT IN HIM.
KEEP POUNDIN' AWAY AT 'IM! REMEMBER WHAT HAPPENED TO THE CAP'N.
HOLD 'IM DOWN! HE'S-- TRYIN' TO BREAK FREE.
CORRECTION-- SWINE--

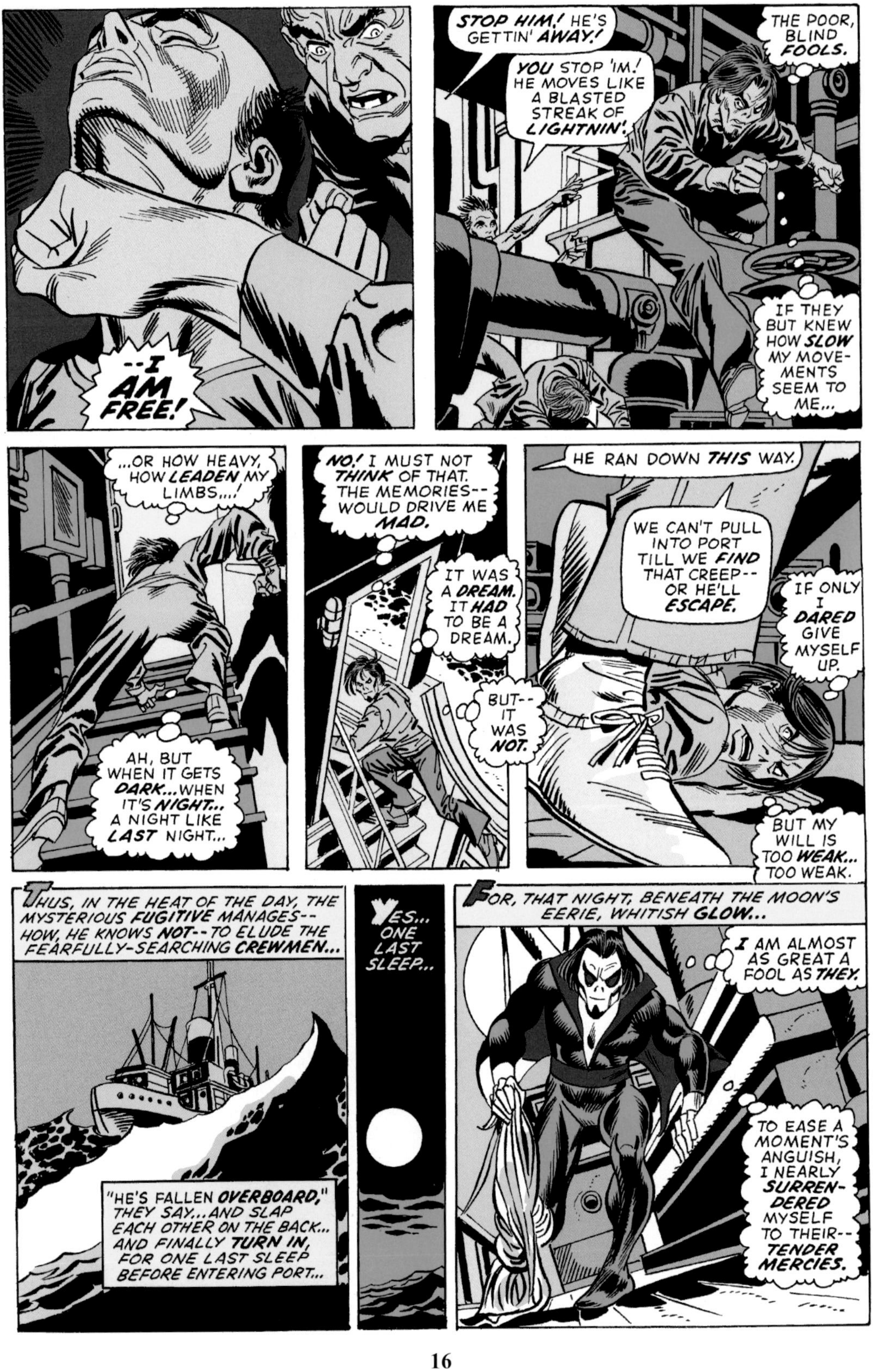
--I AM FREE!
STOP HIM! HE'S GETTIN' AWAY!
YOU STOP 'IM! HE MOVES LIKE A BLASTED STREAK OF LIGHTNIN'!
THE POOR, BLIND FOOLS.
IF THEY BUT KNEW HOW SLOW MY MOVEMENTS SEEM TO ME...
...OR HOW HEAVY, HOW LEADEN MY LIMBS...!
AH, BUT WHEN IT GETS DARK... WHEN IT'S NIGHT... A NIGHT LIKE LAST NIGHT...
NO! I MUST NOT THINK OF THAT. THE MEMORIES--WOULD DRIVE ME MAD.
IT WAS A DREAM. IT HAD TO BE A DREAM.
BUT--IT WAS NOT.
HE RAN DOWN THIS WAY.
WE CAN'T PULL INTO PORT TILL WE FIND THAT CREEP--OR HE'LL ESCAPE.
IF ONLY I DARED GIVE MYSELF UP.
BUT MY WILL IS TOO WEAK... TOO WEAK.
THUS, IN THE HEAT OF THE DAY, THE MYSTERIOUS FUGITIVE MANAGES--HOW, HE KNOWS NOT--TO ELUDE THE FEARFULLY-SEARCHING CREWMEN...
"HE'S FALLEN OVERBOARD," THEY SAY... AND SLAP EACH OTHER ON THE BACK... AND FINALLY TURN IN, FOR ONE LAST SLEEP BEFORE ENTERING PORT...
YES... ONE LAST SLEEP...
FOR, THAT NIGHT, BENEATH THE MOON'S EERIE, WHITISH GLOW...
I AM ALMOST AS GREAT A FOOL AS THEY.
TO EASE A MOMENT'S ANGUISH, I NEARLY SURRENDERED MYSELF TO THEIR--TENDER MERCIES.

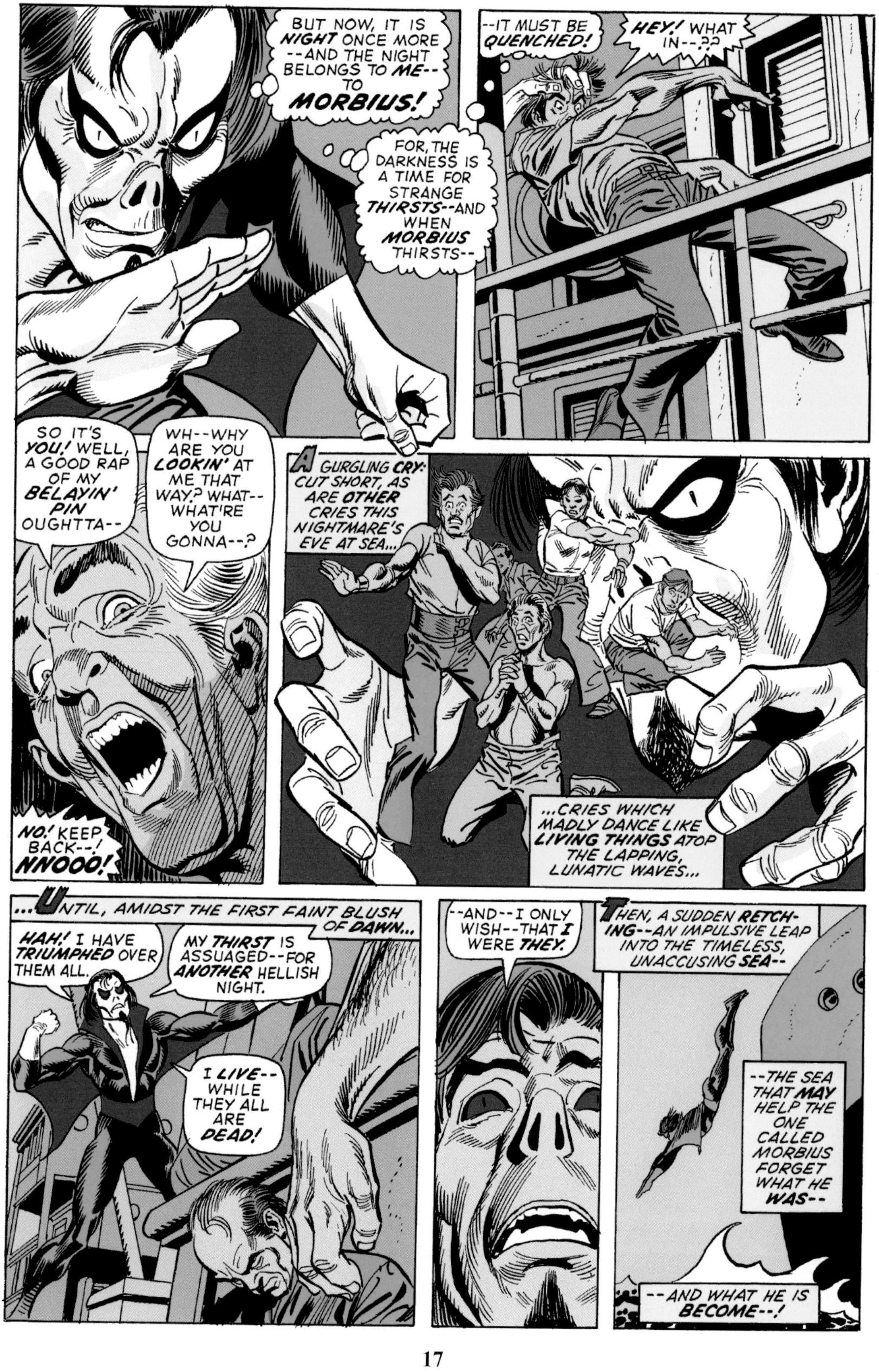
BUT NOW, IT IS NIGHT ONCE MORE --AND THE NIGHT BELONGS TO ME-- TO MORBIUS!
FOR, THE DARKNESS IS A TIME FOR STRANGE THIRSTS--AND WHEN MORBIUS THIRSTS--
--IT MUST BE QUENCHED!
HEY! WHAT IN--??
SO IT'S YOU! WELL, A GOOD RAP OF MY BELAYIN' PIN OUGHTTA--
WH--WHY ARE YOU LOOKIN' AT ME THAT WAY? WHAT-- WHAT'RE YOU GONNA--?
NO! KEEP BACK--! NNOOO!
A GURGLING CRY: CUT SHORT, AS ARE OTHER CRIES THIS NIGHTMARE'S EVE AT SEA...
...CRIES WHICH MADLY DANCE LIKE LIVING THINGS ATOP THE LAPPING, LUNATIC WAVES...
...UNTIL, AMIDST THE FIRST FAINT BLUSH OF DAWN...
HAH! I HAVE TRIUMPHED OVER THEM ALL.
MY THIRST IS ASSUAGED--FOR ANOTHER HELLISH NIGHT.
I LIVE-- WHILE THEY ALL ARE DEAD!
--AND--I ONLY WISH--THAT I WERE THEY.
THEN, A SUDDEN RETCHING--AN IMPULSIVE LEAP INTO THE TIMELESS, UNACCUSING SEA--
--THE SEA THAT MAY HELP THE ONE CALLED MORBIUS FORGET WHAT HE WAS--
--AND WHAT HE IS BECOME--!

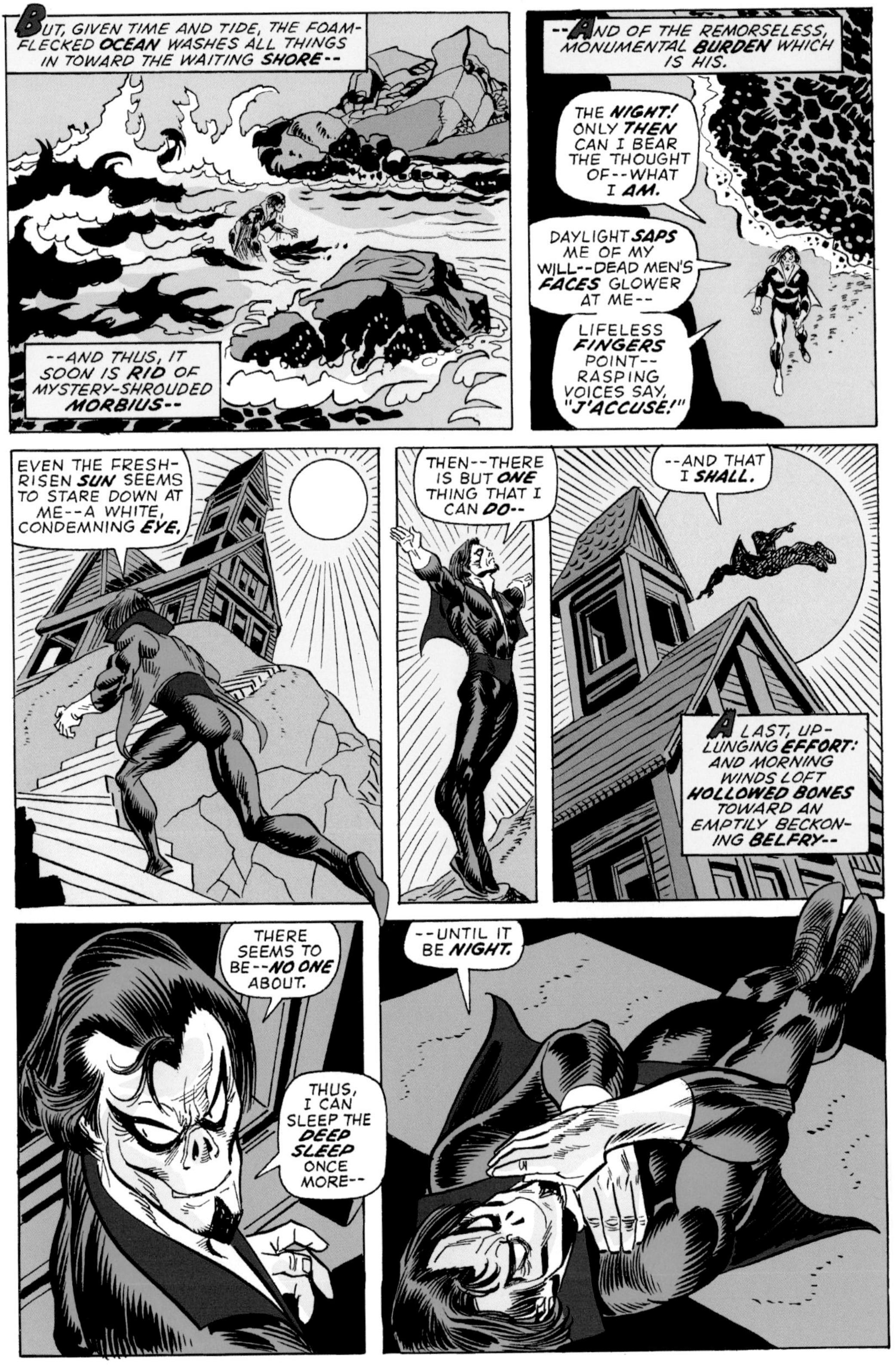

BUT, GIVEN TIME AND TIDE, THE FOAM-FLECKED OCEAN WASHES ALL THINGS IN TOWARD THE WAITING SHORE--
--AND THUS, IT SOON IS RID OF MYSTERY-SHROUDED MORBIUS--
--AND OF THE REMORSELESS, MONUMENTAL BURDEN WHICH IS HIS.
THE NIGHT! ONLY THEN CAN I BEAR THE THOUGHT OF--WHAT I AM.
DAYLIGHT SAPS ME OF MY WILL--DEAD MEN'S FACES GLOWER AT ME--
LIFELESS FINGERS POINT--RASPING VOICES SAY, "J'ACCUSE!"
EVEN THE FRESH-RISEN SUN SEEMS TO STARE DOWN AT ME--A WHITE, CONDEMNING EYE.
THEN--THERE IS BUT ONE THING THAT I CAN DO--
--AND THAT I SHALL.
A LAST, UPLUNGING EFFORT: AND MORNING WINDS LOFT HOLLOWED BONES TOWARD AN EMPTILY BECKONING BELFRY--
THERE SEEMS TO BE--NO ONE ABOUT.
THUS, I CAN SLEEP THE DEEP SLEEP ONCE MORE--
--UNTIL IT BE NIGHT.

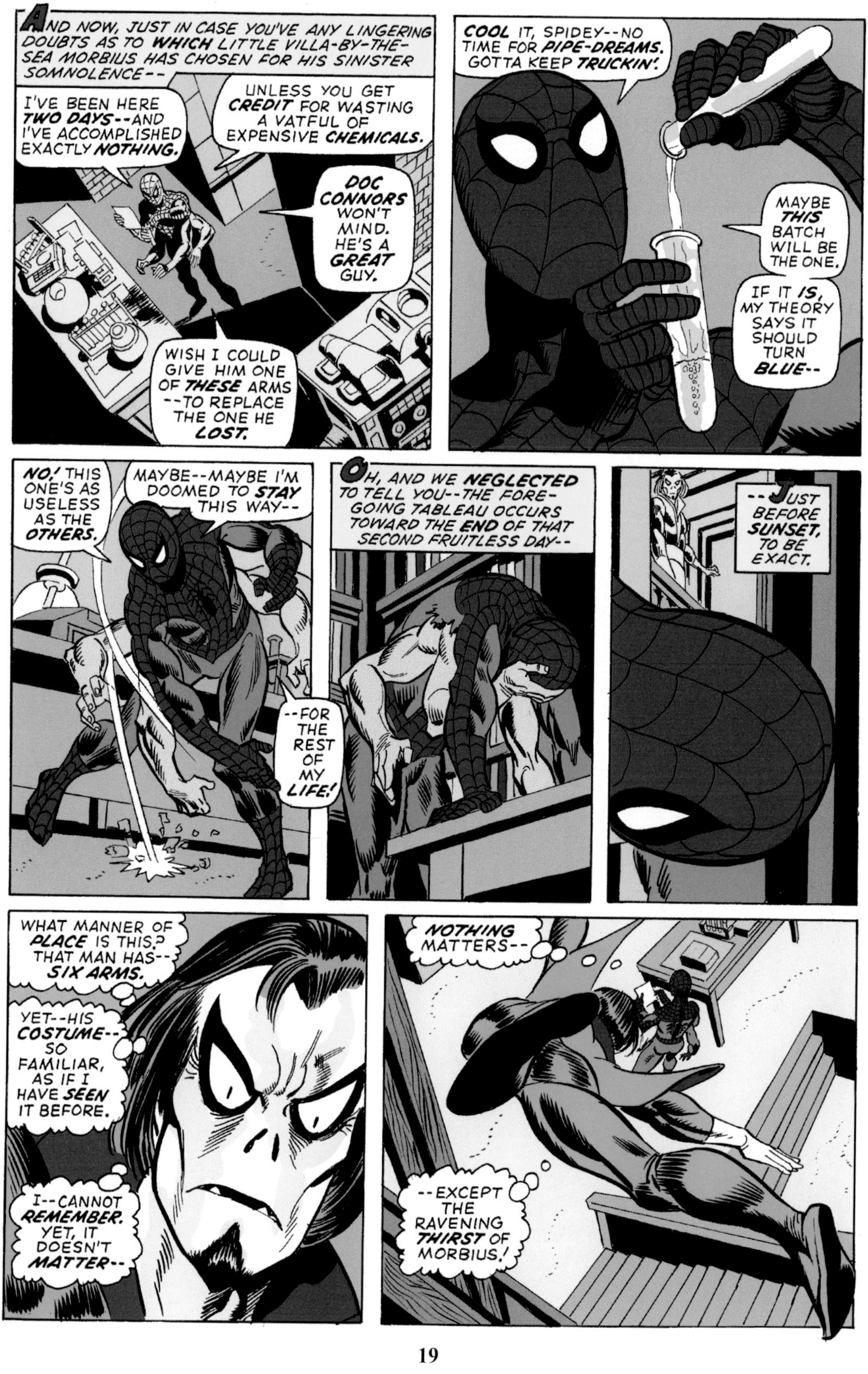
AND NOW, JUST IN CASE YOU'VE ANY LINGERING DOUBTS AS TO WHICH LITTLE VILLA-BY-THE-SEA MORBIUS HAS CHOSEN FOR HIS SINISTER SOMNOLENCE--
I'VE BEEN HERE TWO DAYS--AND I'VE ACCOMPLISHED EXACTLY NOTHING.
UNLESS YOU GET CREDIT FOR WASTING A VATFUL OF EXPENSIVE CHEMICALS.
DOC CONNORS WON'T MIND. HE'S A GREAT GUY.
WISH I COULD GIVE HIM ONE OF THESE ARMS --TO REPLACE THE ONE HE LOST.
COOL IT, SPIDEY--NO TIME FOR PIPE-DREAMS. GOTTA KEEP TRUCKIN'.
MAYBE THIS BATCH WILL BE THE ONE.
IF IT IS, MY THEORY SAYS IT SHOULD TURN BLUE--
NO! THIS ONE'S AS USELESS AS THE OTHERS.
MAYBE--MAYBE I'M DOOMED TO STAY THIS WAY--
--FOR THE REST OF MY LIFE!
OH, AND WE NEGLECTED TO TELL YOU--THE FORE-GOING TABLEAU OCCURS TOWARD THE END OF THAT SECOND FRUITLESS DAY--
--JUST BEFORE SUNSET, TO BE EXACT.
WHAT MANNER OF PLACE IS THIS? THAT MAN HAS--SIX ARMS.
YET--HIS COSTUME--SO FAMILIAR, AS IF I HAVE SEEN IT BEFORE.
I--CANNOT REMEMBER. YET, IT DOESN'T MATTER--
NOTHING MATTERS--
--EXCEPT THE RAVENING THIRST OF MORBIUS!

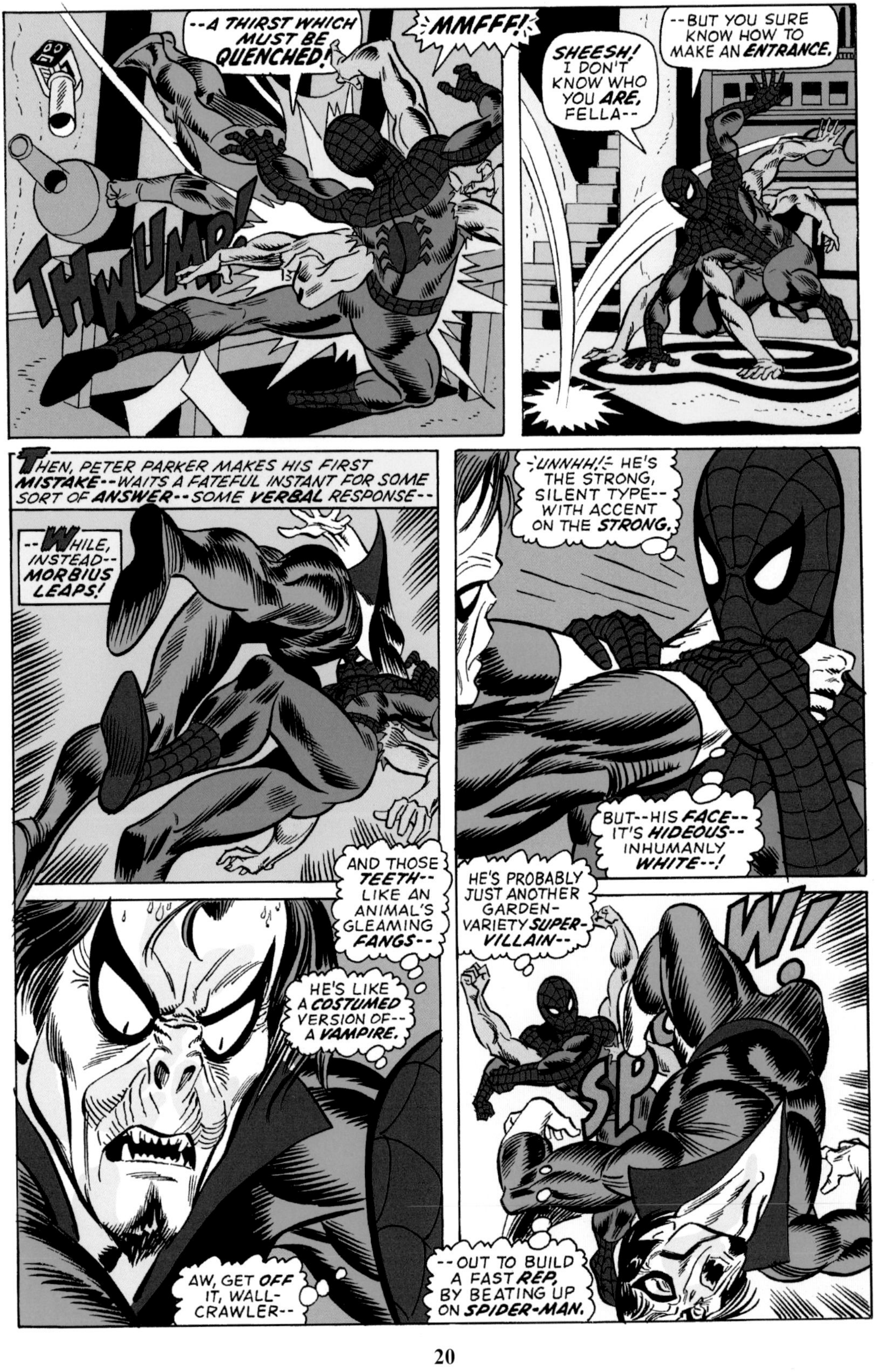

--A THIRST WHICH MUST BE QUENCHED!
THWUMP!
MMFFF!
SHEESH! I DON'T KNOW WHO YOU ARE, FELLA--
--BUT YOU SURE KNOW HOW TO MAKE AN ENTRANCE.
THEN, PETER PARKER MAKES HIS FIRST MISTAKE--WAITS A FATEFUL INSTANT FOR SOME SORT OF ANSWER--SOME VERBAL RESPONSE--
--WHILE, INSTEAD--MORBIUS LEAPS!
UNNHH!-- HE'S THE STRONG, SILENT TYPE--WITH ACCENT ON THE STRONG.
BUT--HIS FACE--IT'S HIDEOUS--INHUMANLY WHITE--!
AND THOSE TEETH--LIKE AN ANIMAL'S GLEAMING FANGS--
HE'S LIKE A COSTUMED VERSION OF--A VAMPIRE.
AW, GET OFF IT, WALL-CRAWLER--
HE'S PROBABLY JUST ANOTHER GARDEN-VARIETY SUPER-VILLAIN--
--OUT TO BUILD A FAST REP, BY BEATING UP ON SPIDER-MAN.

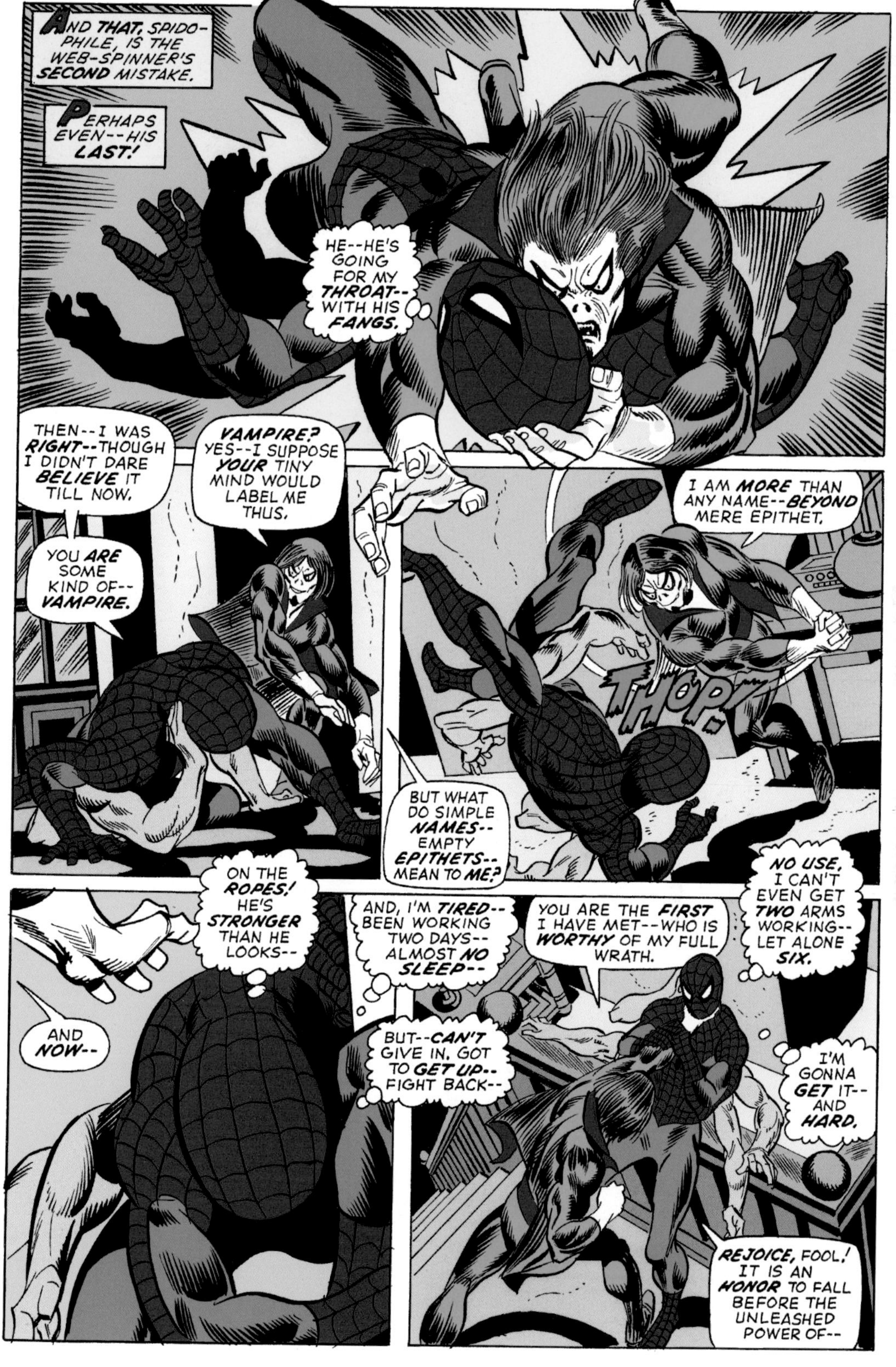
AND THAT, SPIDO-PHILE, IS THE WEB-SPINNER'S SECOND MISTAKE.
PERHAPS EVEN--HIS LAST!
HE--HE'S GOING FOR MY THROAT--WITH HIS FANGS.
THEN--I WAS RIGHT--THOUGH I DIDN'T DARE BELIEVE IT TILL NOW.
YOU ARE SOME KIND OF--VAMPIRE.
VAMPIRE? YES--I SUPPOSE YOUR TINY MIND WOULD LABEL ME THUS.
I AM MORE THAN ANY NAME--BEYOND MERE EPITHET.
THOP!
BUT WHAT DO SIMPLE NAMES--EMPTY EPITHETS--MEAN TO ME?
ON THE ROPES! HE'S STRONGER THAN HE LOOKS--
AND NOW--
AND, I'M TIRED--BEEN WORKING TWO DAYS--ALMOST NO SLEEP--
BUT--CAN'T GIVE IN. GOT TO GET UP--FIGHT BACK--
YOU ARE THE FIRST I HAVE MET--WHO IS WORTHY OF MY FULL WRATH.
NO USE. I CAN'T EVEN GET TWO ARMS WORKING--LET ALONE SIX.
I'M GONNA GET IT--AND HARD.
REJOICE, FOOL! IT IS AN HONOR TO FALL BEFORE THE UNLEASHED POWER OF--

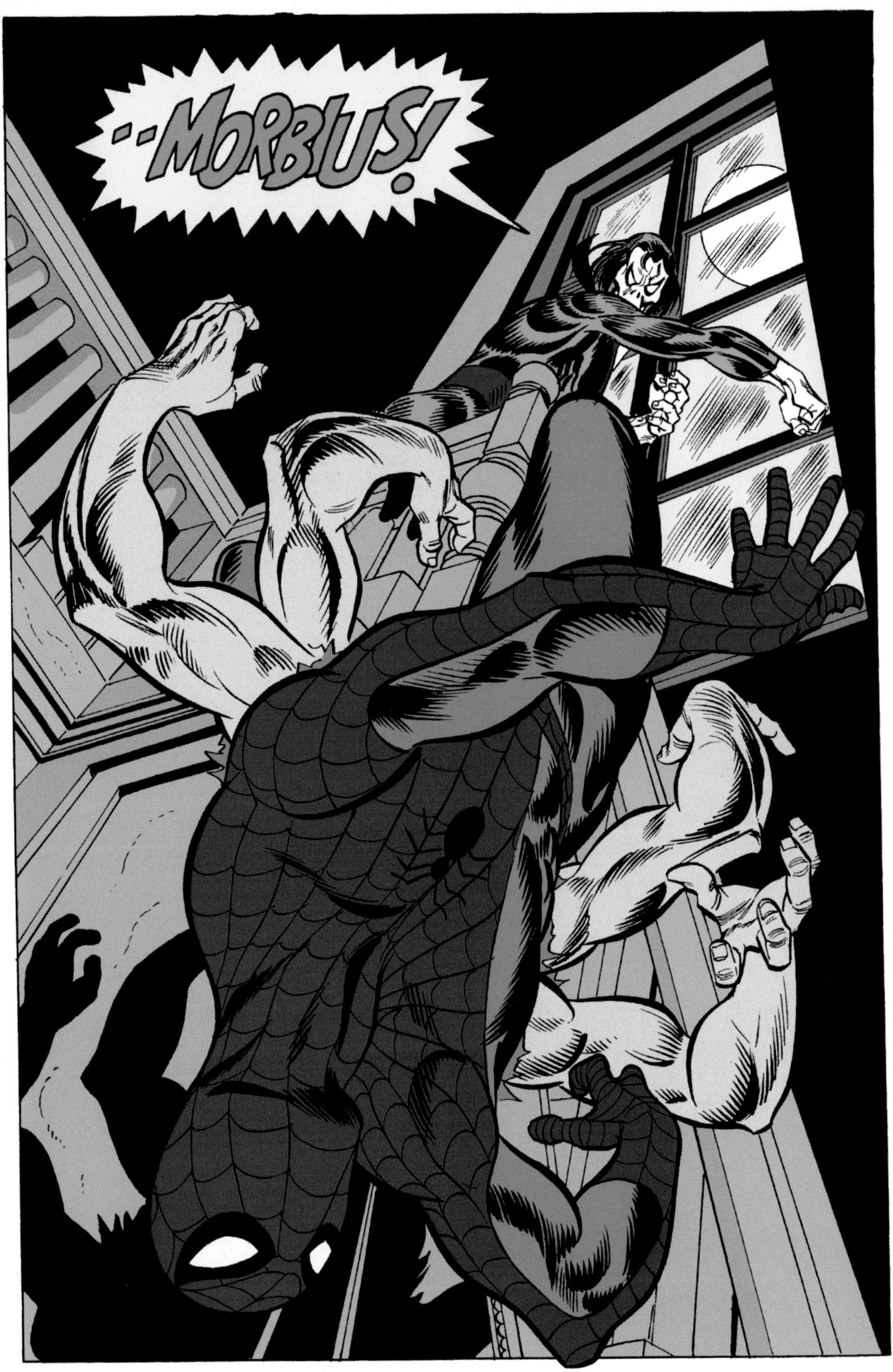
--MORBIUS!

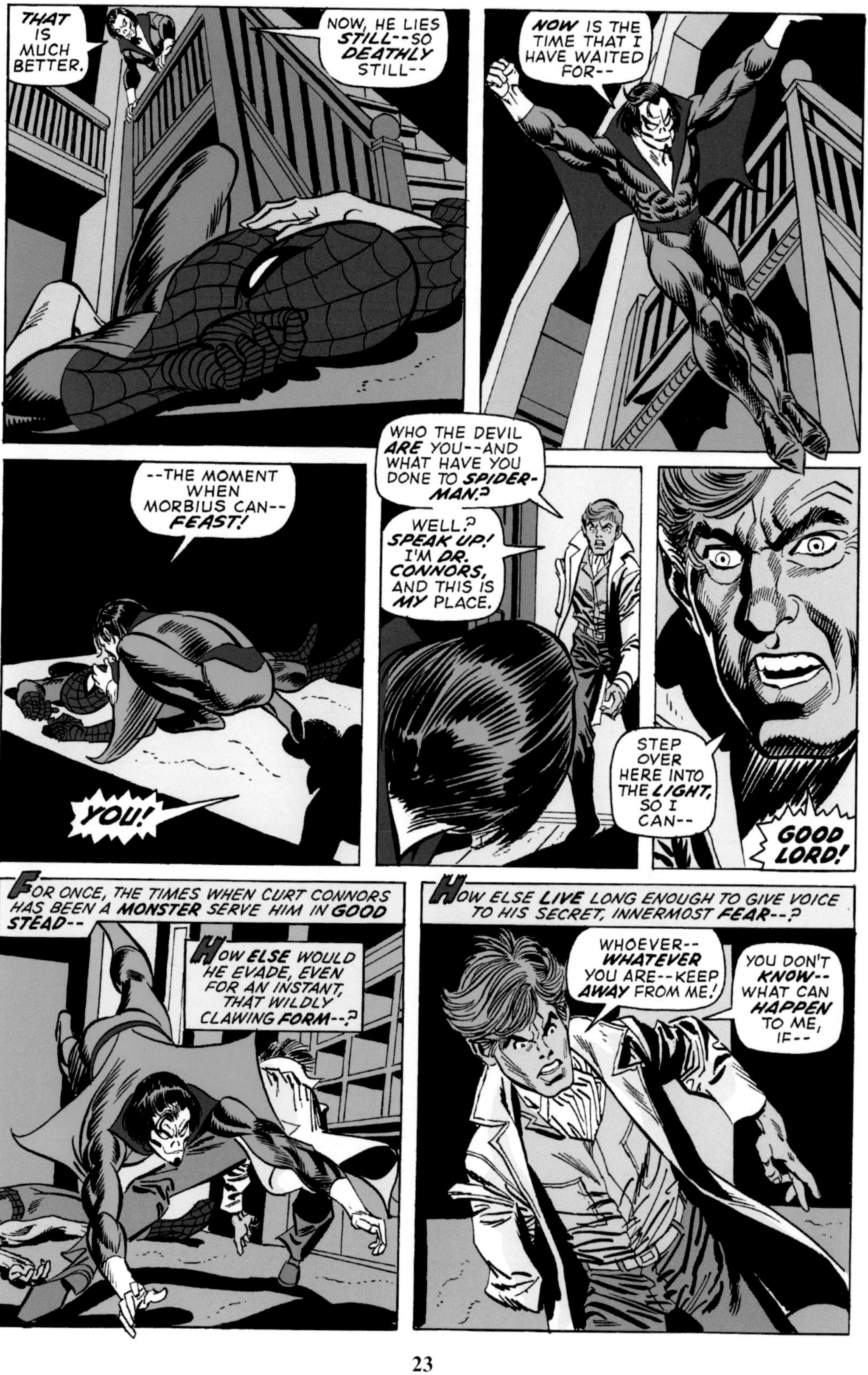
THAT IS MUCH BETTER.
NOW, HE LIES STILL--SO DEATHLY STILL--
NOW IS THE TIME THAT I HAVE WAITED FOR--
--THE MOMENT WHEN MORBIUS CAN--FEAST!
YOU!
WHO THE DEVIL ARE YOU--AND WHAT HAVE YOU DONE TO SPIDER-MAN?
WELL? SPEAK UP! I'M DR. CONNORS, AND THIS IS MY PLACE.
STEP OVER HERE INTO THE LIGHT, SO I CAN--
GOOD LORD!
FOR ONCE, THE TIMES WHEN CURT CONNORS HAS BEEN A MONSTER SERVE HIM IN GOOD STEAD--
HOW ELSE WOULD HE EVADE, EVEN FOR AN INSTANT, THAT WILDLY CLAWING FORM--?
HOW ELSE LIVE LONG ENOUGH TO GIVE VOICE TO HIS SECRET, INNERMOST FEAR--?
WHOEVER--WHATEVER YOU ARE--KEEP AWAY FROM ME!
YOU DON'T KNOW--WHAT CAN HAPPEN TO ME, IF--

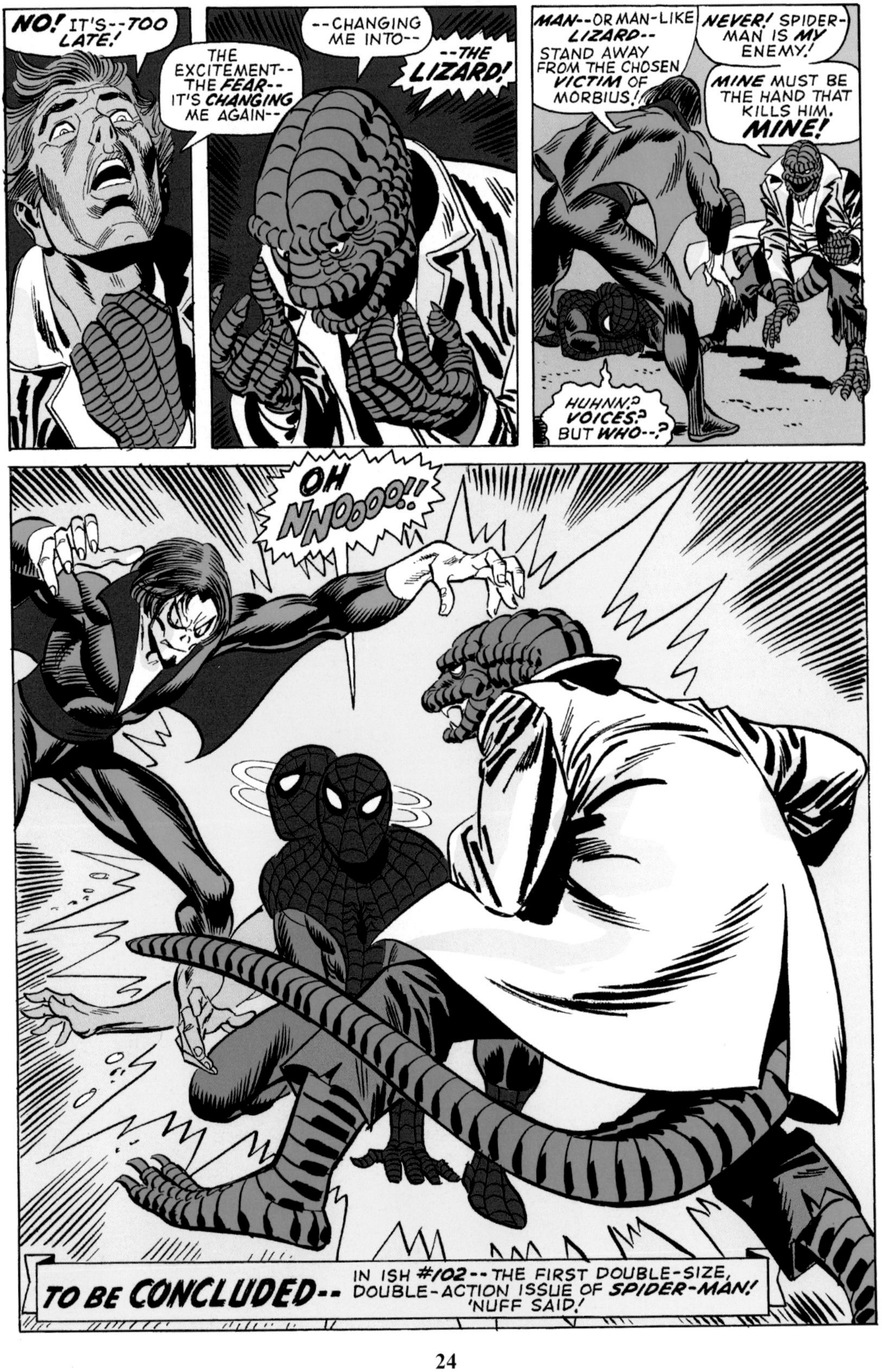
NO! IT'S--TOO LATE!
THE EXCITEMENT--THE FEAR--IT'S CHANGING ME AGAIN--
--CHANGING ME INTO--
--THE LIZARD!
MAN--OR MAN-LIKE LIZARD--STAND AWAY FROM THE CHOSEN VICTIM OF MORBIUS!
NEVER! SPIDER-MAN IS MY ENEMY!
MINE MUST BE THE HAND THAT KILLS HIM. MINE!
HUHNN? VOICES? BUT WHO--?
OH NNOoooo!!
TO BE CONCLUDED--
IN ISH #102--THE FIRST DOUBLE-SIZE, DOUBLE-ACTION ISSUE OF SPIDER-MAN! 'NUFF SAID!

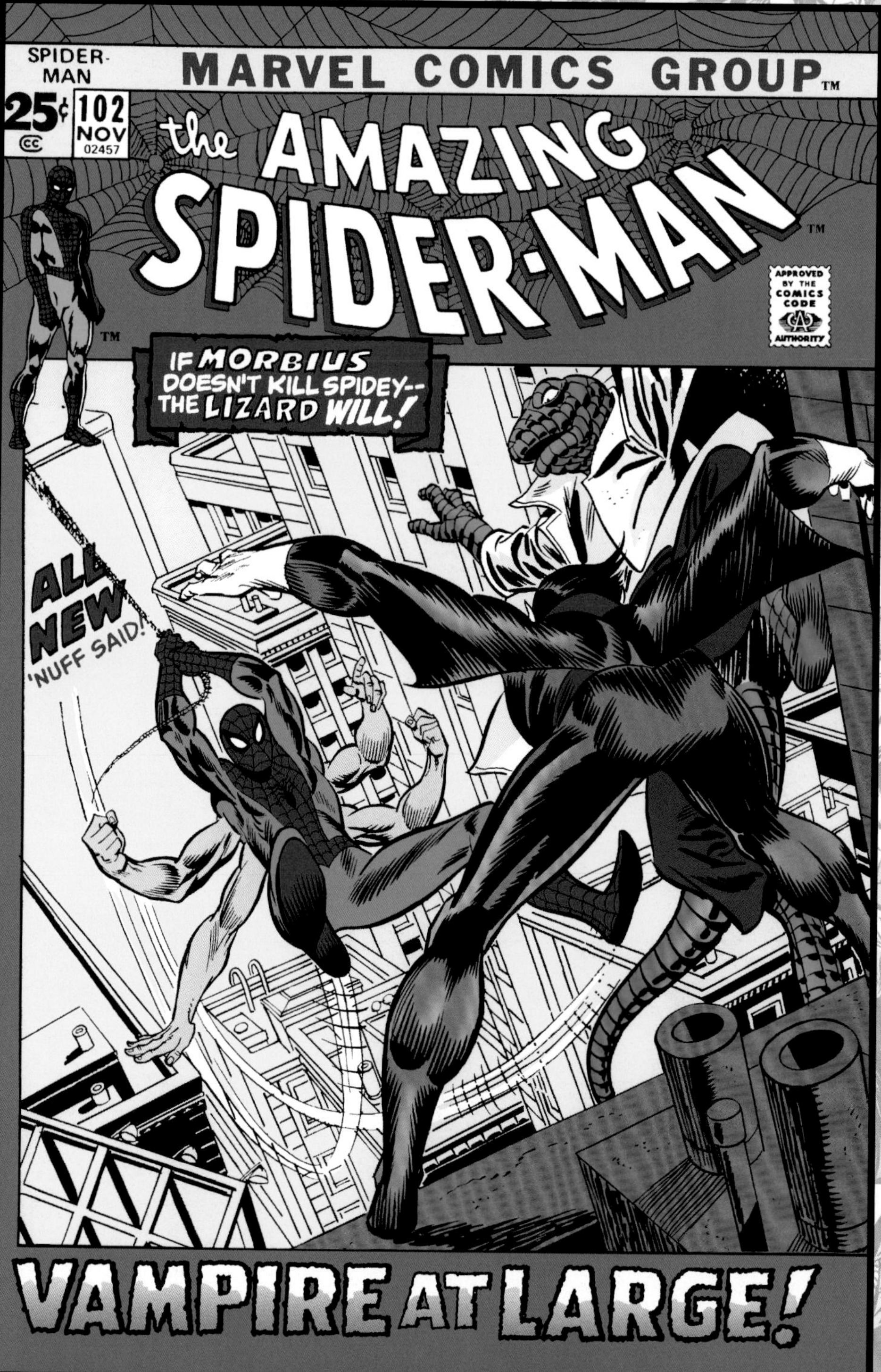
SPIDER-MAN
MARVEL COMICS GROUP
25¢
102
NOV
02457
the AMAZING SPIDER-MAN
APPROVED BY THE COMICS CODE AUTHORITY
IF MORBIUS DOESN'T KILL SPIDEY-- THE LIZARD WILL!
ALL NEW
'NUFF SAID!
VAMPIRE AT LARGE!

AMAZING SPIDER-MAN #102

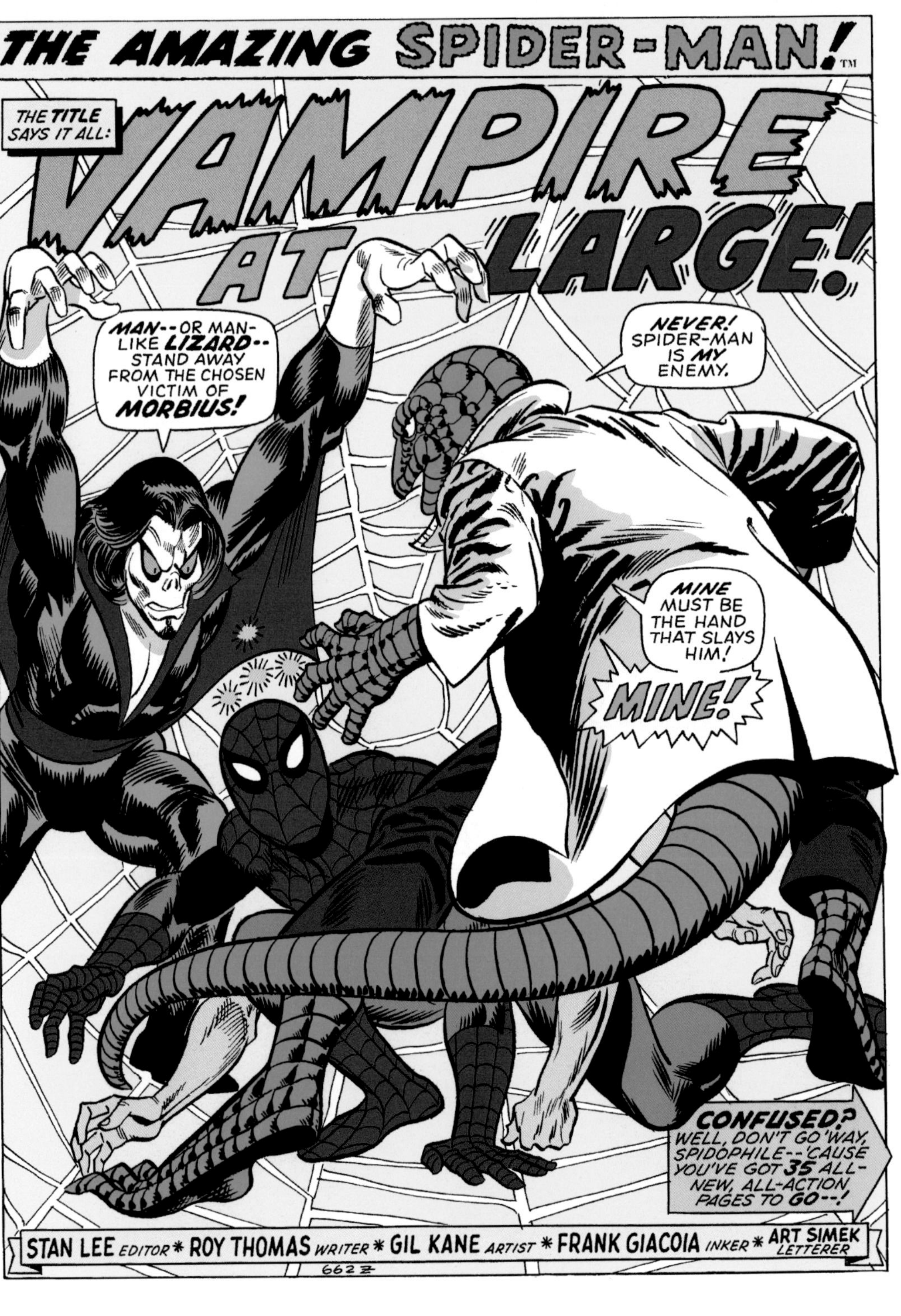
THE AMAZING SPIDER-MAN!™
THE TITLE SAYS IT ALL:
VAMPIRE AT LARGE!
MAN--OR MAN-LIKE LIZARD--STAND AWAY FROM THE CHOSEN VICTIM OF MORBIUS!
NEVER! SPIDER-MAN IS MY ENEMY.
MINE MUST BE THE HAND THAT SLAYS HIM!
MINE!
CONFUSED? WELL, DON'T GO 'WAY, SPIDOPHILE--'CAUSE YOU'VE GOT 35 ALL-NEW, ALL-ACTION PAGES TO GO--!
STAN LEE EDITOR * ROY THOMAS WRITER * GIL KANE ARTIST * FRANK GIACOIA INKER * ART SIMEK LETTERER
662 Z

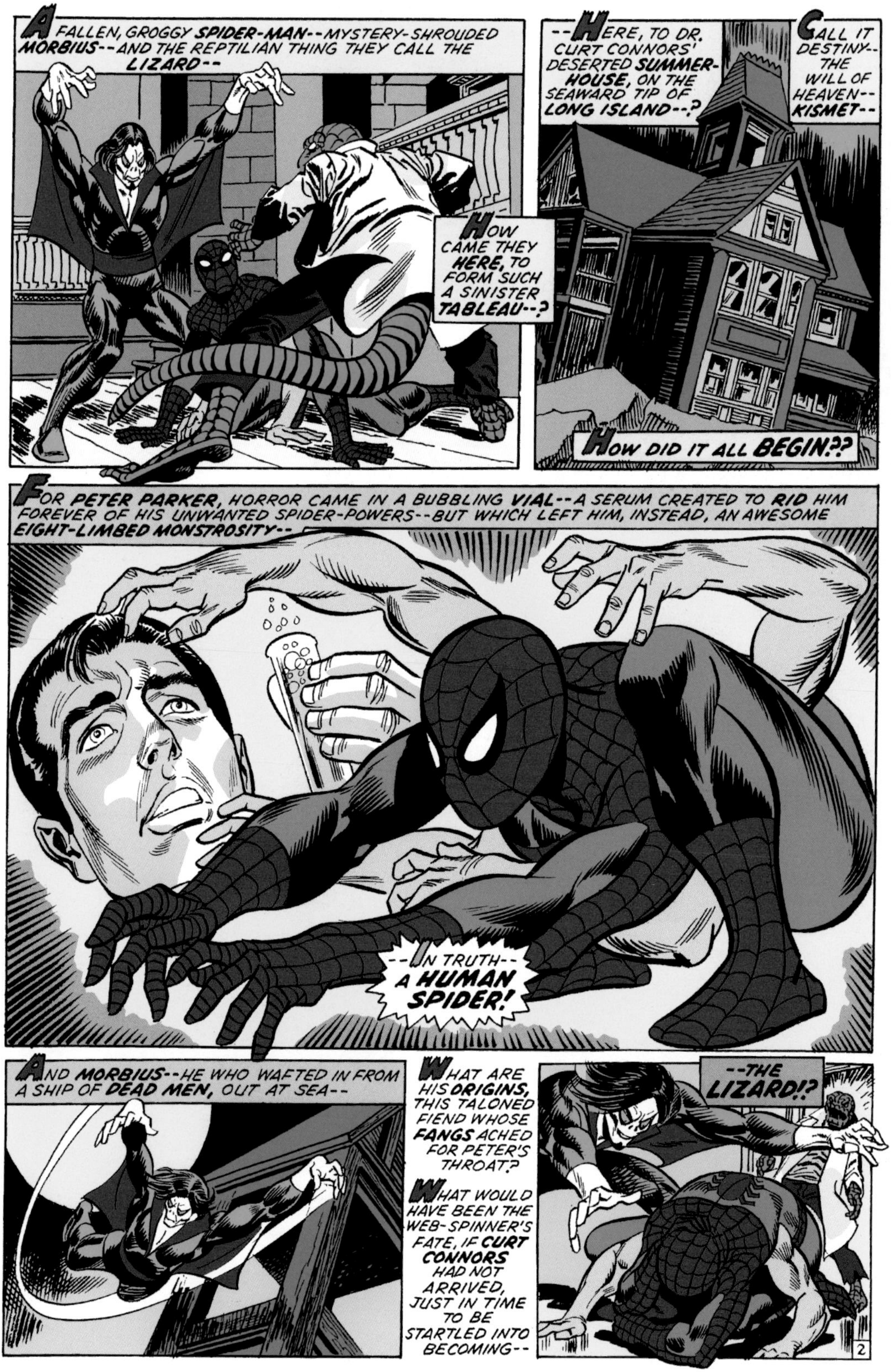
A FALLEN, GROGGY SPIDER-MAN--MYSTERY-SHROUDED MORBIUS--AND THE REPTILIAN THING THEY CALL THE LIZARD--
HOW CAME THEY HERE, TO FORM SUCH A SINISTER TABLEAU--?
--HERE, TO DR. CURT CONNORS' DESERTED SUMMER-HOUSE, ON THE SEAWARD TIP OF LONG ISLAND--?
CALL IT DESTINY--THE WILL OF HEAVEN--KISMET--
HOW DID IT ALL BEGIN??
FOR PETER PARKER, HORROR CAME IN A BUBBLING VIAL--A SERUM CREATED TO RID HIM FOREVER OF HIS UNWANTED SPIDER-POWERS--BUT WHICH LEFT HIM, INSTEAD, AN AWESOME EIGHT-LIMBED MONSTROSITY--
--IN TRUTH--A HUMAN SPIDER!
AND MORBIUS--HE WHO WAFTED IN FROM A SHIP OF DEAD MEN, OUT AT SEA--
WHAT ARE HIS ORIGINS, THIS TALONED FIEND WHOSE FANGS ACHED FOR PETER'S THROAT?
WHAT WOULD HAVE BEEN THE WEB-SPINNER'S FATE, IF CURT CONNORS HAD NOT ARRIVED, JUST IN TIME TO BE STARTLED INTO BECOMING--
--THE LIZARD!?
2

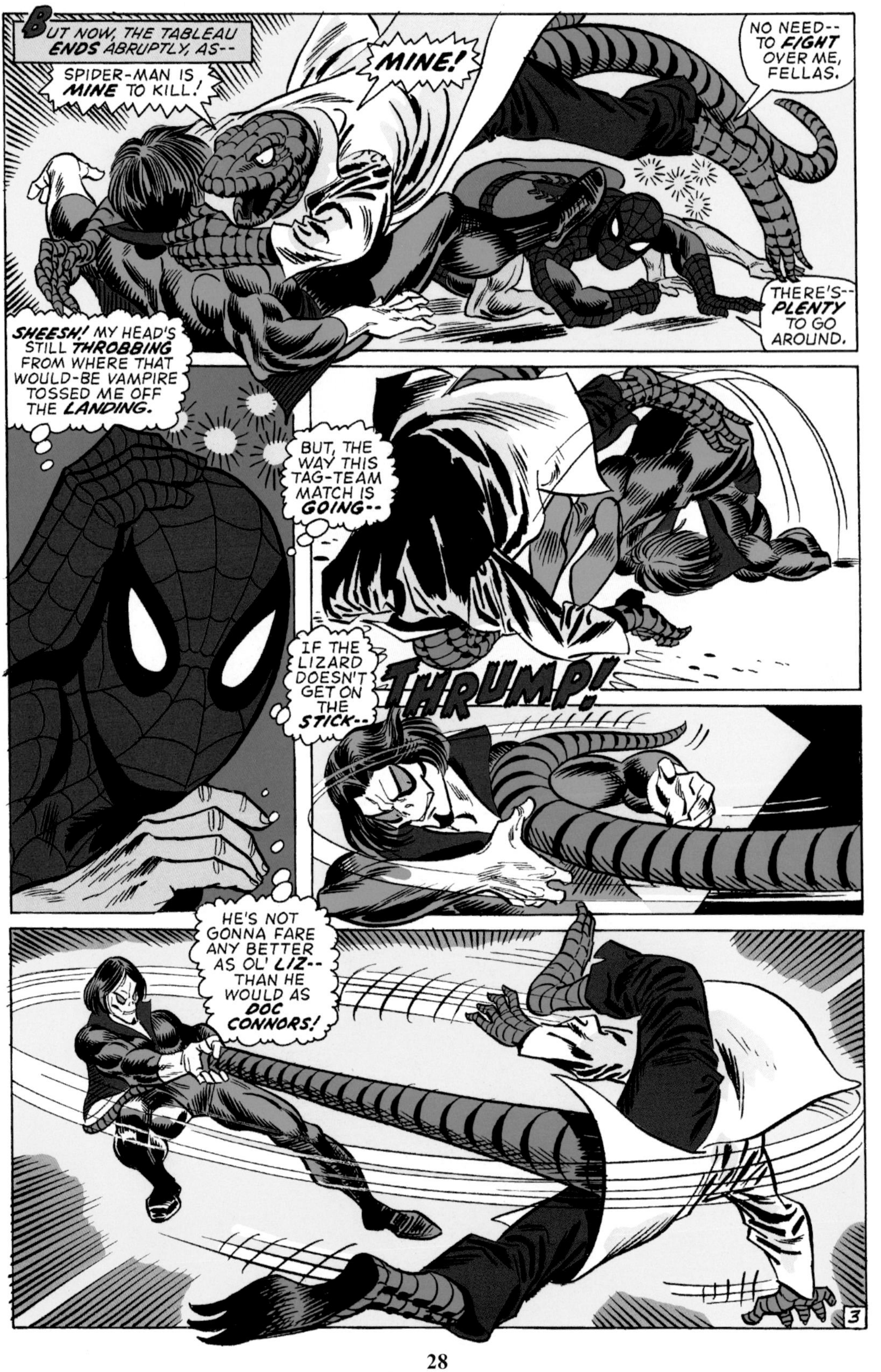
BUT NOW, THE TABLEAU ENDS ABRUPTLY, AS--
SPIDER-MAN IS MINE TO KILL!
MINE!
NO NEED-- TO FIGHT OVER ME, FELLAS.
THERE'S-- PLENTY TO GO AROUND.
SHEESH! MY HEAD'S STILL THROBBING FROM WHERE THAT WOULD-BE VAMPIRE TOSSED ME OFF THE LANDING.
BUT, THE WAY THIS TAG-TEAM MATCH IS GOING--
IF THE LIZARD DOESN'T GET ON THE STICK--
THRUMP!
HE'S NOT GONNA FARE ANY BETTER AS OL' LIZ-- THAN HE WOULD AS DOC CONNORS!
3

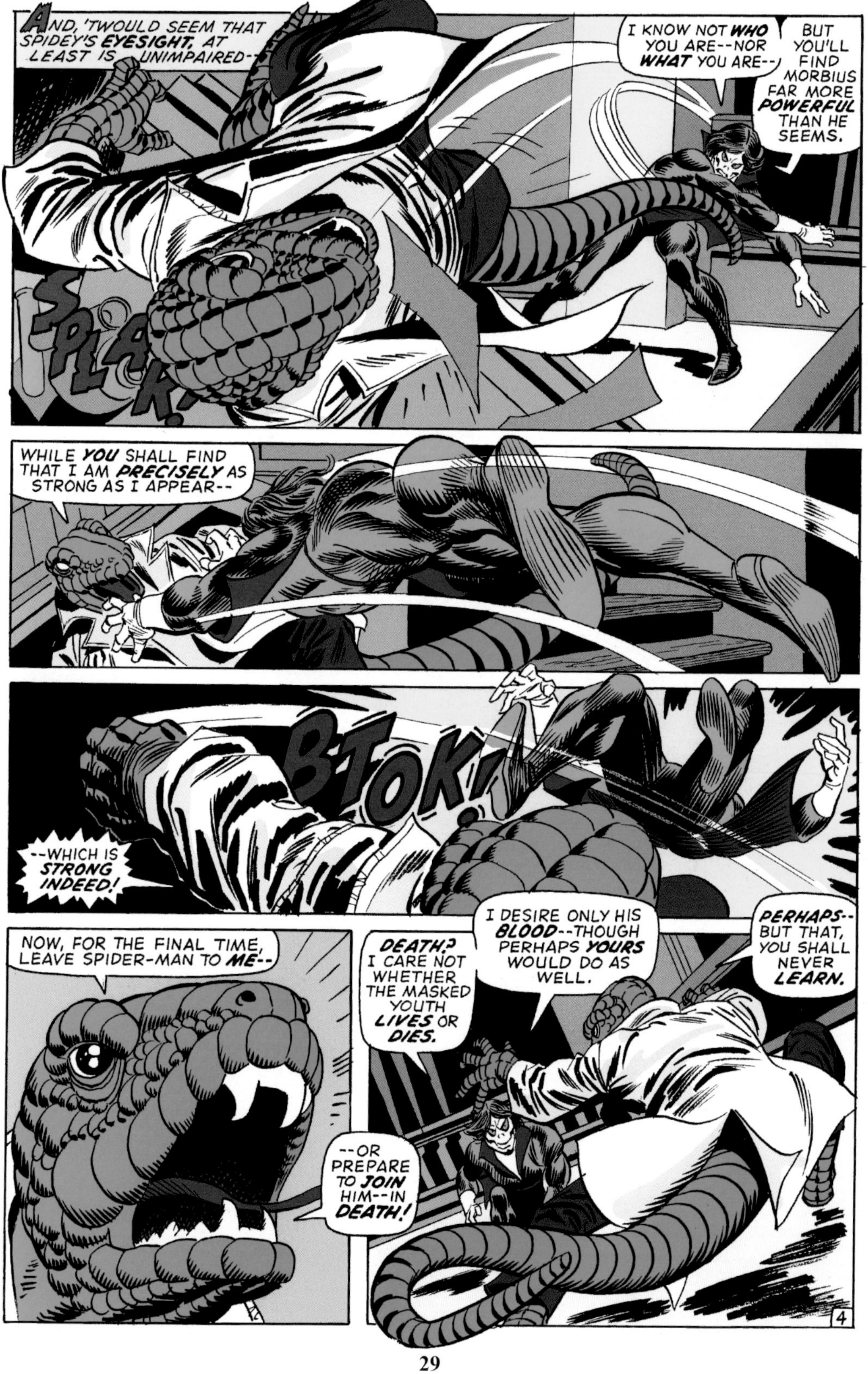
AND, 'TWOULD SEEM THAT SPIDEY'S EYESIGHT, AT LEAST IS UNIMPAIRED--
I KNOW NOT WHO YOU ARE--NOR WHAT YOU ARE--
BUT YOU'LL FIND MORBIUS FAR MORE POWERFUL THAN HE SEEMS.
SPLAK!
WHILE YOU SHALL FIND THAT I AM PRECISELY AS STRONG AS I APPEAR--
BTOK!
--WHICH IS STRONG INDEED!
NOW, FOR THE FINAL TIME, LEAVE SPIDER-MAN TO ME--
--OR PREPARE TO JOIN HIM--IN DEATH!
DEATH? I CARE NOT WHETHER THE MASKED YOUTH LIVES OR DIES.
I DESIRE ONLY HIS BLOOD--THOUGH PERHAPS YOURS WOULD DO AS WELL.
PERHAPS--BUT THAT, YOU SHALL NEVER LEARN.
4

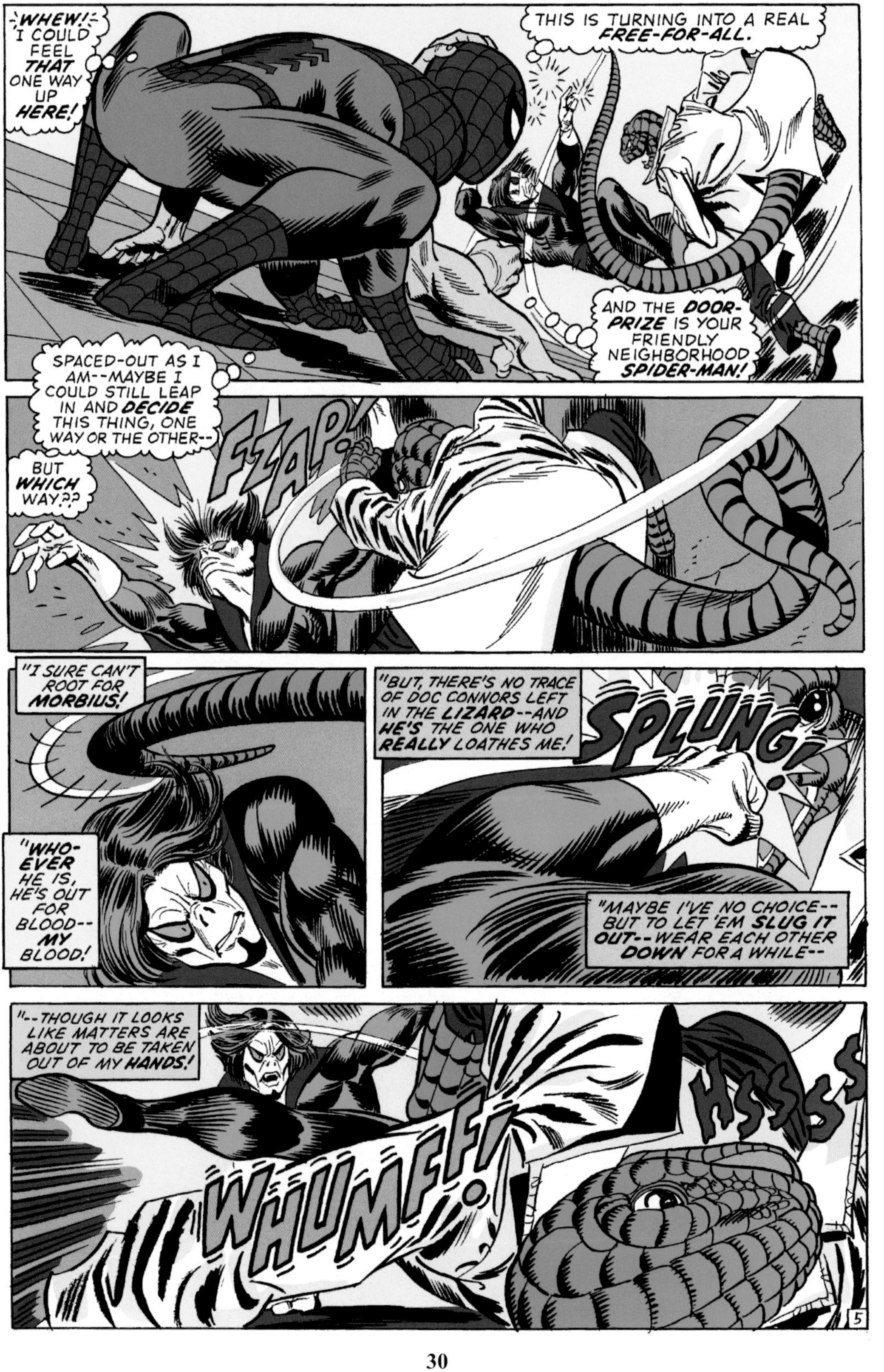
WHEW! I COULD FEEL THAT ONE WAY UP HERE!
THIS IS TURNING INTO A REAL FREE-FOR-ALL.
AND THE DOOR-PRIZE IS YOUR FRIENDLY NEIGHBORHOOD SPIDER-MAN!
SPACED-OUT AS I AM--MAYBE I COULD STILL LEAP IN AND DECIDE THIS THING, ONE WAY OR THE OTHER--
BUT WHICH WAY??
FZAP!
"I SURE CAN'T ROOT FOR MORBIUS!
"WHO-EVER HE IS, HE'S OUT FOR BLOOD--MY BLOOD!
"BUT, THERE'S NO TRACE OF DOC CONNORS LEFT IN THE LIZARD--AND HE'S THE ONE WHO REALLY LOATHES ME!
SPLUNG!
"MAYBE I'VE NO CHOICE--BUT TO LET 'EM SLUG IT OUT--WEAR EACH OTHER DOWN FOR A WHILE--
"--THOUGH IT LOOKS LIKE MATTERS ARE ABOUT TO BE TAKEN OUT OF MY HANDS!
HSSSSS
WHUMFF!
5

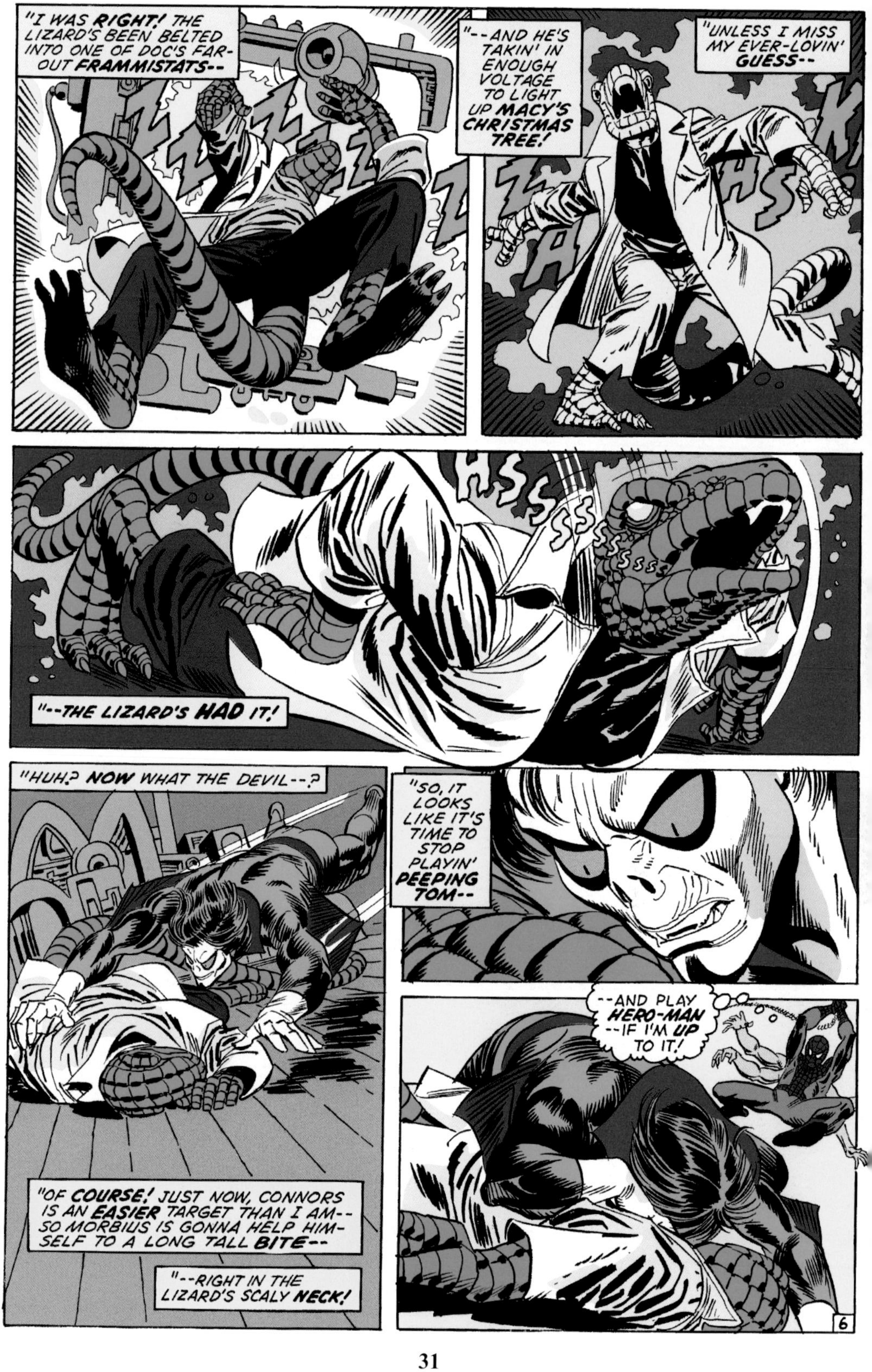
"I WAS RIGHT! THE LIZARD'S BEEN BELTED INTO ONE OF DOC'S FAR-OUT FRAMMISTATS--
"--AND HE'S TAKIN' IN ENOUGH VOLTAGE TO LIGHT UP MACY'S CHRISTMAS TREE!
"UNLESS I MISS MY EVER-LOVIN' GUESS--
"--THE LIZARD'S HAD IT!
"HUH? NOW WHAT THE DEVIL--?
"OF COURSE! JUST NOW, CONNORS IS AN EASIER TARGET THAN I AM--SO MORBIUS IS GONNA HELP HIMSELF TO A LONG TALL BITE--
"--RIGHT IN THE LIZARD'S SCALY NECK!
"SO, IT LOOKS LIKE IT'S TIME TO STOP PLAYIN' PEEPING TOM--
--AND PLAY HERO-MAN --IF I'M UP TO IT!
6

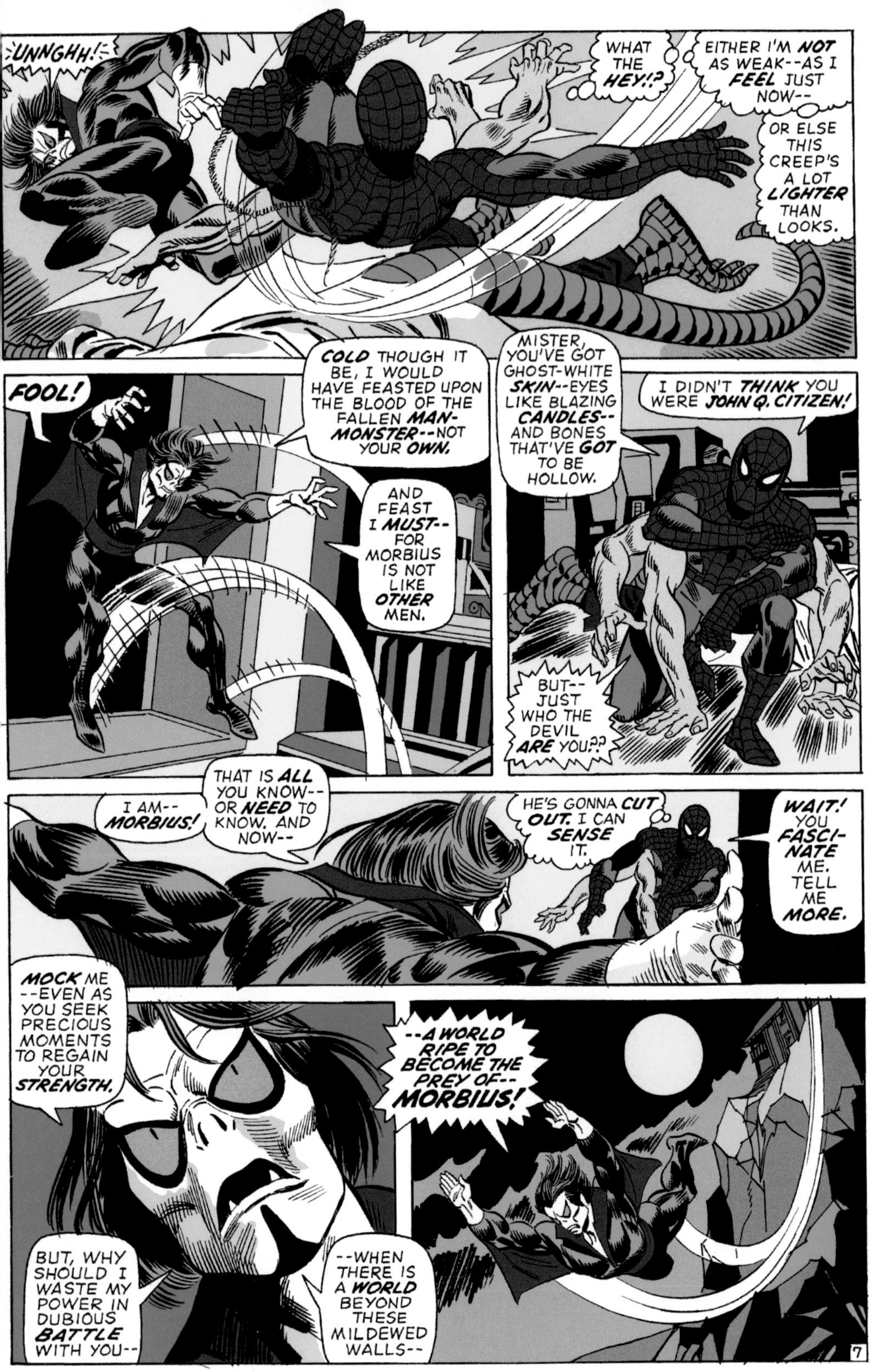
UNNGHH!
WHAT THE HEY!?
EITHER I'M NOT AS WEAK--AS I FEEL JUST NOW--
OR ELSE THIS CREEP'S A LOT LIGHTER THAN LOOKS.
FOOL!
COLD THOUGH IT BE, I WOULD HAVE FEASTED UPON THE BLOOD OF THE FALLEN MAN-MONSTER--NOT YOUR OWN.
AND FEAST I MUST--FOR MORBIUS IS NOT LIKE OTHER MEN.
MISTER, YOU'VE GOT GHOST-WHITE SKIN--EYES LIKE BLAZING CANDLES--AND BONES THAT'VE GOT TO BE HOLLOW.
I DIDN'T THINK YOU WERE JOHN Q. CITIZEN!
BUT--JUST WHO THE DEVIL ARE YOU??
I AM--MORBIUS!
THAT IS ALL YOU KNOW--OR NEED TO KNOW. AND NOW--
HE'S GONNA CUT OUT. I CAN SENSE IT.
WAIT! YOU FASCINATE ME. TELL ME MORE.
MOCK ME--EVEN AS YOU SEEK PRECIOUS MOMENTS TO REGAIN YOUR STRENGTH.
BUT, WHY SHOULD I WASTE MY POWER IN DUBIOUS BATTLE WITH YOU--
--WHEN THERE IS A WORLD BEYOND THESE MILDEWED WALLS--
--A WORLD RIPE TO BECOME THE PREY OF--MORBIUS!
7

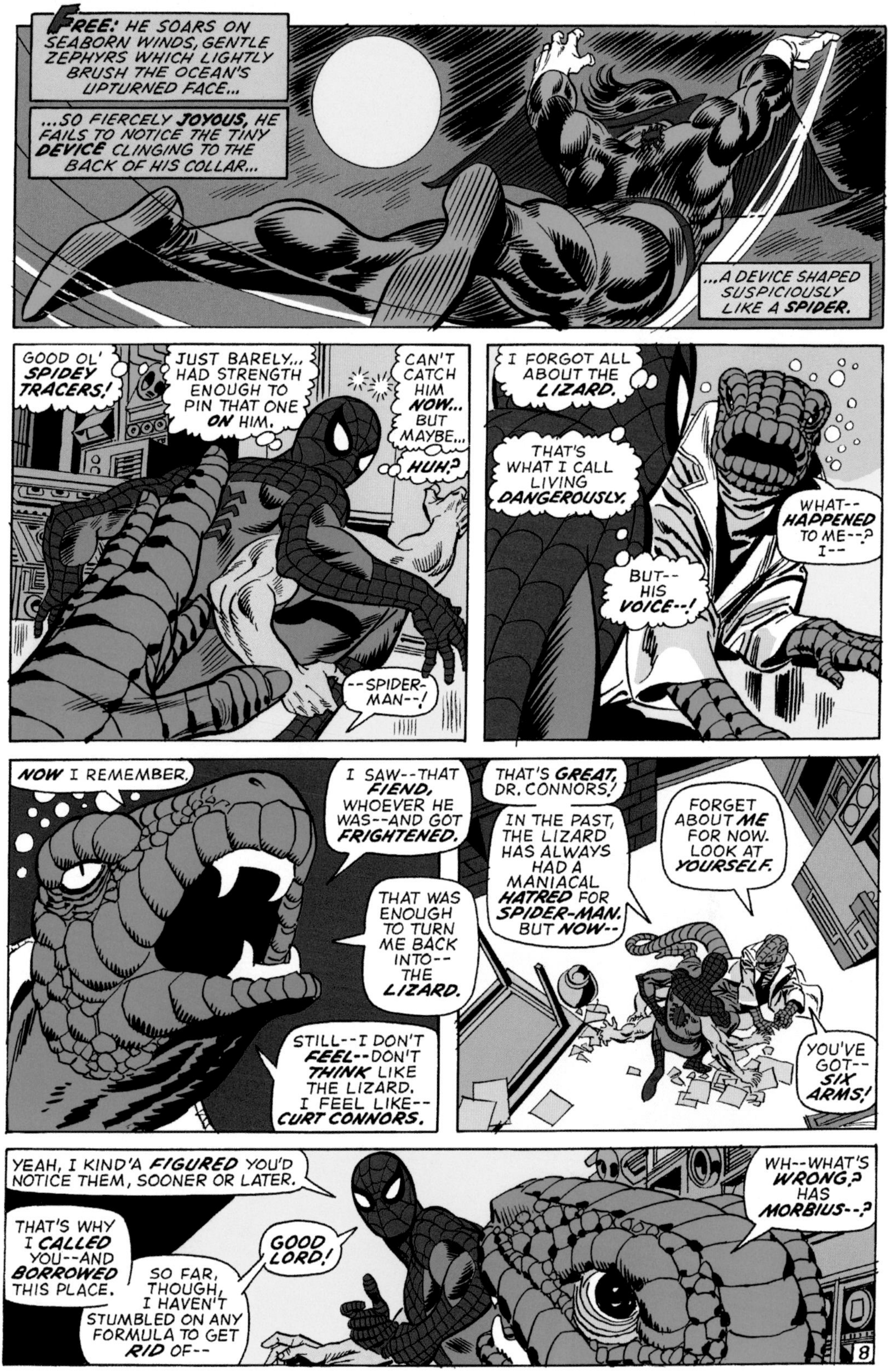
FREE: HE SOARS ON SEABORN WINDS, GENTLE ZEPHYRS WHICH LIGHTLY BRUSH THE OCEAN'S UPTURNED FACE...
...SO FIERCELY JOYOUS, HE FAILS TO NOTICE THE TINY DEVICE CLINGING TO THE BACK OF HIS COLLAR...
...A DEVICE SHAPED SUSPICIOUSLY LIKE A SPIDER.
GOOD OL' SPIDEY TRACERS!
JUST BARELY... HAD STRENGTH ENOUGH TO PIN THAT ONE ON HIM.
CAN'T CATCH HIM NOW... BUT MAYBE... HUH?
--SPIDER-MAN--!
I FORGOT ALL ABOUT THE LIZARD.
THAT'S WHAT I CALL LIVING DANGEROUSLY.
WHAT--HAPPENED TO ME--? I--
BUT--HIS VOICE--!
NOW I REMEMBER.
I SAW--THAT FIEND, WHOEVER HE WAS--AND GOT FRIGHTENED.
THAT WAS ENOUGH TO TURN ME BACK INTO--THE LIZARD.
STILL--I DON'T FEEL--DON'T THINK LIKE THE LIZARD. I FEEL LIKE--CURT CONNORS.
THAT'S GREAT, DR. CONNORS!
IN THE PAST, THE LIZARD HAS ALWAYS HAD A MANIACAL HATRED FOR SPIDER-MAN. BUT NOW--
FORGET ABOUT ME FOR NOW. LOOK AT YOURSELF.
YOU'VE GOT--SIX ARMS!
YEAH, I KIND'A FIGURED YOU'D NOTICE THEM, SOONER OR LATER.
THAT'S WHY I CALLED YOU--AND BORROWED THIS PLACE.
SO FAR, THOUGH, I HAVEN'T STUMBLED ON ANY FORMULA TO GET RID OF--
GOOD LORD!
WH--WHAT'S WRONG? HAS MORBIUS--?
8

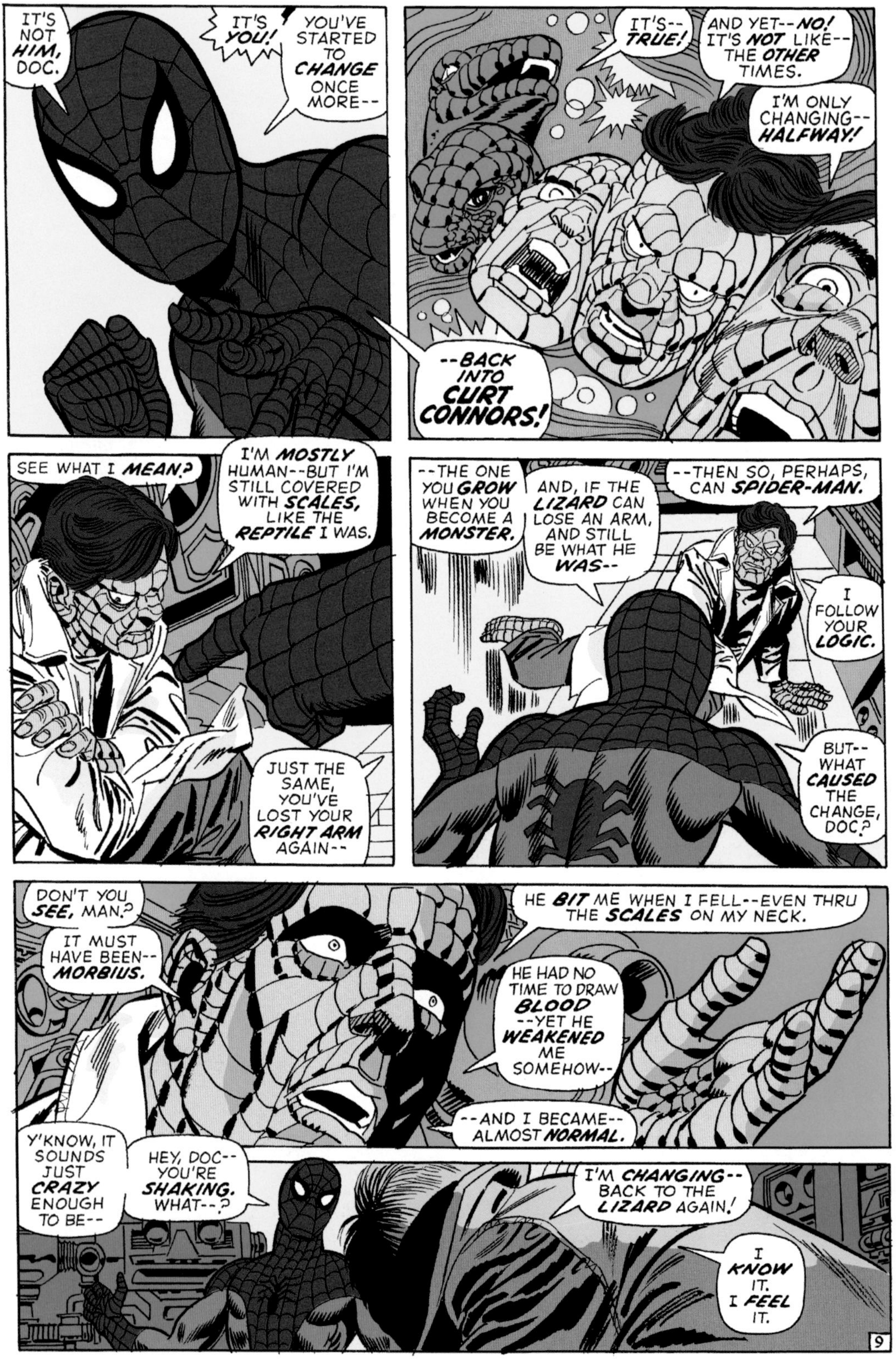

IT'S NOT HIM, DOC.
IT'S YOU!
YOU'VE STARTED TO CHANGE ONCE MORE--
--BACK INTO CURT CONNORS!
IT'S--TRUE!
AND YET--NO! IT'S NOT LIKE--THE OTHER TIMES.
I'M ONLY CHANGING--HALFWAY!
SEE WHAT I MEAN?
I'M MOSTLY HUMAN--BUT I'M STILL COVERED WITH SCALES, LIKE THE REPTILE I WAS.
JUST THE SAME, YOU'VE LOST YOUR RIGHT ARM AGAIN--
--THE ONE YOU GROW WHEN YOU BECOME A MONSTER.
AND, IF THE LIZARD CAN LOSE AN ARM, AND STILL BE WHAT HE WAS--
--THEN SO, PERHAPS, CAN SPIDER-MAN.
I FOLLOW YOUR LOGIC.
BUT--WHAT CAUSED THE CHANGE, DOC?
DON'T YOU SEE, MAN?
IT MUST HAVE BEEN--MORBIUS.
HE BIT ME WHEN I FELL--EVEN THRU THE SCALES ON MY NECK.
HE HAD NO TIME TO DRAW BLOOD--YET HE WEAKENED ME SOMEHOW--
--AND I BECAME--ALMOST NORMAL.
Y'KNOW, IT SOUNDS JUST CRAZY ENOUGH TO BE--
HEY, DOC--YOU'RE SHAKING. WHAT--?
I'M CHANGING--BACK TO THE LIZARD AGAIN!
I KNOW IT. I FEEL IT.
9

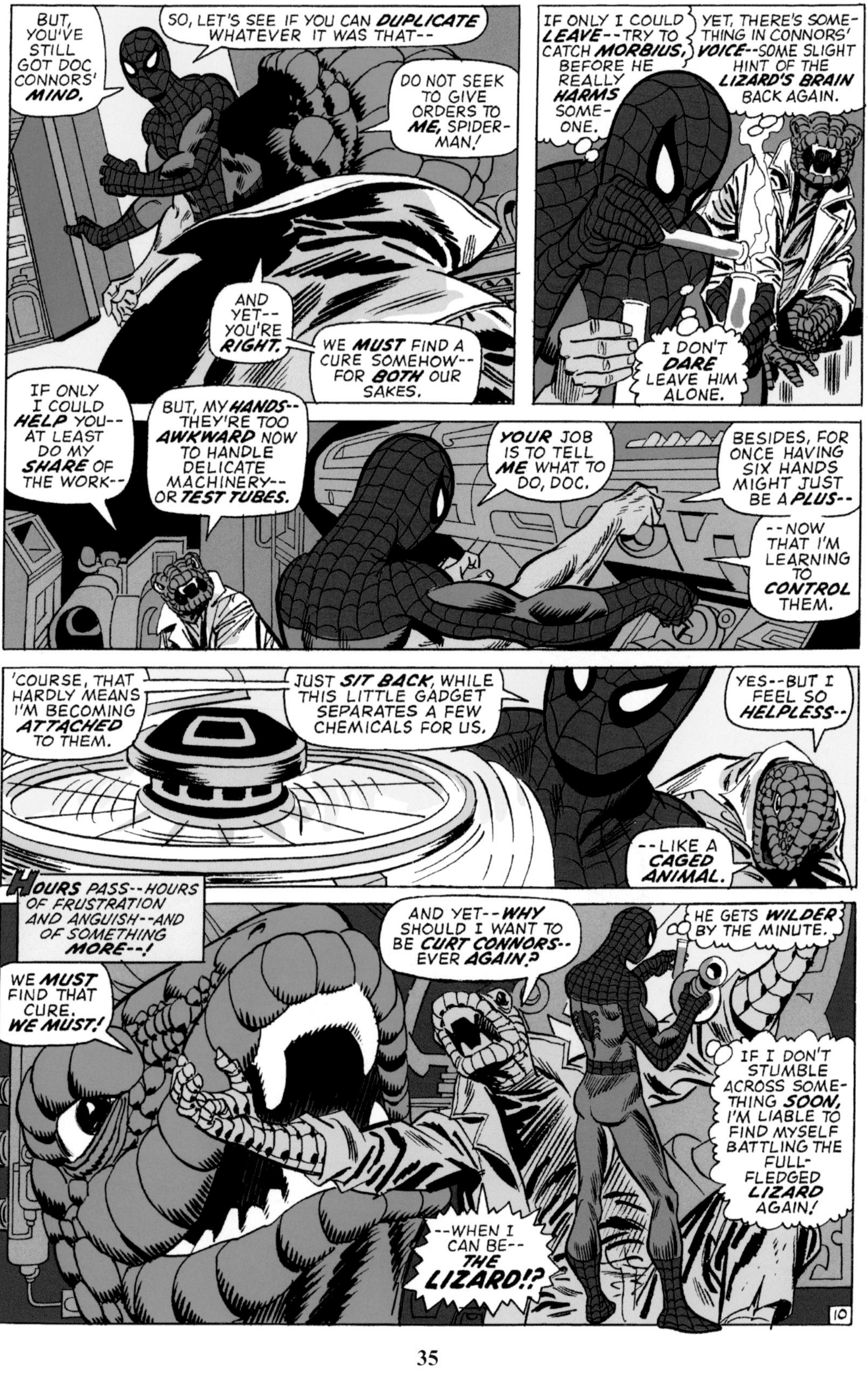
BUT, YOU'VE STILL GOT DOC CONNORS' MIND.
SO, LET'S SEE IF YOU CAN DUPLICATE WHATEVER IT WAS THAT--
DO NOT SEEK TO GIVE ORDERS TO ME, SPIDER-MAN!
AND YET--YOU'RE RIGHT.
WE MUST FIND A CURE SOMEHOW--FOR BOTH OUR SAKES.
IF ONLY I COULD LEAVE--TRY TO CATCH MORBIUS, BEFORE HE REALLY HARMS SOME-ONE.
YET, THERE'S SOME-THING IN CONNORS' VOICE--SOME SLIGHT HINT OF THE LIZARD'S BRAIN BACK AGAIN.
I DON'T DARE LEAVE HIM ALONE.
IF ONLY I COULD HELP YOU--AT LEAST DO MY SHARE OF THE WORK--
BUT, MY HANDS--THEY'RE TOO AWKWARD NOW TO HANDLE DELICATE MACHINERY--OR TEST TUBES.
YOUR JOB IS TO TELL ME WHAT TO DO, DOC.
BESIDES, FOR ONCE HAVING SIX HANDS MIGHT JUST BE A PLUS--
--NOW THAT I'M LEARNING TO CONTROL THEM.
'COURSE, THAT HARDLY MEANS I'M BECOMING ATTACHED TO THEM.
JUST SIT BACK, WHILE THIS LITTLE GADGET SEPARATES A FEW CHEMICALS FOR US.
YES--BUT I FEEL SO HELPLESS--
--LIKE A CAGED ANIMAL.
HOURS PASS--HOURS OF FRUSTRATION AND ANGUISH--AND OF SOMETHING MORE--!
WE MUST FIND THAT CURE. WE MUST!
AND YET--WHY SHOULD I WANT TO BE CURT CONNORS--EVER AGAIN?
--WHEN I CAN BE--THE LIZARD!?
HE GETS WILDER BY THE MINUTE.
IF I DON'T STUMBLE ACROSS SOME-THING SOON, I'M LIABLE TO FIND MYSELF BATTLING THE FULL-FLEDGED LIZARD AGAIN!
10

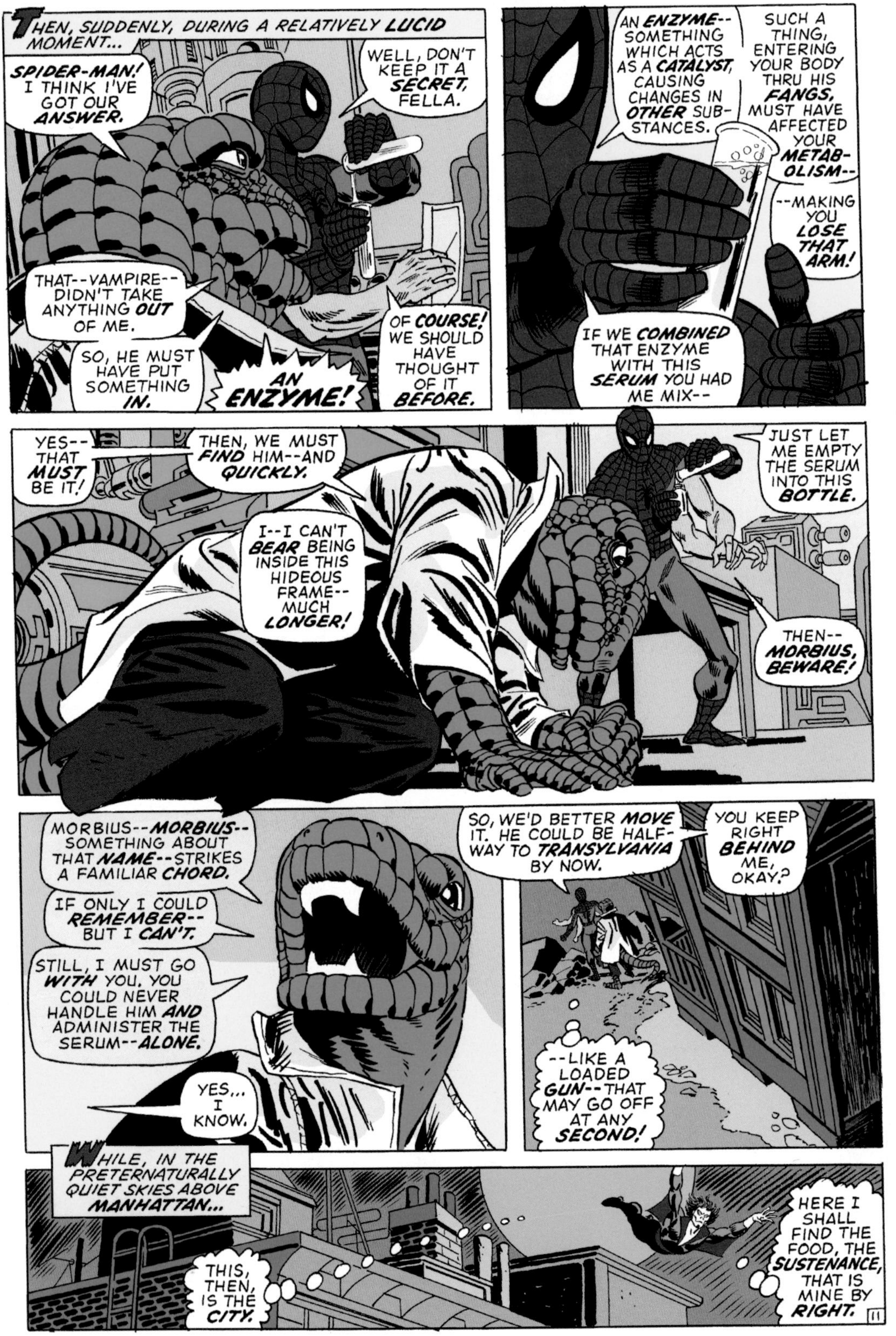
THEN, SUDDENLY, DURING A RELATIVELY LUCID MOMENT...
SPIDER-MAN! I THINK I'VE GOT OUR ANSWER.
WELL, DON'T KEEP IT A SECRET, FELLA.
THAT--VAMPIRE--DIDN'T TAKE ANYTHING OUT OF ME.
SO, HE MUST HAVE PUT SOMETHING IN.
AN ENZYME!
OF COURSE! WE SHOULD HAVE THOUGHT OF IT BEFORE.
AN ENZYME--SOMETHING WHICH ACTS AS A CATALYST, CAUSING CHANGES IN OTHER SUBSTANCES.
SUCH A THING, ENTERING YOUR BODY THRU HIS FANGS, MUST HAVE AFFECTED YOUR METABOLISM--
--MAKING YOU LOSE THAT ARM!
IF WE COMBINED THAT ENZYME WITH THIS SERUM YOU HAD ME MIX--
YES--THAT MUST BE IT!
THEN, WE MUST FIND HIM--AND QUICKLY.
JUST LET ME EMPTY THE SERUM INTO THIS BOTTLE.
I--I CAN'T BEAR BEING INSIDE THIS HIDEOUS FRAME--MUCH LONGER!
THEN--MORBIUS, BEWARE!
MORBIUS--MORBIUS--SOMETHING ABOUT THAT NAME--STRIKES A FAMILIAR CHORD.
IF ONLY I COULD REMEMBER--BUT I CAN'T.
STILL, I MUST GO WITH YOU. YOU COULD NEVER HANDLE HIM AND ADMINISTER THE SERUM--ALONE.
YES,... I KNOW.
SO, WE'D BETTER MOVE IT. HE COULD BE HALF-WAY TO TRANSYLVANIA BY NOW.
YOU KEEP RIGHT BEHIND ME, OKAY?
--LIKE A LOADED GUN--THAT MAY GO OFF AT ANY SECOND!
WHILE, IN THE PRETERNATURALLY QUIET SKIES ABOVE MANHATTAN...
THIS, THEN, IS THE CITY.
HERE I SHALL FIND THE FOOD, THE SUSTENANCE, THAT IS MINE BY RIGHT.
11

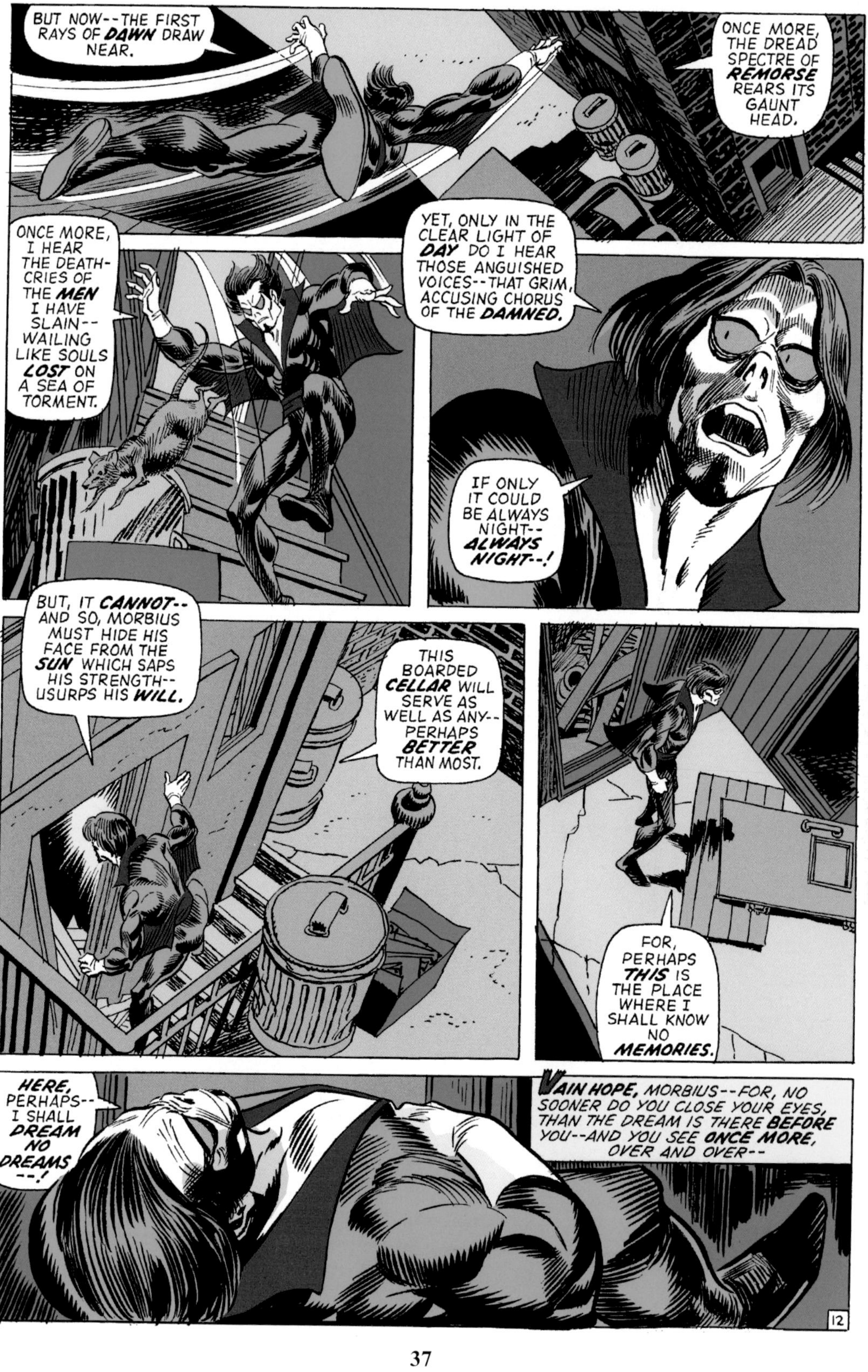

BUT NOW--THE FIRST RAYS OF DAWN DRAW NEAR.
ONCE MORE, THE DREAD SPECTRE OF REMORSE REARS ITS GAUNT HEAD.
ONCE MORE, I HEAR THE DEATH-CRIES OF THE MEN I HAVE SLAIN--WAILING LIKE SOULS LOST ON A SEA OF TORMENT.
YET, ONLY IN THE CLEAR LIGHT OF DAY DO I HEAR THOSE ANGUISHED VOICES--THAT GRIM, ACCUSING CHORUS OF THE DAMNED.
IF ONLY IT COULD BE ALWAYS NIGHT--ALWAYS NIGHT--!
BUT, IT CANNOT--AND SO, MORBIUS MUST HIDE HIS FACE FROM THE SUN WHICH SAPS HIS STRENGTH--USURPS HIS WILL.
THIS BOARDED CELLAR WILL SERVE AS WELL AS ANY--PERHAPS BETTER THAN MOST.
FOR, PERHAPS THIS IS THE PLACE WHERE I SHALL KNOW NO MEMORIES.
HERE, PERHAPS--I SHALL DREAM NO DREAMS--!
VAIN HOPE, MORBIUS--FOR, NO SOONER DO YOU CLOSE YOUR EYES, THAN THE DREAM IS THERE BEFORE YOU--AND YOU SEE ONCE MORE, OVER AND OVER--
12

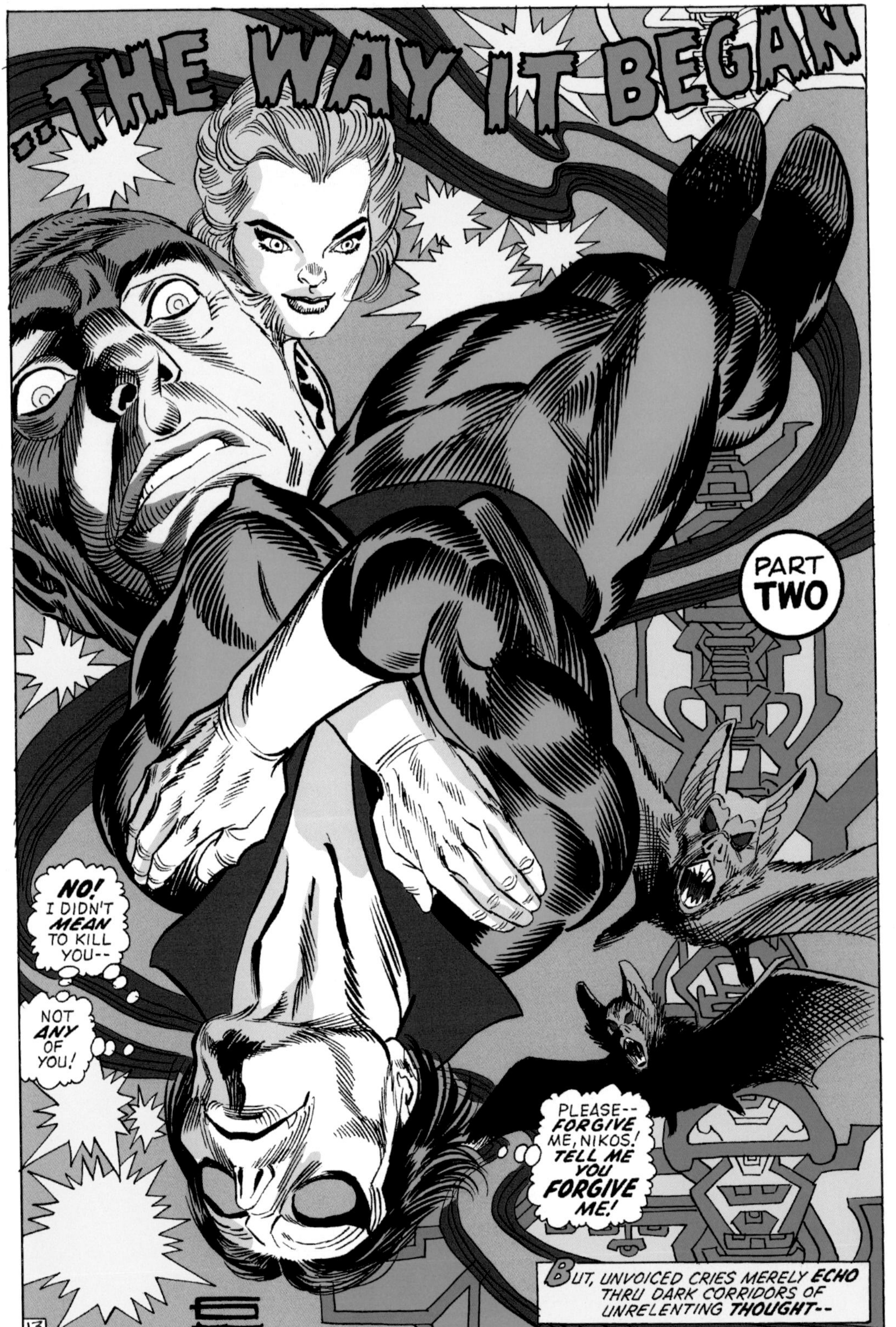

..THE WAY IT BEGAN
PART TWO
NO! I DIDN'T MEAN TO KILL YOU--
NOT ANY OF YOU!
PLEASE-- FORGIVE ME, NIKOS! TELL ME YOU FORGIVE ME!
BUT, UNVOICED CRIES MERELY ECHO THRU DARK CORRIDORS OF UNRELENTING THOUGHT--
13

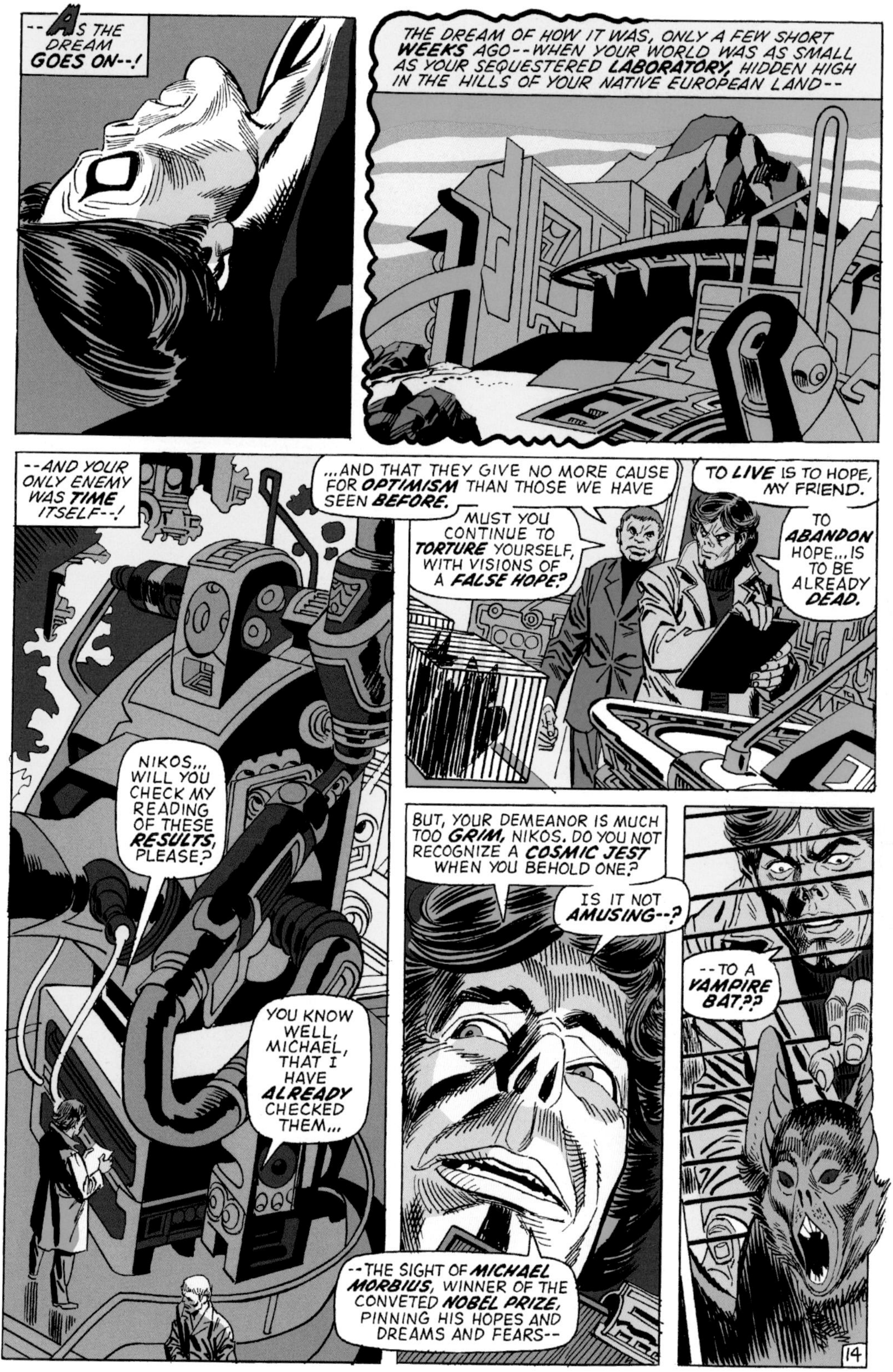
--As the dream goes on--!
The dream of how it was, only a few short weeks ago--when your world was as small as your sequestered laboratory, hidden high in the hills of your native European land--
--And your only enemy was time itself--!
Nikos... will you check my reading of these results, please?
You know well, Michael, that I have already checked them...
...And that they give no more cause for optimism than those we have seen before.
Must you continue to torture yourself, with visions of a false hope?
To live is to hope, my friend.
To abandon hope... is to be already dead.
But, your demeanor is much too grim, Nikos. Do you not recognize a cosmic jest when you behold one?
Is it not amusing--?
--The sight of Michael Morbius, winner of the conveted Nobel Prize, pinning his hopes and dreams and fears--
--To a vampire bat??
14

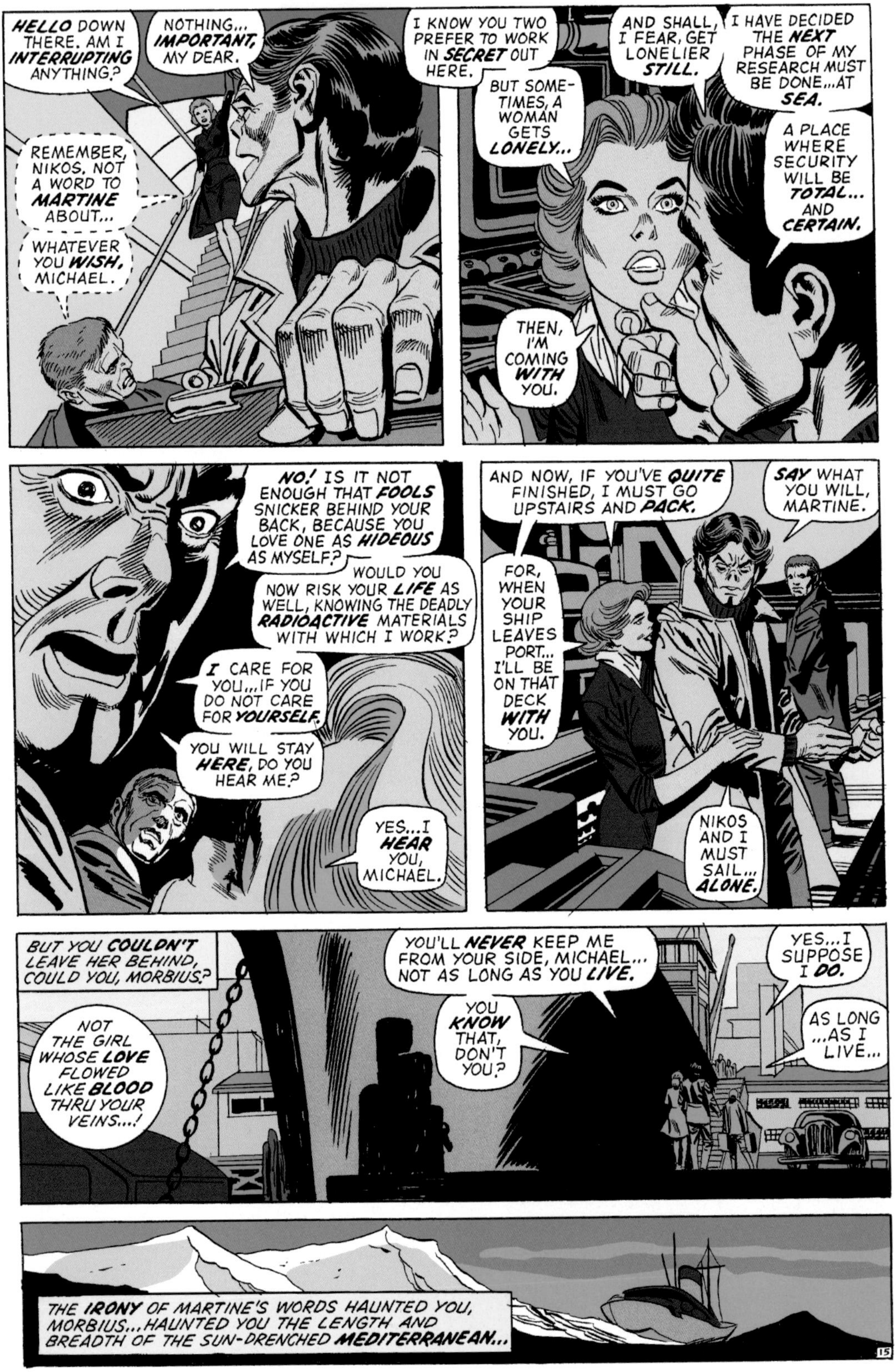
HELLO DOWN THERE. AM I INTERRUPTING ANYTHING?
NOTHING... IMPORTANT, MY DEAR.
REMEMBER, NIKOS. NOT A WORD TO MARTINE ABOUT...
WHATEVER YOU WISH, MICHAEL.
I KNOW YOU TWO PREFER TO WORK IN SECRET OUT HERE.
BUT SOMETIMES, A WOMAN GETS LONELY...
AND SHALL, I FEAR, GET LONELIER STILL.
I HAVE DECIDED THE NEXT PHASE OF MY RESEARCH MUST BE DONE...AT SEA.
A PLACE WHERE SECURITY WILL BE TOTAL... AND CERTAIN.
THEN, I'M COMING WITH YOU.
NO! IS IT NOT ENOUGH THAT FOOLS SNICKER BEHIND YOUR BACK, BECAUSE YOU LOVE ONE AS HIDEOUS AS MYSELF?
WOULD YOU NOW RISK YOUR LIFE AS WELL, KNOWING THE DEADLY RADIOACTIVE MATERIALS WITH WHICH I WORK?
I CARE FOR YOU... IF YOU DO NOT CARE FOR YOURSELF.
YOU WILL STAY HERE, DO YOU HEAR ME?
YES...I HEAR YOU, MICHAEL.
AND NOW, IF YOU'VE QUITE FINISHED, I MUST GO UPSTAIRS AND PACK.
SAY WHAT YOU WILL, MARTINE.
FOR, WHEN YOUR SHIP LEAVES PORT... I'LL BE ON THAT DECK WITH YOU.
NIKOS AND I MUST SAIL... ALONE.
BUT YOU COULDN'T LEAVE HER BEHIND, COULD YOU, MORBIUS?
NOT THE GIRL WHOSE LOVE FLOWED LIKE BLOOD THRU YOUR VEINS...!
YOU'LL NEVER KEEP ME FROM YOUR SIDE, MICHAEL... NOT AS LONG AS YOU LIVE.
YOU KNOW THAT, DON'T YOU?
YES...I SUPPOSE I DO.
AS LONG ...AS I LIVE...
THE IRONY OF MARTINE'S WORDS HAUNTED YOU, MORBIUS... HAUNTED YOU THE LENGTH AND BREADTH OF THE SUN-DRENCHED MEDITERRANEAN...
15

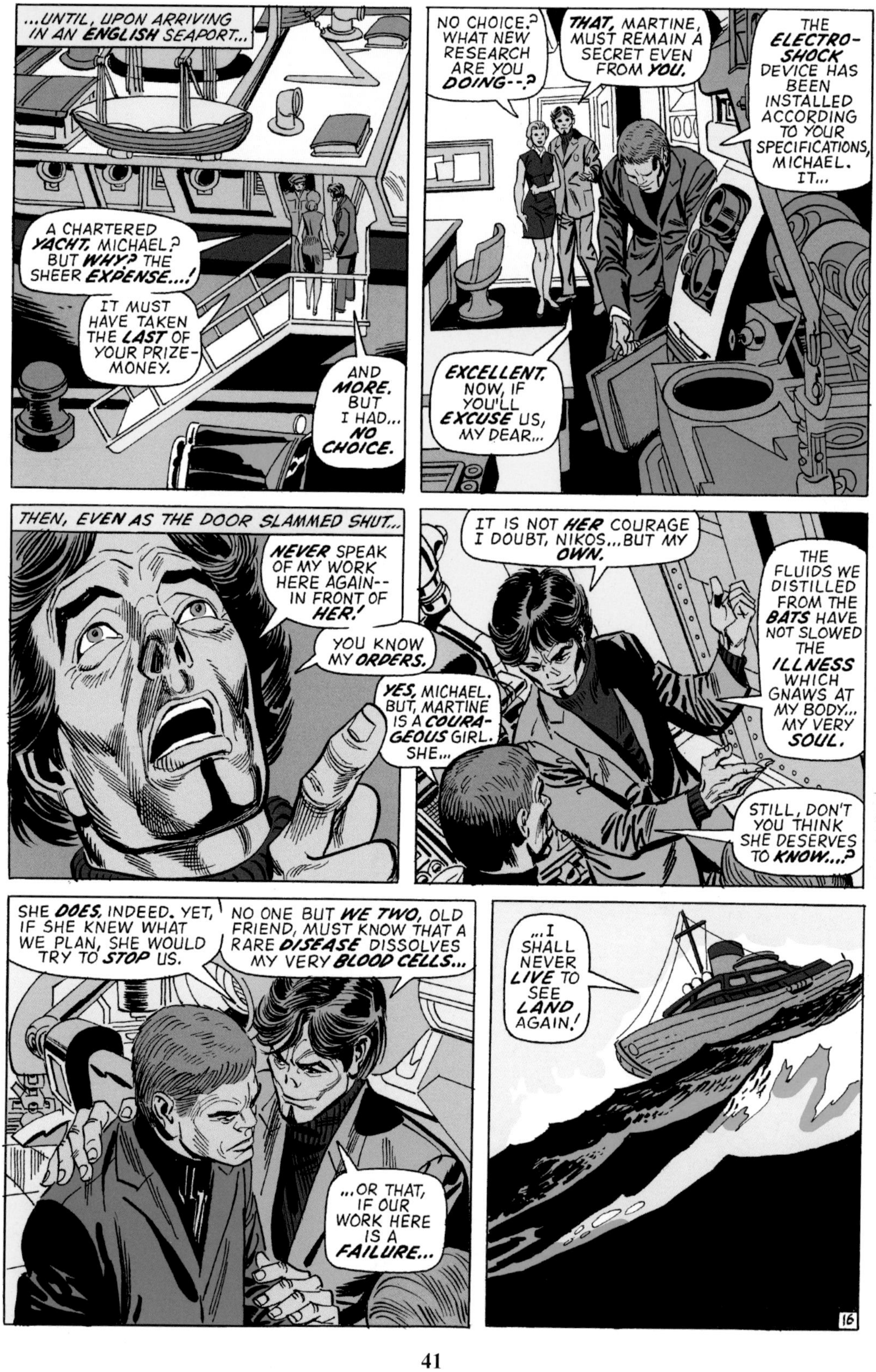
...UNTIL, UPON ARRIVING IN AN ENGLISH SEAPORT...
A CHARTERED YACHT, MICHAEL? BUT WHY? THE SHEER EXPENSE...!
IT MUST HAVE TAKEN THE LAST OF YOUR PRIZE-MONEY.
AND MORE. BUT I HAD... NO CHOICE.
NO CHOICE? WHAT NEW RESEARCH ARE YOU DOING--?
THAT, MARTINE, MUST REMAIN A SECRET EVEN FROM YOU.
THE ELECTRO-SHOCK DEVICE HAS BEEN INSTALLED ACCORDING TO YOUR SPECIFICATIONS, MICHAEL. IT...
EXCELLENT. NOW, IF YOU'LL EXCUSE US, MY DEAR...
THEN, EVEN AS THE DOOR SLAMMED SHUT...
NEVER SPEAK OF MY WORK HERE AGAIN-- IN FRONT OF HER!
YOU KNOW MY ORDERS.
YES, MICHAEL. BUT, MARTINE IS A COURAGEOUS GIRL. SHE...
IT IS NOT HER COURAGE I DOUBT, NIKOS... BUT MY OWN.
THE FLUIDS WE DISTILLED FROM THE BATS HAVE NOT SLOWED THE ILLNESS WHICH GNAWS AT MY BODY... MY VERY SOUL.
STILL, DON'T YOU THINK SHE DESERVES TO KNOW...?
SHE DOES, INDEED. YET, IF SHE KNEW WHAT WE PLAN, SHE WOULD TRY TO STOP US.
NO ONE BUT WE TWO, OLD FRIEND, MUST KNOW THAT A RARE DISEASE DISSOLVES MY VERY BLOOD CELLS...
...OR THAT, IF OUR WORK HERE IS A FAILURE...
...I SHALL NEVER LIVE TO SEE LAND AGAIN!
16

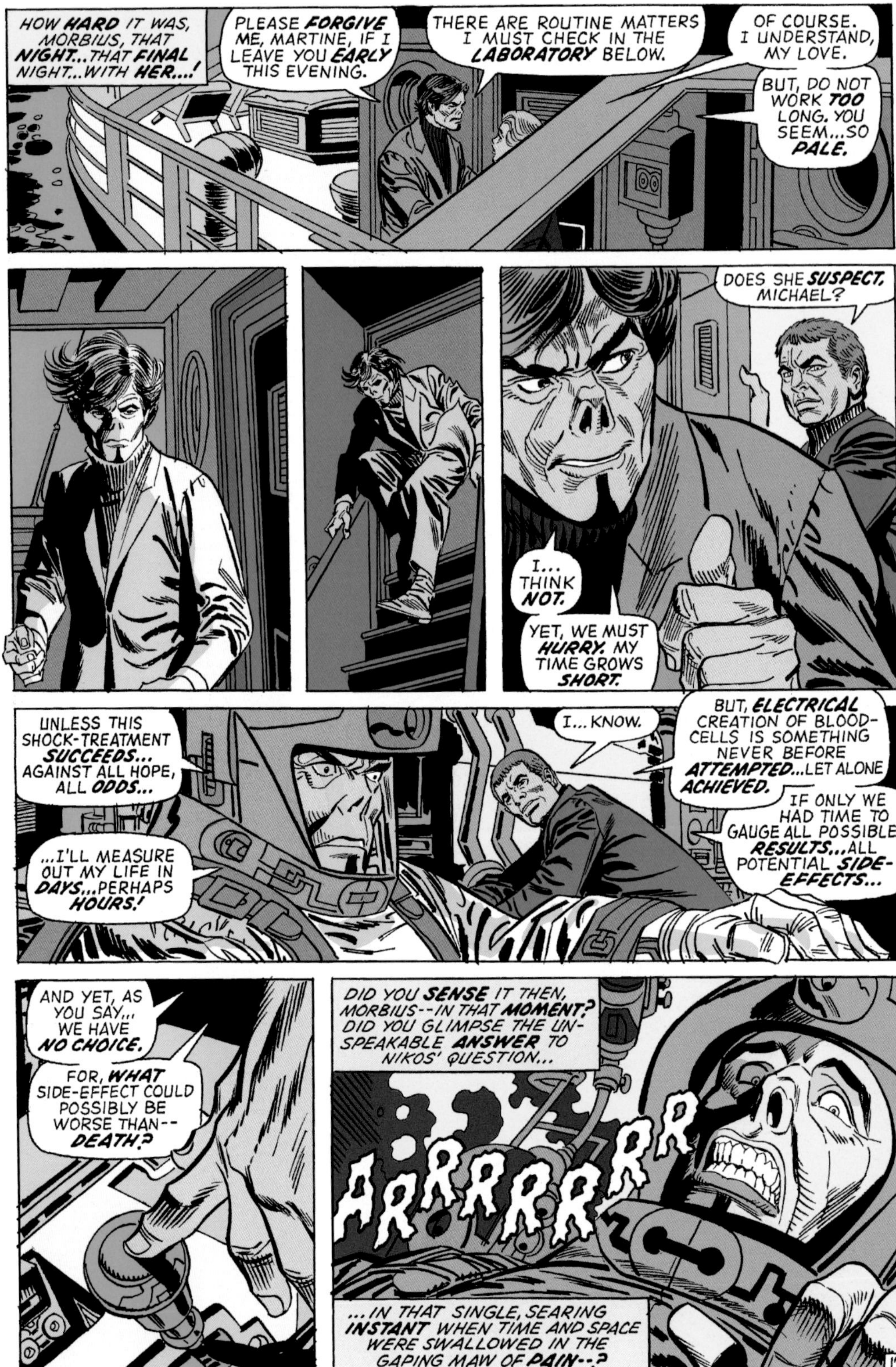
HOW HARD IT WAS, MORBIUS, THAT NIGHT...THAT FINAL NIGHT...WITH HER...!
PLEASE FORGIVE ME, MARTINE, IF I LEAVE YOU EARLY THIS EVENING.
THERE ARE ROUTINE MATTERS I MUST CHECK IN THE LABORATORY BELOW.
OF COURSE. I UNDERSTAND, MY LOVE.
BUT, DO NOT WORK TOO LONG. YOU SEEM...SO PALE.
DOES SHE SUSPECT, MICHAEL?
I... THINK NOT.
YET, WE MUST HURRY. MY TIME GROWS SHORT.
UNLESS THIS SHOCK-TREATMENT SUCCEEDS... AGAINST ALL HOPE, ALL ODDS...
...I'LL MEASURE OUT MY LIFE IN DAYS...PERHAPS HOURS!
I... KNOW.
BUT, ELECTRICAL CREATION OF BLOOD-CELLS IS SOMETHING NEVER BEFORE ATTEMPTED...LET ALONE ACHIEVED.
IF ONLY WE HAD TIME TO GAUGE ALL POSSIBLE RESULTS...ALL POTENTIAL SIDE-EFFECTS...
AND YET, AS YOU SAY... WE HAVE NO CHOICE.
FOR, WHAT SIDE-EFFECT COULD POSSIBLY BE WORSE THAN--DEATH?
DID YOU SENSE IT THEN, MORBIUS--IN THAT MOMENT? DID YOU GLIMPSE THE UN-SPEAKABLE ANSWER TO NIKOS' QUESTION...
ARRRRRRRR
...IN THAT SINGLE, SEARING INSTANT WHEN TIME AND SPACE WERE SWALLOWED IN THE GAPING MAW OF PAIN--?
17

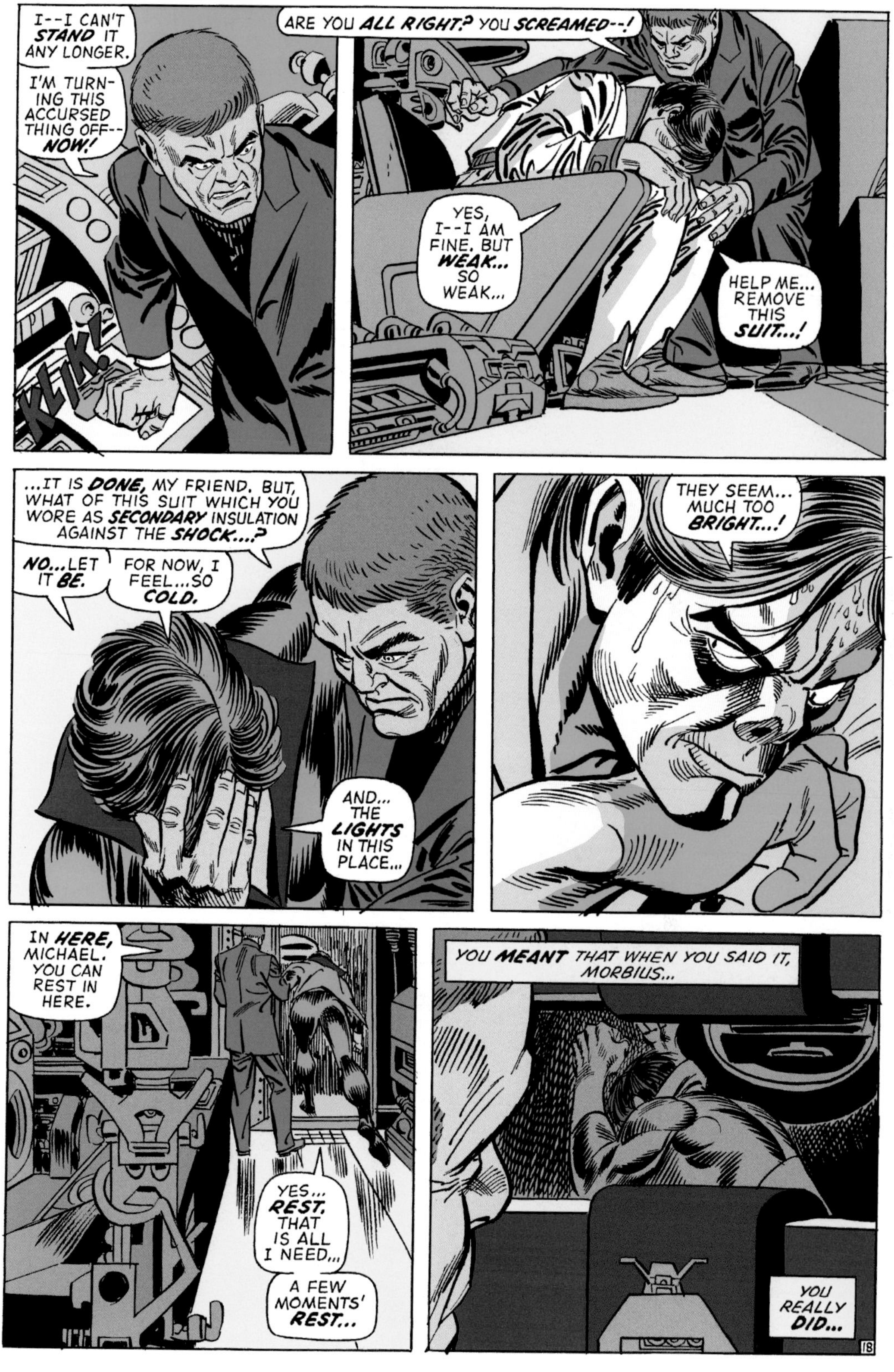
I--I CAN'T STAND IT ANY LONGER.
I'M TURNING THIS ACCURSED THING OFF-- NOW!
KLIK!
ARE YOU ALL RIGHT? YOU SCREAMED--!
YES, I--I AM FINE. BUT WEAK... SO WEAK...
HELP ME... REMOVE THIS SUIT...!
...IT IS DONE, MY FRIEND. BUT, WHAT OF THIS SUIT WHICH YOU WORE AS SECONDARY INSULATION AGAINST THE SHOCK...?
NO... LET IT BE.
FOR NOW, I FEEL... SO COLD.
AND... THE LIGHTS IN THIS PLACE...
THEY SEEM... MUCH TOO BRIGHT...!
IN HERE, MICHAEL. YOU CAN REST IN HERE.
YES... REST. THAT IS ALL I NEED...
A FEW MOMENTS' REST...
YOU MEANT THAT WHEN YOU SAID IT, MORBIUS...
YOU REALLY DID...
18

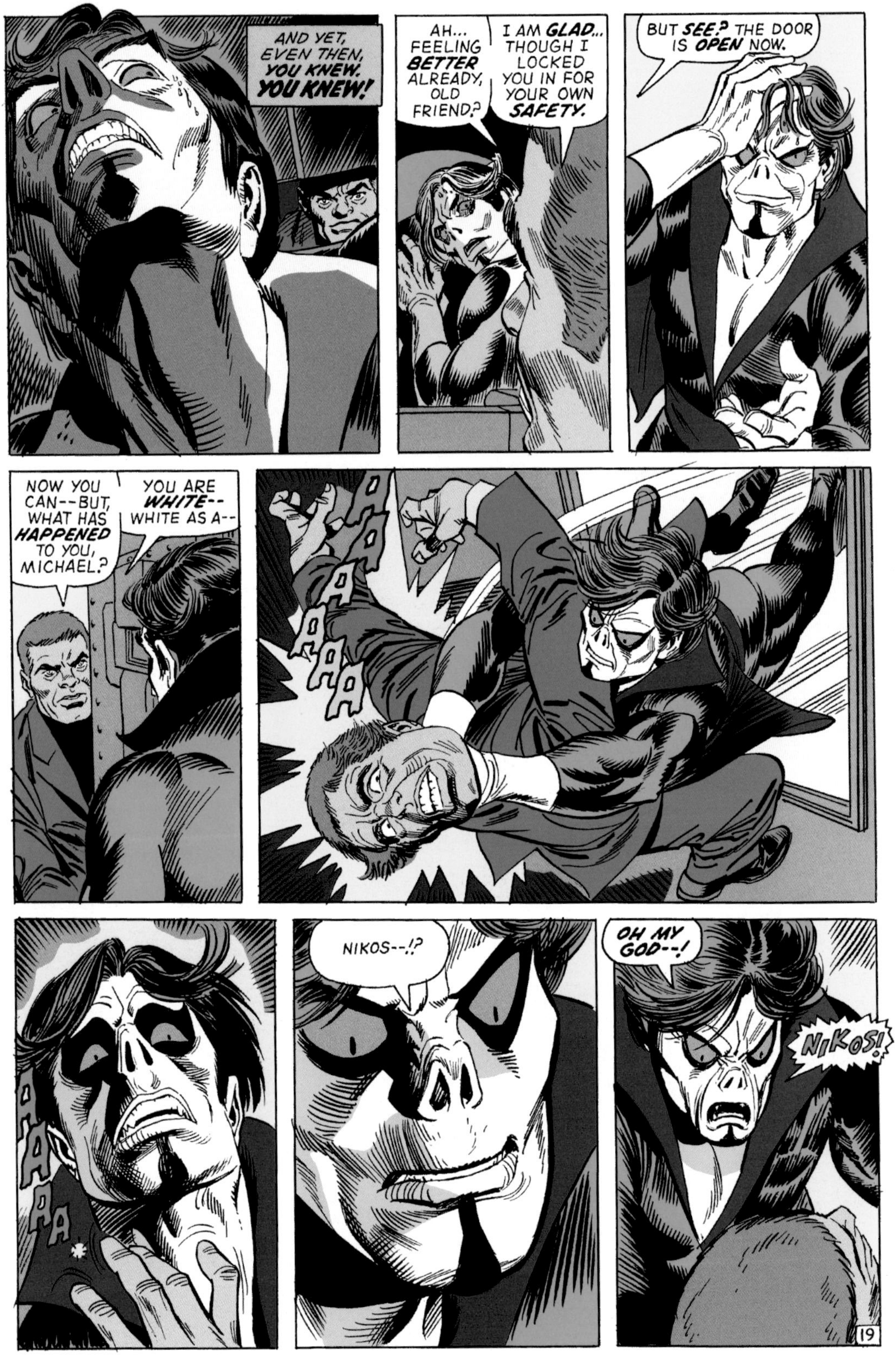
AND YET, EVEN THEN, YOU KNEW. YOU KNEW!
AH... FEELING BETTER ALREADY, OLD FRIEND?
I AM GLAD... THOUGH I LOCKED YOU IN FOR YOUR OWN SAFETY.
BUT SEE? THE DOOR IS OPEN NOW.
NOW YOU CAN--BUT, WHAT HAS HAPPENED TO YOU, MICHAEL?
YOU ARE WHITE--WHITE AS A--
NIKOS--!?
OH MY GOD--!
NIKOS!
19

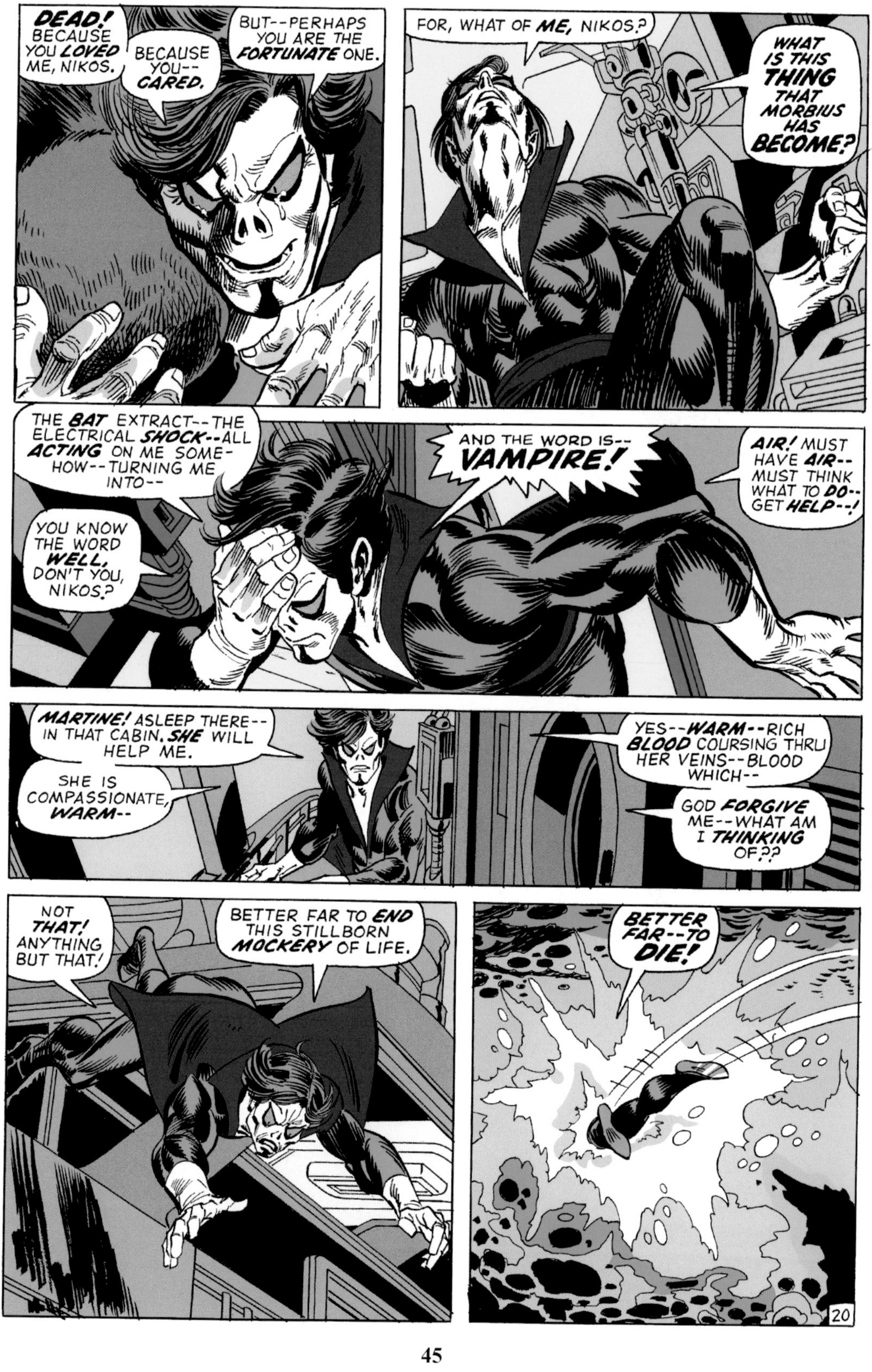
DEAD! BECAUSE YOU LOVED ME, NIKOS.
BECAUSE YOU-- CARED.
BUT--PERHAPS YOU ARE THE FORTUNATE ONE.
FOR, WHAT OF ME, NIKOS?
WHAT IS THIS THING THAT MORBIUS HAS BECOME?
THE BAT EXTRACT--THE ELECTRICAL SHOCK--ALL ACTING ON ME SOMEHOW--TURNING ME INTO--
YOU KNOW THE WORD WELL, DON'T YOU, NIKOS?
AND THE WORD IS-- VAMPIRE!
AIR! MUST HAVE AIR-- MUST THINK WHAT TO DO-- GET HELP--!
MARTINE! ASLEEP THERE-- IN THAT CABIN. SHE WILL HELP ME.
SHE IS COMPASSIONATE, WARM--
YES--WARM--RICH BLOOD COURSING THRU HER VEINS--BLOOD WHICH--
GOD FORGIVE ME--WHAT AM I THINKING OF??
NOT THAT! ANYTHING BUT THAT!
BETTER FAR TO END THIS STILLBORN MOCKERY OF LIFE.
BETTER FAR--TO DIE!
20

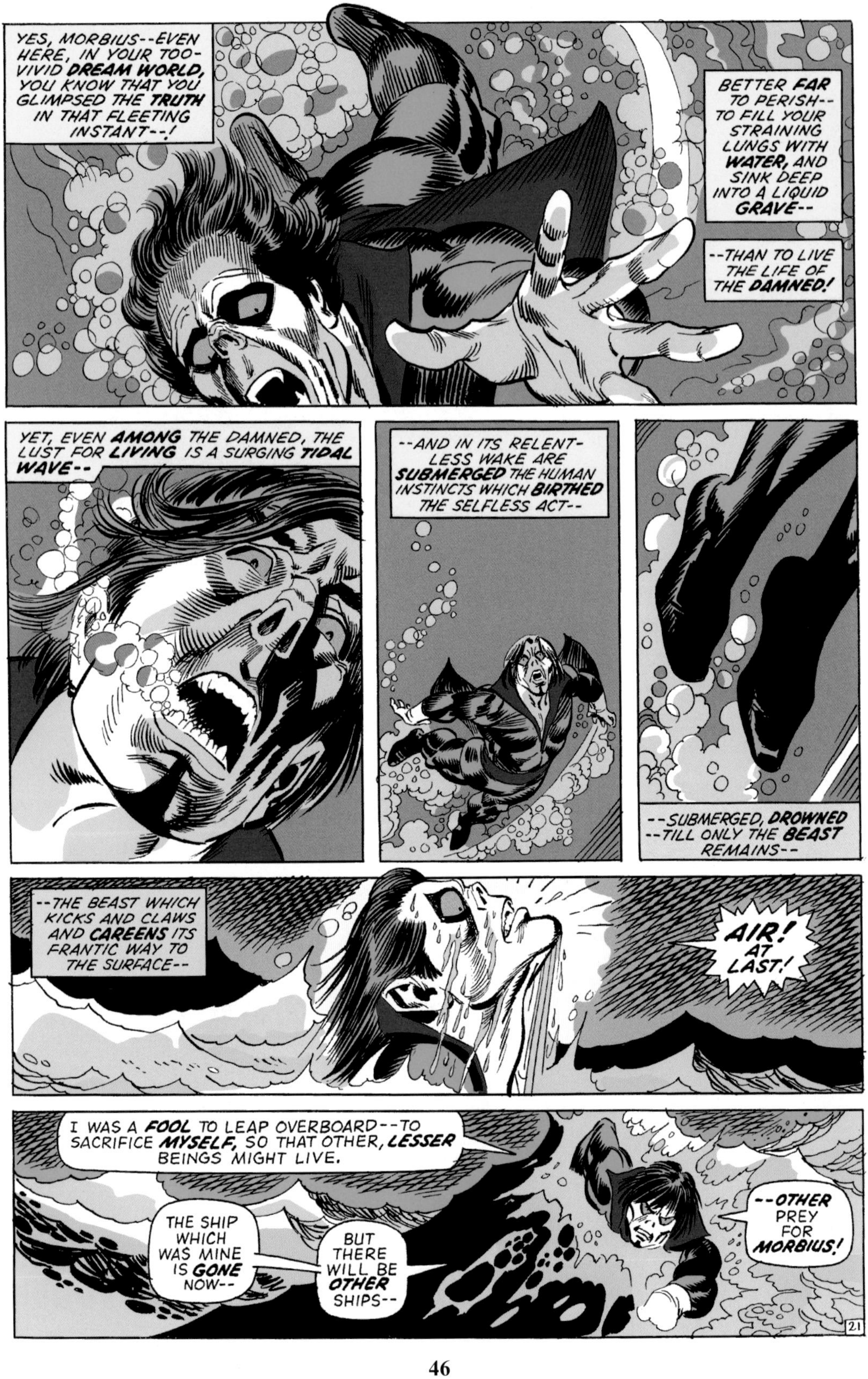
YES, MORBIUS--EVEN HERE, IN YOUR TOO-VIVID DREAM WORLD, YOU KNOW THAT YOU GLIMPSED THE TRUTH IN THAT FLEETING INSTANT--!
BETTER FAR TO PERISH-- TO FILL YOUR STRAINING LUNGS WITH WATER, AND SINK DEEP INTO A LIQUID GRAVE--
--THAN TO LIVE THE LIFE OF THE DAMNED!
YET, EVEN AMONG THE DAMNED, THE LUST FOR LIVING IS A SURGING TIDAL WAVE--
--AND IN ITS RELENTLESS WAKE ARE SUBMERGED THE HUMAN INSTINCTS WHICH BIRTHED THE SELFLESS ACT--
--SUBMERGED, DROWNED --TILL ONLY THE BEAST REMAINS--
--THE BEAST WHICH KICKS AND CLAWS AND CAREENS ITS FRANTIC WAY TO THE SURFACE--
AIR! AT LAST!
I WAS A FOOL TO LEAP OVERBOARD--TO SACRIFICE MYSELF, SO THAT OTHER, LESSER BEINGS MIGHT LIVE.
THE SHIP WHICH WAS MINE IS GONE NOW--
BUT THERE WILL BE OTHER SHIPS--
--OTHER PREY FOR MORBIUS!
21

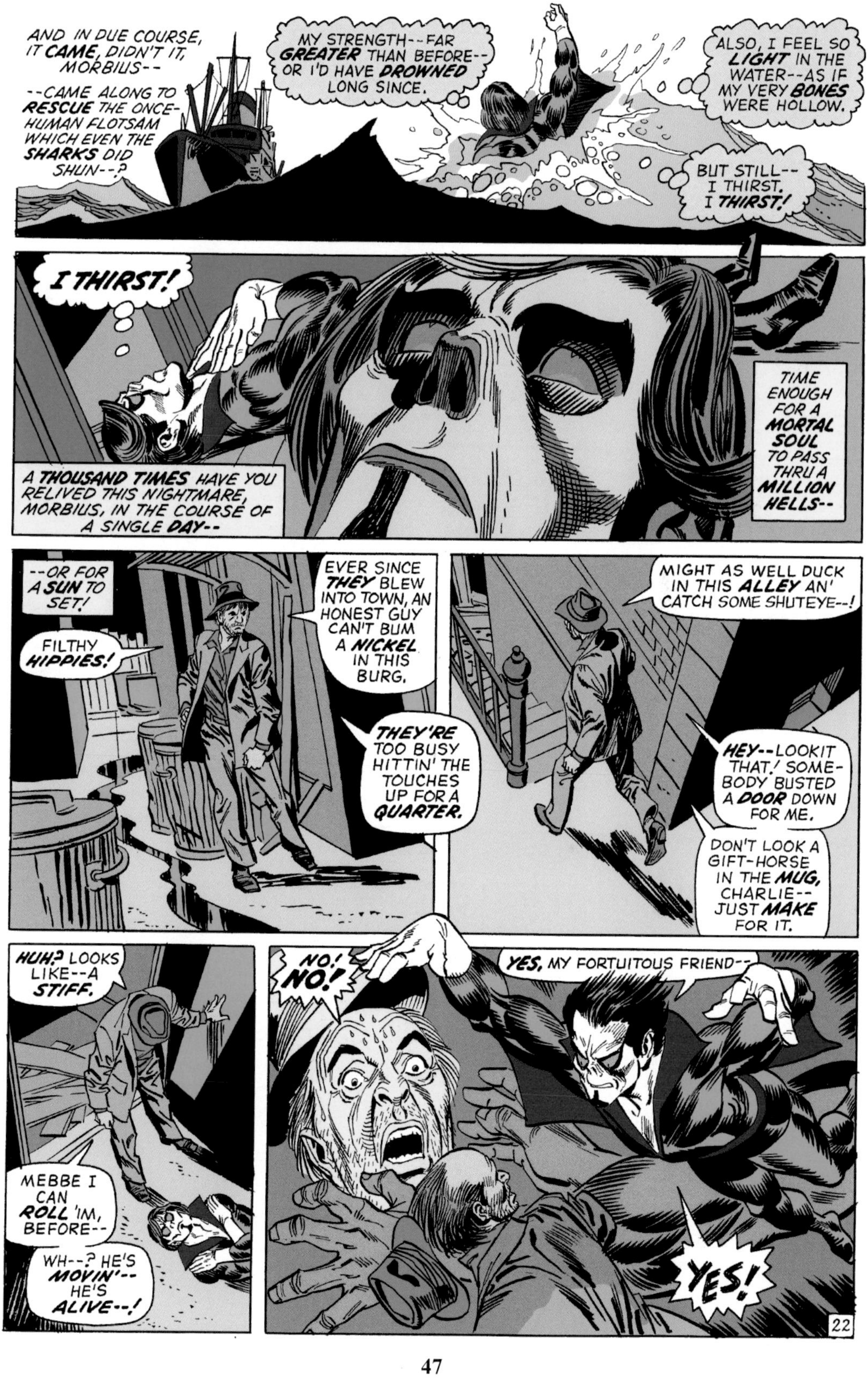
AND IN DUE COURSE, IT CAME, DIDN'T IT, MORBIUS--
--CAME ALONG TO RESCUE THE ONCE-HUMAN FLOTSAM WHICH EVEN THE SHARKS DID SHUN--?
MY STRENGTH--FAR GREATER THAN BEFORE--OR I'D HAVE DROWNED LONG SINCE.
ALSO, I FEEL SO LIGHT IN THE WATER--AS IF MY VERY BONES WERE HOLLOW.
BUT STILL--I THIRST. I THIRST!
I THIRST!
A THOUSAND TIMES HAVE YOU RELIVED THIS NIGHTMARE, MORBIUS, IN THE COURSE OF A SINGLE DAY--
TIME ENOUGH FOR A MORTAL SOUL TO PASS THRU A MILLION HELLS--
--OR FOR A SUN TO SET!
FILTHY HIPPIES!
EVER SINCE THEY BLEW INTO TOWN, AN HONEST GUY CAN'T BUM A NICKEL IN THIS BURG.
THEY'RE TOO BUSY HITTIN' THE TOUCHES UP FOR A QUARTER.
MIGHT AS WELL DUCK IN THIS ALLEY AN' CATCH SOME SHUTEYE--!
HEY--LOOKIT THAT! SOMEBODY BUSTED A DOOR DOWN FOR ME.
DON'T LOOK A GIFT-HORSE IN THE MUG, CHARLIE--JUST MAKE FOR IT.
HUH? LOOKS LIKE--A STIFF.
MEBBE I CAN ROLL 'IM, BEFORE--
WH--? HE'S MOVIN'--HE'S ALIVE--!
NO! NO!
YES, MY FORTUITOUS FRIEND--
YES!
22

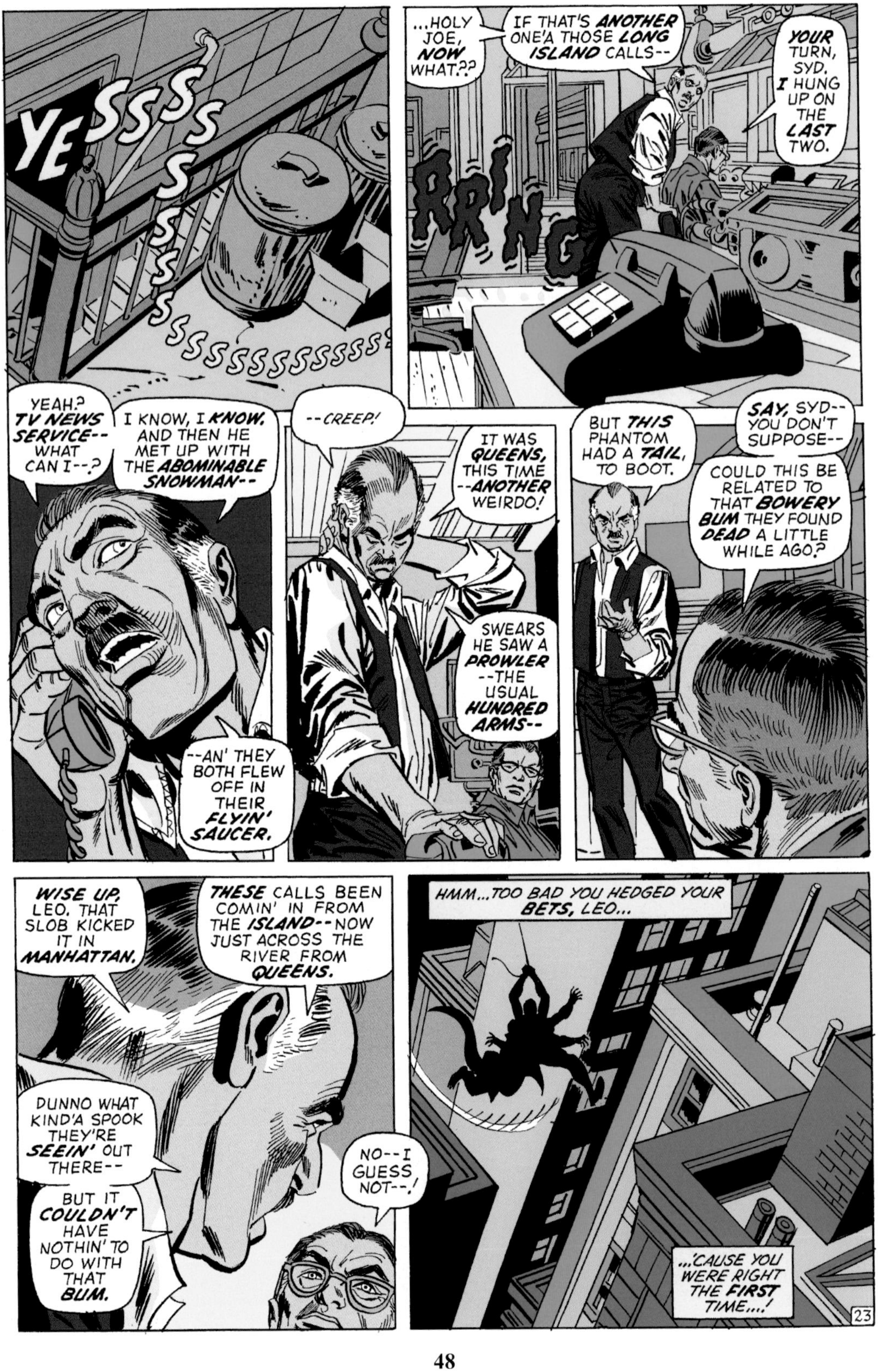
YESSSSS
SSSSSSSSSSSSSSSSS!
...HOLY JOE, NOW WHAT??
IF THAT'S ANOTHER ONE'A THOSE LONG ISLAND CALLS--
YOUR TURN, SYD. I HUNG UP ON THE LAST TWO.
RRING
YEAH? TV NEWS SERVICE-- WHAT CAN I--?
I KNOW, I KNOW. AND THEN HE MET UP WITH THE ABOMINABLE SNOWMAN--
--AN' THEY BOTH FLEW OFF IN THEIR FLYIN' SAUCER.
--CREEP!
IT WAS QUEENS, THIS TIME --ANOTHER WEIRDO!
SWEARS HE SAW A PROWLER --THE USUAL HUNDRED ARMS--
BUT THIS PHANTOM HAD A TAIL, TO BOOT.
SAY, SYD-- YOU DON'T SUPPOSE--
COULD THIS BE RELATED TO THAT BOWERY BUM THEY FOUND DEAD A LITTLE WHILE AGO?
WISE UP, LEO. THAT SLOB KICKED IT IN MANHATTAN.
THESE CALLS BEEN COMIN' IN FROM THE ISLAND--NOW JUST ACROSS THE RIVER FROM QUEENS.
DUNNO WHAT KIND'A SPOOK THEY'RE SEEIN' OUT THERE--
BUT IT COULDN'T HAVE NOTHIN' TO DO WITH THAT BUM.
NO--I GUESS NOT--!
HMM...TOO BAD YOU HEDGED YOUR BETS, LEO...
...'CAUSE YOU WERE RIGHT THE FIRST TIME...!
23

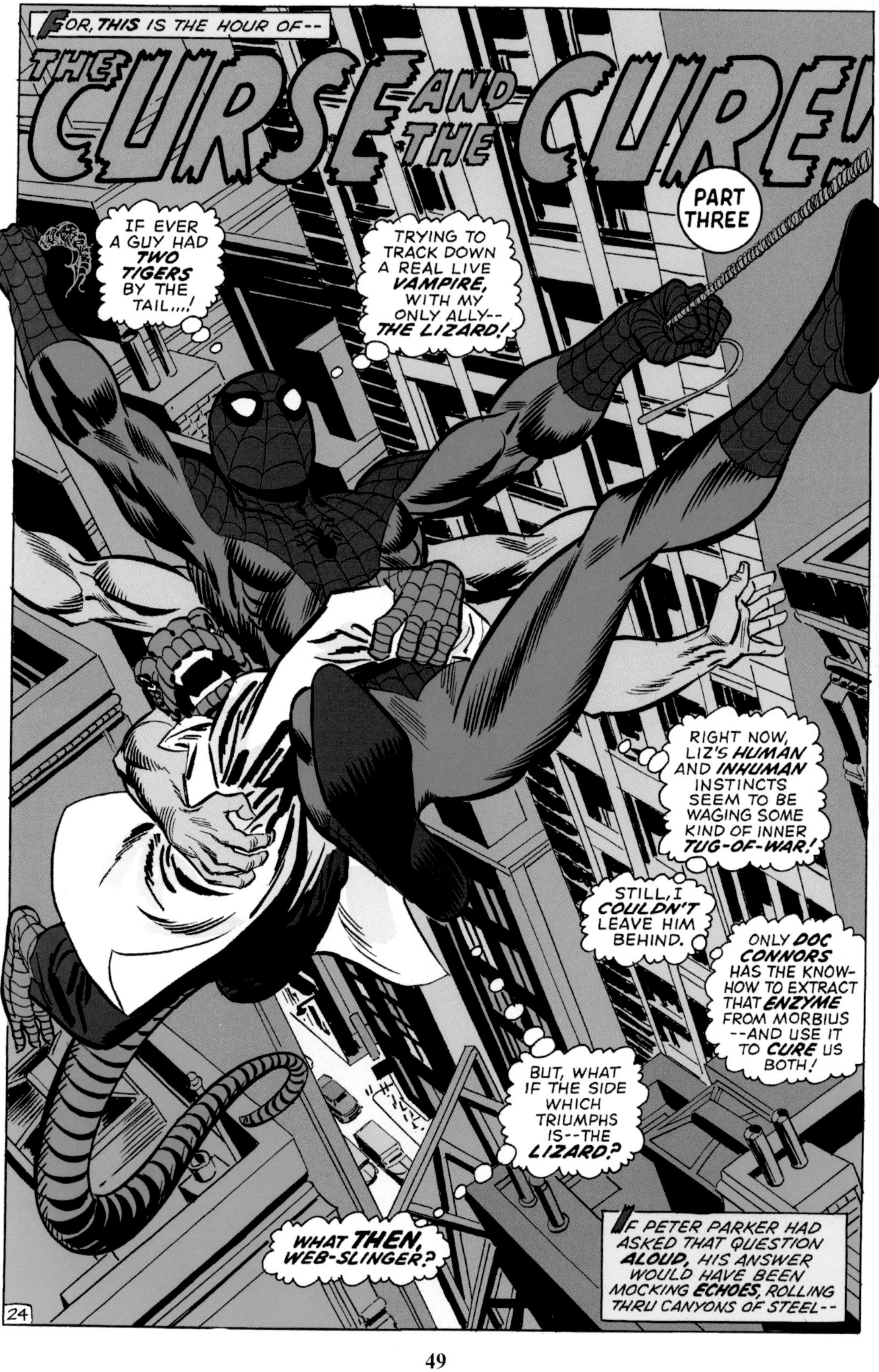
FOR, THIS IS THE HOUR OF--
THE CURSE AND THE CURE!
PART THREE
IF EVER A GUY HAD TWO TIGERS BY THE TAIL...!
TRYING TO TRACK DOWN A REAL LIVE VAMPIRE, WITH MY ONLY ALLY-- THE LIZARD!
RIGHT NOW, LIZ'S HUMAN AND INHUMAN INSTINCTS SEEM TO BE WAGING SOME KIND OF INNER TUG-OF-WAR!
STILL, I COULDN'T LEAVE HIM BEHIND.
ONLY DOC CONNORS HAS THE KNOW-HOW TO EXTRACT THAT ENZYME FROM MORBIUS --AND USE IT TO CURE US BOTH!
BUT, WHAT IF THE SIDE WHICH TRIUMPHS IS--THE LIZARD?
WHAT THEN, WEB-SLINGER?
IF PETER PARKER HAD ASKED THAT QUESTION ALOUD, HIS ANSWER WOULD HAVE BEEN MOCKING ECHOES, ROLLING THRU CANYONS OF STEEL--
24

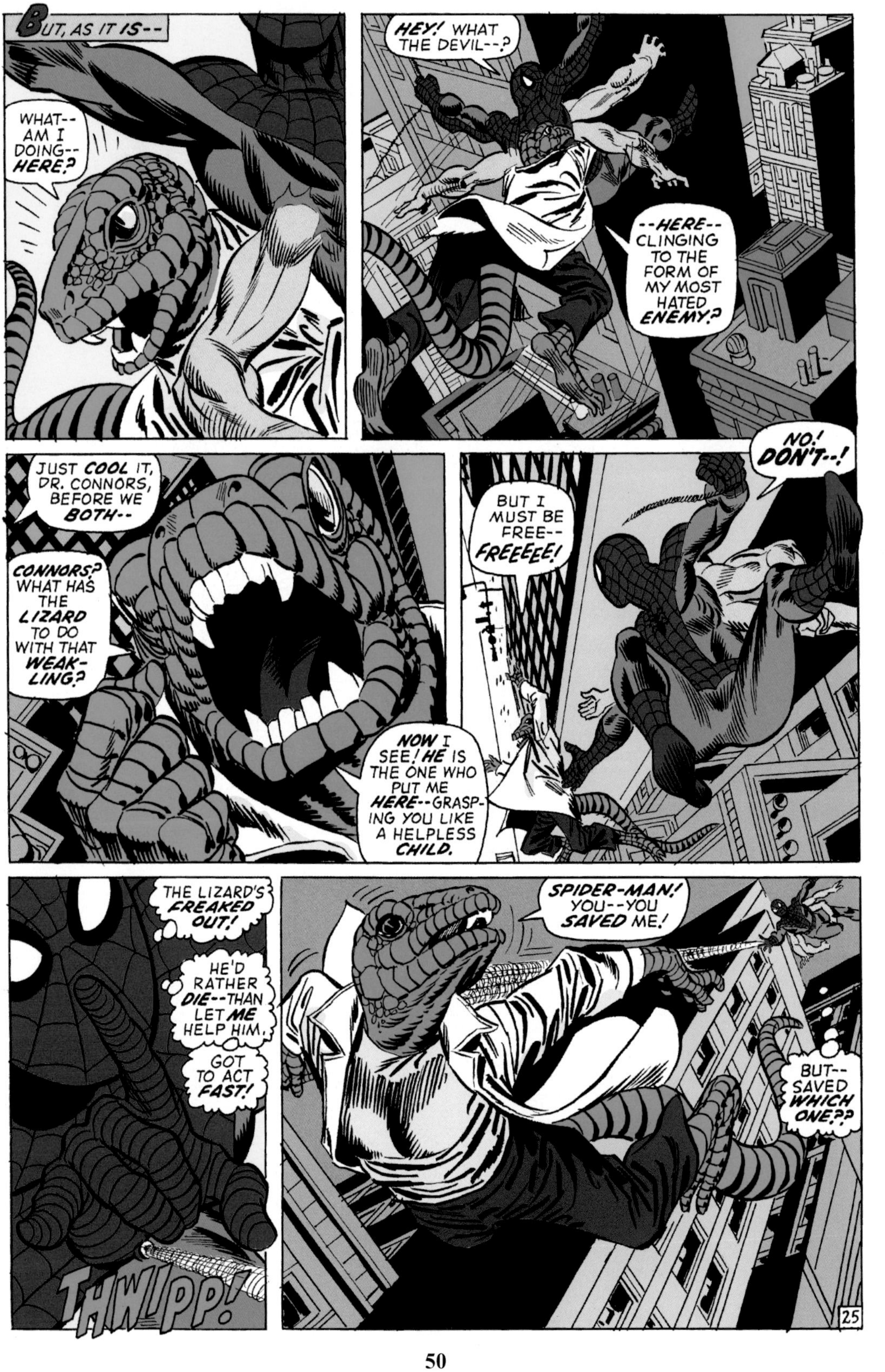
BUT, AS IT IS--
WHAT-- AM I DOING-- HERE?
HEY! WHAT THE DEVIL--?
--HERE-- CLINGING TO THE FORM OF MY MOST HATED ENEMY?
JUST COOL IT, DR. CONNORS, BEFORE WE BOTH--
CONNORS? WHAT HAS THE LIZARD TO DO WITH THAT WEAK-LING?
BUT I MUST BE FREE-- FREEEEE!
NO! DON'T--!
NOW I SEE! HE IS THE ONE WHO PUT ME HERE--GRASP-ING YOU LIKE A HELPLESS CHILD.
THE LIZARD'S FREAKED OUT!
HE'D RATHER DIE--THAN LET ME HELP HIM.
GOT TO ACT FAST!
THWIPP!
SPIDER-MAN! YOU--YOU SAVED ME!
BUT-- SAVED WHICH ONE??
25

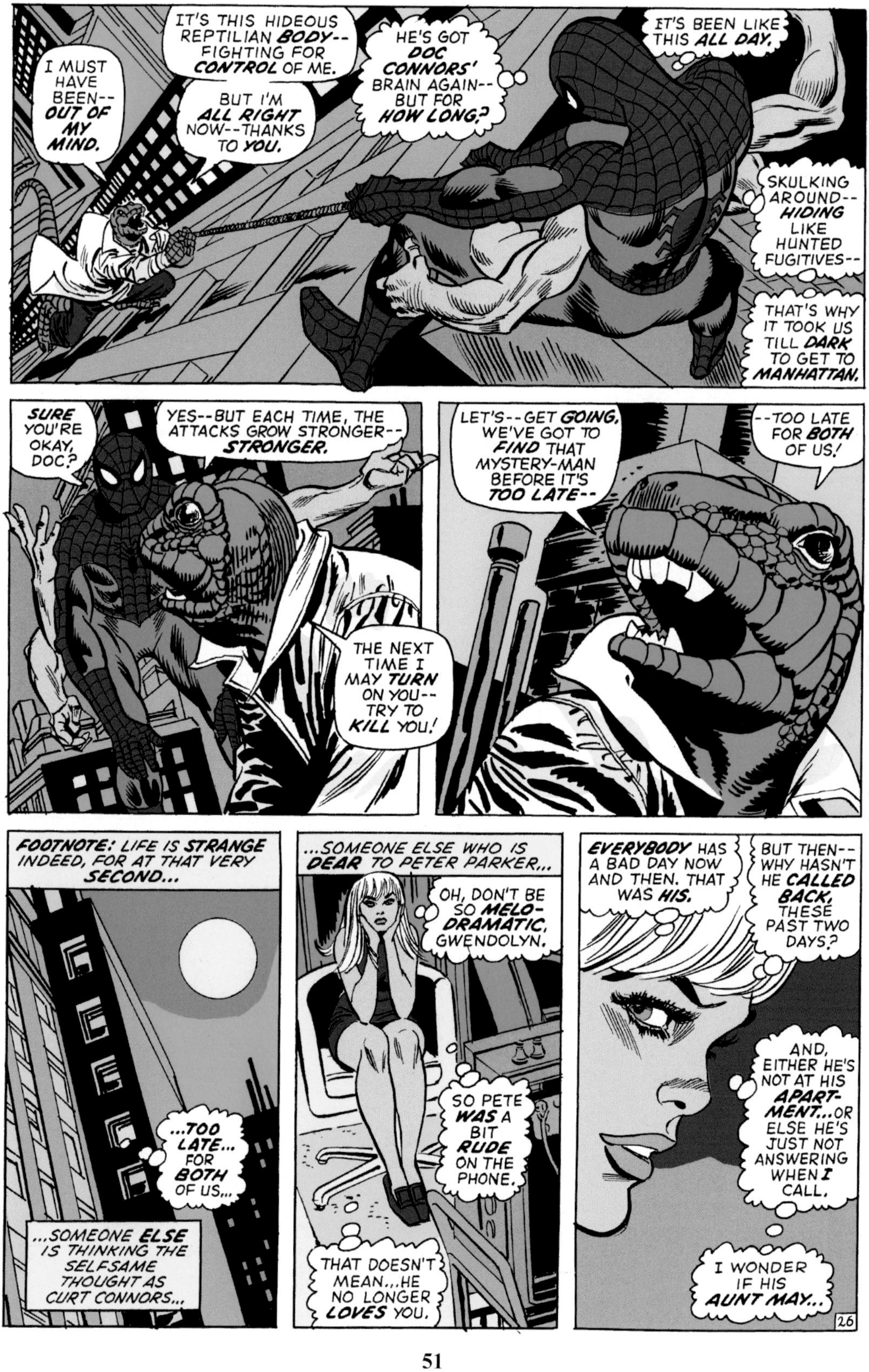
I MUST HAVE BEEN-- OUT OF MY MIND.
IT'S THIS HIDEOUS REPTILIAN BODY-- FIGHTING FOR CONTROL OF ME.
BUT I'M ALL RIGHT NOW--THANKS TO YOU.
HE'S GOT DOC CONNORS' BRAIN AGAIN-- BUT FOR HOW LONG?
IT'S BEEN LIKE THIS ALL DAY.
SKULKING AROUND-- HIDING LIKE HUNTED FUGITIVES--
THAT'S WHY IT TOOK US TILL DARK TO GET TO MANHATTAN.
SURE YOU'RE OKAY, DOC?
YES--BUT EACH TIME, THE ATTACKS GROW STRONGER-- STRONGER.
THE NEXT TIME I MAY TURN ON YOU-- TRY TO KILL YOU!
LET'S--GET GOING. WE'VE GOT TO FIND THAT MYSTERY-MAN BEFORE IT'S TOO LATE--
--TOO LATE FOR BOTH OF US!
FOOTNOTE: LIFE IS STRANGE INDEED, FOR AT THAT VERY SECOND...
...TOO LATE... FOR BOTH OF US...
...SOMEONE ELSE IS THINKING THE SELFSAME THOUGHT AS CURT CONNORS...
...SOMEONE ELSE WHO IS DEAR TO PETER PARKER...
OH, DON'T BE SO MELO-DRAMATIC, GWENDOLYN.
SO PETE WAS A BIT RUDE ON THE PHONE.
THAT DOESN'T MEAN...HE NO LONGER LOVES YOU.
EVERYBODY HAS A BAD DAY NOW AND THEN. THAT WAS HIS.
BUT THEN-- WHY HASN'T HE CALLED BACK, THESE PAST TWO DAYS?
AND, EITHER HE'S NOT AT HIS APART-MENT...OR ELSE HE'S JUST NOT ANSWERING WHEN I CALL.
I WONDER IF HIS AUNT MAY...
26

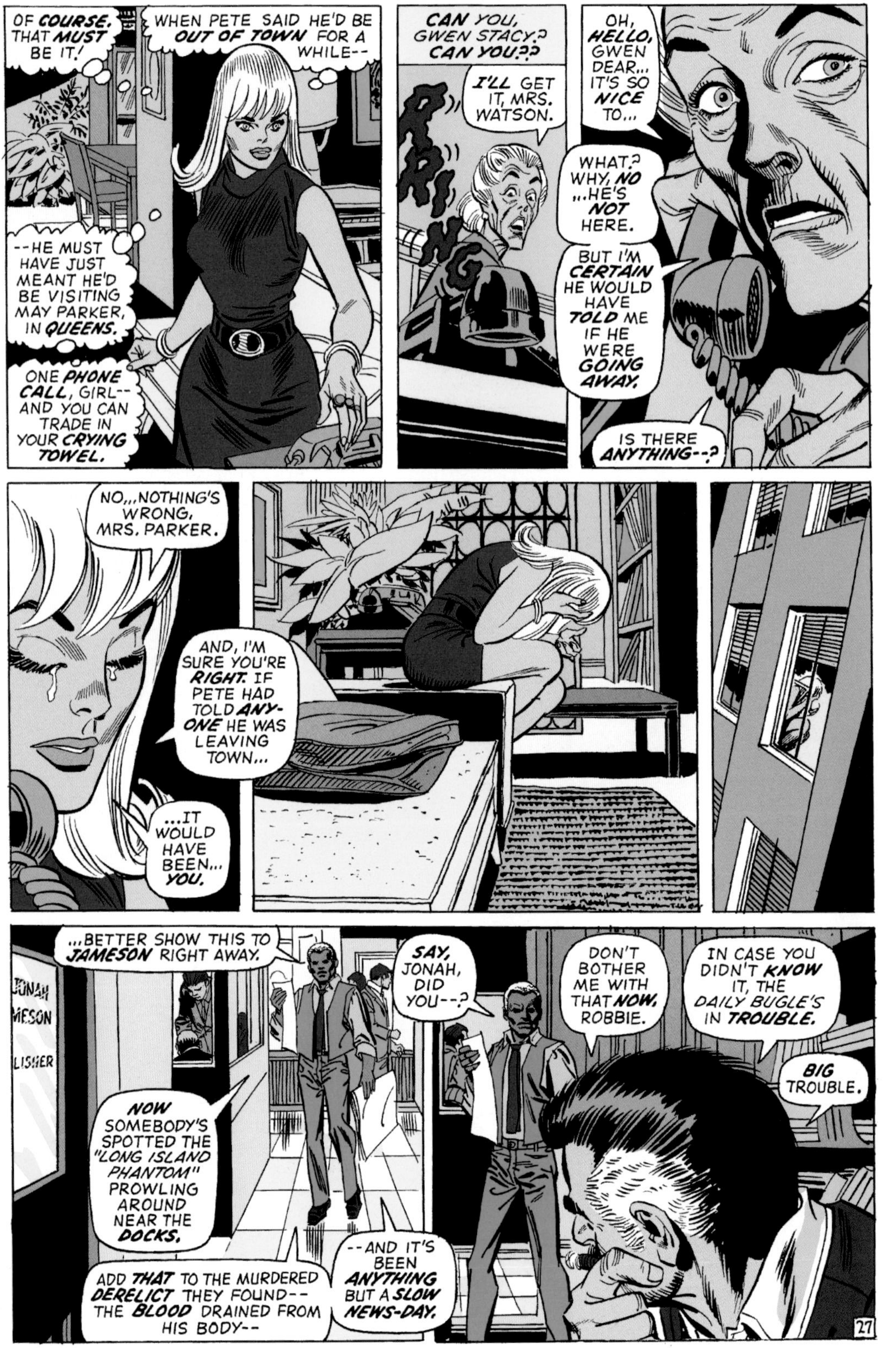
OF COURSE. THAT MUST BE IT!
WHEN PETE SAID HE'D BE OUT OF TOWN FOR A WHILE--
--HE MUST HAVE JUST MEANT HE'D BE VISITING MAY PARKER, IN QUEENS.
ONE PHONE CALL, GIRL-- AND YOU CAN TRADE IN YOUR CRYING TOWEL.
CAN YOU, GWEN STACY? CAN YOU??
I'LL GET IT, MRS. WATSON.
RRING
OH, HELLO, GWEN DEAR... IT'S SO NICE TO...
WHAT? WHY, NO ...HE'S NOT HERE.
BUT I'M CERTAIN HE WOULD HAVE TOLD ME IF HE WERE GOING AWAY.
IS THERE ANYTHING--?
NO... NOTHING'S WRONG, MRS. PARKER.
AND, I'M SURE YOU'RE RIGHT. IF PETE HAD TOLD ANYONE HE WAS LEAVING TOWN...
...IT WOULD HAVE BEEN... YOU.
...BETTER SHOW THIS TO JAMESON RIGHT AWAY.
JONAH
MESON
LISHER
NOW SOMEBODY'S SPOTTED THE "LONG ISLAND PHANTOM" PROWLING AROUND NEAR THE DOCKS.
ADD THAT TO THE MURDERED DERELICT THEY FOUND-- THE BLOOD DRAINED FROM HIS BODY--
SAY, JONAH, DID YOU--?
DON'T BOTHER ME WITH THAT NOW, ROBBIE.
IN CASE YOU DIDN'T KNOW IT, THE DAILY BUGLE'S IN TROUBLE.
BIG TROUBLE.
--AND IT'S BEEN ANYTHING BUT A SLOW NEWS-DAY.
27

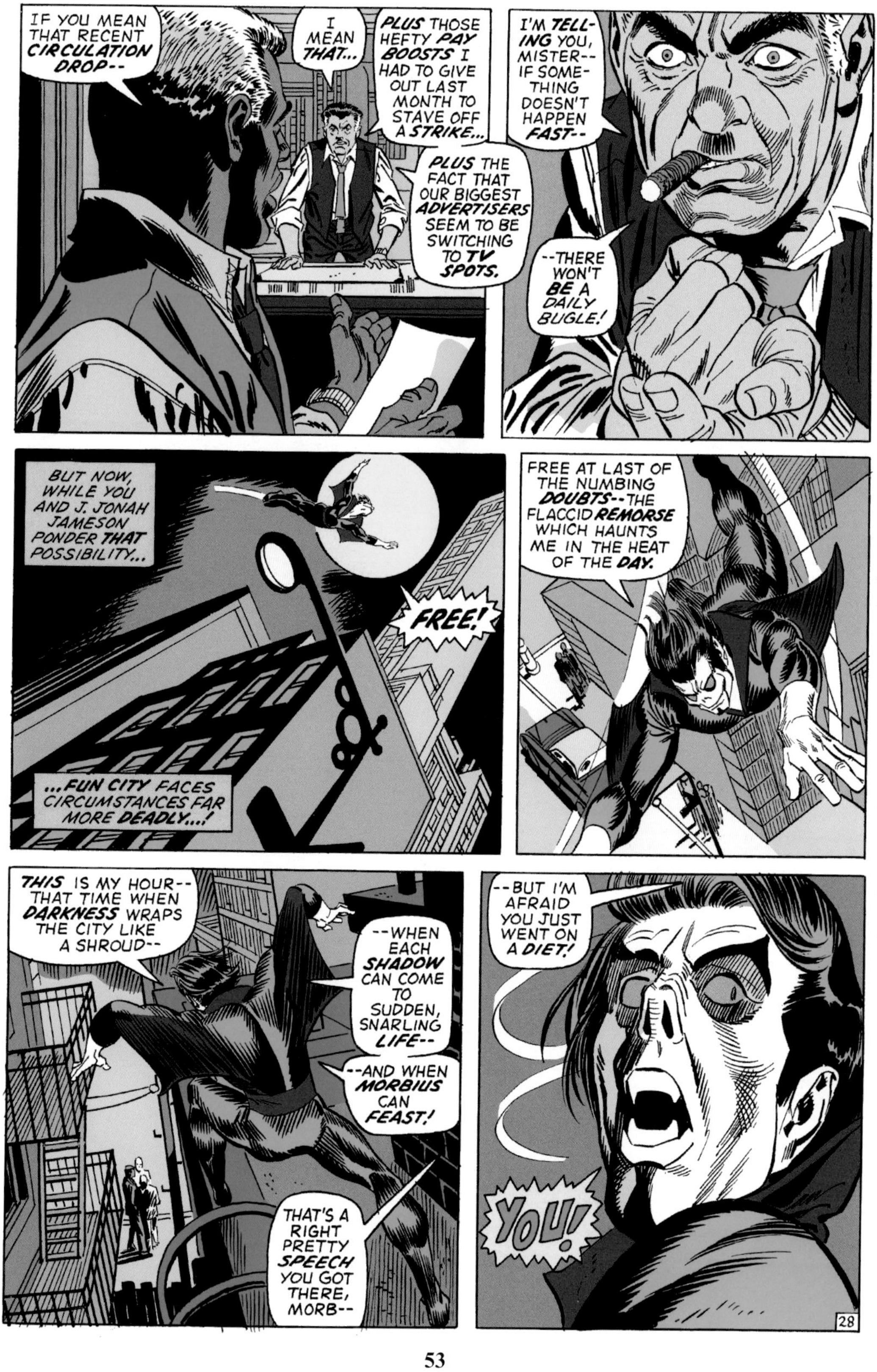
IF YOU MEAN THAT RECENT CIRCULATION DROP--
I MEAN THAT...
PLUS THOSE HEFTY PAY BOOSTS I HAD TO GIVE OUT LAST MONTH TO STAVE OFF A STRIKE...
PLUS THE FACT THAT OUR BIGGEST ADVERTISERS SEEM TO BE SWITCHING TO TV SPOTS.
I'M TELLING YOU, MISTER--IF SOMETHING DOESN'T HAPPEN FAST--
--THERE WON'T BE A DAILY BUGLE!
BUT NOW, WHILE YOU AND J. JONAH JAMESON PONDER THAT POSSIBILITY...
FREE!
...FUN CITY FACES CIRCUMSTANCES FAR MORE DEADLY...!
FREE AT LAST OF THE NUMBING DOUBTS--THE FLACCID REMORSE WHICH HAUNTS ME IN THE HEAT OF THE DAY.
THIS IS MY HOUR--THAT TIME WHEN DARKNESS WRAPS THE CITY LIKE A SHROUD--
--WHEN EACH SHADOW CAN COME TO SUDDEN, SNARLING LIFE--
--AND WHEN MORBIUS CAN FEAST!
THAT'S A RIGHT PRETTY SPEECH YOU GOT THERE, MORB--
--BUT I'M AFRAID YOU JUST WENT ON A DIET!
YOU!
28

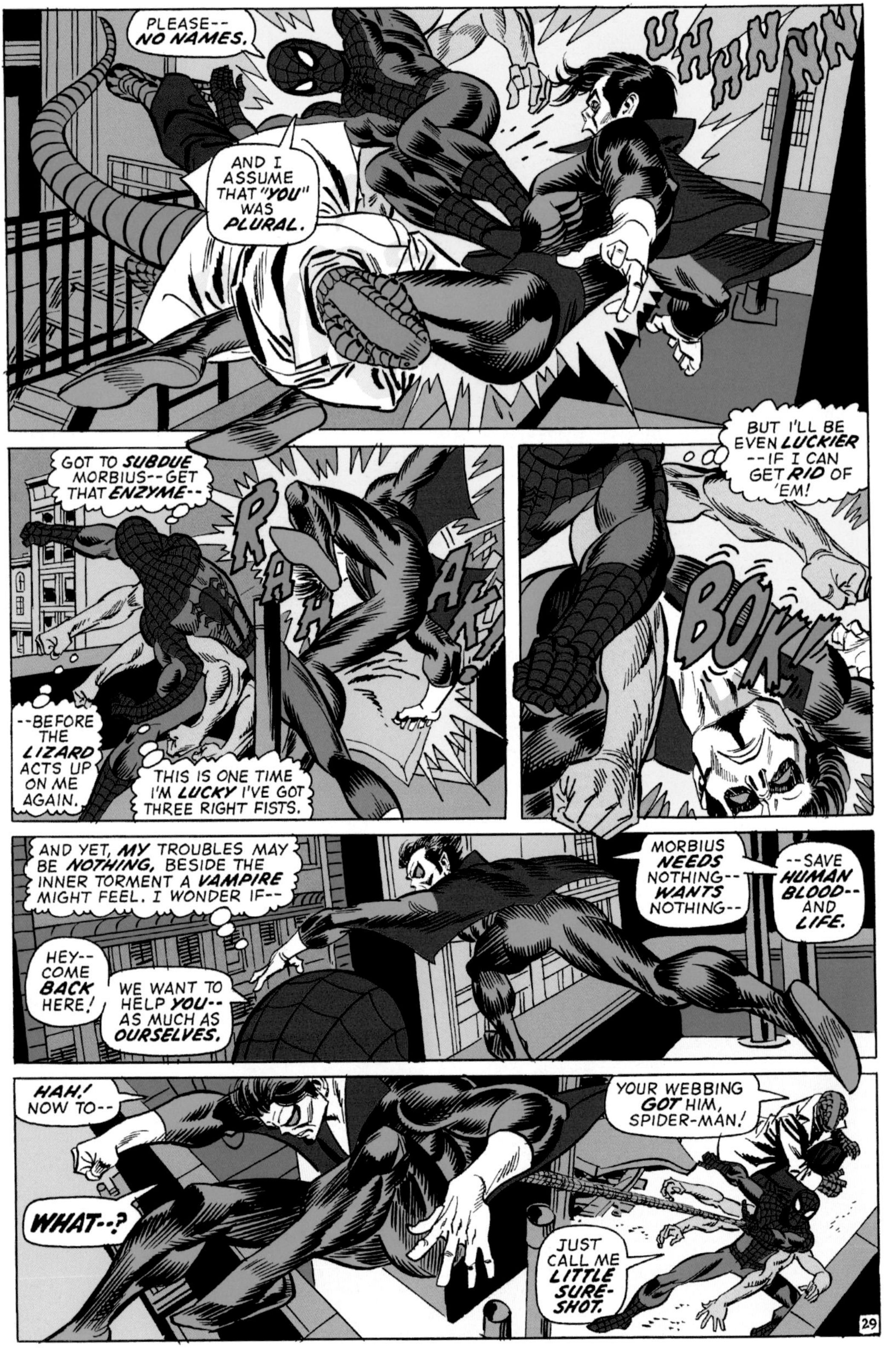
PLEASE--
NO NAMES.
UHHNNN
AND I ASSUME THAT "YOU" WAS PLURAL.
GOT TO SUBDUE MORBIUS--GET THAT ENZYME--
RAKK!
--BEFORE THE LIZARD ACTS UP ON ME AGAIN.
THIS IS ONE TIME I'M LUCKY I'VE GOT THREE RIGHT FISTS.
BUT I'LL BE EVEN LUCKIER --IF I CAN GET RID OF 'EM!
BOK!
AND YET, MY TROUBLES MAY BE NOTHING, BESIDE THE INNER TORMENT A VAMPIRE MIGHT FEEL. I WONDER IF--
MORBIUS NEEDS NOTHING-- WANTS NOTHING--
--SAVE HUMAN BLOOD-- AND LIFE.
HEY-- COME BACK HERE!
WE WANT TO HELP YOU-- AS MUCH AS OURSELVES.
HAH! NOW TO--
WHAT--?
YOUR WEBBING GOT HIM, SPIDER-MAN!
JUST CALL ME LITTLE SURE-SHOT.
29

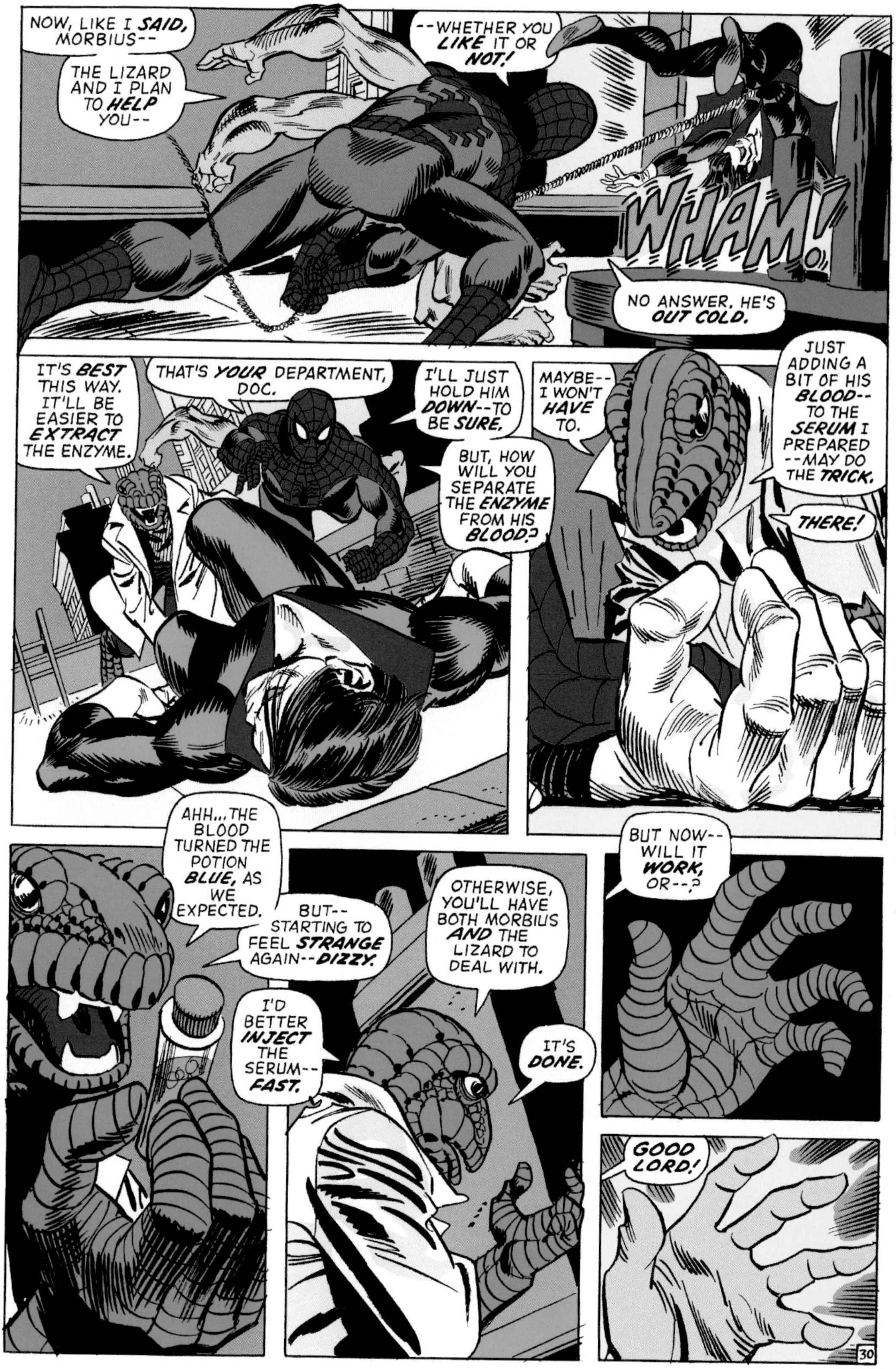
NOW, LIKE I SAID, MORBIUS--
THE LIZARD AND I PLAN TO HELP YOU--
--WHETHER YOU LIKE IT OR NOT!
WHAM!
NO ANSWER. HE'S OUT COLD.
IT'S BEST THIS WAY. IT'LL BE EASIER TO EXTRACT THE ENZYME.
THAT'S YOUR DEPARTMENT, DOC.
I'LL JUST HOLD HIM DOWN--TO BE SURE.
BUT, HOW WILL YOU SEPARATE THE ENZYME FROM HIS BLOOD?
MAYBE--I WON'T HAVE TO.
JUST ADDING A BIT OF HIS BLOOD--TO THE SERUM I PREPARED--MAY DO THE TRICK.
THERE!
AHH...THE BLOOD TURNED THE POTION BLUE, AS WE EXPECTED.
BUT--STARTING TO FEEL STRANGE AGAIN--DIZZY.
I'D BETTER INJECT THE SERUM--FAST.
OTHERWISE, YOU'LL HAVE BOTH MORBIUS AND THE LIZARD TO DEAL WITH.
IT'S DONE.
BUT NOW--WILL IT WORK, OR--?
GOOD LORD!
30

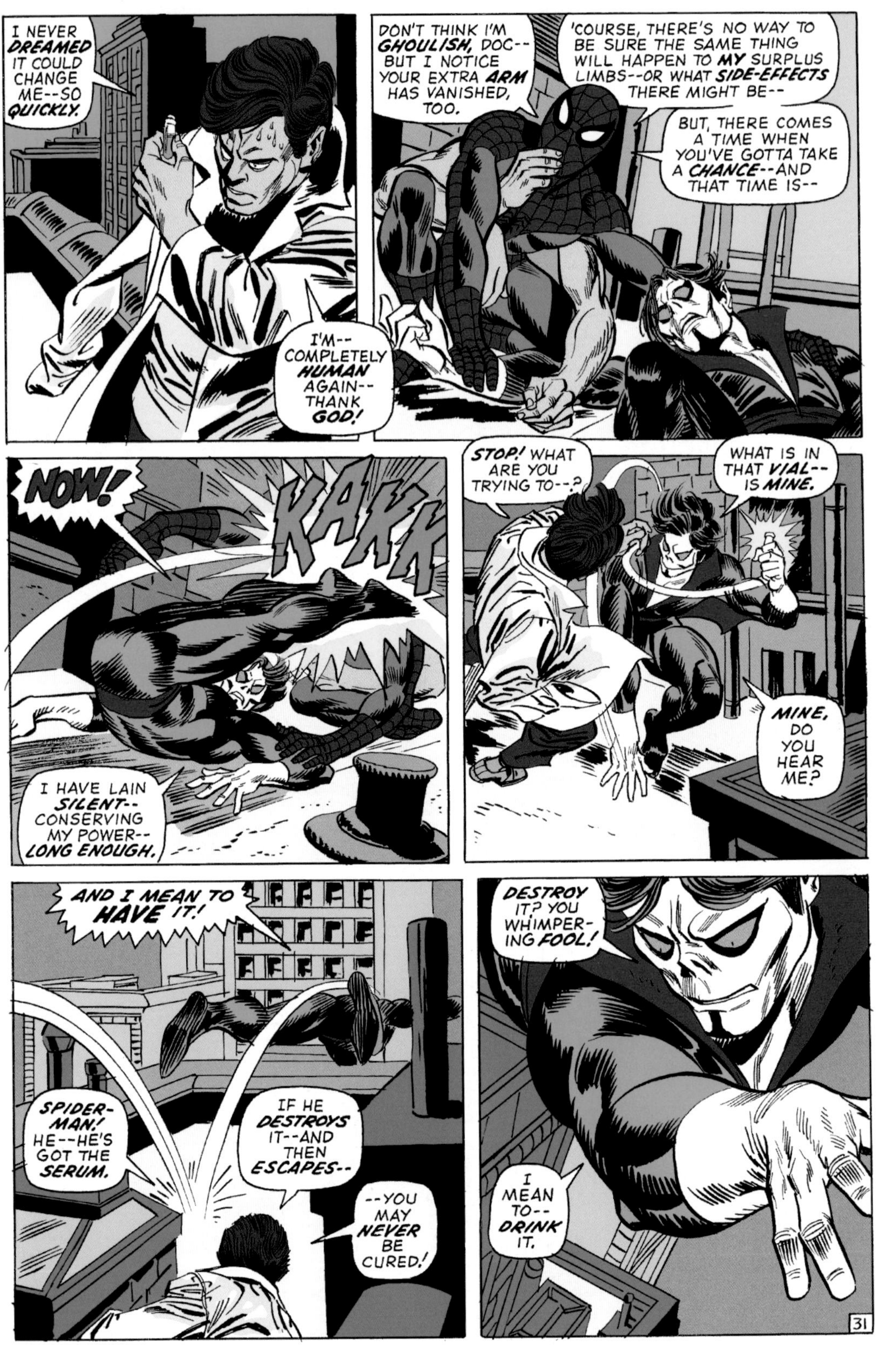
I NEVER DREAMED IT COULD CHANGE ME--SO QUICKLY.
I'M--COMPLETELY HUMAN AGAIN--THANK GOD!
DON'T THINK I'M GHOULISH, DOC--BUT I NOTICE YOUR EXTRA ARM HAS VANISHED, TOO.
'COURSE, THERE'S NO WAY TO BE SURE THE SAME THING WILL HAPPEN TO MY SURPLUS LIMBS--OR WHAT SIDE-EFFECTS THERE MIGHT BE--
BUT, THERE COMES A TIME WHEN YOU'VE GOTTA TAKE A CHANCE--AND THAT TIME IS--
NOW!
KAKK
I HAVE LAIN SILENT--CONSERVING MY POWER--LONG ENOUGH.
STOP! WHAT ARE YOU TRYING TO--?
WHAT IS IN THAT VIAL--IS MINE.
MINE, DO YOU HEAR ME?
AND I MEAN TO HAVE IT!
SPIDER-MAN! HE--HE'S GOT THE SERUM.
IF HE DESTROYS IT--AND THEN ESCAPES--
--YOU MAY NEVER BE CURED!
DESTROY IT? YOU WHIMPERING FOOL!
I MEAN TO--DRINK IT.
31

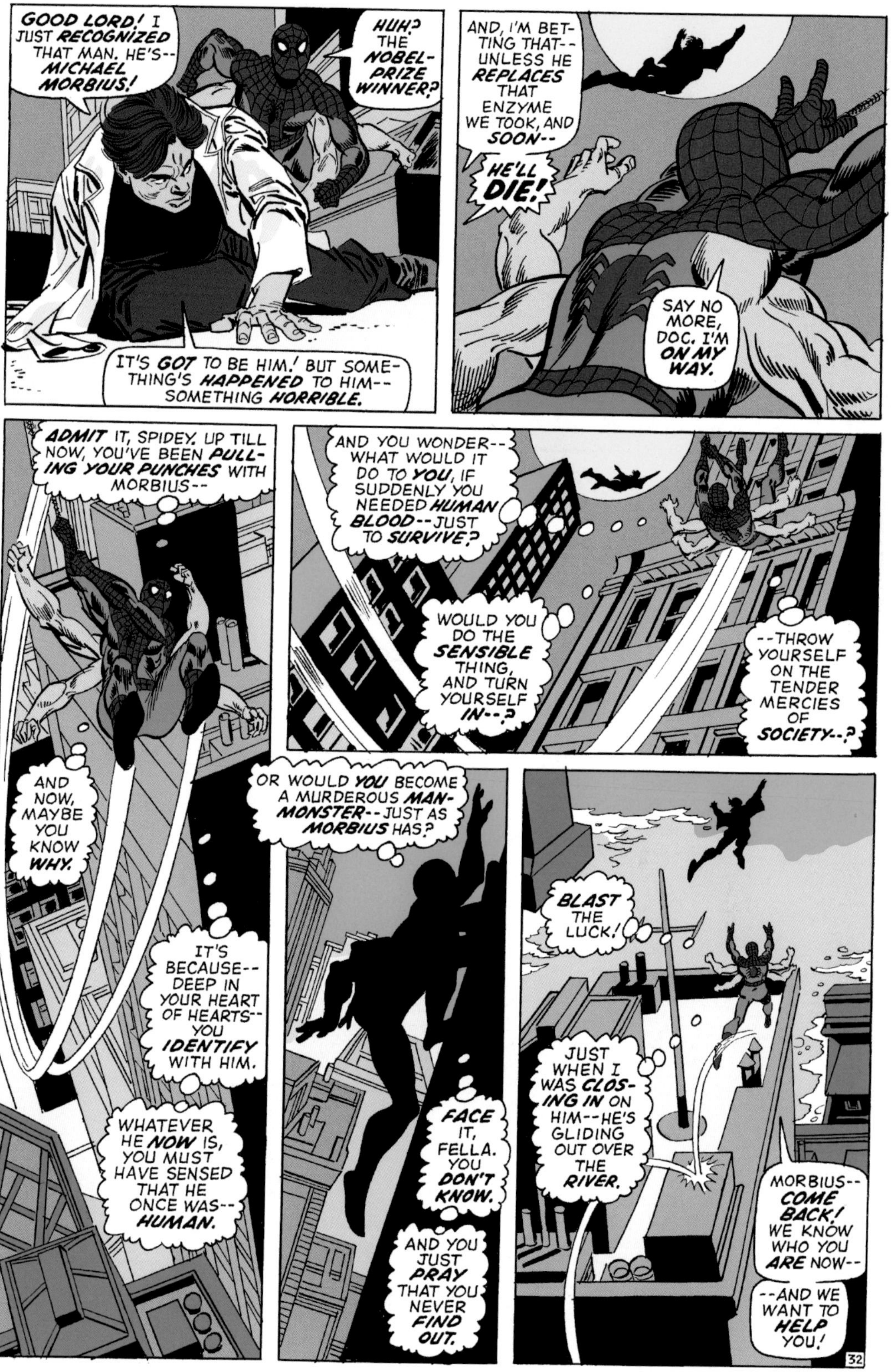
GOOD LORD! I JUST RECOGNIZED THAT MAN. HE'S-- MICHAEL MORBIUS!
HUH? THE NOBEL-PRIZE WINNER?
IT'S GOT TO BE HIM! BUT SOMETHING'S HAPPENED TO HIM-- SOMETHING HORRIBLE.
AND, I'M BETTING THAT-- UNLESS HE REPLACES THAT ENZYME WE TOOK, AND SOON--
HE'LL DIE!
SAY NO MORE, DOC. I'M ON MY WAY.
ADMIT IT, SPIDEY. UP TILL NOW, YOU'VE BEEN PULLING YOUR PUNCHES WITH MORBIUS--
AND NOW, MAYBE YOU KNOW WHY.
IT'S BECAUSE-- DEEP IN YOUR HEART OF HEARTS-- YOU IDENTIFY WITH HIM.
WHATEVER HE NOW IS, YOU MUST HAVE SENSED THAT HE ONCE WAS-- HUMAN.
AND YOU WONDER-- WHAT WOULD IT DO TO YOU, IF SUDDENLY YOU NEEDED HUMAN BLOOD--JUST TO SURVIVE?
WOULD YOU DO THE SENSIBLE THING, AND TURN YOURSELF IN--?
--THROW YOURSELF ON THE TENDER MERCIES OF SOCIETY--?
OR WOULD YOU BECOME A MURDEROUS MAN-MONSTER--JUST AS MORBIUS HAS?
FACE IT, FELLA. YOU DON'T KNOW.
AND YOU JUST PRAY THAT YOU NEVER FIND OUT.
BLAST THE LUCK!
JUST WHEN I WAS CLOSING IN ON HIM--HE'S GLIDING OUT OVER THE RIVER.
MORBIUS-- COME BACK! WE KNOW WHO YOU ARE NOW--
--AND WE WANT TO HELP YOU!
32

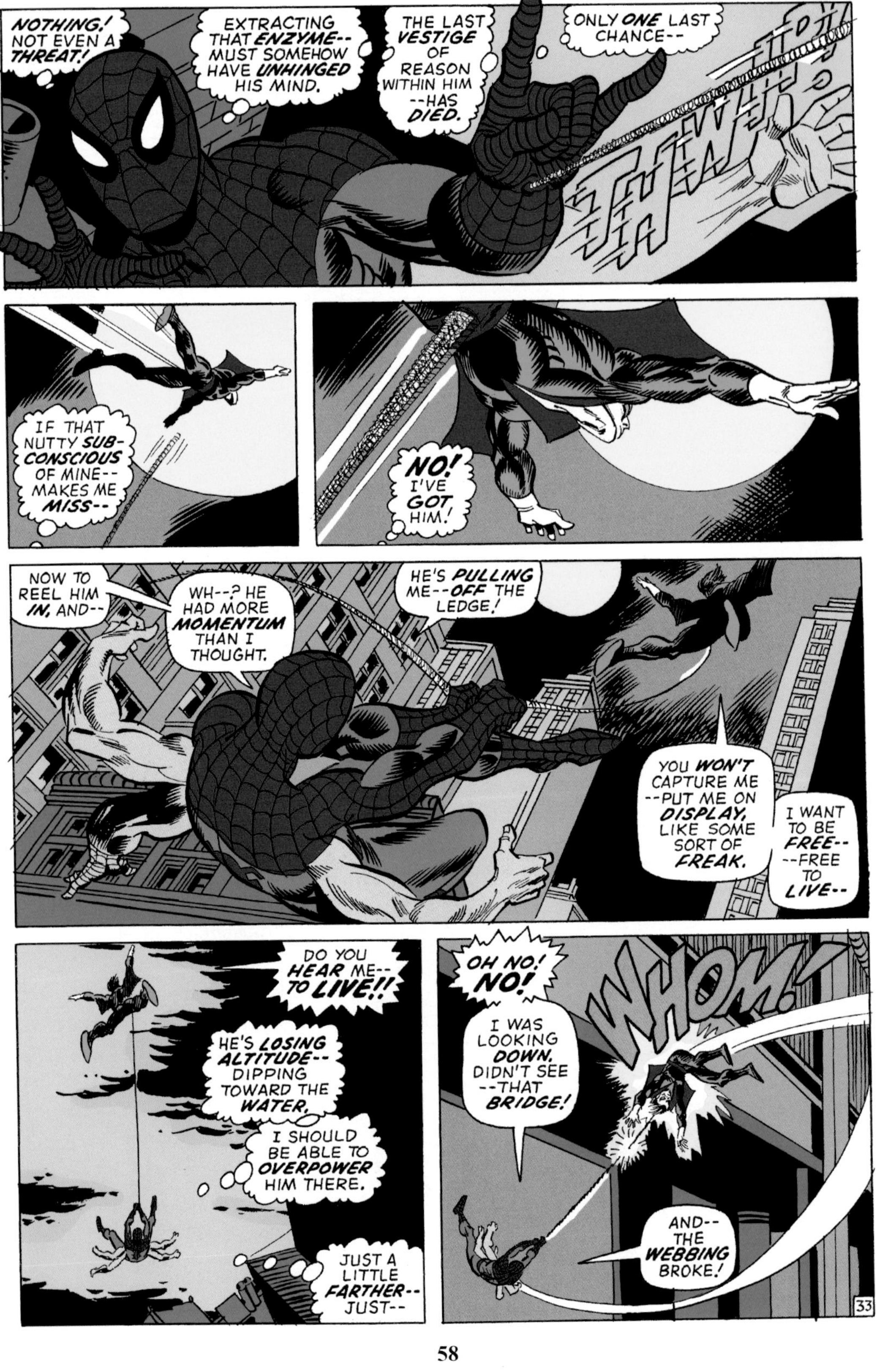
NOTHING! NOT EVEN A THREAT!
EXTRACTING THAT ENZYME-- MUST SOMEHOW HAVE UNHINGED HIS MIND.
THE LAST VESTIGE OF REASON WITHIN HIM --HAS DIED.
ONLY ONE LAST CHANCE--
THWIP
IF THAT NUTTY SUB-CONSCIOUS OF MINE-- MAKES ME MISS--
NO! I'VE GOT HIM!
NOW TO REEL HIM IN, AND--
WH--? HE HAD MORE MOMENTUM THAN I THOUGHT.
HE'S PULLING ME--OFF THE LEDGE!
YOU WON'T CAPTURE ME --PUT ME ON DISPLAY, LIKE SOME SORT OF FREAK.
I WANT TO BE FREE-- --FREE TO LIVE--
DO YOU HEAR ME-- TO LIVE!!
HE'S LOSING ALTITUDE-- DIPPING TOWARD THE WATER.
I SHOULD BE ABLE TO OVERPOWER HIM THERE.
JUST A LITTLE FARTHER-- JUST--
OH NO! NO!
I WAS LOOKING DOWN. DIDN'T SEE --THAT BRIDGE!
WHOM!
AND-- THE WEBBING BROKE!
33

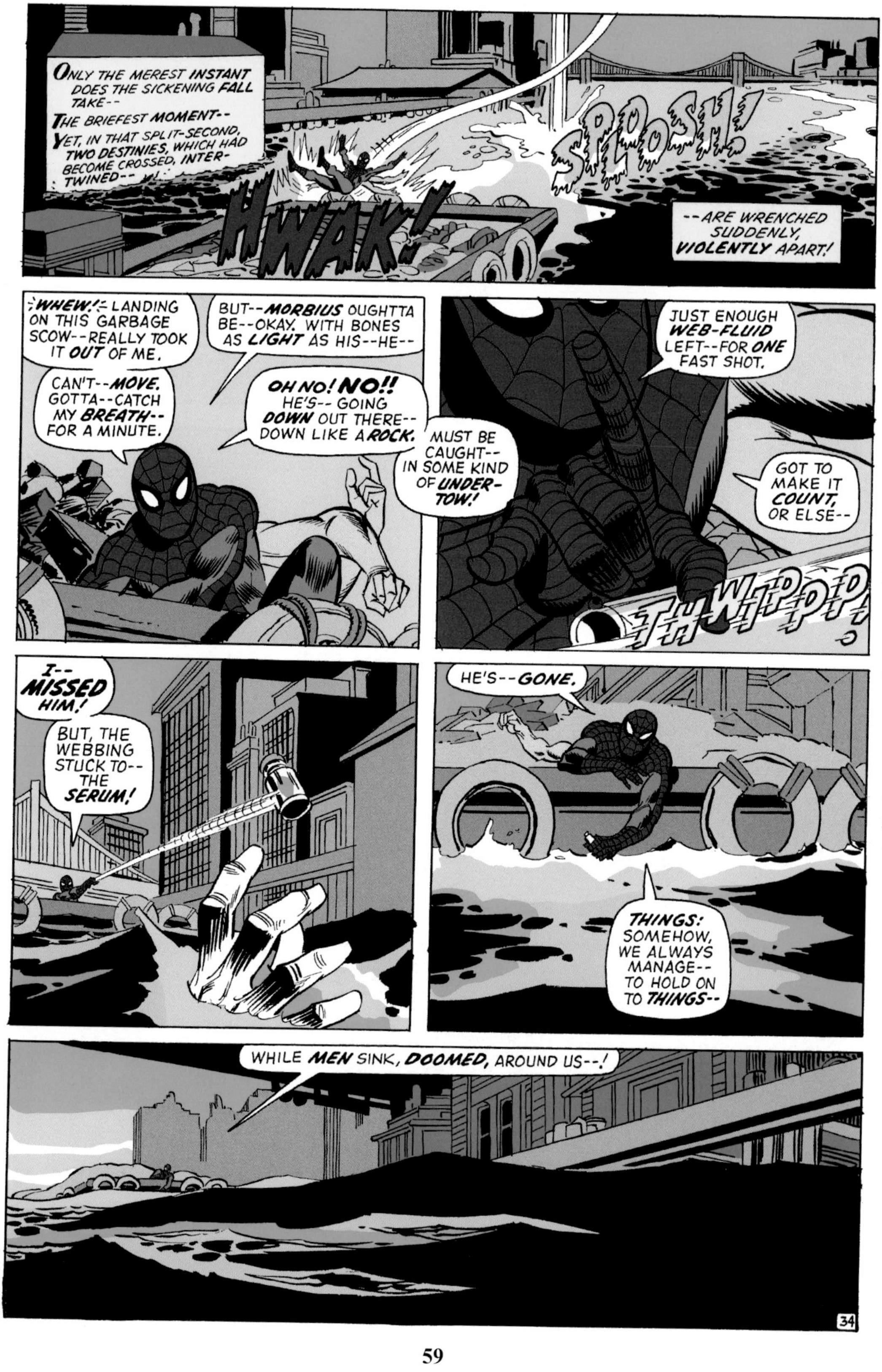
ONLY THE MEREST INSTANT DOES THE SICKENING FALL TAKE--
THE BRIEFEST MOMENT--
YET, IN THAT SPLIT-SECOND, TWO DESTINIES, WHICH HAD BECOME CROSSED, INTER-TWINED--
SPLOSH!
HWAK!
--ARE WRENCHED SUDDENLY, VIOLENTLY APART!
WHEW! LANDING ON THIS GARBAGE SCOW--REALLY TOOK IT OUT OF ME.
CAN'T--MOVE. GOTTA--CATCH MY BREATH-- FOR A MINUTE.
BUT--MORBIUS OUGHTTA BE--OKAY. WITH BONES AS LIGHT AS HIS--HE--
OH NO! NO!! HE'S-- GOING DOWN OUT THERE-- DOWN LIKE A ROCK.
MUST BE CAUGHT-- IN SOME KIND OF UNDER-TOW!
JUST ENOUGH WEB-FLUID LEFT--FOR ONE FAST SHOT.
GOT TO MAKE IT COUNT, OR ELSE--
THWIPPP!
I-- MISSED HIM!
BUT, THE WEBBING STUCK TO-- THE SERUM!
HE'S--GONE.
THINGS: SOMEHOW, WE ALWAYS MANAGE-- TO HOLD ON TO THINGS--
WHILE MEN SINK, DOOMED, AROUND US--!
34

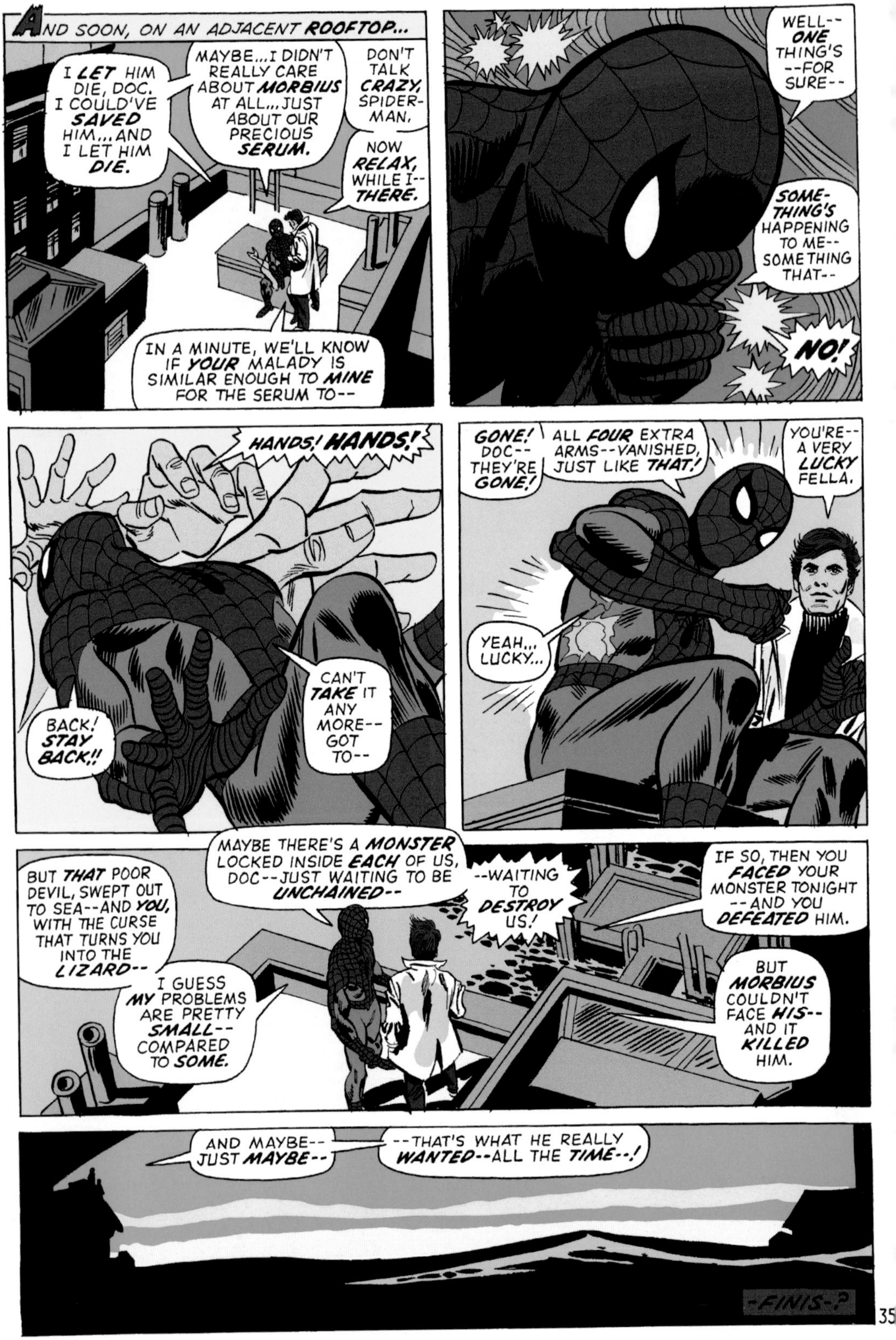
AND SOON, ON AN ADJACENT ROOFTOP...
I LET HIM DIE, DOC. I COULD'VE SAVED HIM... AND I LET HIM DIE.
MAYBE... I DIDN'T REALLY CARE ABOUT MORBIUS AT ALL... JUST ABOUT OUR PRECIOUS SERUM.
DON'T TALK CRAZY, SPIDER-MAN.
NOW RELAX, WHILE I-- THERE.
IN A MINUTE, WE'LL KNOW IF YOUR MALADY IS SIMILAR ENOUGH TO MINE FOR THE SERUM TO--
WELL-- ONE THING'S --FOR SURE--
SOME-THING'S HAPPENING TO ME-- SOMETHING THAT--
NO!
HANDS! HANDS!
CAN'T TAKE IT ANY MORE-- GOT TO--
BACK! STAY BACK!!
GONE! DOC-- THEY'RE GONE!
ALL FOUR EXTRA ARMS--VANISHED, JUST LIKE THAT!
YOU'RE-- A VERY LUCKY FELLA.
YEAH... LUCKY...
BUT THAT POOR DEVIL, SWEPT OUT TO SEA--AND YOU, WITH THE CURSE THAT TURNS YOU INTO THE LIZARD--
I GUESS MY PROBLEMS ARE PRETTY SMALL-- COMPARED TO SOME.
MAYBE THERE'S A MONSTER LOCKED INSIDE EACH OF US, DOC--JUST WAITING TO BE UNCHAINED--
--WAITING TO DESTROY US!
IF SO, THEN YOU FACED YOUR MONSTER TONIGHT --AND YOU DEFEATED HIM.
BUT MORBIUS COULDN'T FACE HIS-- AND IT KILLED HIM.
AND MAYBE-- JUST MAYBE--
--THAT'S WHAT HE REALLY WANTED--ALL THE TIME--!
-FINIS-?
35

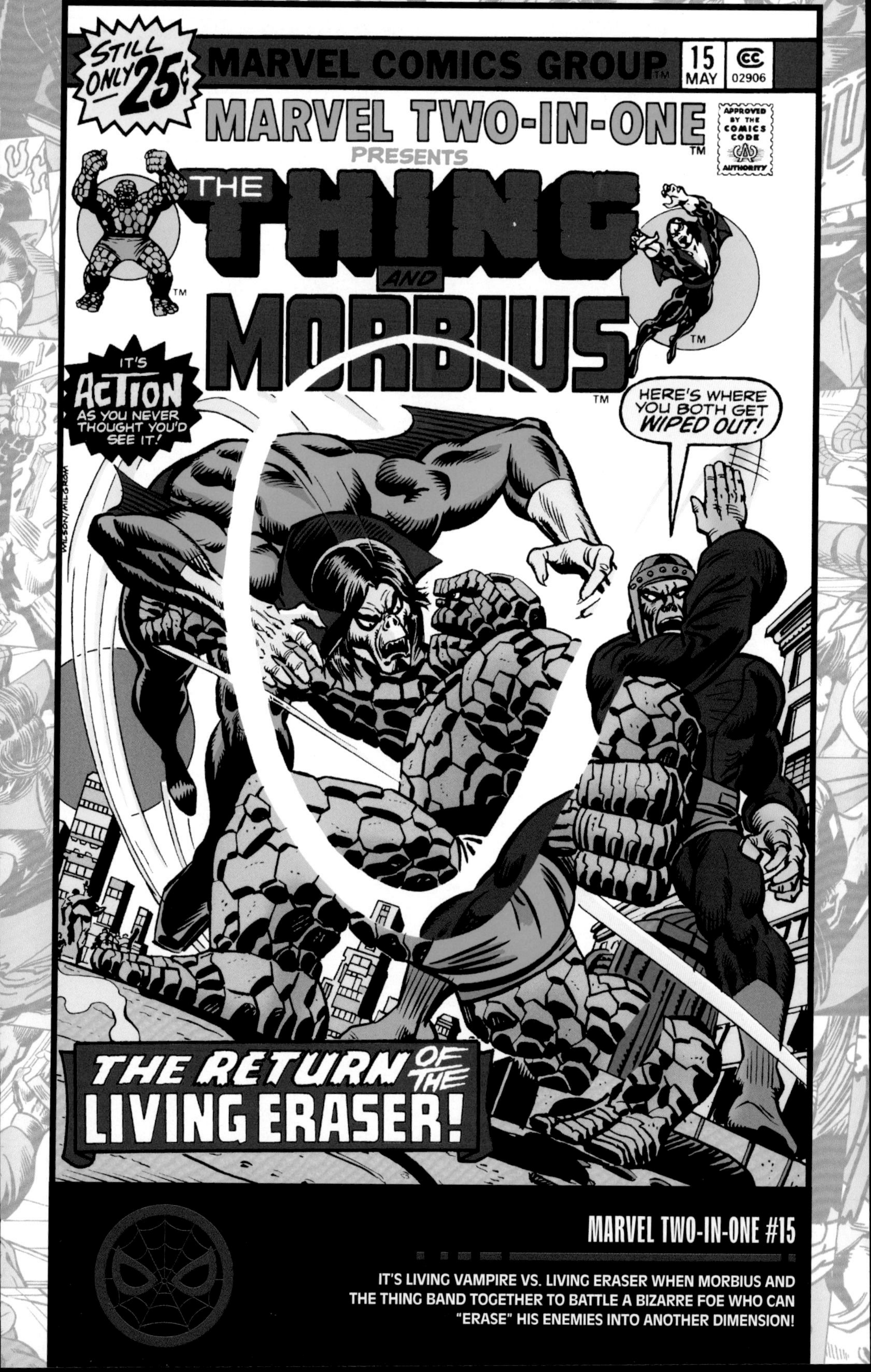
STILL ONLY 25¢
MARVEL COMICS GROUP
15 MAY
CC 02906
MARVEL TWO-IN-ONE
PRESENTS
APPROVED BY THE COMICS CODE AUTHORITY
THE THING AND MORBIUS
IT'S ACTION AS YOU NEVER THOUGHT YOU'D SEE IT!
HERE'S WHERE YOU BOTH GET WIPED OUT!
THE RETURN OF THE LIVING ERASER!

MARVEL TWO-IN-ONE #15

IT'S LIVING VAMPIRE VS. LIVING ERASER WHEN MORBIUS AND THE THING BAND TOGETHER TO BATTLE A BIZARRE FOE WHO CAN "ERASE" HIS ENEMIES INTO ANOTHER DIMENSION!

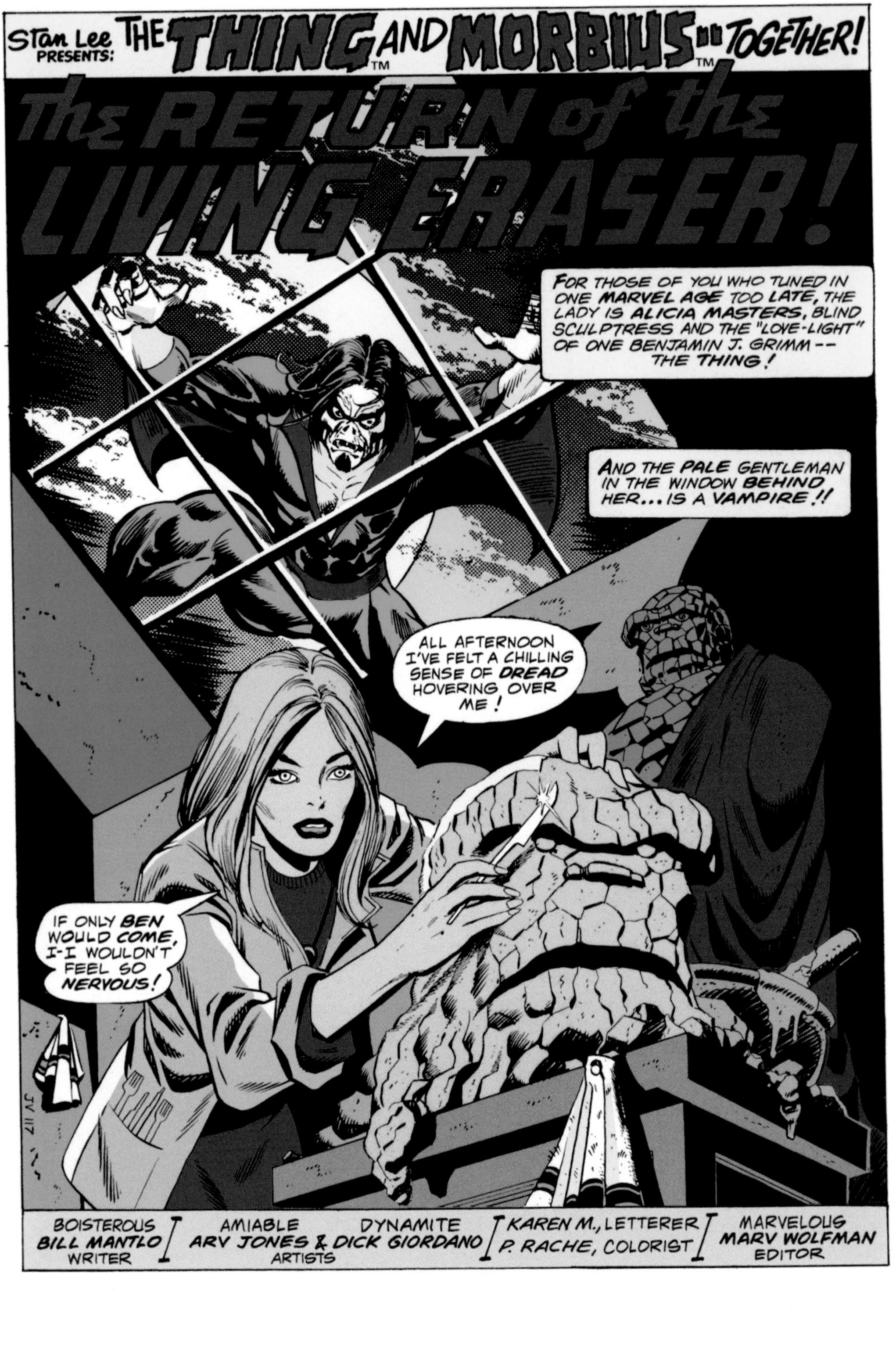

Stan Lee PRESENTS: THE THING AND MORBIUS ... TOGETHER!
The RETURN of the LIVING ERASER!
FOR THOSE OF YOU WHO TUNED IN ONE MARVEL AGE TOO LATE, THE LADY IS ALICIA MASTERS, BLIND SCULPTRESS AND THE "LOVE-LIGHT" OF ONE BENJAMIN J. GRIMM -- THE THING!
AND THE PALE GENTLEMAN IN THE WINDOW BEHIND HER... IS A VAMPIRE!!
ALL AFTERNOON I'VE FELT A CHILLING SENSE OF DREAD HOVERING OVER ME!
IF ONLY BEN WOULD COME, I-I WOULDN'T FEEL SO NERVOUS!
BOISTEROUS BILL MANTLO WRITER
AMIABLE ARV JONES & DYNAMITE DICK GIORDANO ARTISTS
KAREN M., LETTERER P. RACHE, COLORIST
MARVELOUS MARV WOLFMAN EDITOR

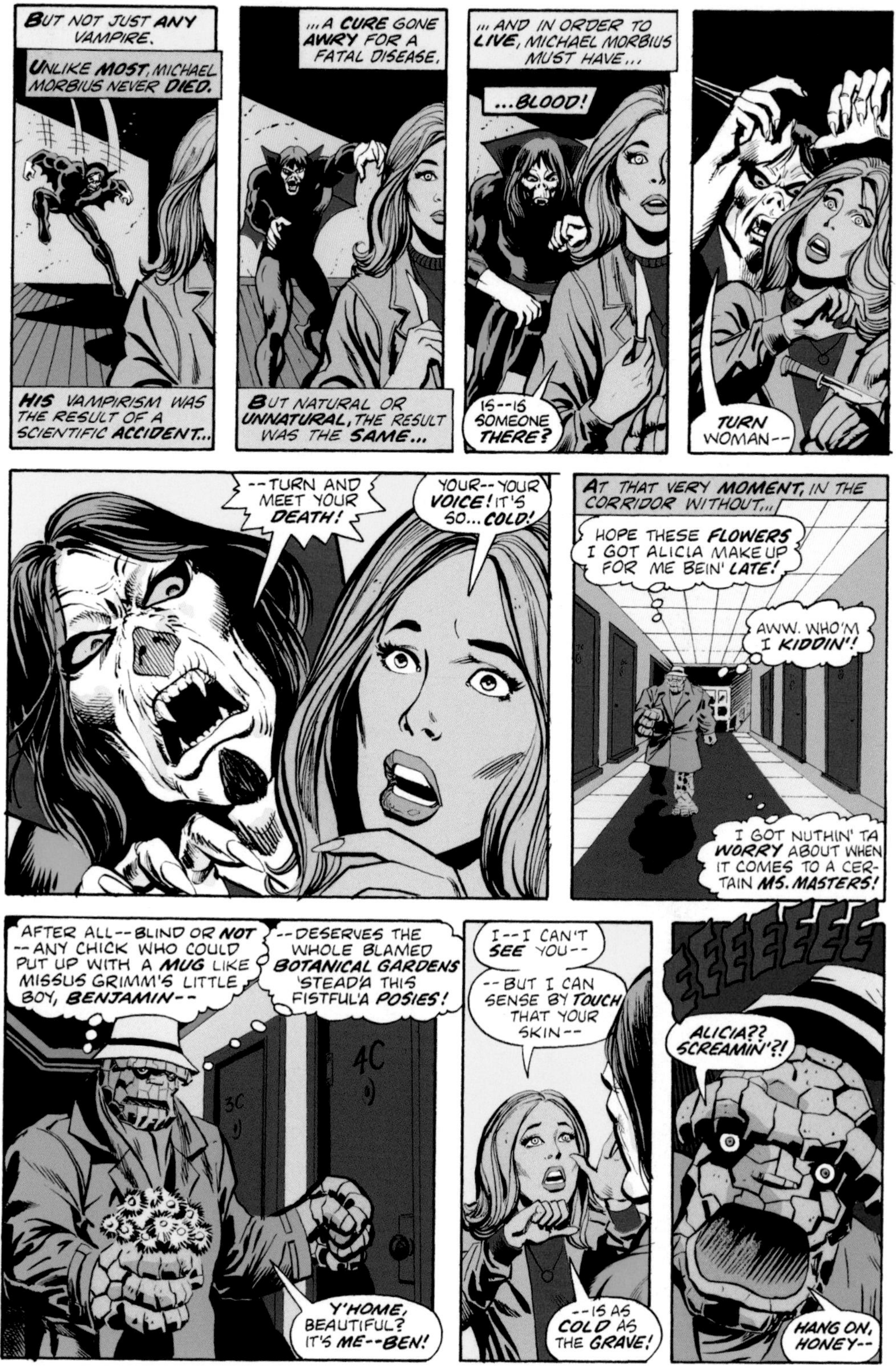
BUT NOT JUST ANY VAMPIRE.
UNLIKE MOST, MICHAEL MORBIUS NEVER DIED.
HIS VAMPIRISM WAS THE RESULT OF A SCIENTIFIC ACCIDENT...
...A CURE GONE AWRY FOR A FATAL DISEASE.
BUT NATURAL OR UNNATURAL, THE RESULT WAS THE SAME...
...AND IN ORDER TO LIVE, MICHAEL MORBIUS MUST HAVE...
...BLOOD!
IS--IS SOMEONE THERE?
TURN WOMAN--
--TURN AND MEET YOUR DEATH!
YOUR--YOUR VOICE! IT'S SO...COLD!
AT THAT VERY MOMENT, IN THE CORRIDOR WITHOUT...
HOPE THESE FLOWERS I GOT ALICIA MAKE UP FOR ME BEIN' LATE!
AWW. WHO'M I KIDDIN'!
I GOT NUTHIN' TA WORRY ABOUT WHEN IT COMES TO A CERTAIN MS. MASTERS!
AFTER ALL--BLIND OR NOT--ANY CHICK WHO COULD PUT UP WITH A MUG LIKE MISSUS GRIMM'S LITTLE BOY, BENJAMIN--
--DESERVES THE WHOLE BLAMED BOTANICAL GARDENS 'STEAD'A THIS FISTFUL'A POSIES!
Y'HOME, BEAUTIFUL? IT'S ME--BEN!
I--I CAN'T SEE YOU--
--BUT I CAN SENSE BY TOUCH THAT YOUR SKIN--
--IS AS COLD AS THE GRAVE!
EEEEEEE
ALICIA?? SCREAMIN'?!
HANG ON, HONEY--

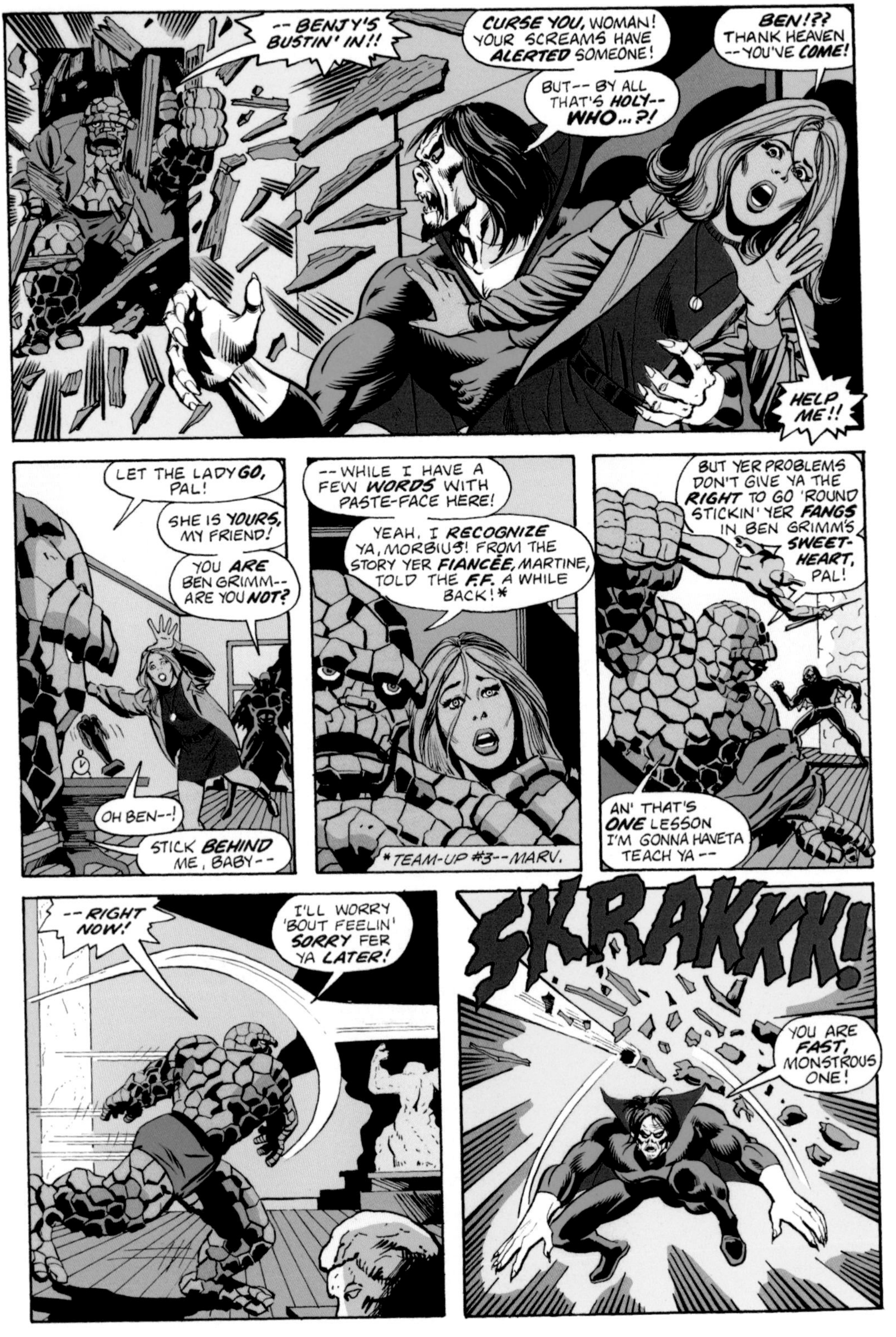

-- BENJY'S BUSTIN' IN!!
CURSE YOU, WOMAN! YOUR SCREAMS HAVE ALERTED SOMEONE!
BUT-- BY ALL THAT'S HOLY-- WHO...?!
BEN!?? THANK HEAVEN --YOU'VE COME!
HELP ME!!
LET THE LADY GO, PAL!
SHE IS YOURS, MY FRIEND!
YOU ARE BEN GRIMM-- ARE YOU NOT?
OH BEN--!
STICK BEHIND ME, BABY--
-- WHILE I HAVE A FEW WORDS WITH PASTE-FACE HERE!
YEAH, I RECOGNIZE YA, MORBIUS! FROM THE STORY YER FIANCÉE, MARTINE, TOLD THE F.F. A WHILE BACK!*
*TEAM-UP #3--MARV.
BUT YER PROBLEMS DON'T GIVE YA THE RIGHT TO GO 'ROUND STICKIN' YER FANGS IN BEN GRIMM'S SWEET-HEART, PAL!
AN' THAT'S ONE LESSON I'M GONNA HAVETA TEACH YA --
-- RIGHT NOW!
I'LL WORRY 'BOUT FEELIN' SORRY FER YA LATER!
SKRAKKK!
YOU ARE FAST, MONSTROUS ONE!

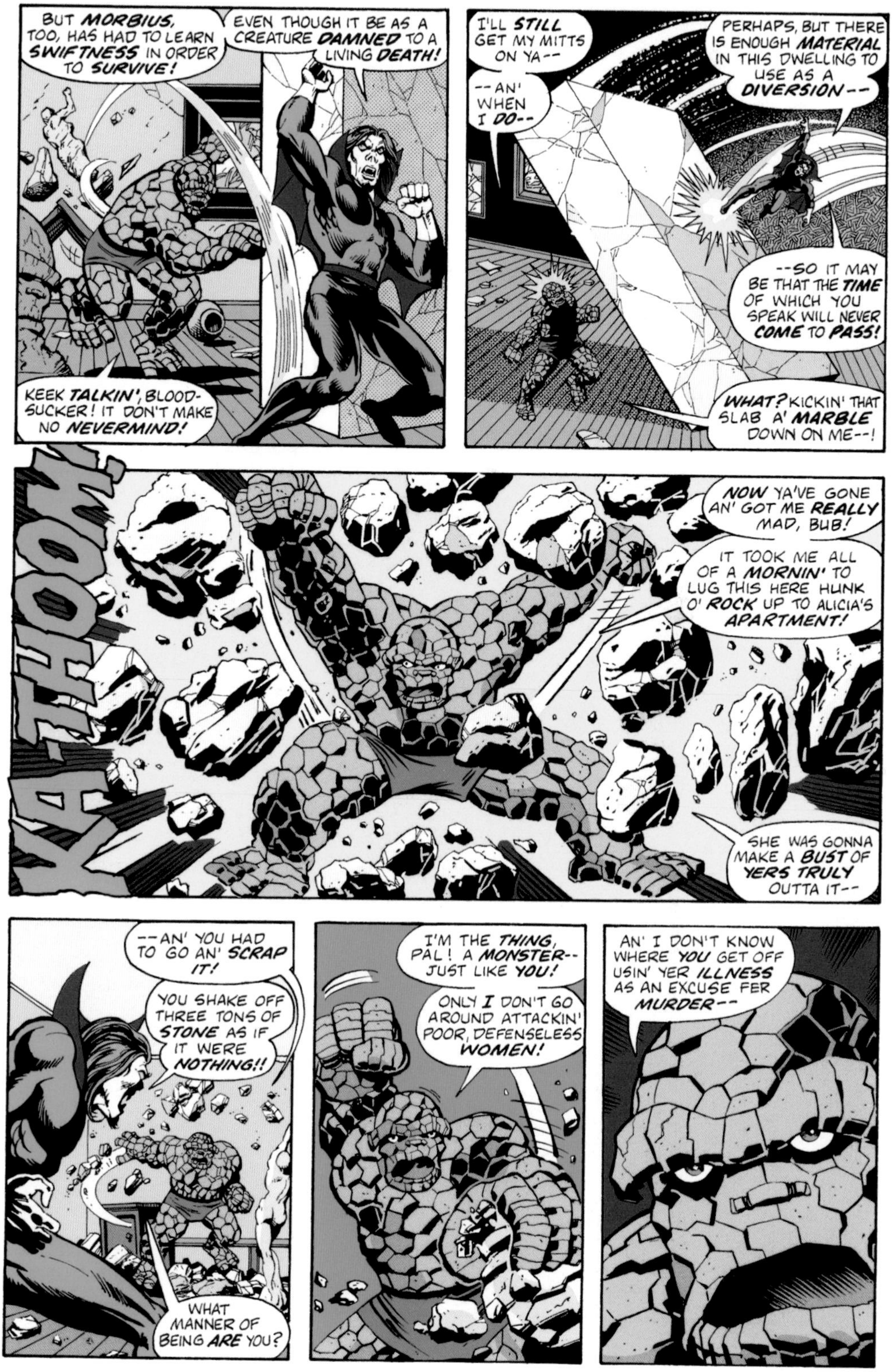
BUT MORBIUS, TOO, HAS HAD TO LEARN SWIFTNESS IN ORDER TO SURVIVE!
EVEN THOUGH IT BE AS A CREATURE DAMNED TO A LIVING DEATH!
KEEK TALKIN', BLOOD-SUCKER! IT DON'T MAKE NO NEVERMIND!
I'LL STILL GET MY MITTS ON YA--
--AN' WHEN I DO--
PERHAPS, BUT THERE IS ENOUGH MATERIAL IN THIS DWELLING TO USE AS A DIVERSION--
--SO IT MAY BE THAT THE TIME OF WHICH YOU SPEAK WILL NEVER COME TO PASS!
WHAT? KICKIN' THAT SLAB A' MARBLE DOWN ON ME--!
KA-THOOM!
NOW YA'VE GONE AN' GOT ME REALLY MAD, BUB!
IT TOOK ME ALL OF A MORNIN' TO LUG THIS HERE HUNK O' ROCK UP TO ALICIA'S APARTMENT!
SHE WAS GONNA MAKE A BUST OF YERS TRULY OUTTA IT--
--AN' YOU HAD TO GO AN' SCRAP IT!
YOU SHAKE OFF THREE TONS OF STONE AS IF IT WERE NOTHING!!
WHAT MANNER OF BEING ARE YOU?
I'M THE THING, PAL! A MONSTER--JUST LIKE YOU!
ONLY I DON'T GO AROUND ATTACKIN' POOR, DEFENSELESS WOMEN!
AN' I DON'T KNOW WHERE YOU GET OFF USIN' YER ILLNESS AS AN EXCUSE FER MURDER--

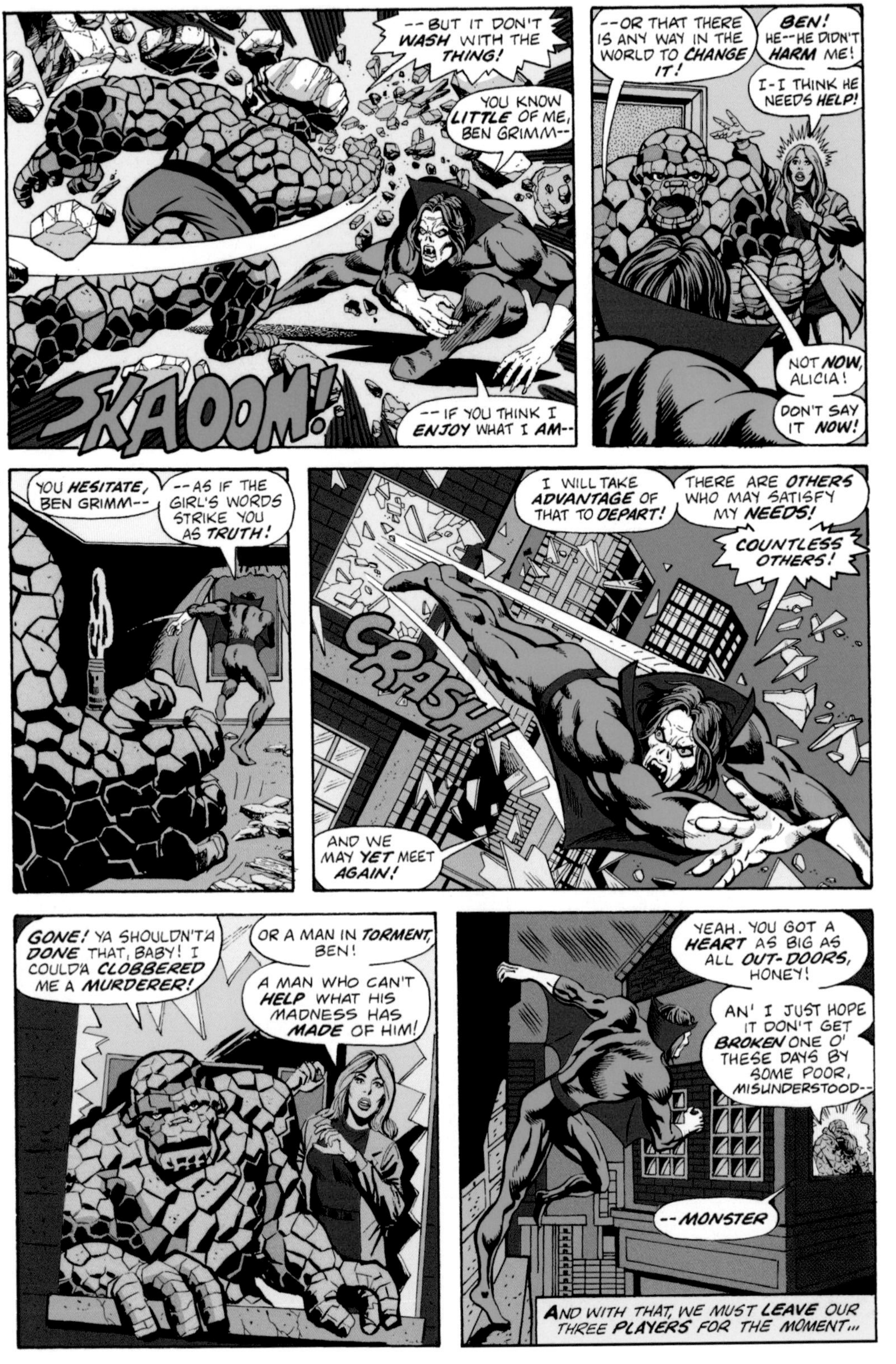
--BUT IT DON'T WASH WITH THE THING!
YOU KNOW LITTLE OF ME, BEN GRIMM--
--IF YOU THINK I ENJOY WHAT I AM--
SKAOOM!
--OR THAT THERE IS ANY WAY IN THE WORLD TO CHANGE IT!
BEN! HE--HE DIDN'T HARM ME!
I-I THINK HE NEEDS HELP!
NOT NOW, ALICIA!
DON'T SAY IT NOW!
YOU HESITATE, BEN GRIMM--
--AS IF THE GIRL'S WORDS STRIKE YOU AS TRUTH!
I WILL TAKE ADVANTAGE OF THAT TO DEPART!
THERE ARE OTHERS WHO MAY SATISFY MY NEEDS!
COUNTLESS OTHERS!
CRASH!
AND WE MAY YET MEET AGAIN!
GONE! YA SHOULDN'T'A DONE THAT, BABY! I COULD'A CLOBBERED ME A MURDERER!
OR A MAN IN TORMENT, BEN!
A MAN WHO CAN'T HELP WHAT HIS MADNESS HAS MADE OF HIM!
YEAH. YOU GOT A HEART AS BIG AS ALL OUT-DOORS, HONEY!
AN' I JUST HOPE IT DON'T GET BROKEN ONE O' THESE DAYS BY SOME POOR, MISUNDERSTOOD--
--MONSTER
AND WITH THAT, WE MUST LEAVE OUR THREE PLAYERS FOR THE MOMENT...

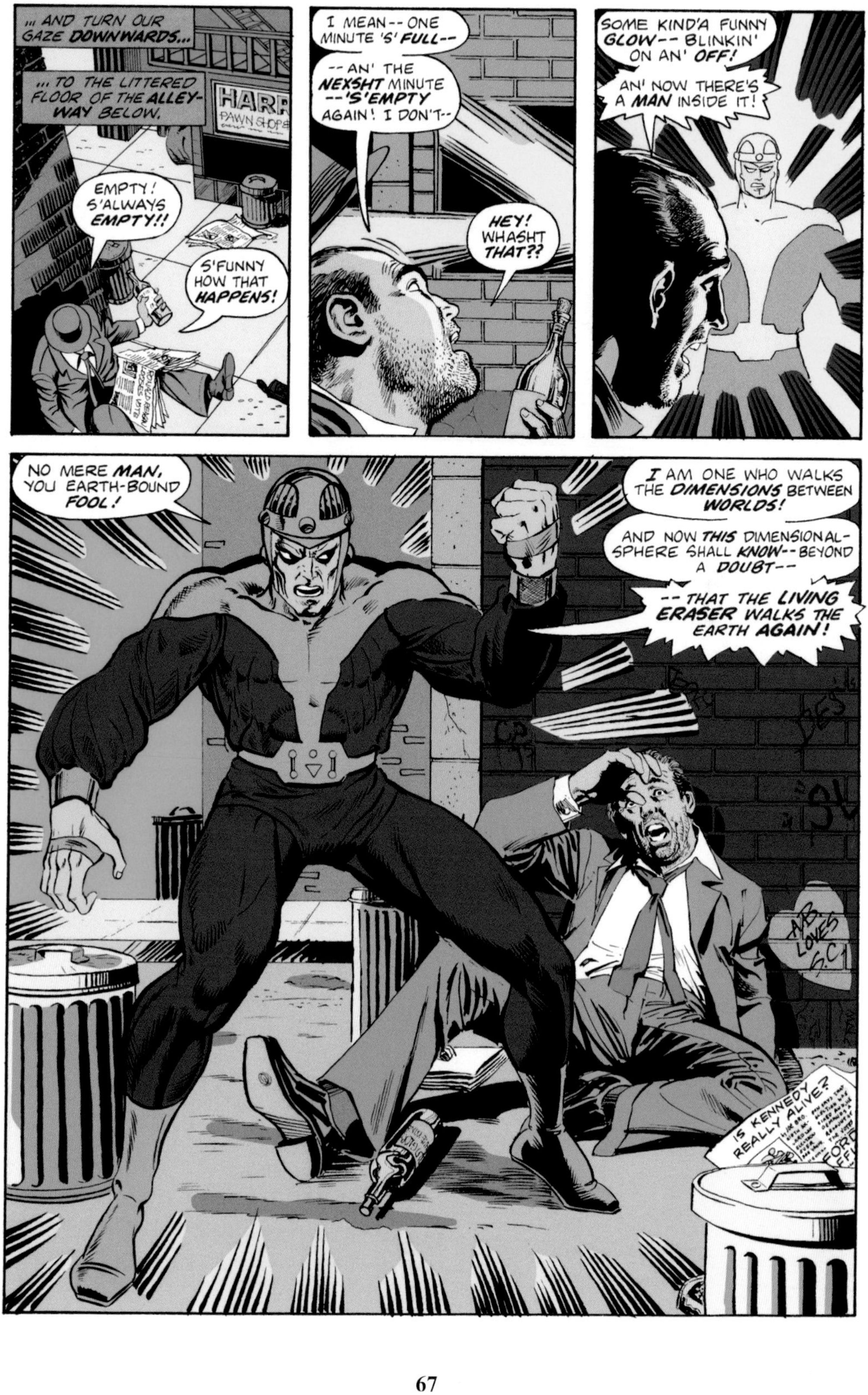
... AND TURN OUR GAZE DOWNWARDS...
... TO THE LITTERED FLOOR OF THE ALLEY-WAY BELOW.
HARR
PAWN SHOP
EMPTY! S'ALWAYS EMPTY!!
S'FUNNY HOW THAT HAPPENS!
I MEAN -- ONE MINUTE 'S' FULL --
-- AN' THE NEXSHT MINUTE -- 'S'EMPTY AGAIN! I DON'T --
HEY! WHASHT THAT??
SOME KIND'A FUNNY GLOW -- BLINKIN' ON AN' OFF!
AN' NOW THERE'S A MAN INSIDE IT!
NO MERE MAN, YOU EARTH-BOUND FOOL!
I AM ONE WHO WALKS THE DIMENSIONS BETWEEN WORLDS!
AND NOW THIS DIMENSIONAL-SPHERE SHALL KNOW -- BEYOND A DOUBT --
-- THAT THE LIVING ERASER WALKS THE EARTH AGAIN!
A.B. LOVES S.C.
IS KENNEDY REALLY ALIVE?
FORD

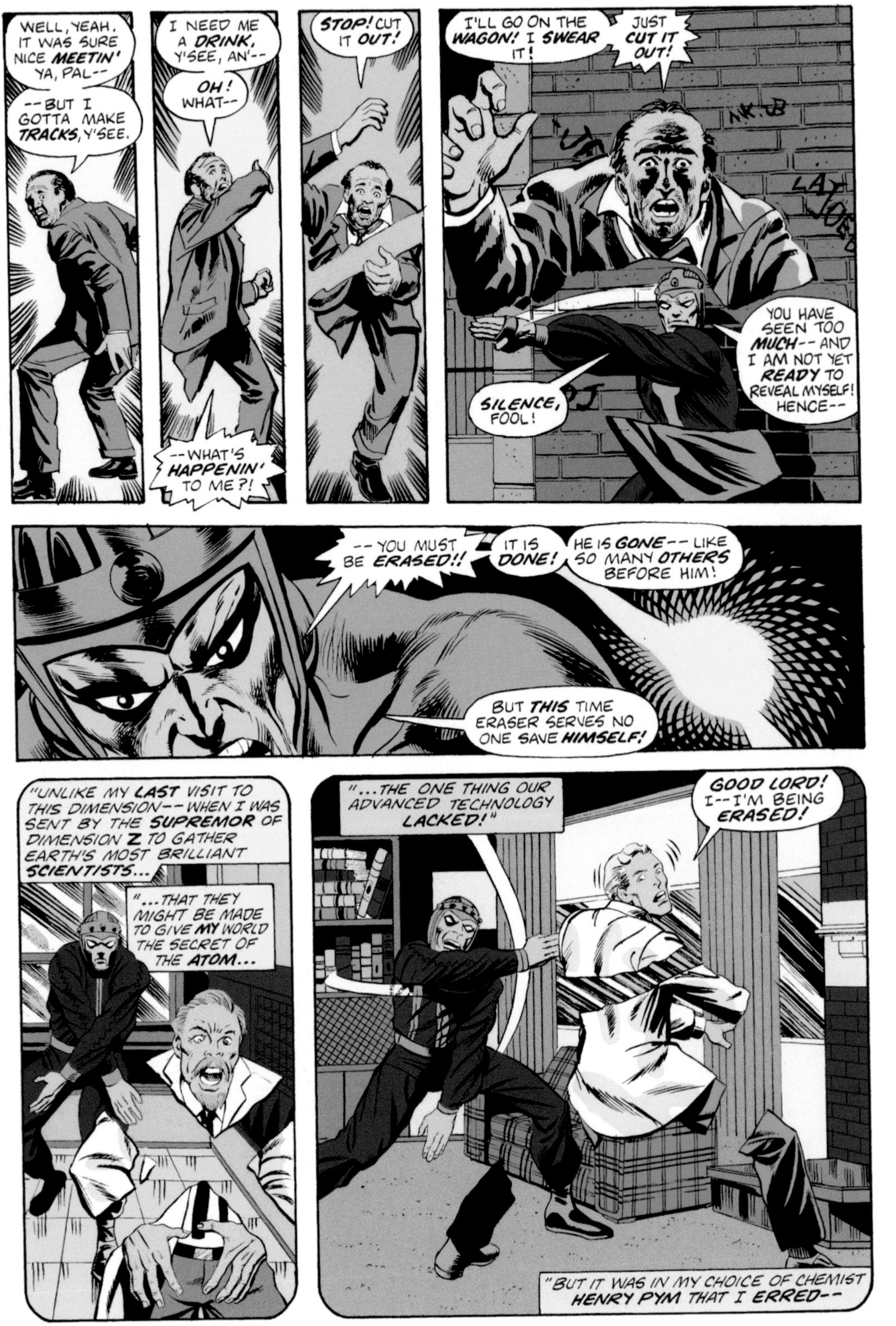

WELL, YEAH. IT WAS SURE NICE MEETIN' YA, PAL--
--BUT I GOTTA MAKE TRACKS, Y'SEE.
I NEED ME A DRINK, Y'SEE, AN'--
OH! WHAT--
--WHAT'S HAPPENIN' TO ME?!
STOP! CUT IT OUT!
I'LL GO ON THE WAGON! I SWEAR IT!
JUST CUT IT OUT!
SILENCE, FOOL!
YOU HAVE SEEN TOO MUCH-- AND I AM NOT YET READY TO REVEAL MYSELF! HENCE--
--YOU MUST BE ERASED!!
IT IS DONE!
HE IS GONE-- LIKE SO MANY OTHERS BEFORE HIM!
BUT THIS TIME ERASER SERVES NO ONE SAVE HIMSELF!
"UNLIKE MY LAST VISIT TO THIS DIMENSION-- WHEN I WAS SENT BY THE SUPREMOR OF DIMENSION Z TO GATHER EARTH'S MOST BRILLIANT SCIENTISTS...
"...THAT THEY MIGHT BE MADE TO GIVE MY WORLD THE SECRET OF THE ATOM...
"...THE ONE THING OUR ADVANCED TECHNOLOGY LACKED!"
GOOD LORD! I--I'M BEING ERASED!
"BUT IT WAS IN MY CHOICE OF CHEMIST HENRY PYM THAT I ERRED--

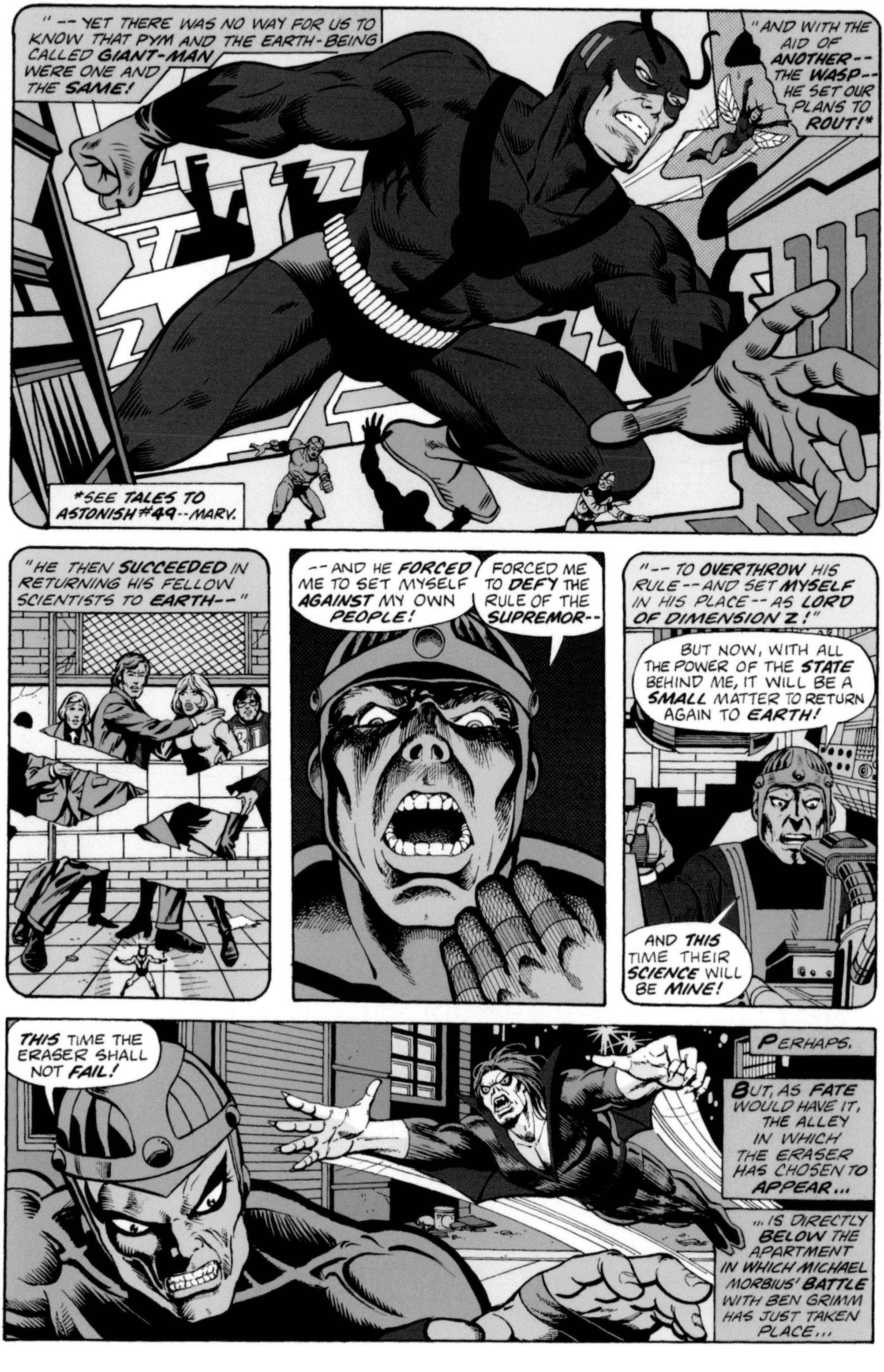
"--YET THERE WAS NO WAY FOR US TO KNOW THAT PYM AND THE EARTH-BEING CALLED GIANT-MAN WERE ONE AND THE SAME!
"AND WITH THE AID OF ANOTHER-- THE WASP-- HE SET OUR PLANS TO ROUT!*
*SEE TALES TO ASTONISH #49--MARV.
"HE THEN SUCCEEDED IN RETURNING HIS FELLOW SCIENTISTS TO EARTH--"
--AND HE FORCED ME TO SET MYSELF AGAINST MY OWN PEOPLE!
FORCED ME TO DEFY THE RULE OF THE SUPREMOR--
"--TO OVERTHROW HIS RULE--AND SET MYSELF IN HIS PLACE--AS LORD OF DIMENSION Z!"
BUT NOW, WITH ALL THE POWER OF THE STATE BEHIND ME, IT WILL BE A SMALL MATTER TO RETURN AGAIN TO EARTH!
AND THIS TIME THEIR SCIENCE WILL BE MINE!
THIS TIME THE ERASER SHALL NOT FAIL!
PERHAPS.
BUT, AS FATE WOULD HAVE IT, THE ALLEY IN WHICH THE ERASER HAS CHOSEN TO APPEAR...
...IS DIRECTLY BELOW THE APARTMENT IN WHICH MICHAEL MORBIUS' BATTLE WITH BEN GRIMM HAS JUST TAKEN PLACE...

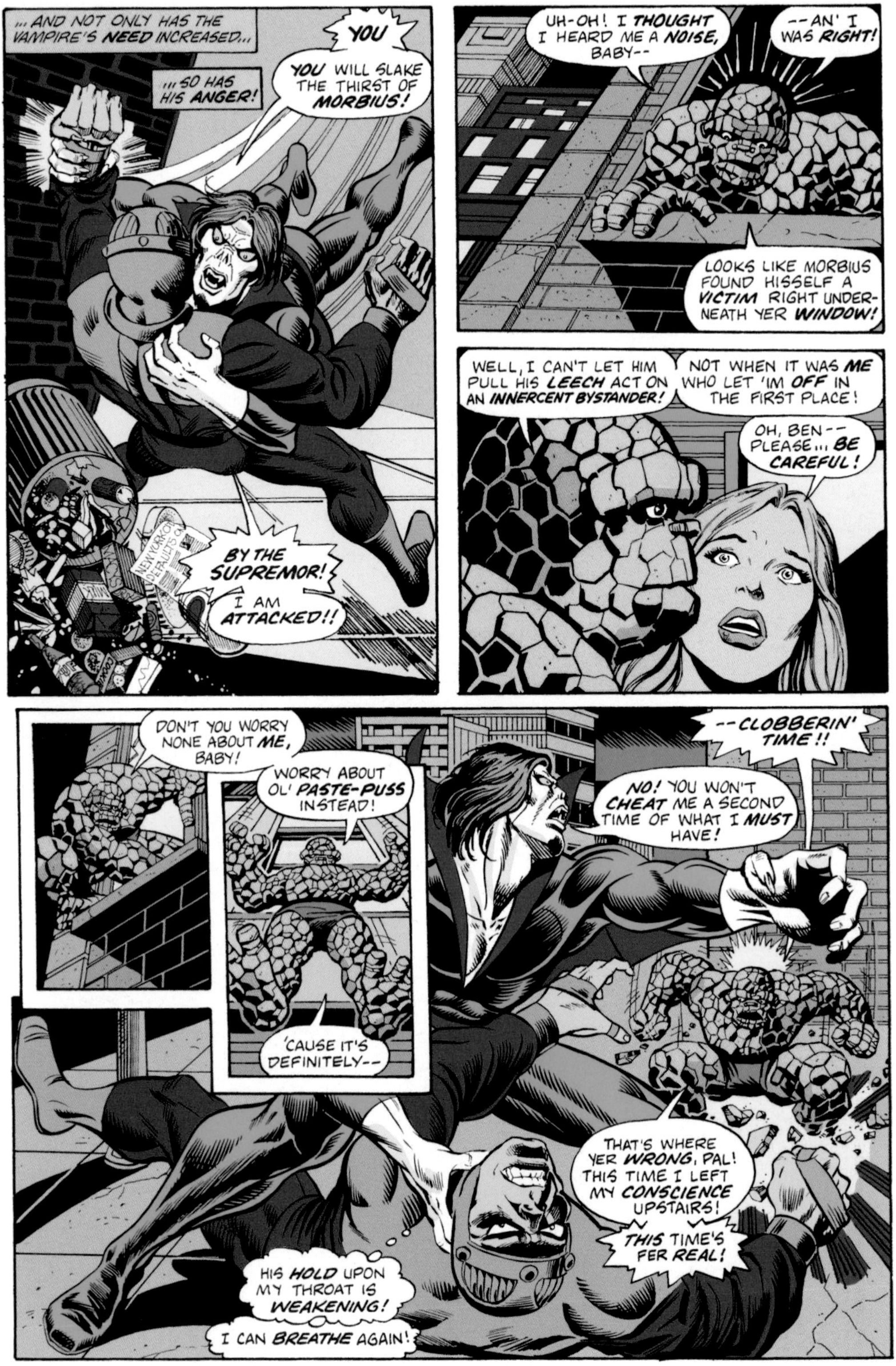

...AND NOT ONLY HAS THE VAMPIRE'S NEED INCREASED...
...SO HAS HIS ANGER!
YOU
YOU WILL SLAKE THE THIRST OF MORBIUS!
NEW YORK DEFAULTS ON
BY THE SUPREMOR!
I AM ATTACKED!!
UH-OH! I THOUGHT I HEARD ME A NOISE, BABY--
--AN' I WAS RIGHT!
LOOKS LIKE MORBIUS FOUND HISSELF A VICTIM RIGHT UNDERNEATH YER WINDOW!
WELL, I CAN'T LET HIM PULL HIS LEECH ACT ON AN INNERCENT BYSTANDER!
NOT WHEN IT WAS ME WHO LET 'IM OFF IN THE FIRST PLACE!
OH, BEN-- PLEASE... BE CAREFUL!
DON'T YOU WORRY NONE ABOUT ME, BABY!
WORRY ABOUT OL' PASTE-PUSS INSTEAD!
'CAUSE IT'S DEFINITELY--
--CLOBBERIN' TIME!!
NO! YOU WON'T CHEAT ME A SECOND TIME OF WHAT I MUST HAVE!
THAT'S WHERE YER WRONG, PAL! THIS TIME I LEFT MY CONSCIENCE UPSTAIRS!
THIS TIME'S FER REAL!
HIS HOLD UPON MY THROAT IS WEAKENING!
I CAN BREATHE AGAIN!

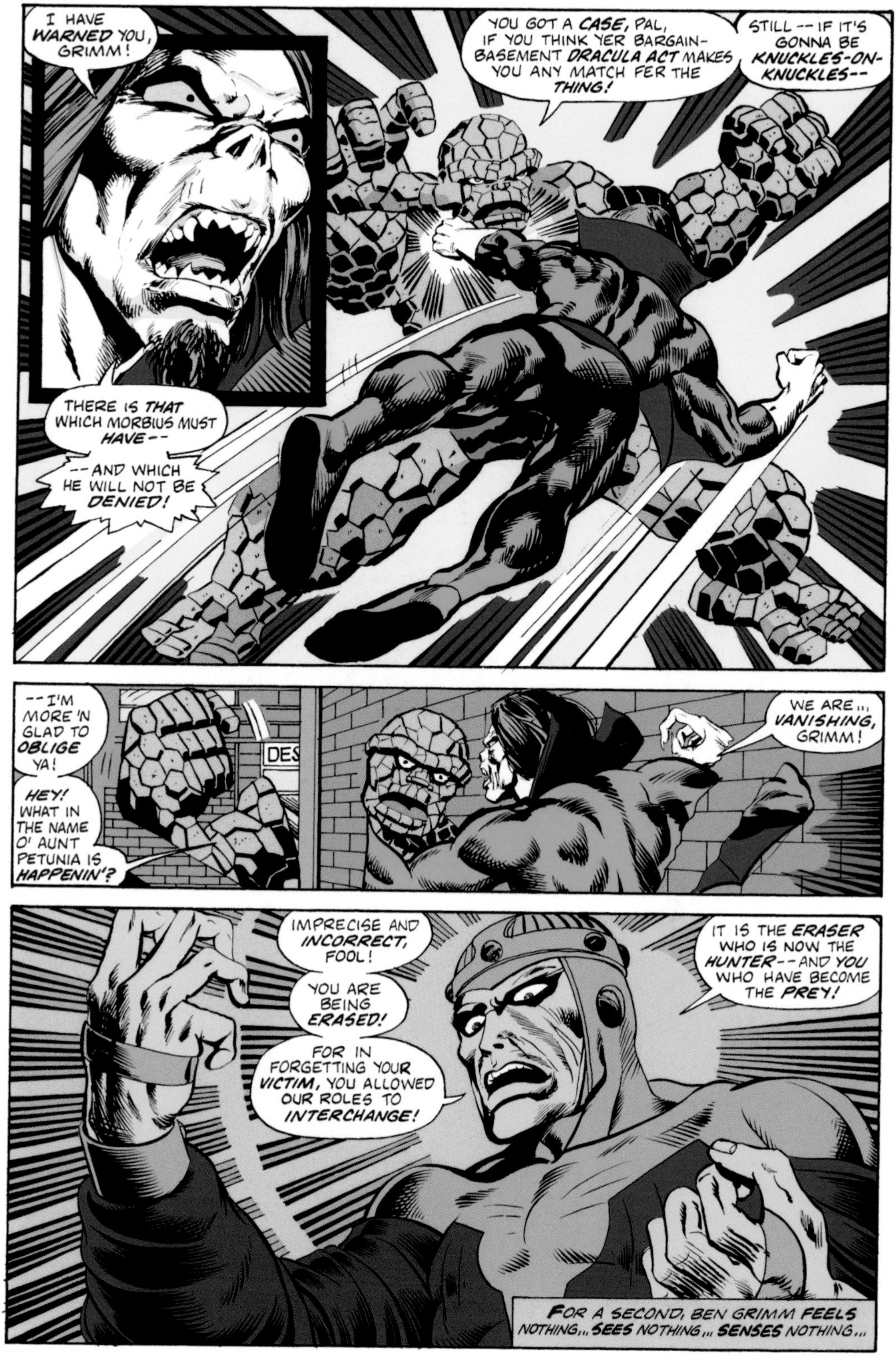
I HAVE WARNED YOU, GRIMM!
YOU GOT A CASE, PAL, IF YOU THINK YER BARGAIN-BASEMENT DRACULA ACT MAKES YOU ANY MATCH FER THE THING!
STILL -- IF IT'S GONNA BE KNUCKLES-ON-KNUCKLES--
THERE IS THAT WHICH MORBIUS MUST HAVE--
--AND WHICH HE WILL NOT BE DENIED!
--I'M MORE 'N GLAD TO OBLIGE YA!
HEY! WHAT IN THE NAME O' AUNT PETUNIA IS HAPPENIN'?
WE ARE... VANISHING, GRIMM!
IMPRECISE AND INCORRECT, FOOL!
YOU ARE BEING ERASED!
FOR IN FORGETTING YOUR VICTIM, YOU ALLOWED OUR ROLES TO INTERCHANGE!
IT IS THE ERASER WHO IS NOW THE HUNTER--AND YOU WHO HAVE BECOME THE PREY!
FOR A SECOND, BEN GRIMM FEELS NOTHING... SEES NOTHING... SENSES NOTHING...

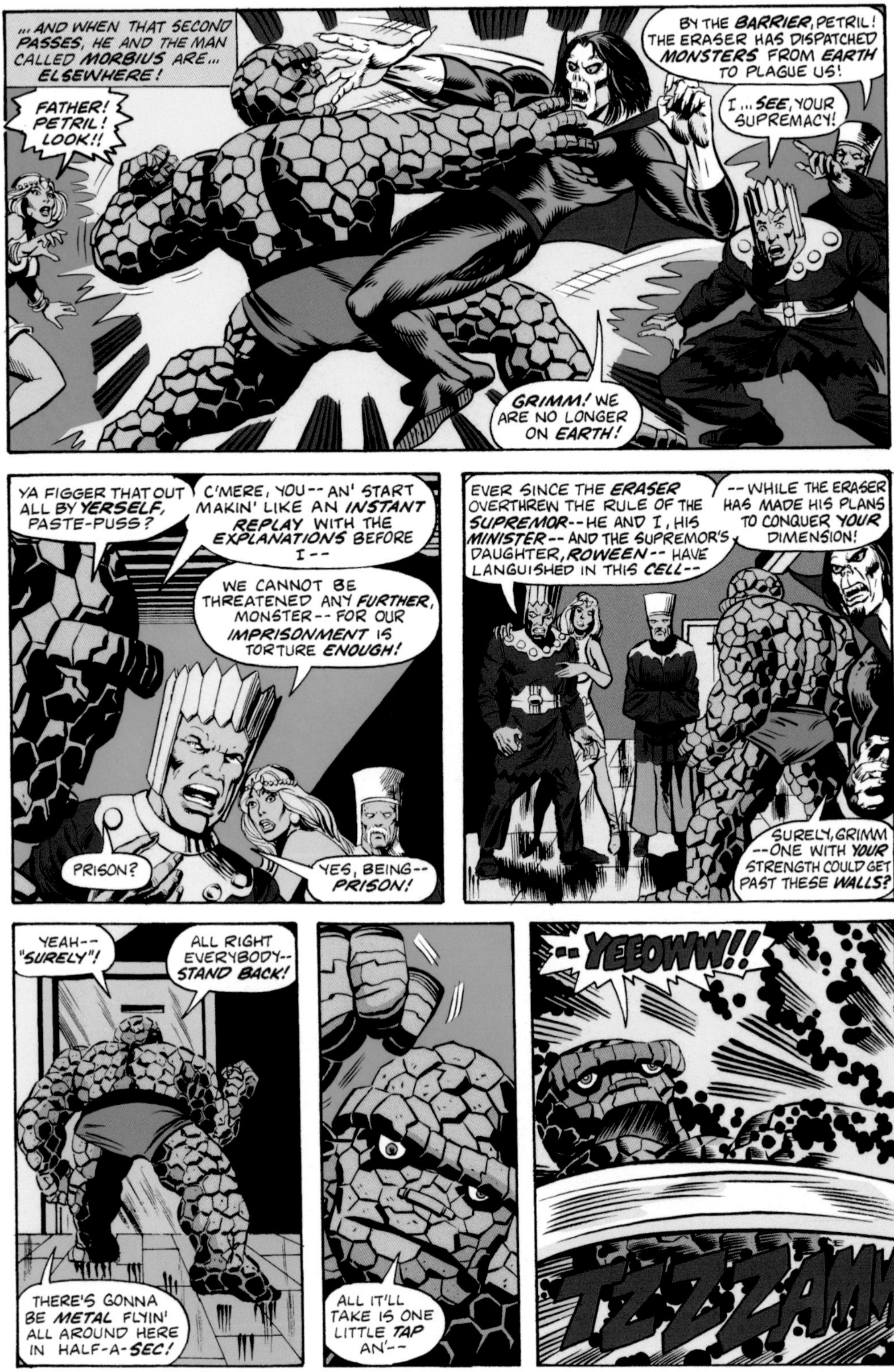
...AND WHEN THAT SECOND PASSES, HE AND THE MAN CALLED MORBIUS ARE... ELSEWHERE!
FATHER! PETRIL! LOOK!!
BY THE BARRIER, PETRIL! THE ERASER HAS DISPATCHED MONSTERS FROM EARTH TO PLAGUE US!
I... SEE, YOUR SUPREMACY!
GRIMM! WE ARE NO LONGER ON EARTH!
YA FIGGER THAT OUT ALL BY YERSELF, PASTE-PUSS?
C'MERE, YOU-- AN' START MAKIN' LIKE AN INSTANT REPLAY WITH THE EXPLANATIONS BEFORE I--
WE CANNOT BE THREATENED ANY FURTHER, MONSTER-- FOR OUR IMPRISONMENT IS TORTURE ENOUGH!
PRISON?
YES, BEING-- PRISON!
EVER SINCE THE ERASER OVERTHREW THE RULE OF THE SUPREMOR-- HE AND I, HIS MINISTER-- AND THE SUPREMOR'S DAUGHTER, ROWEEN-- HAVE LANGUISHED IN THIS CELL--
--WHILE THE ERASER HAS MADE HIS PLANS TO CONQUER YOUR DIMENSION!
SURELY, GRIMM --ONE WITH YOUR STRENGTH COULD GET PAST THESE WALLS?
YEAH-- "SURELY"!
ALL RIGHT EVERYBODY-- STAND BACK!
THERE'S GONNA BE METAL FLYIN' ALL AROUND HERE IN HALF-A-SEC!
ALL IT'LL TAKE IS ONE LITTLE TAP AN'--
--YEEOWW!!
TZZZAMM

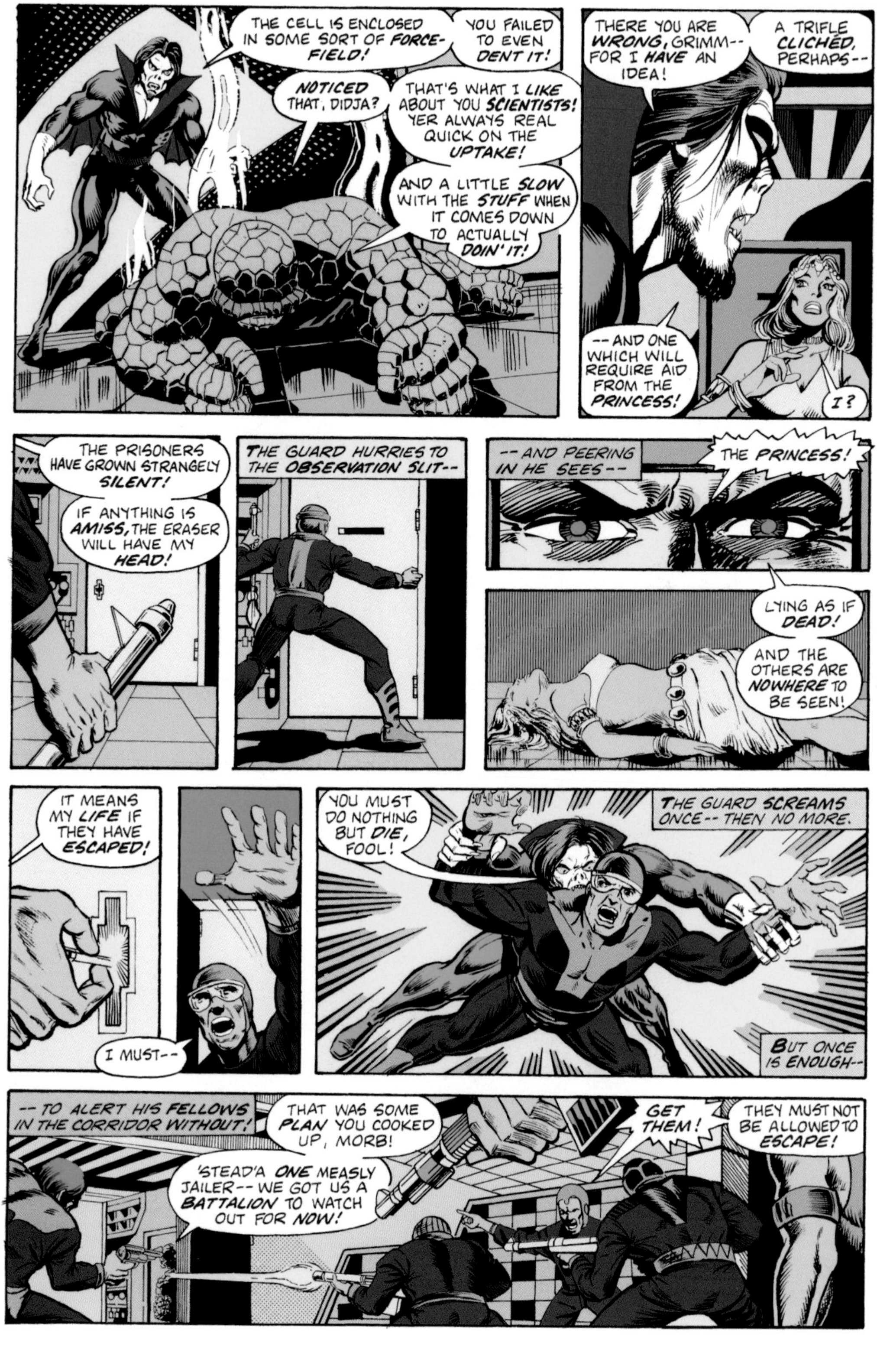
THE CELL IS ENCLOSED IN SOME SORT OF FORCE-FIELD!
YOU FAILED TO EVEN DENT IT!
NOTICED THAT, DIDJA?
THAT'S WHAT I LIKE ABOUT YOU SCIENTISTS! YER ALWAYS REAL QUICK ON THE UPTAKE!
AND A LITTLE SLOW WITH THE STUFF WHEN IT COMES DOWN TO ACTUALLY DOIN' IT!
THERE YOU ARE WRONG, GRIMM-- FOR I HAVE AN IDEA!
A TRIFLE CLICHÉD, PERHAPS--
--AND ONE WHICH WILL REQUIRE AID FROM THE PRINCESS!
I?
THE PRISONERS HAVE GROWN STRANGELY SILENT!
IF ANYTHING IS AMISS, THE ERASER WILL HAVE MY HEAD!
THE GUARD HURRIES TO THE OBSERVATION SLIT--
--AND PEERING IN HE SEES--
THE PRINCESS!
LYING AS IF DEAD!
AND THE OTHERS ARE NOWHERE TO BE SEEN!
IT MEANS MY LIFE IF THEY HAVE ESCAPED!
I MUST--
YOU MUST DO NOTHING BUT DIE, FOOL!
THE GUARD SCREAMS ONCE-- THEN NO MORE.
BUT ONCE IS ENOUGH--
--TO ALERT HIS FELLOWS IN THE CORRIDOR WITHOUT!
THAT WAS SOME PLAN YOU COOKED UP, MORB!
'STEAD'A ONE MEASLY JAILER-- WE GOT US A BATTALION TO WATCH OUT FOR NOW!
GET THEM!
THEY MUST NOT BE ALLOWED TO ESCAPE!

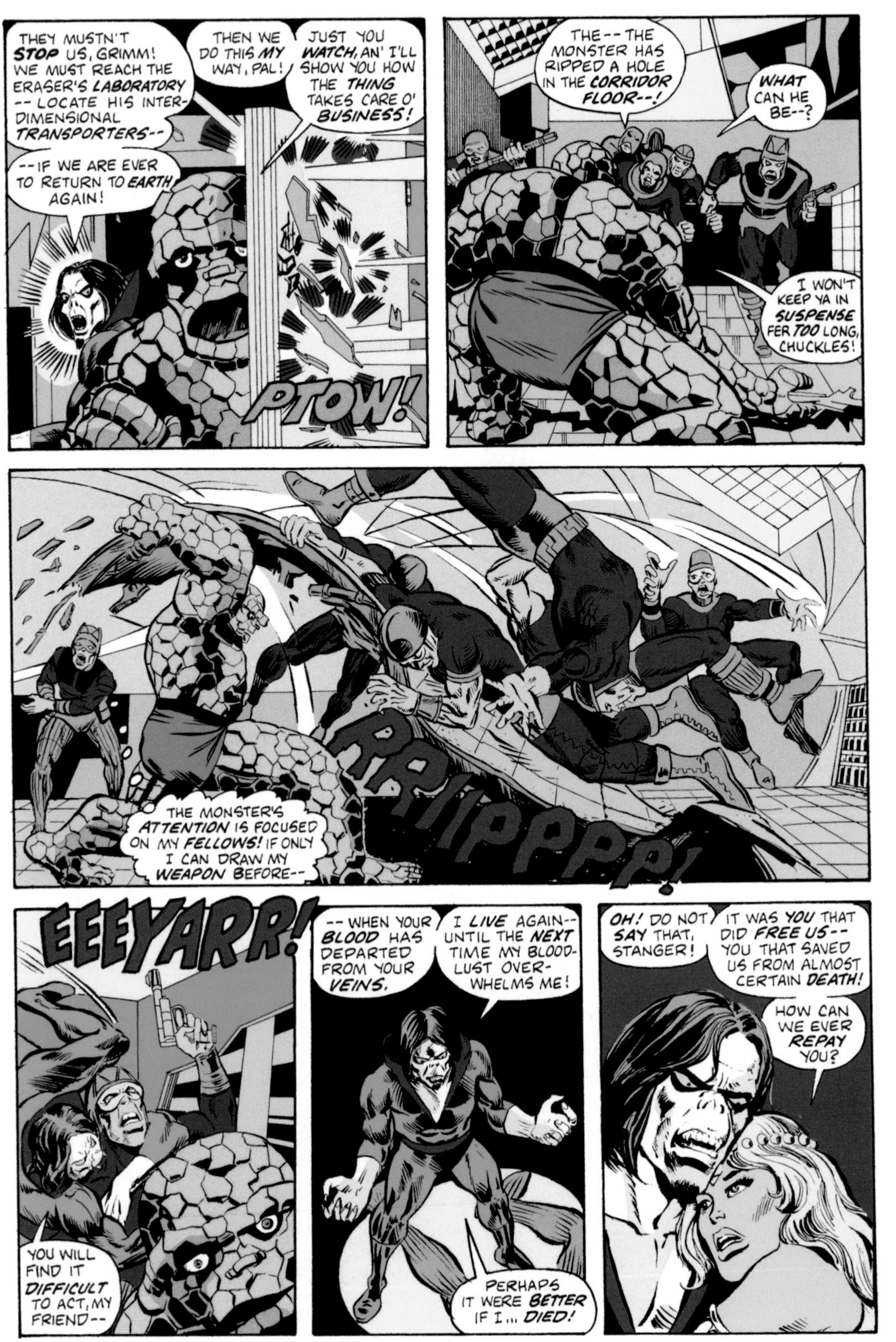

THEY MUSTN'T **STOP** US, GRIMM! WE MUST REACH THE ERASER'S **LABORATORY** -- LOCATE HIS INTER-DIMENSIONAL **TRANSPORTERS**--
--IF WE ARE EVER TO RETURN TO **EARTH** AGAIN!
THEN WE DO THIS **MY** WAY, PAL!
JUST YOU **WATCH**, AN' I'LL SHOW YOU HOW THE **THING** TAKES CARE O' **BUSINESS**!
PTOW!
THE--THE MONSTER HAS RIPPED A HOLE IN THE **CORRIDOR FLOOR**--!
WHAT CAN HE BE--?
I WON'T KEEP YA IN **SUSPENSE** FER **TOO** LONG, CHUCKLES!
THE MONSTER'S **ATTENTION** IS FOCUSED ON MY **FELLOWS**! IF ONLY I CAN DRAW MY **WEAPON** BEFORE--
RRIIPPPPP!
EEEYARR!
YOU WILL FIND IT **DIFFICULT** TO ACT, MY FRIEND--
--WHEN YOUR **BLOOD** HAS DEPARTED FROM YOUR **VEINS**.
I **LIVE** AGAIN--UNTIL THE **NEXT** TIME MY BLOOD-LUST OVER-WHELMS ME!
PERHAPS IT WERE **BETTER** IF I... **DIED**!
OH! DO NOT **SAY** THAT, STANGER!
IT WAS **YOU** THAT DID **FREE US**-- YOU THAT SAVED US FROM ALMOST CERTAIN **DEATH**!
HOW CAN WE EVER **REPAY** YOU?

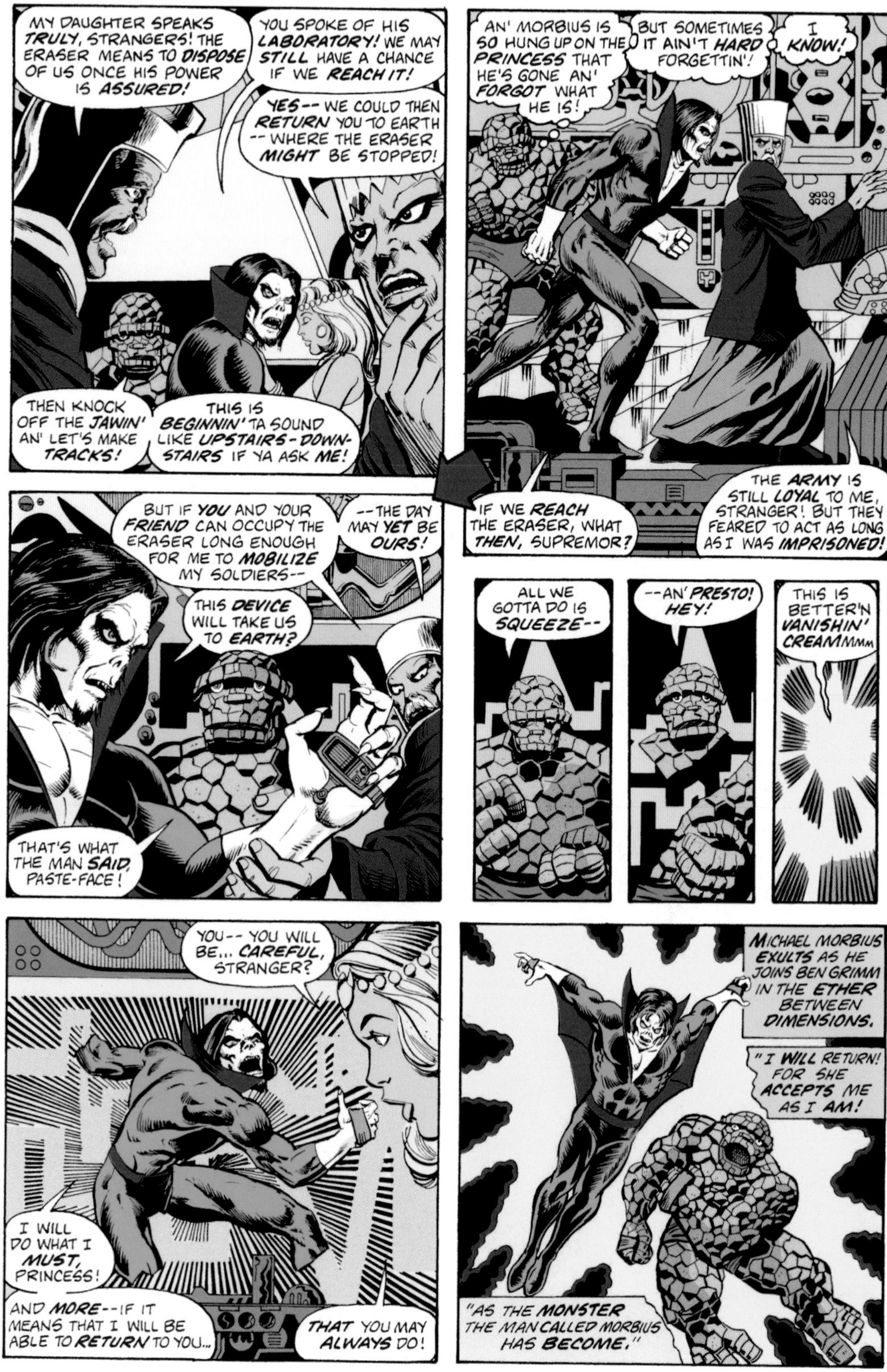
MY DAUGHTER SPEAKS TRULY, STRANGERS! THE ERASER MEANS TO DISPOSE OF US ONCE HIS POWER IS ASSURED!
YOU SPOKE OF HIS LABORATORY! WE MAY STILL HAVE A CHANCE IF WE REACH IT!
YES-- WE COULD THEN RETURN YOU TO EARTH -- WHERE THE ERASER MIGHT BE STOPPED!
THEN KNOCK OFF THE JAWIN' AN' LET'S MAKE TRACKS!
THIS IS BEGINNIN' TA SOUND LIKE UPSTAIRS-DOWNSTAIRS IF YA ASK ME!
AN' MORBIUS IS SO HUNG UP ON THE PRINCESS THAT HE'S GONE AN' FORGOT WHAT HE IS!
BUT SOMETIMES IT AIN'T HARD FORGETTIN'!
I KNOW!
IF WE REACH THE ERASER, WHAT THEN, SUPREMOR?
THE ARMY IS STILL LOYAL TO ME, STRANGER! BUT THEY FEARED TO ACT AS LONG AS I WAS IMPRISONED!
BUT IF YOU AND YOUR FRIEND CAN OCCUPY THE ERASER LONG ENOUGH FOR ME TO MOBILIZE MY SOLDIERS--
--THE DAY MAY YET BE OURS!
THIS DEVICE WILL TAKE US TO EARTH?
THAT'S WHAT THE MAN SAID, PASTE-FACE!
ALL WE GOTTA DO IS SQUEEZE--
--AN' PRESTO! HEY!
THIS IS BETTER'N VANISHIN' CREAMMMM
YOU-- YOU WILL BE... CAREFUL, STRANGER?
I WILL DO WHAT I MUST, PRINCESS!
AND MORE--IF IT MEANS THAT I WILL BE ABLE TO RETURN TO YOU...
THAT YOU MAY ALWAYS DO!
MICHAEL MORBIUS EXULTS AS HE JOINS BEN GRIMM IN THE ETHER BETWEEN DIMENSIONS.
"I WILL RETURN! FOR SHE ACCEPTS ME AS I AM!
"AS THE MONSTER THE MAN CALLED MORBIUS HAS BECOME."

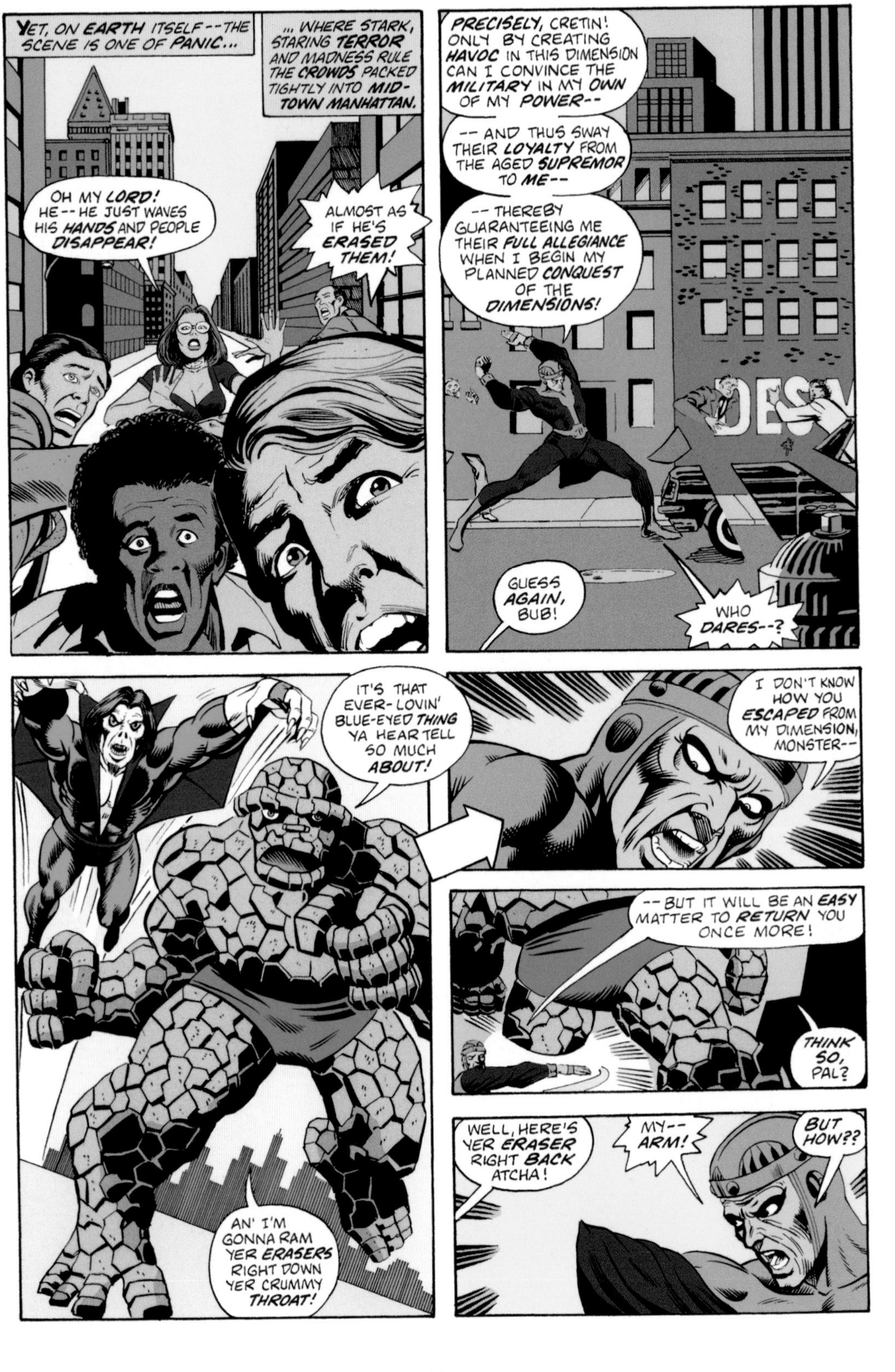
YET, ON EARTH ITSELF--THE SCENE IS ONE OF PANIC...
...WHERE STARK, STARING TERROR AND MADNESS RULE THE CROWDS PACKED TIGHTLY INTO MID-TOWN MANHATTAN.
OH MY LORD! HE--HE JUST WAVES HIS HANDS AND PEOPLE DISAPPEAR!
ALMOST AS IF HE'S ERASED THEM!
PRECISELY, CRETIN! ONLY BY CREATING HAVOC IN THIS DIMENSION CAN I CONVINCE THE MILITARY IN MY OWN OF MY POWER--
--AND THUS SWAY THEIR LOYALTY FROM THE AGED SUPREMOR TO ME--
--THEREBY GUARANTEEING ME THEIR FULL ALLEGIANCE WHEN I BEGIN MY PLANNED CONQUEST OF THE DIMENSIONS!
GUESS AGAIN, BUB!
WHO DARES--?
IT'S THAT EVER-LOVIN' BLUE-EYED THING YA HEAR TELL SO MUCH ABOUT!
AN' I'M GONNA RAM YER ERASERS RIGHT DOWN YER CRUMMY THROAT!
I DON'T KNOW HOW YOU ESCAPED FROM MY DIMENSION, MONSTER--
--BUT IT WILL BE AN EASY MATTER TO RETURN YOU ONCE MORE!
THINK SO, PAL?
WELL, HERE'S YER ERASER RIGHT BACK ATCHA!
MY--ARM!
BUT HOW??

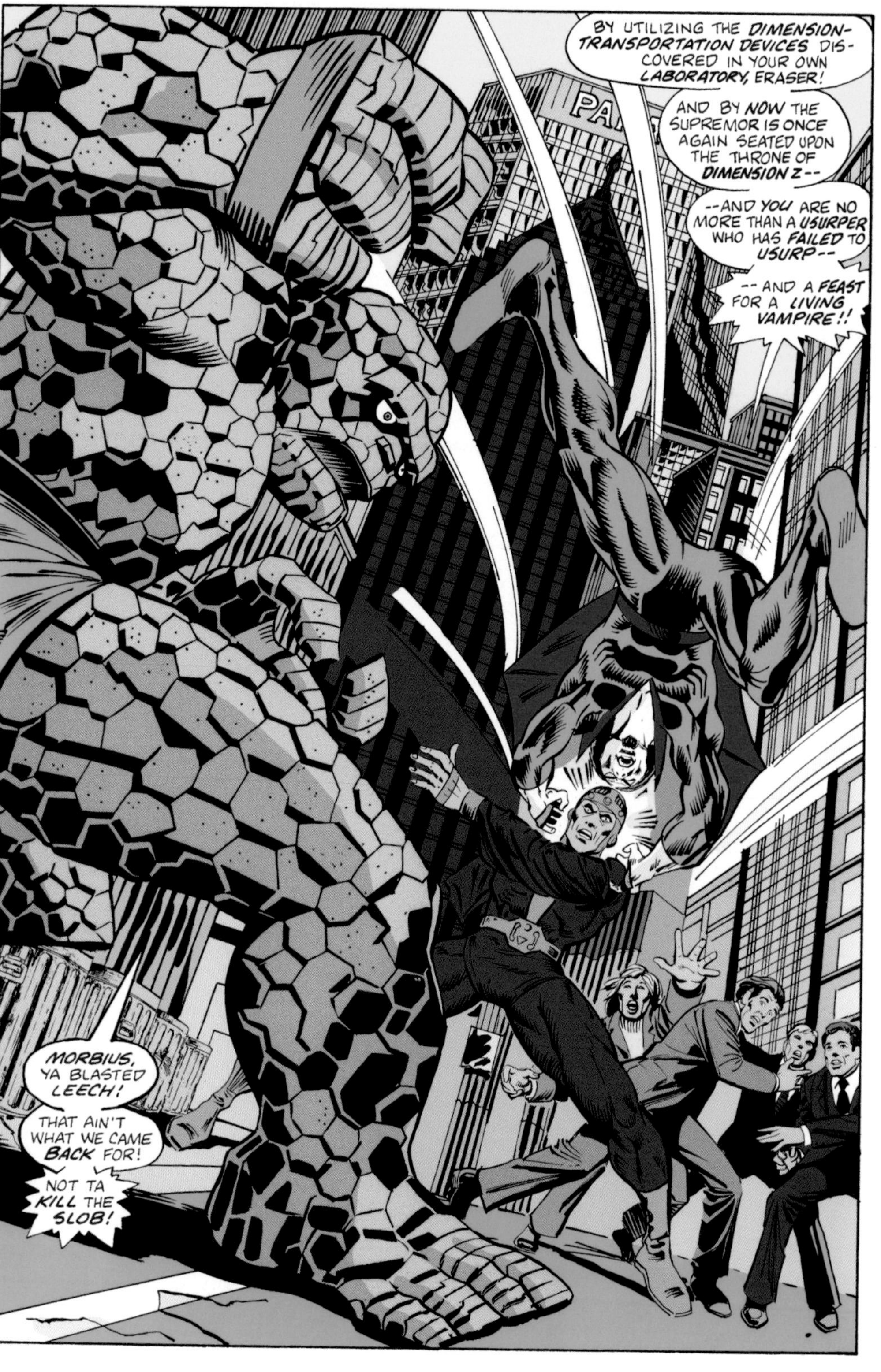
BY UTILIZING THE DIMENSION-TRANSPORTATION DEVICES DISCOVERED IN YOUR OWN LABORATORY, ERASER!
AND BY NOW THE SUPREMOR IS ONCE AGAIN SEATED UPON THE THRONE OF DIMENSION Z--
--AND YOU ARE NO MORE THAN A USURPER WHO HAS FAILED TO USURP--
-- AND A FEAST FOR A LIVING VAMPIRE!!
MORBIUS, YA BLASTED LEECH!
THAT AIN'T WHAT WE CAME BACK FOR!
NOT TA KILL THE SLOB!

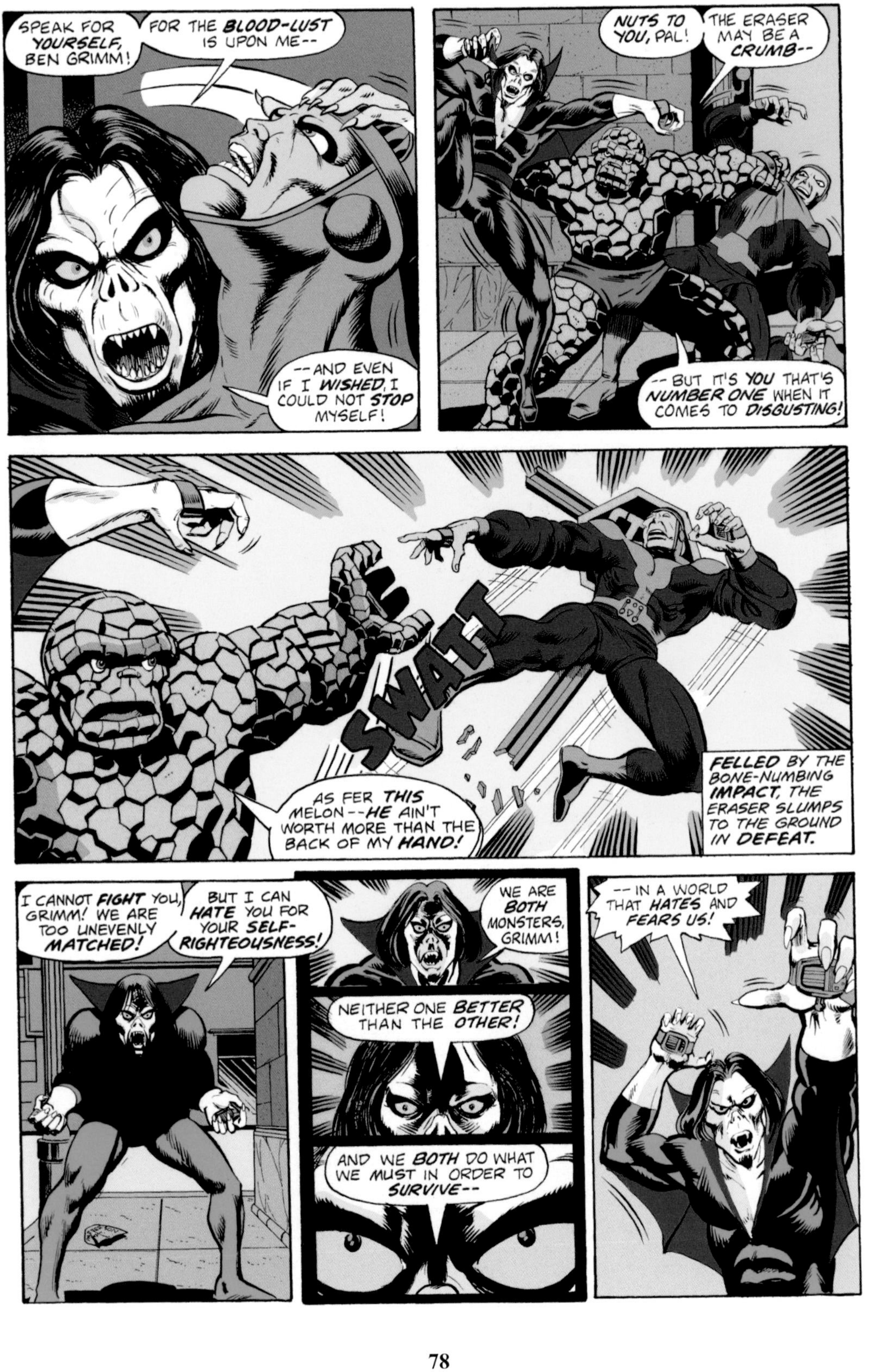
SPEAK FOR YOURSELF, BEN GRIMM!
FOR THE BLOOD-LUST IS UPON ME--
--AND EVEN IF I WISHED, I COULD NOT STOP MYSELF!
NUTS TO YOU, PAL!
THE ERASER MAY BE A CRUMB--
-- BUT IT'S YOU THAT'S NUMBER ONE WHEN IT COMES TO DISGUSTING!
SWATT
AS FER THIS MELON--HE AIN'T WORTH MORE THAN THE BACK OF MY HAND!
FELLED BY THE BONE-NUMBING IMPACT, THE ERASER SLUMPS TO THE GROUND IN DEFEAT.
I CANNOT FIGHT YOU, GRIMM! WE ARE TOO UNEVENLY MATCHED!
BUT I CAN HATE YOU FOR YOUR SELF-RIGHTEOUSNESS!
WE ARE BOTH MONSTERS, GRIMM!
NEITHER ONE BETTER THAN THE OTHER!
AND WE BOTH DO WHAT WE MUST IN ORDER TO SURVIVE--
-- IN A WORLD THAT HATES AND FEARS US!

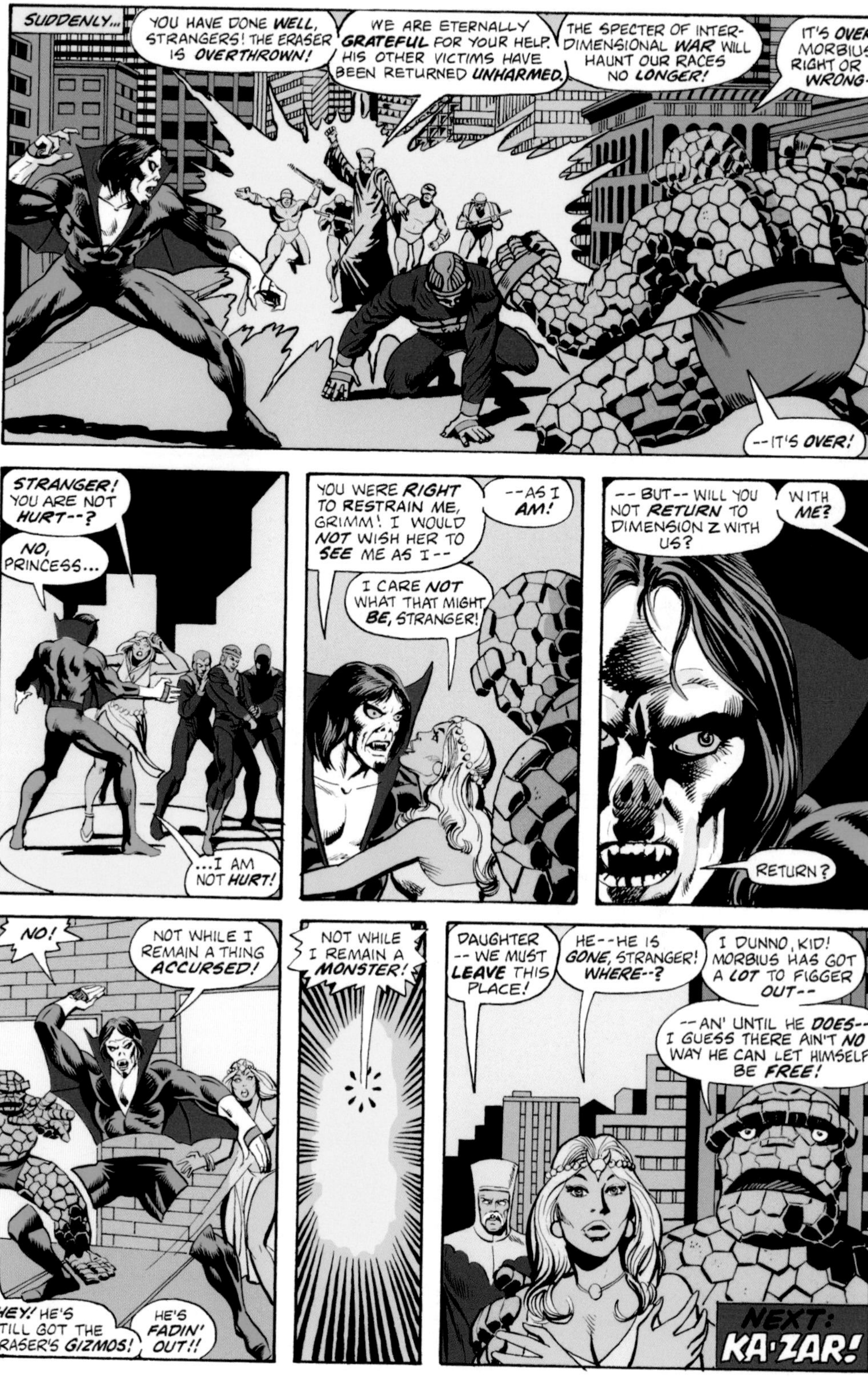
SUDDENLY...
YOU HAVE DONE WELL, STRANGERS! THE ERASER IS OVERTHROWN!
WE ARE ETERNALLY GRATEFUL FOR YOUR HELP. HIS OTHER VICTIMS HAVE BEEN RETURNED UNHARMED.
THE SPECTER OF INTER-DIMENSIONAL WAR WILL HAUNT OUR RACES NO LONGER!
IT'S OVER, MORBIUS! RIGHT OR WRONG--
--IT'S OVER!
STRANGER! YOU ARE NOT HURT--?
NO, PRINCESS...
...I AM NOT HURT!
YOU WERE RIGHT TO RESTRAIN ME, GRIMM! I WOULD NOT WISH HER TO SEE ME AS I--
--AS I AM!
I CARE NOT WHAT THAT MIGHT BE, STRANGER!
-- BUT-- WILL YOU NOT RETURN TO DIMENSION Z WITH US?
WITH ME?
RETURN?
NO!
NOT WHILE I REMAIN A THING ACCURSED!
HEY! HE'S STILL GOT THE ERASER'S GIZMOS!
HE'S FADIN' OUT!!
NOT WHILE I REMAIN A MONSTER!
DAUGHTER -- WE MUST LEAVE THIS PLACE!
HE--HE IS GONE, STRANGER! WHERE--?
I DUNNO, KID! MORBIUS HAS GOT A LOT TO FIGGER OUT--
--AN' UNTIL HE DOES-- I GUESS THERE AIN'T NO WAY HE CAN LET HIMSELF BE FREE!
NEXT: KA-ZAR!

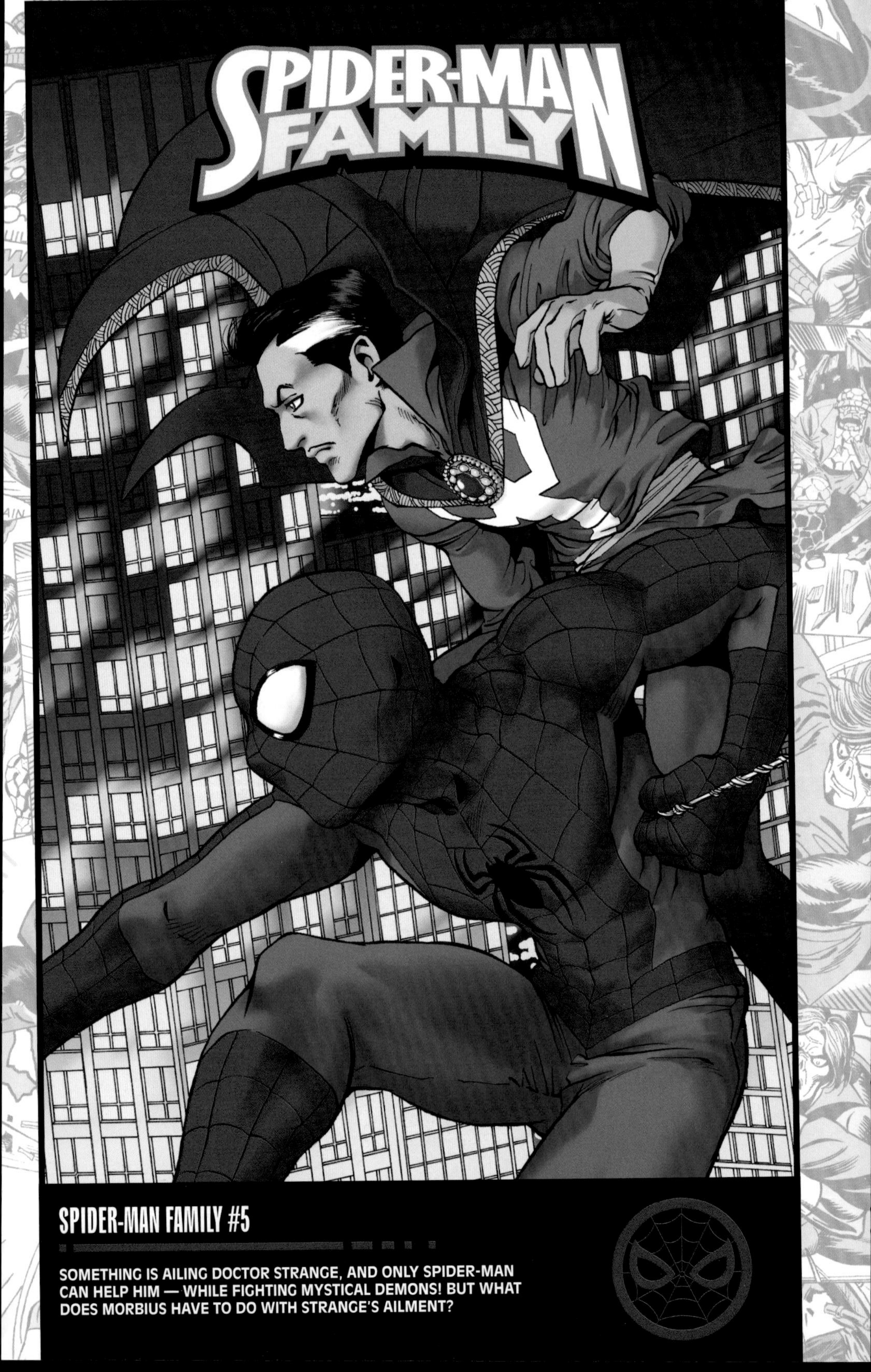
SPIDER-MAN
FAMILY

SPIDER-MAN FAMILY #5

SOMETHING IS AILING DOCTOR STRANGE, AND ONLY SPIDER-MAN CAN HELP HIM — WHILE FIGHTING MYSTICAL DEMONS! BUT WHAT DOES MORBIUS HAVE TO DO WITH STRANGE'S AILMENT?

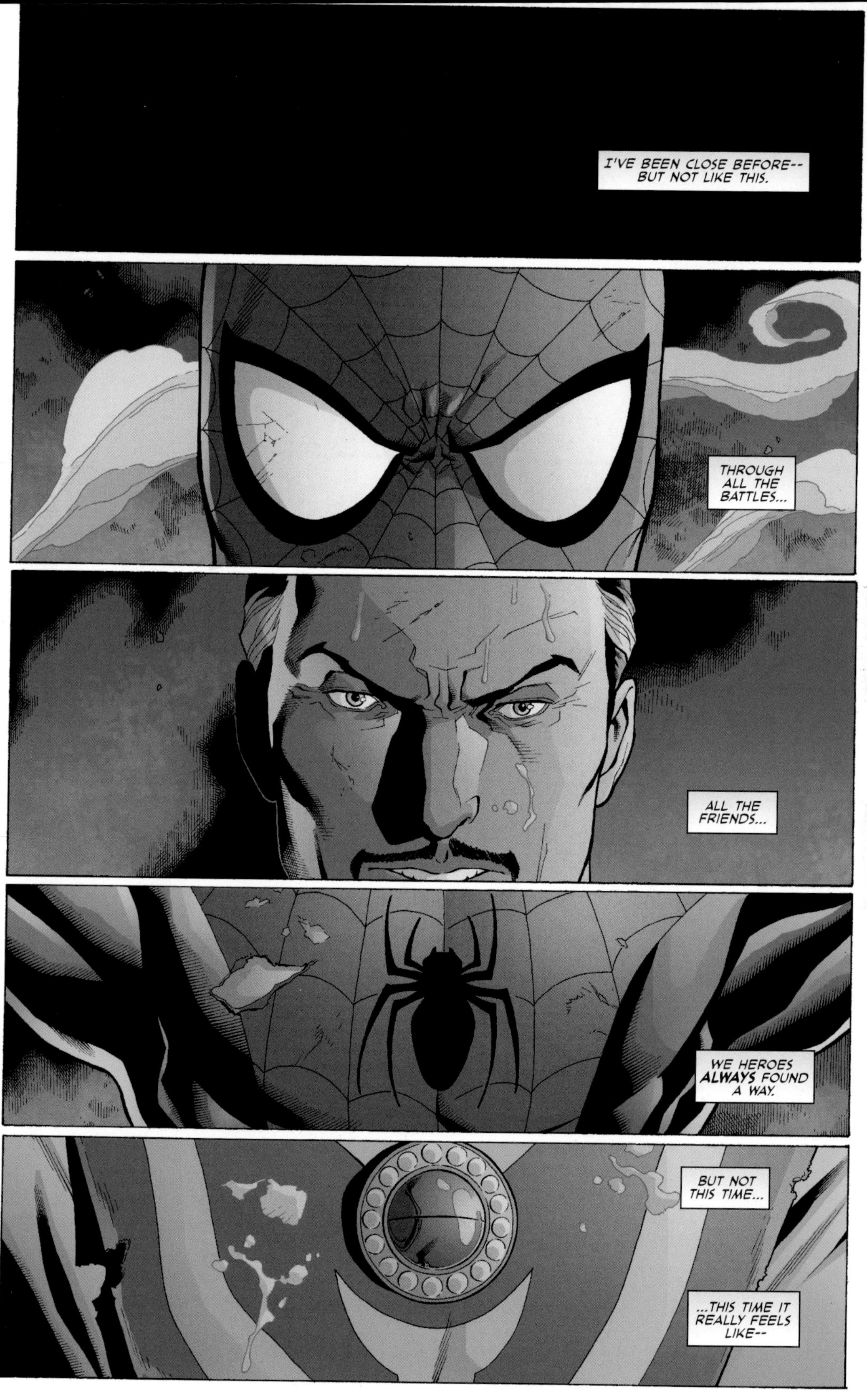
I'VE BEEN CLOSE BEFORE-- BUT NOT LIKE THIS.
THROUGH ALL THE BATTLES...
ALL THE FRIENDS...
WE HEROES **ALWAYS** FOUND A WAY.
BUT NOT THIS TIME...
...THIS TIME IT REALLY FEELS LIKE--

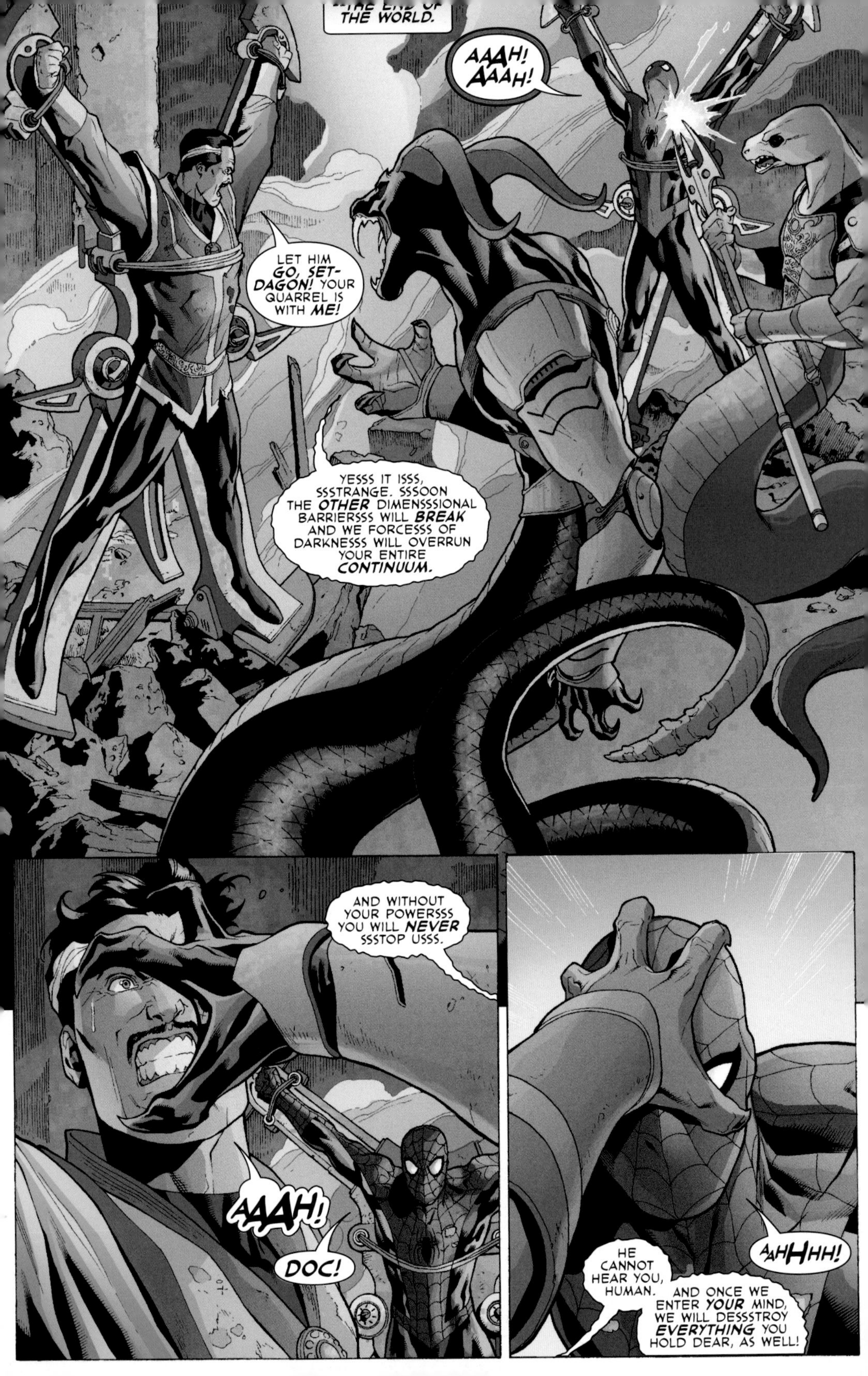
...THE END OF THE WORLD.
AAAH! AAAH!
LET HIM GO, SET-DAGON! YOUR QUARREL IS WITH ME!
YESSS IT ISSS, SSSTRANGE. SSSOON THE OTHER DIMENSSSIONAL BARRIERSSS WILL BREAK AND WE FORCESSS OF DARKNESSS WILL OVERRUN YOUR ENTIRE CONTINUUM.
AND WITHOUT YOUR POWERSSS YOU WILL NEVER SSSTOP USSS.
AAAH!
DOC!
AAHHHH!
HE CANNOT HEAR YOU, HUMAN.
AND ONCE WE ENTER YOUR MIND, WE WILL DESSSTROY EVERYTHING YOU HOLD DEAR, AS WELL!

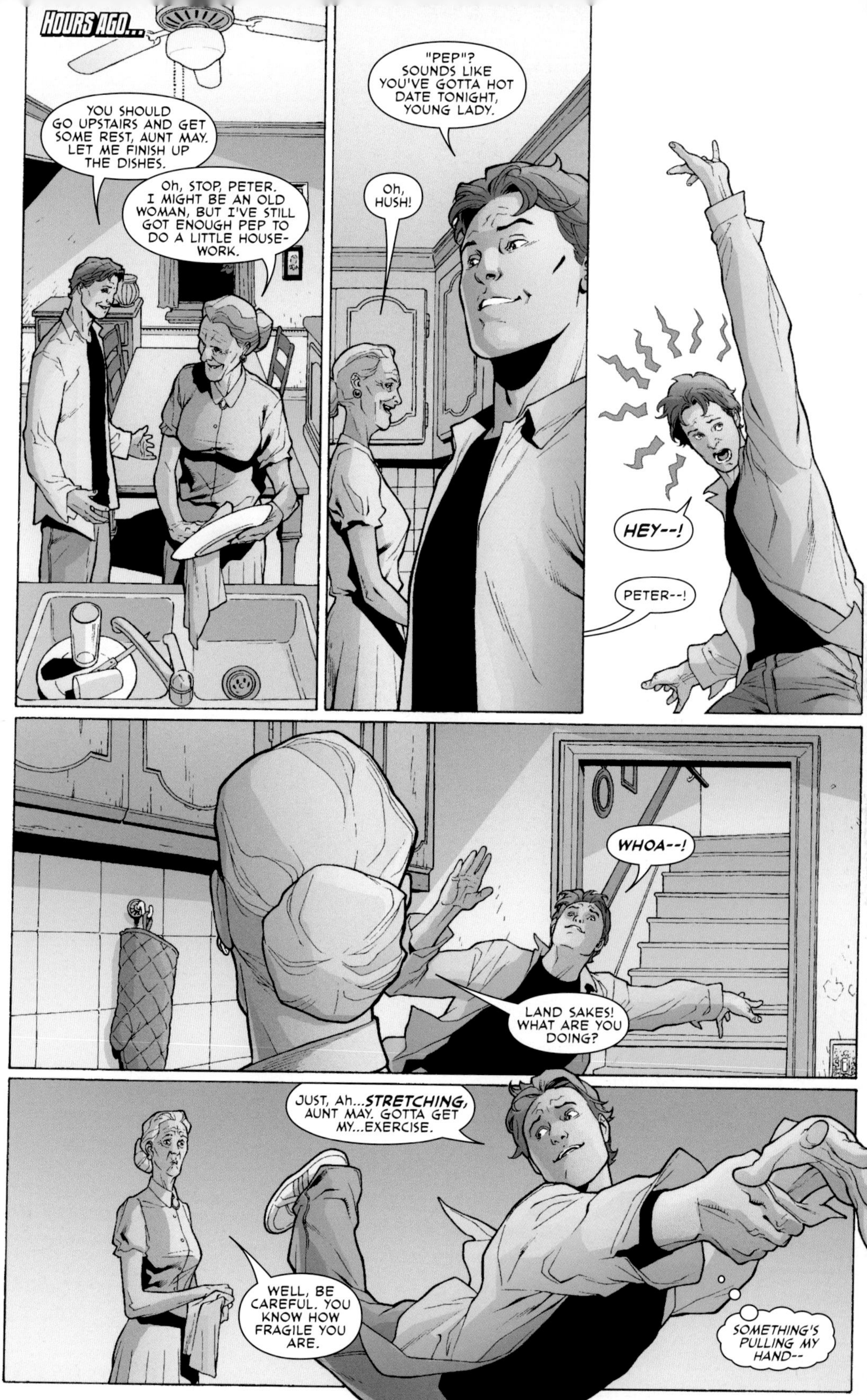
HOURS AGO...
YOU SHOULD GO UPSTAIRS AND GET SOME REST, AUNT MAY. LET ME FINISH UP THE DISHES.
Oh, STOP, PETER. I MIGHT BE AN OLD WOMAN, BUT I'VE STILL GOT ENOUGH PEP TO DO A LITTLE HOUSE-WORK.
"PEP"? SOUNDS LIKE YOU'VE GOTTA HOT DATE TONIGHT, YOUNG LADY.
Oh, HUSH!
HEY--!
PETER--!
WHOA--!
LAND SAKES! WHAT ARE YOU DOING?
JUST, Ah...STRETCHING, AUNT MAY. GOTTA GET MY...EXERCISE.
WELL, BE CAREFUL. YOU KNOW HOW FRAGILE YOU ARE.
SOMETHING'S PULLING MY HAND--

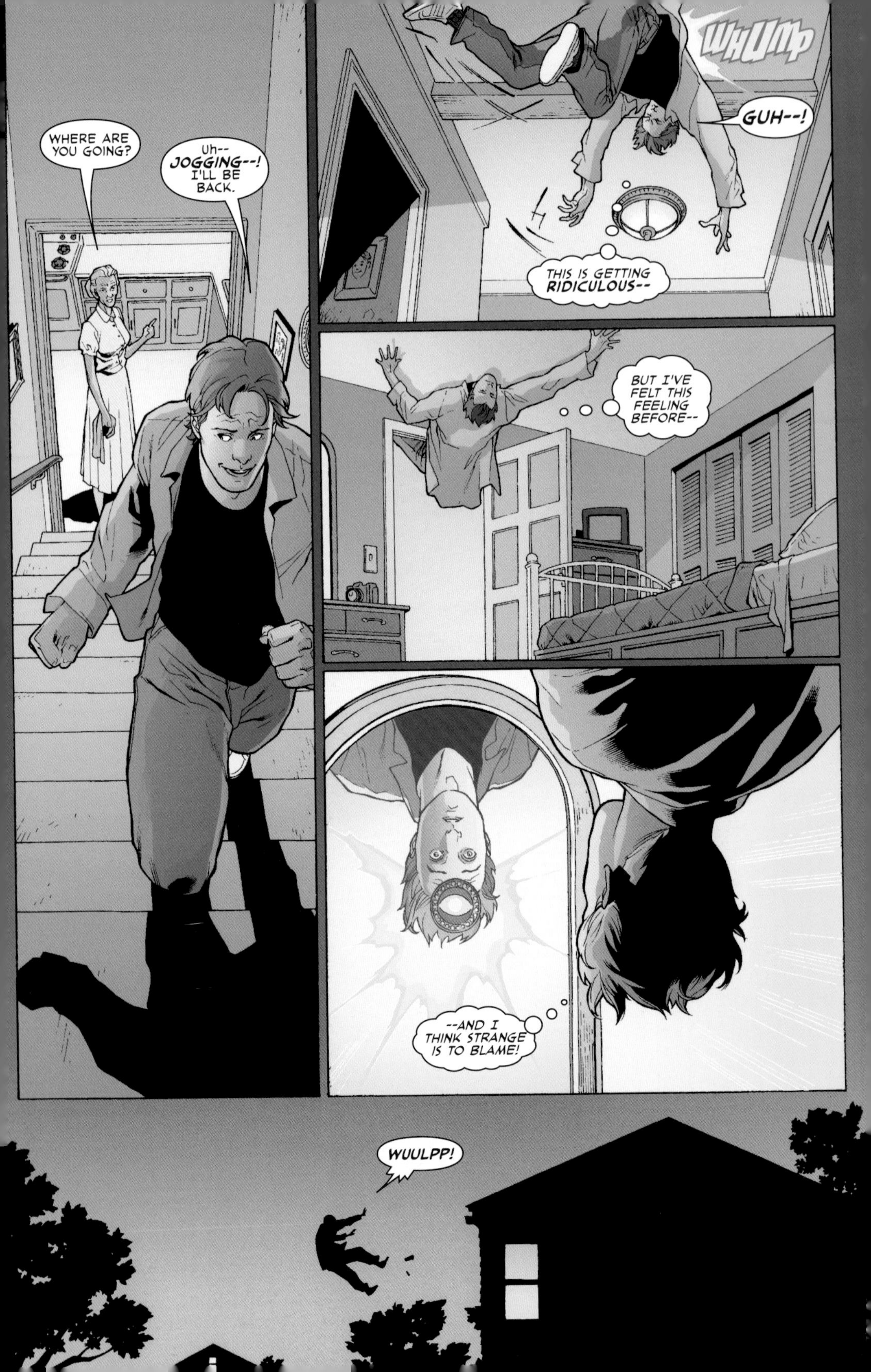
WHERE ARE YOU GOING?
Uh-- JOGGING--! I'LL BE BACK.
WHUMP
GUH--!
THIS IS GETTING RIDICULOUS--
BUT I'VE FELT THIS FEELING BEFORE--
--AND I THINK STRANGE IS TO BLAME!
WUULPP!

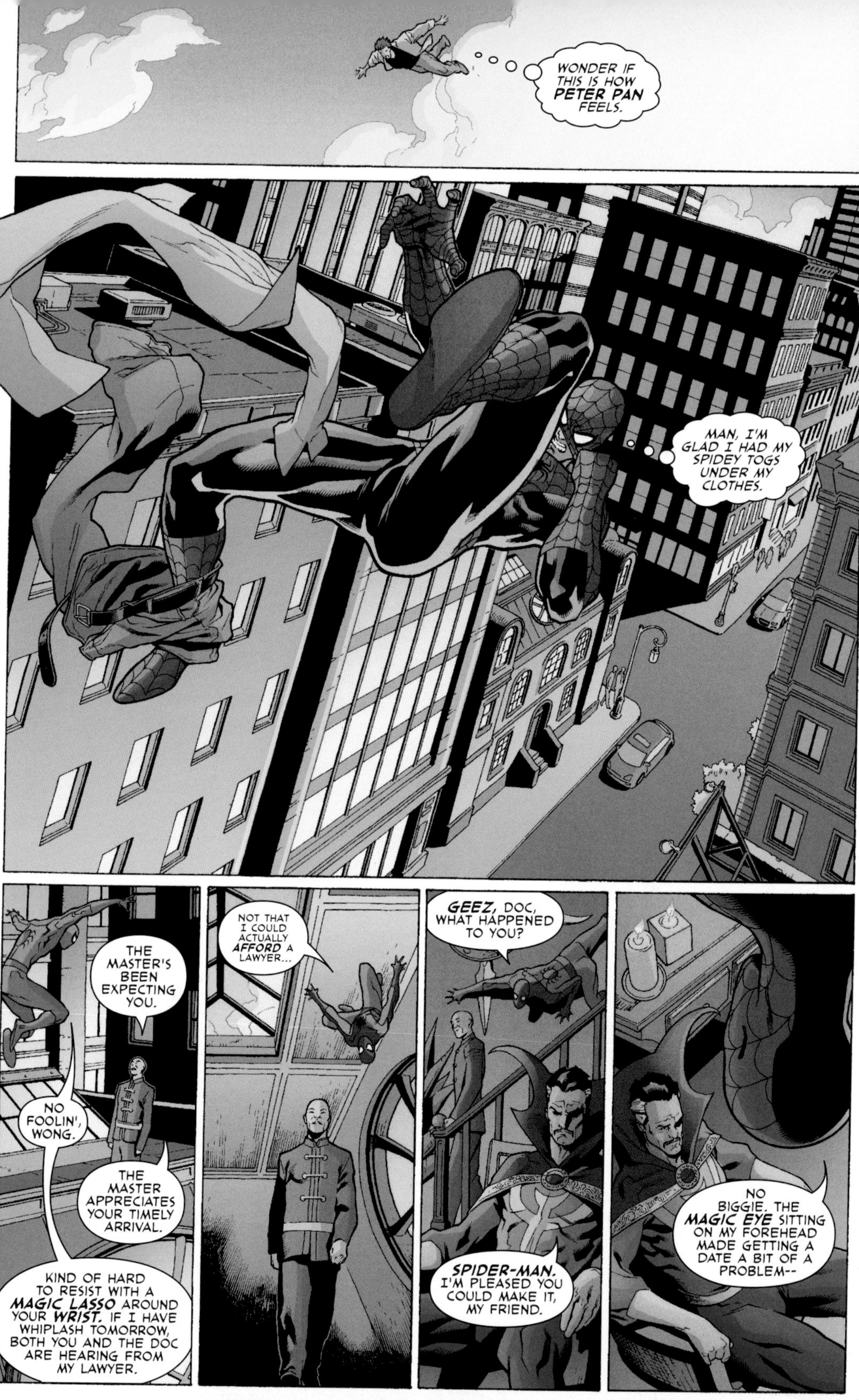
WONDER IF THIS IS HOW PETER PAN FEELS.
MAN, I'M GLAD I HAD MY SPIDEY TOGS UNDER MY CLOTHES.
THE MASTER'S BEEN EXPECTING YOU.
NO FOOLIN', WONG.
THE MASTER APPRECIATES YOUR TIMELY ARRIVAL.
KIND OF HARD TO RESIST WITH A MAGIC LASSO AROUND YOUR WRIST. IF I HAVE WHIPLASH TOMORROW, BOTH YOU AND THE DOC ARE HEARING FROM MY LAWYER.
NOT THAT I COULD ACTUALLY AFFORD A LAWYER...
GEEZ, DOC, WHAT HAPPENED TO YOU?
SPIDER-MAN. I'M PLEASED YOU COULD MAKE IT, MY FRIEND.
NO BIGGIE. THE MAGIC EYE SITTING ON MY FOREHEAD MADE GETTING A DATE A BIT OF A PROBLEM--

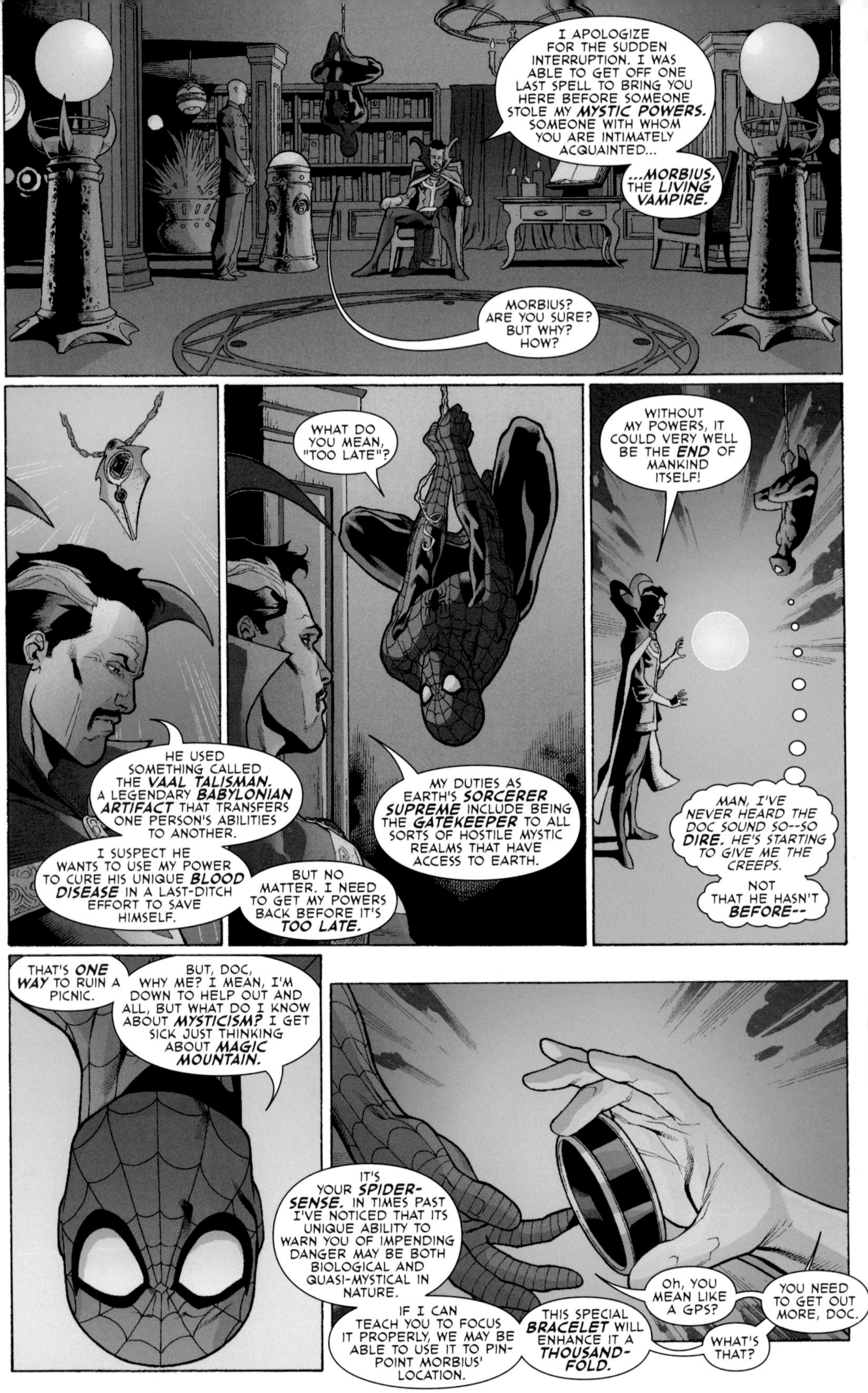

I APOLOGIZE FOR THE SUDDEN INTERRUPTION. I WAS ABLE TO GET OFF ONE LAST SPELL TO BRING YOU HERE BEFORE SOMEONE STOLE MY MYSTIC POWERS. SOMEONE WITH WHOM YOU ARE INTIMATELY ACQUAINTED...
...MORBIUS, THE LIVING VAMPIRE.
MORBIUS? ARE YOU SURE? BUT WHY? HOW?
HE USED SOMETHING CALLED THE VAAL TALISMAN. A LEGENDARY BABYLONIAN ARTIFACT THAT TRANSFERS ONE PERSON'S ABILITIES TO ANOTHER.
I SUSPECT HE WANTS TO USE MY POWER TO CURE HIS UNIQUE BLOOD DISEASE IN A LAST-DITCH EFFORT TO SAVE HIMSELF.
BUT NO MATTER. I NEED TO GET MY POWERS BACK BEFORE IT'S TOO LATE.
WHAT DO YOU MEAN, "TOO LATE"?
MY DUTIES AS EARTH'S SORCERER SUPREME INCLUDE BEING THE GATEKEEPER TO ALL SORTS OF HOSTILE MYSTIC REALMS THAT HAVE ACCESS TO EARTH.
WITHOUT MY POWERS, IT COULD VERY WELL BE THE END OF MANKIND ITSELF!
MAN, I'VE NEVER HEARD THE DOC SOUND SO--SO DIRE. HE'S STARTING TO GIVE ME THE CREEPS.
NOT THAT HE HASN'T BEFORE--
THAT'S ONE WAY TO RUIN A PICNIC.
BUT, DOC, WHY ME? I MEAN, I'M DOWN TO HELP OUT AND ALL, BUT WHAT DO I KNOW ABOUT MYSTICISM? I GET SICK JUST THINKING ABOUT MAGIC MOUNTAIN.
IT'S YOUR SPIDER-SENSE. IN TIMES PAST I'VE NOTICED THAT ITS UNIQUE ABILITY TO WARN YOU OF IMPENDING DANGER MAY BE BOTH BIOLOGICAL AND QUASI-MYSTICAL IN NATURE.
IF I CAN TEACH YOU TO FOCUS IT PROPERLY, WE MAY BE ABLE TO USE IT TO PIN-POINT MORBIUS' LOCATION.
THIS SPECIAL BRACELET WILL ENHANCE IT A THOUSAND-FOLD.
OH, YOU MEAN LIKE A GPS?
WHAT'S THAT?
YOU NEED TO GET OUT MORE, DOC.

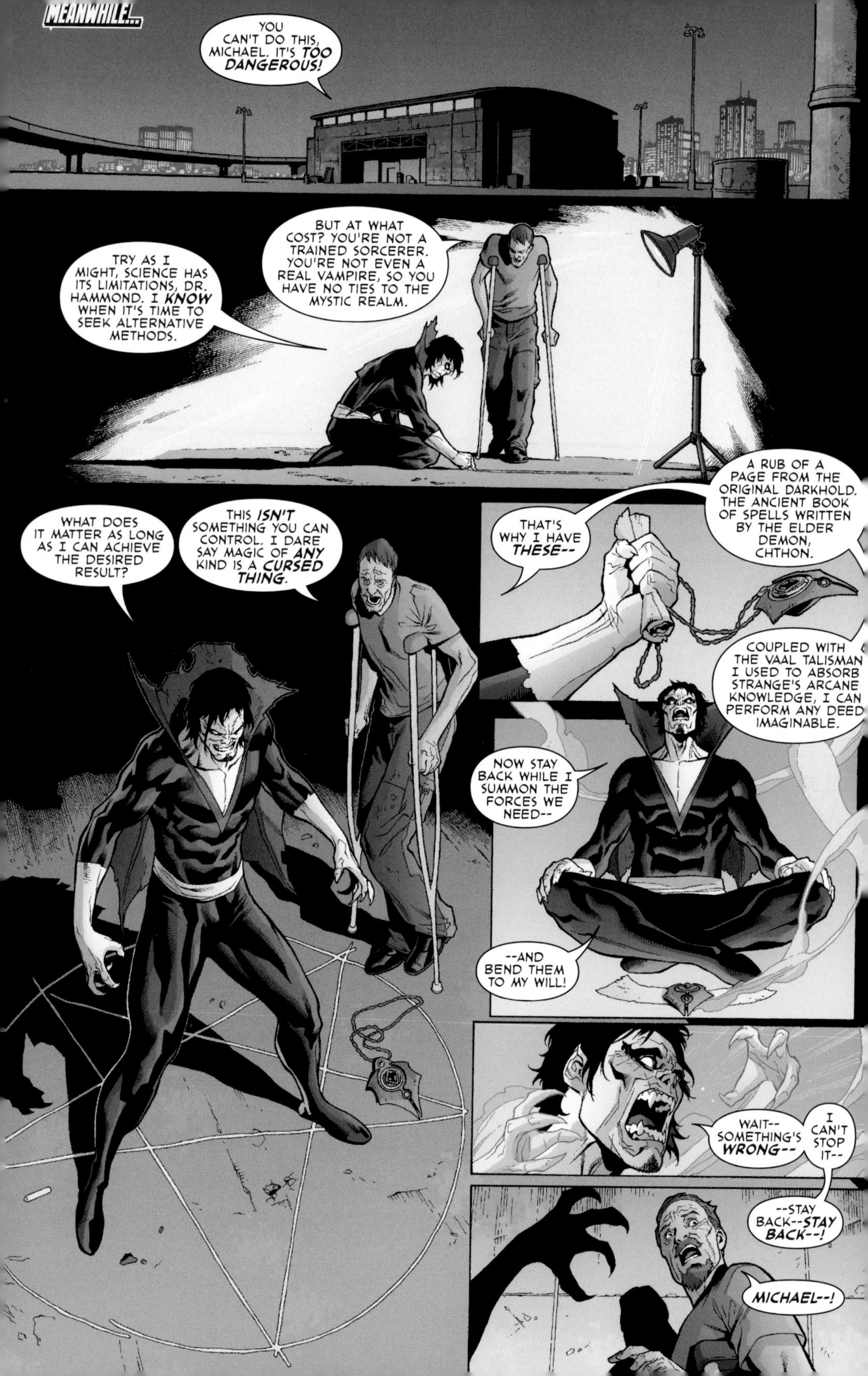
MEANWHILE...
YOU CAN'T DO THIS, MICHAEL. IT'S TOO DANGEROUS!
TRY AS I MIGHT, SCIENCE HAS ITS LIMITATIONS, DR. HAMMOND. I KNOW WHEN IT'S TIME TO SEEK ALTERNATIVE METHODS.
BUT AT WHAT COST? YOU'RE NOT A TRAINED SORCERER. YOU'RE NOT EVEN A REAL VAMPIRE, SO YOU HAVE NO TIES TO THE MYSTIC REALM.
WHAT DOES IT MATTER AS LONG AS I CAN ACHIEVE THE DESIRED RESULT?
THIS ISN'T SOMETHING YOU CAN CONTROL. I DARE SAY MAGIC OF ANY KIND IS A CURSED THING.
THAT'S WHY I HAVE THESE--
A RUB OF A PAGE FROM THE ORIGINAL DARKHOLD. THE ANCIENT BOOK OF SPELLS WRITTEN BY THE ELDER DEMON, CHTHON.
COUPLED WITH THE VAAL TALISMAN I USED TO ABSORB STRANGE'S ARCANE KNOWLEDGE, I CAN PERFORM ANY DEED IMAGINABLE.
NOW STAY BACK WHILE I SUMMON THE FORCES WE NEED--
--AND BEND THEM TO MY WILL!
WAIT-- SOMETHING'S WRONG--
I CAN'T STOP IT--
--STAY BACK--STAY BACK--!
MICHAEL--!

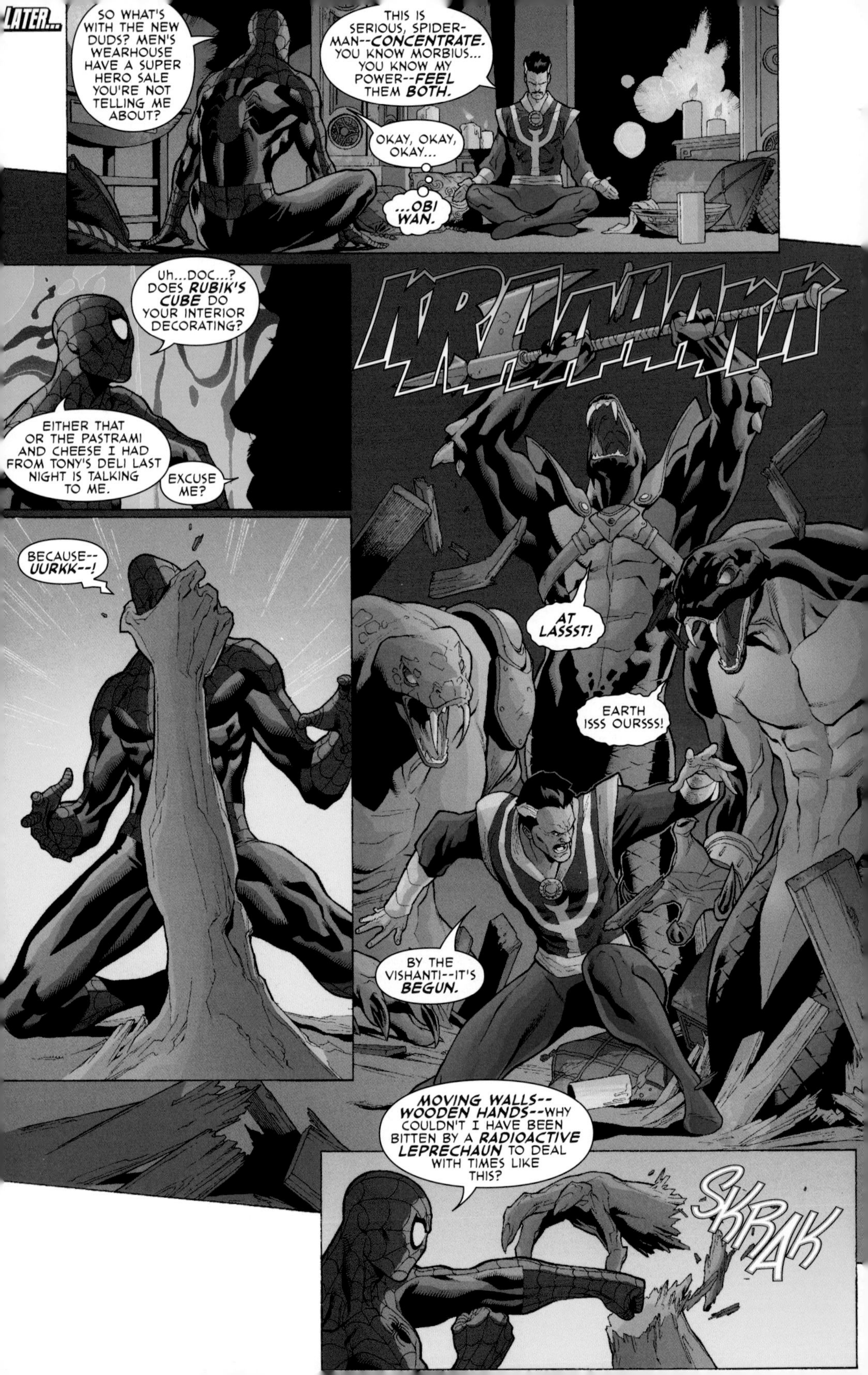
LATER...
SO WHAT'S WITH THE NEW DUDS? MEN'S WEARHOUSE HAVE A SUPER HERO SALE YOU'RE NOT TELLING ME ABOUT?
THIS IS SERIOUS, SPIDER-MAN--CONCENTRATE. YOU KNOW MORBIUS... YOU KNOW MY POWER--FEEL THEM BOTH.
OKAY, OKAY, OKAY...
...OBI WAN.
Uh...DOC...? DOES RUBIK'S CUBE DO YOUR INTERIOR DECORATING?
EITHER THAT OR THE PASTRAMI AND CHEESE I HAD FROM TONY'S DELI LAST NIGHT IS TALKING TO ME.
EXCUSE ME?
KRAAKAKK
BECAUSE--UURKK--!
AT LASSST!
EARTH ISSS OURSSS!
BY THE VISHANTI--IT'S BEGUN.
MOVING WALLS--WOODEN HANDS--WHY COULDN'T I HAVE BEEN BITTEN BY A RADIOACTIVE LEPRECHAUN TO DEAL WITH TIMES LIKE THIS?
SKRAK

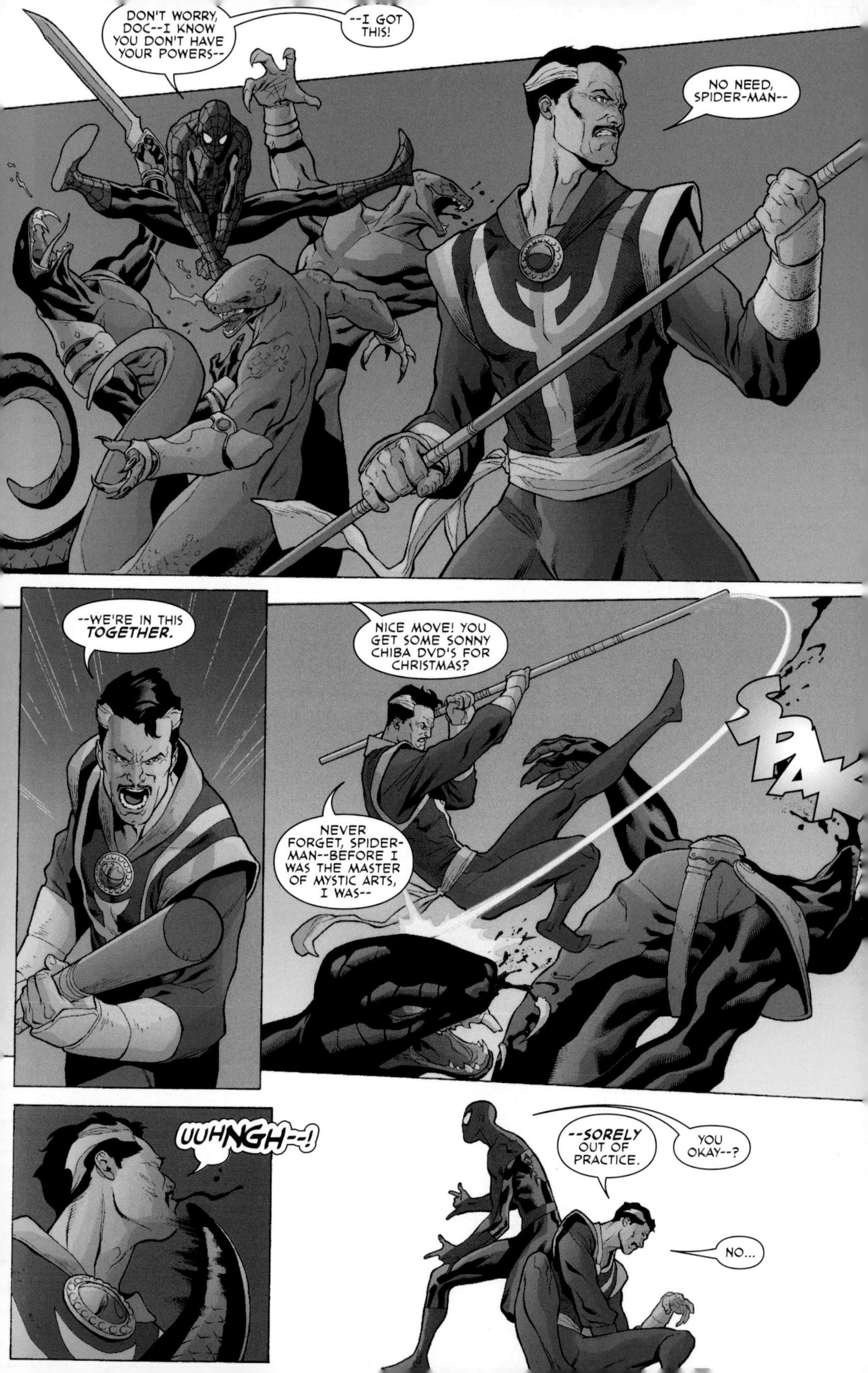
DON'T WORRY, DOC--I KNOW YOU DON'T HAVE YOUR POWERS--
--I GOT THIS!
NO NEED, SPIDER-MAN--
--WE'RE IN THIS *TOGETHER.*
NICE MOVE! YOU GET SOME SONNY CHIBA DVD'S FOR CHRISTMAS?
NEVER FORGET, SPIDER-MAN--BEFORE I WAS THE MASTER OF MYSTIC ARTS, I WAS--
SPAK
UUHNGH--!
--*SORELY* OUT OF PRACTICE.
YOU OKAY--?
NO...

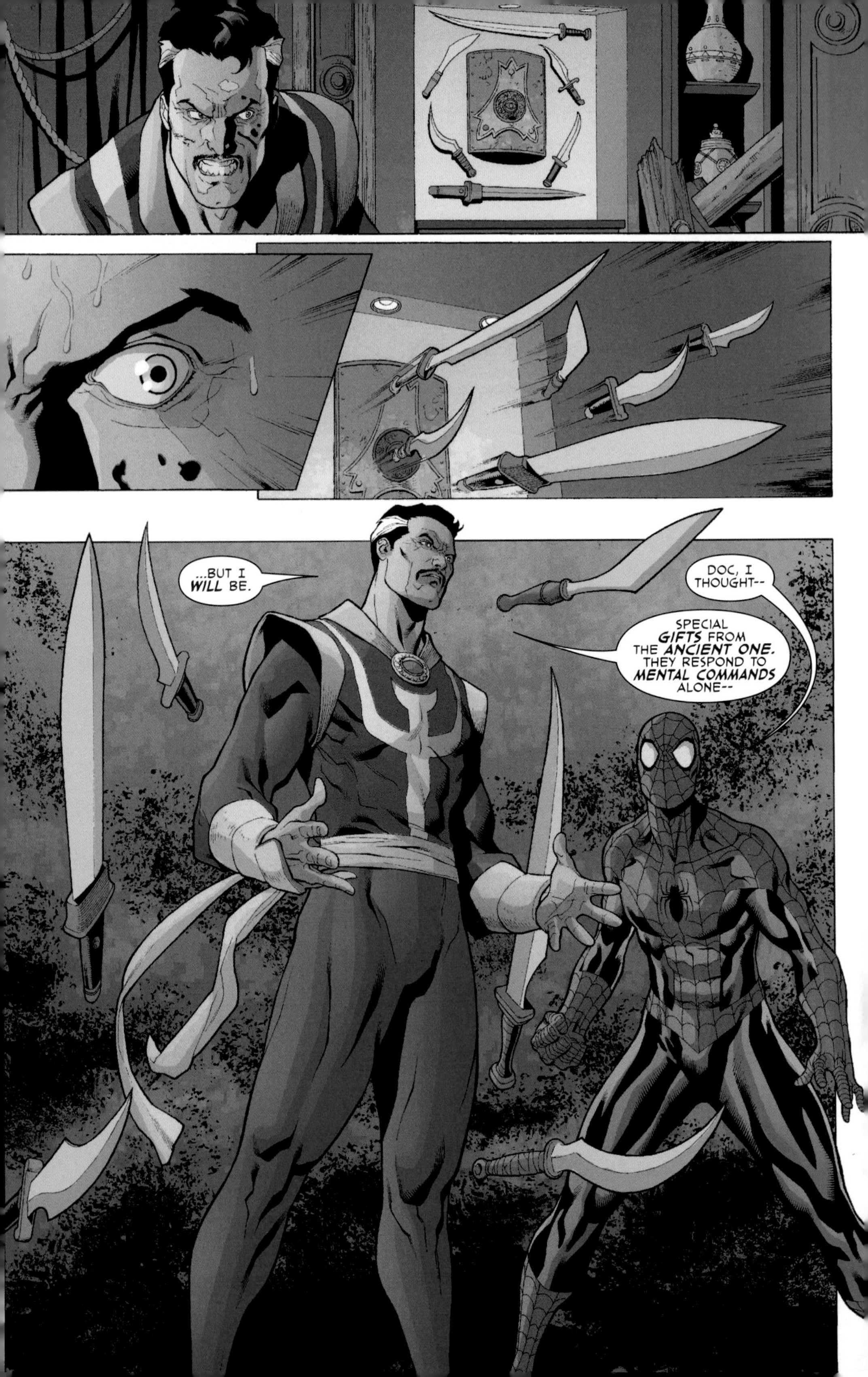
...BUT I WILL BE.
DOC, I THOUGHT--
SPECIAL GIFTS FROM THE ANCIENT ONE. THEY RESPOND TO MENTAL COMMANDS ALONE--

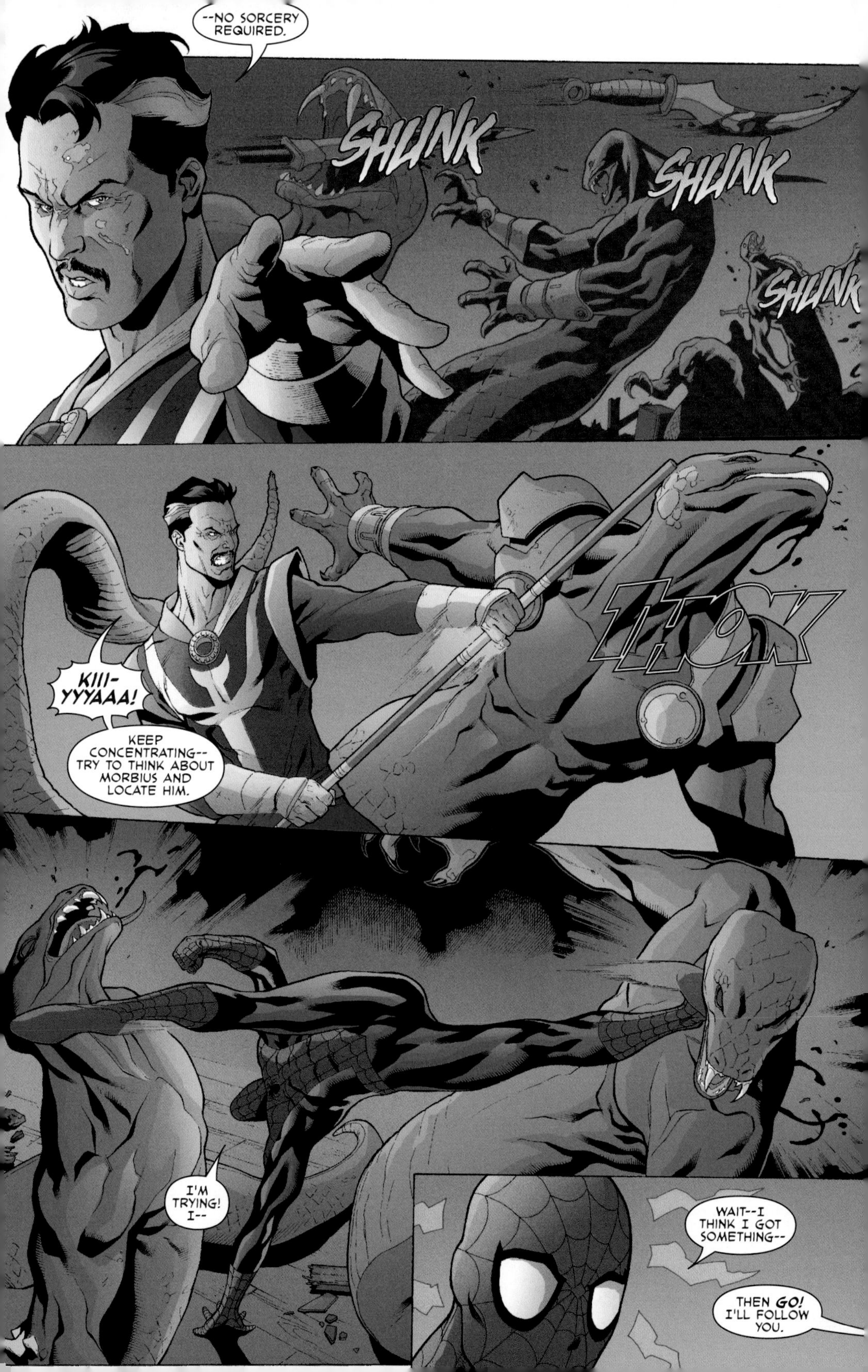
--NO SORCERY REQUIRED.
SHUNK
SHUNK
SHUNK
THOK
KIII-YYYAAA!
KEEP CONCENTRATING-- TRY TO THINK ABOUT MORBIUS AND LOCATE HIM.
I'M TRYING! I--
WAIT--I THINK I GOT SOMETHING--
THEN GO! I'LL FOLLOW YOU.

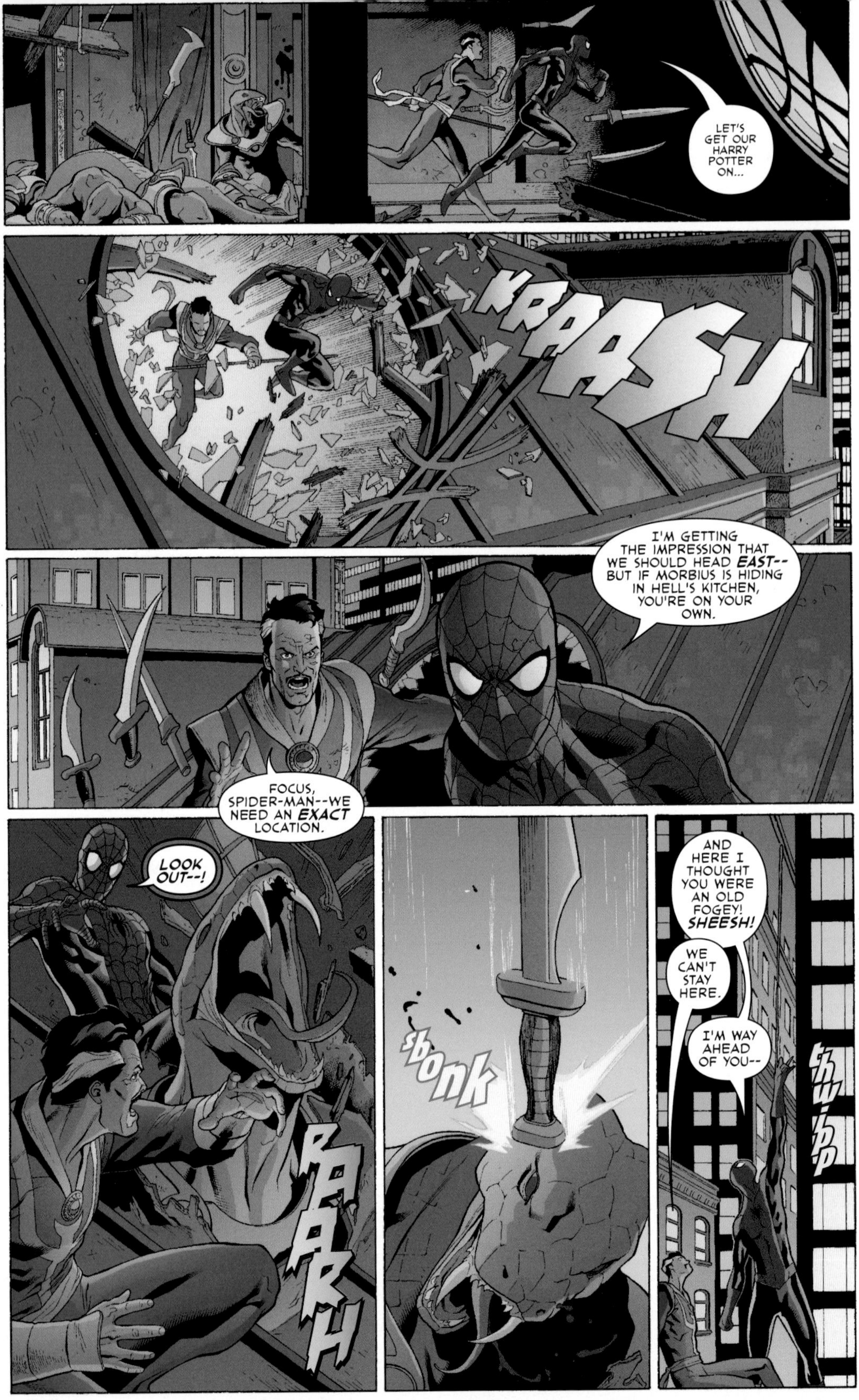
LET'S GET OUR HARRY POTTER ON...
KRAASH
I'M GETTING THE IMPRESSION THAT WE SHOULD HEAD EAST-- BUT IF MORBIUS IS HIDING IN HELL'S KITCHEN, YOU'RE ON YOUR OWN.
FOCUS, SPIDER-MAN--WE NEED AN EXACT LOCATION.
LOOK OUT--!
RAARH
sbonk
AND HERE I THOUGHT YOU WERE AN OLD FOGEY! SHEESH!
WE CAN'T STAY HERE.
I'M WAY AHEAD OF YOU--
thwipp

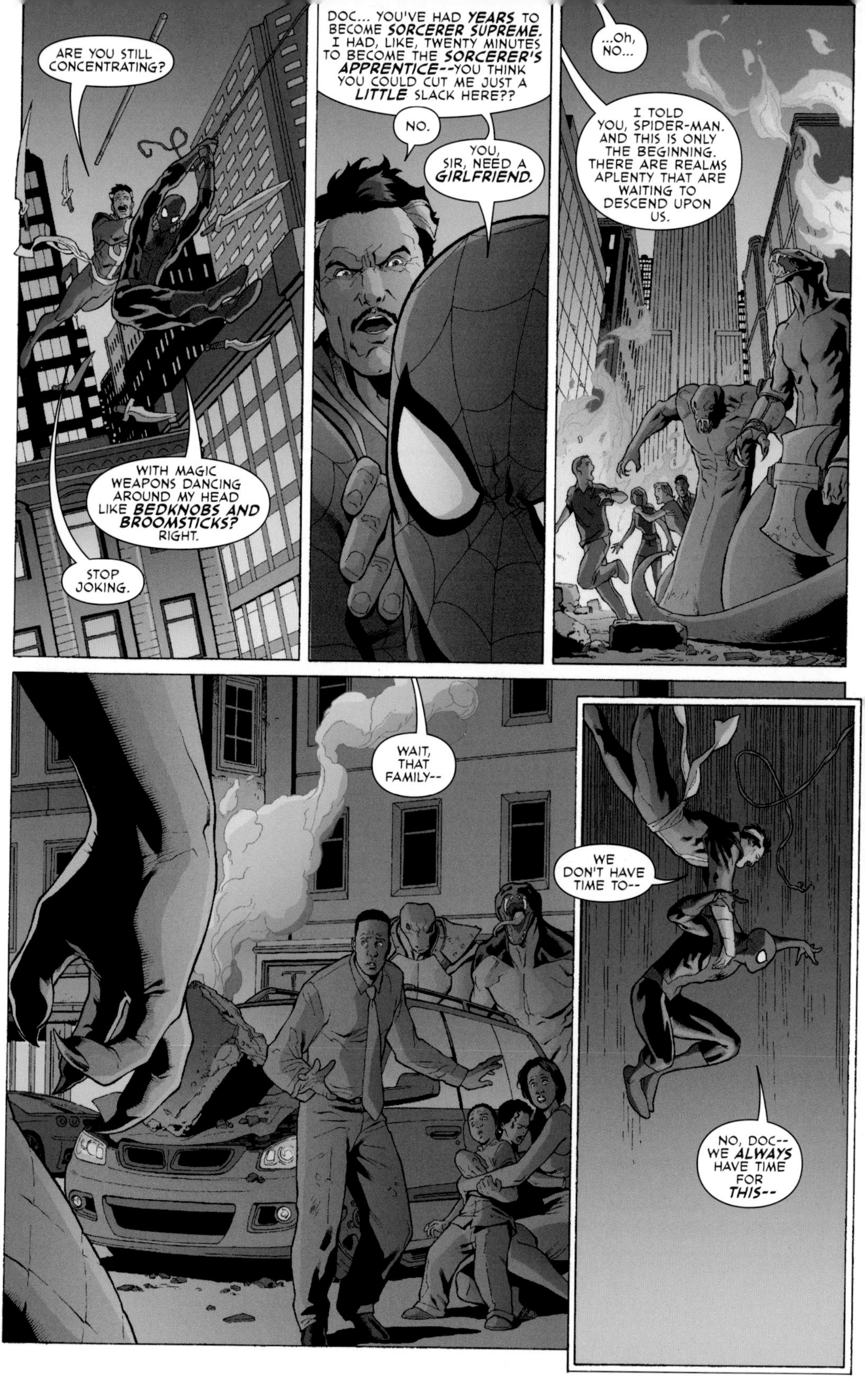
ARE YOU STILL CONCENTRATING?
WITH MAGIC WEAPONS DANCING AROUND MY HEAD LIKE BEDKNOBS AND BROOMSTICKS? RIGHT.
STOP JOKING.
DOC... YOU'VE HAD YEARS TO BECOME SORCERER SUPREME. I HAD, LIKE, TWENTY MINUTES TO BECOME THE SORCERER'S APPRENTICE--YOU THINK YOU COULD CUT ME JUST A LITTLE SLACK HERE??
NO.
YOU, SIR, NEED A GIRLFRIEND.
...OH, NO...
I TOLD YOU, SPIDER-MAN. AND THIS IS ONLY THE BEGINNING. THERE ARE REALMS APLENTY THAT ARE WAITING TO DESCEND UPON US.
WAIT, THAT FAMILY--
WE DON'T HAVE TIME TO--
NO, DOC-- WE ALWAYS HAVE TIME FOR THIS--

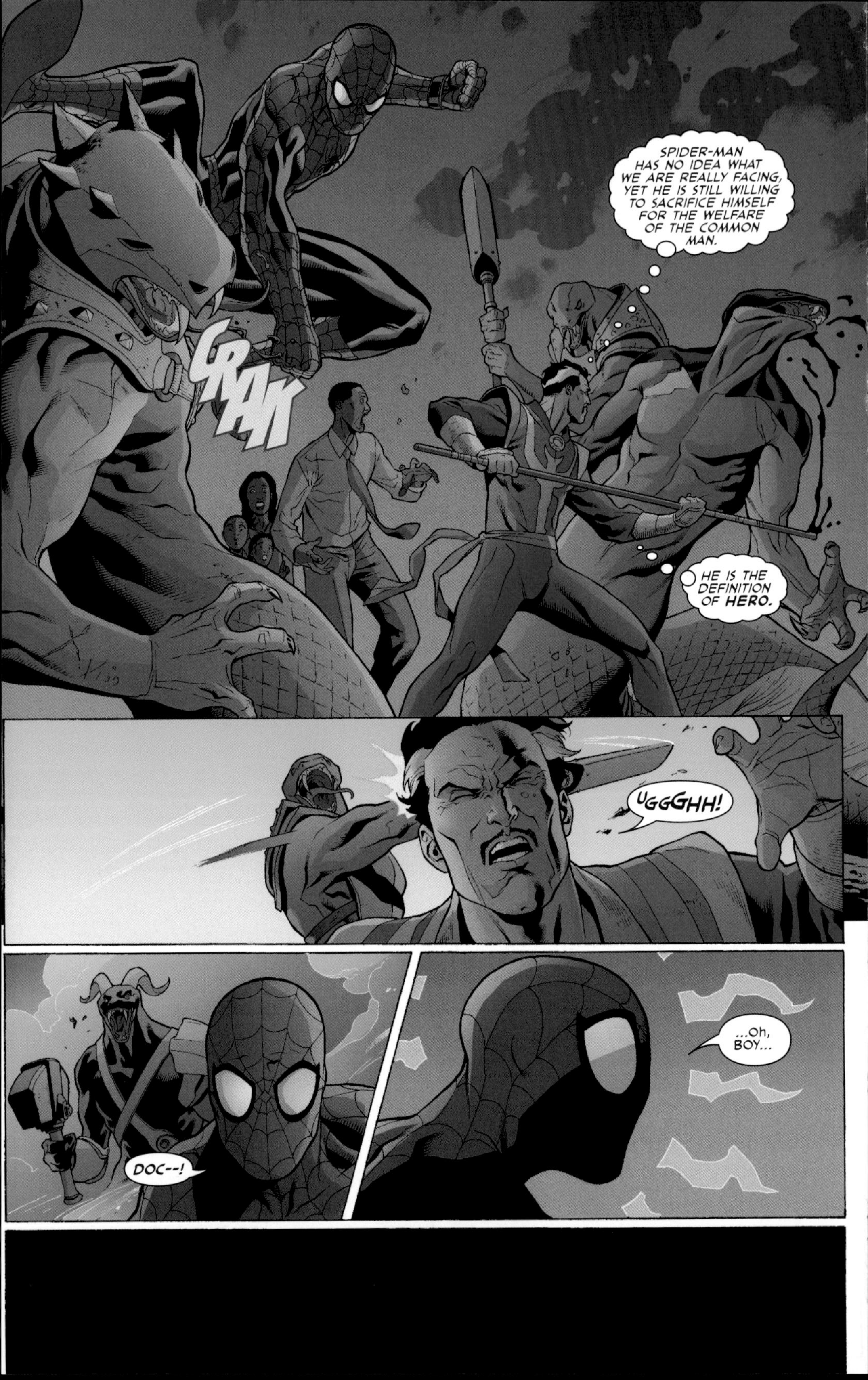
SPIDER-MAN HAS NO IDEA WHAT WE ARE REALLY FACING, YET HE IS STILL WILLING TO SACRIFICE HIMSELF FOR THE WELFARE OF THE COMMON MAN.
CRAK
HE IS THE DEFINITION OF HERO.
UGGGHH!
DOC--!
...OH, BOY...

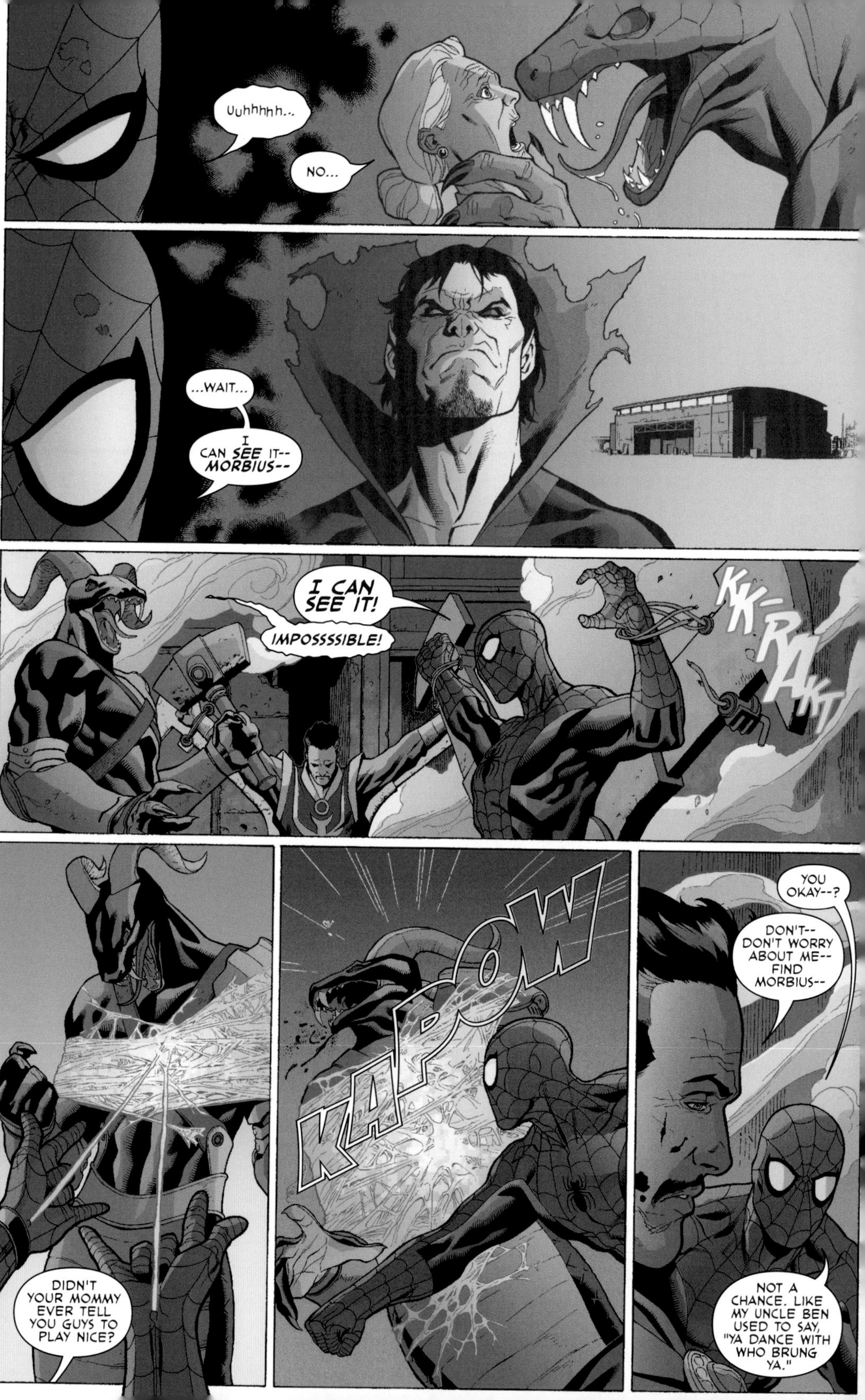
Uuhhhhh...
NO...
...WAIT...
I CAN SEE IT-- MORBIUS--
I CAN SEE IT!
IMPOSSSSIBLE!
KK-RAKT!
DIDN'T YOUR MOMMY EVER TELL YOU GUYS TO PLAY NICE?
KA-POW
YOU OKAY--?
DON'T-- DON'T WORRY ABOUT ME-- FIND MORBIUS--
NOT A CHANCE. LIKE MY UNCLE BEN USED TO SAY, "YA DANCE WITH WHO BRUNG YA."

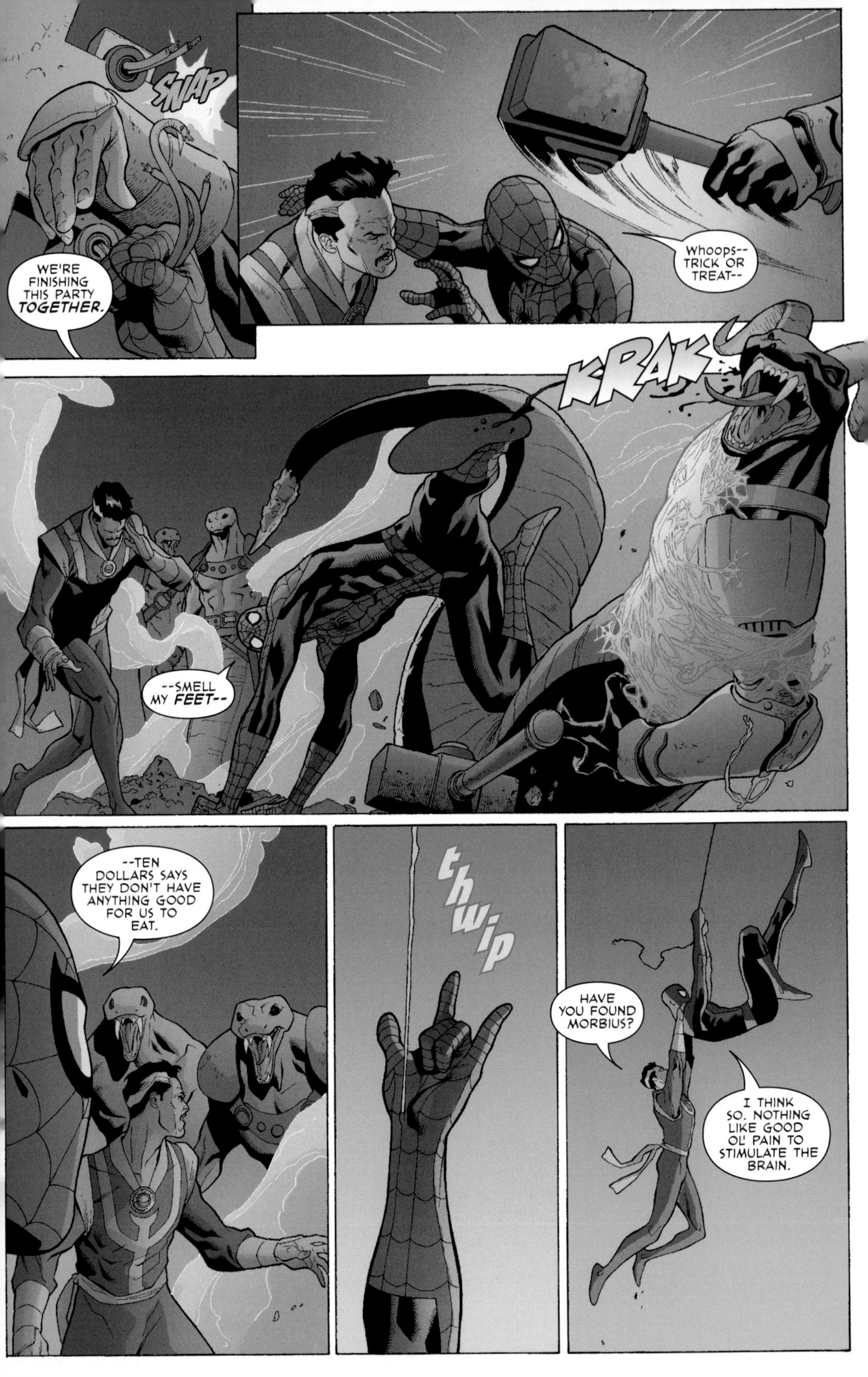
SNAP
WE'RE FINISHING THIS PARTY TOGETHER.
Whoops-- TRICK OR TREAT--
KRAK
--SMELL MY FEET--
--TEN DOLLARS SAYS THEY DON'T HAVE ANYTHING GOOD FOR US TO EAT.
thwip
HAVE YOU FOUND MORBIUS?
I THINK SO. NOTHING LIKE GOOD OL' PAIN TO STIMULATE THE BRAIN.

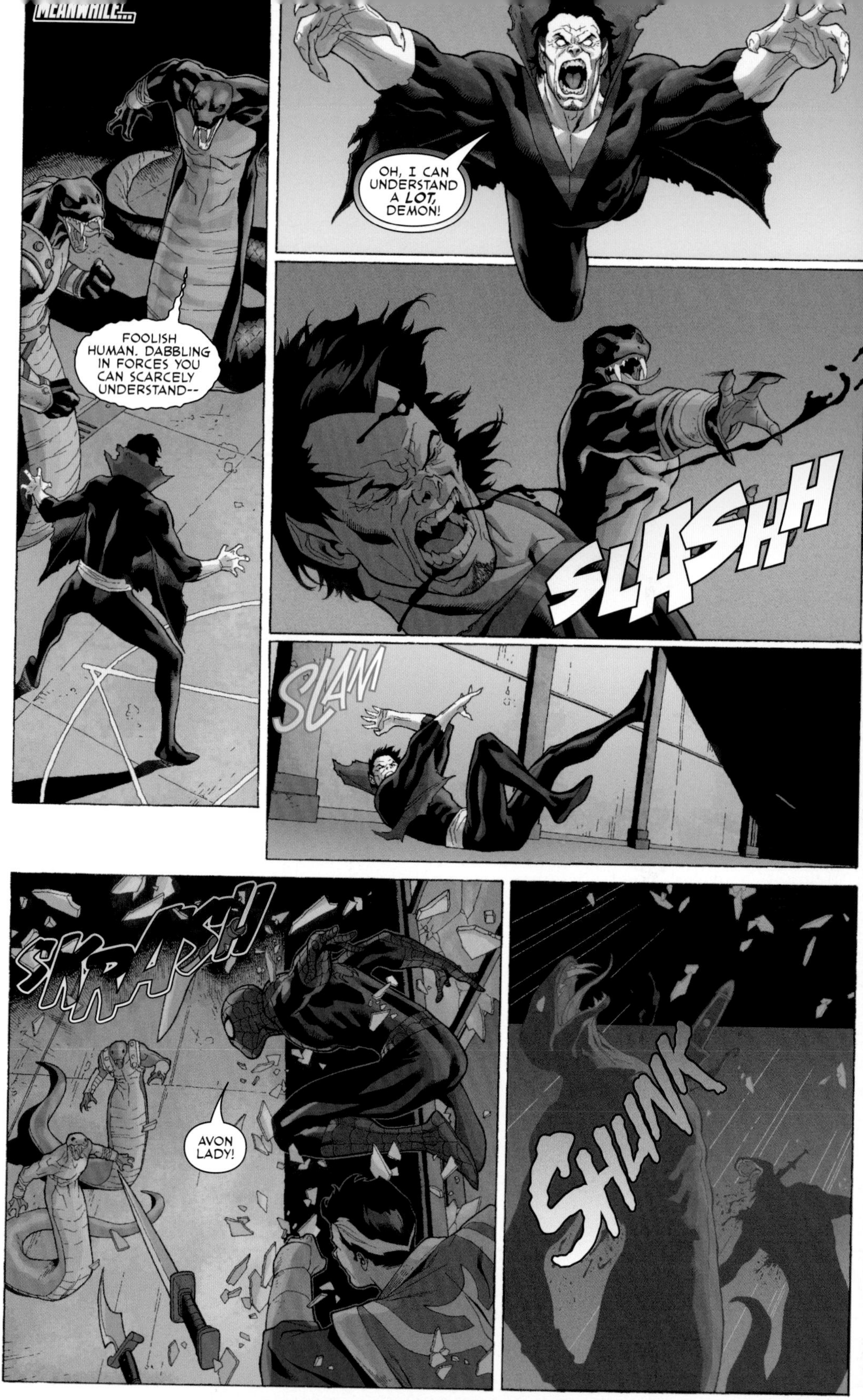
MEANWHILE...
FOOLISH HUMAN. DABBLING IN FORCES YOU CAN SCARCELY UNDERSTAND--
OH, I CAN UNDERSTAND A LOT, DEMON!
SLASHH
SLAM
SKRASH
AVON LADY!
SHUNK

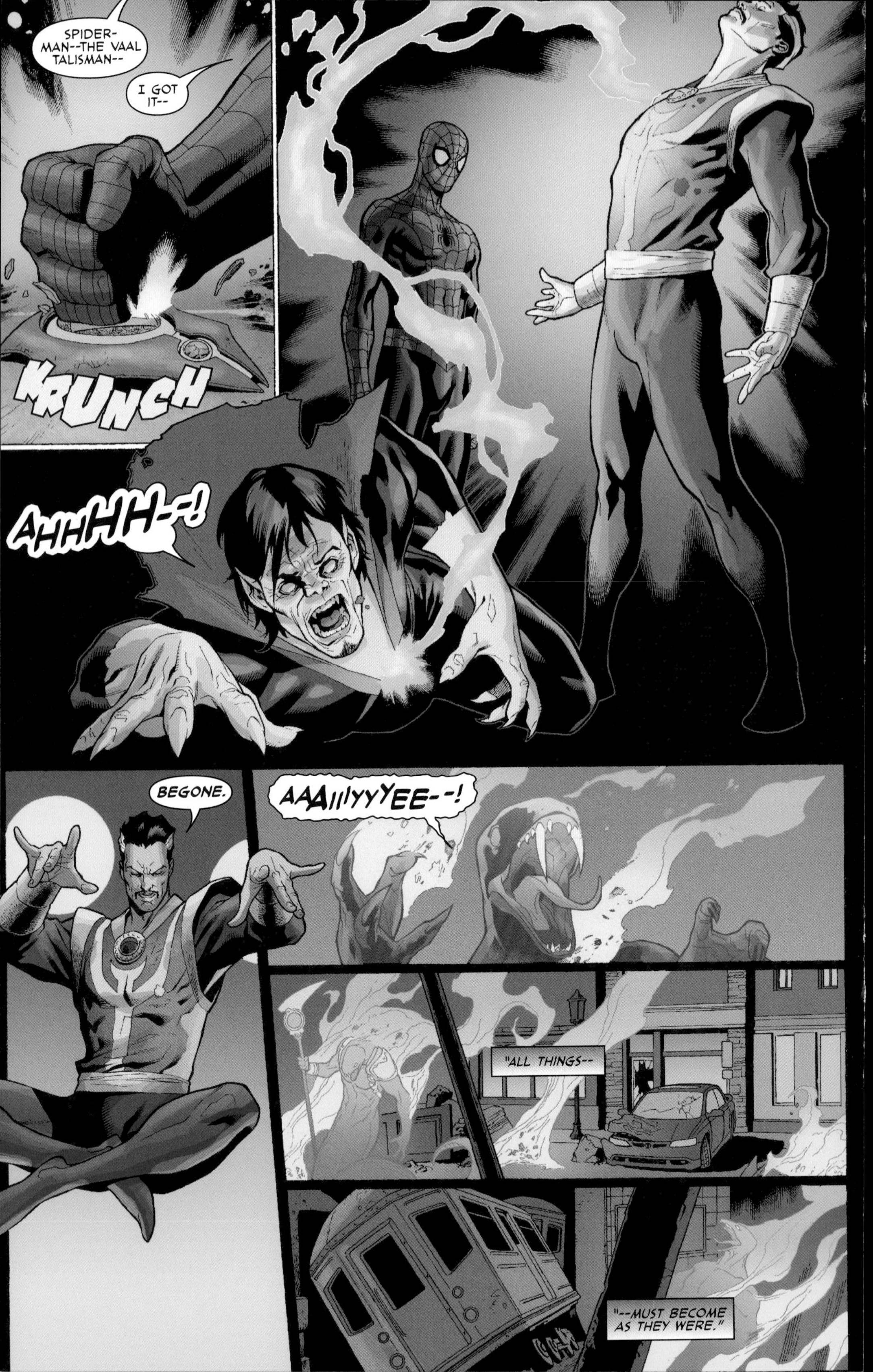

SPIDER-MAN--THE VAAL TALISMAN--
I GOT IT--
KRUNCH
AHHHH--!
BEGONE.
AAAIIIYYYEE--!
"ALL THINGS--
"--MUST BECOME AS THEY WERE."

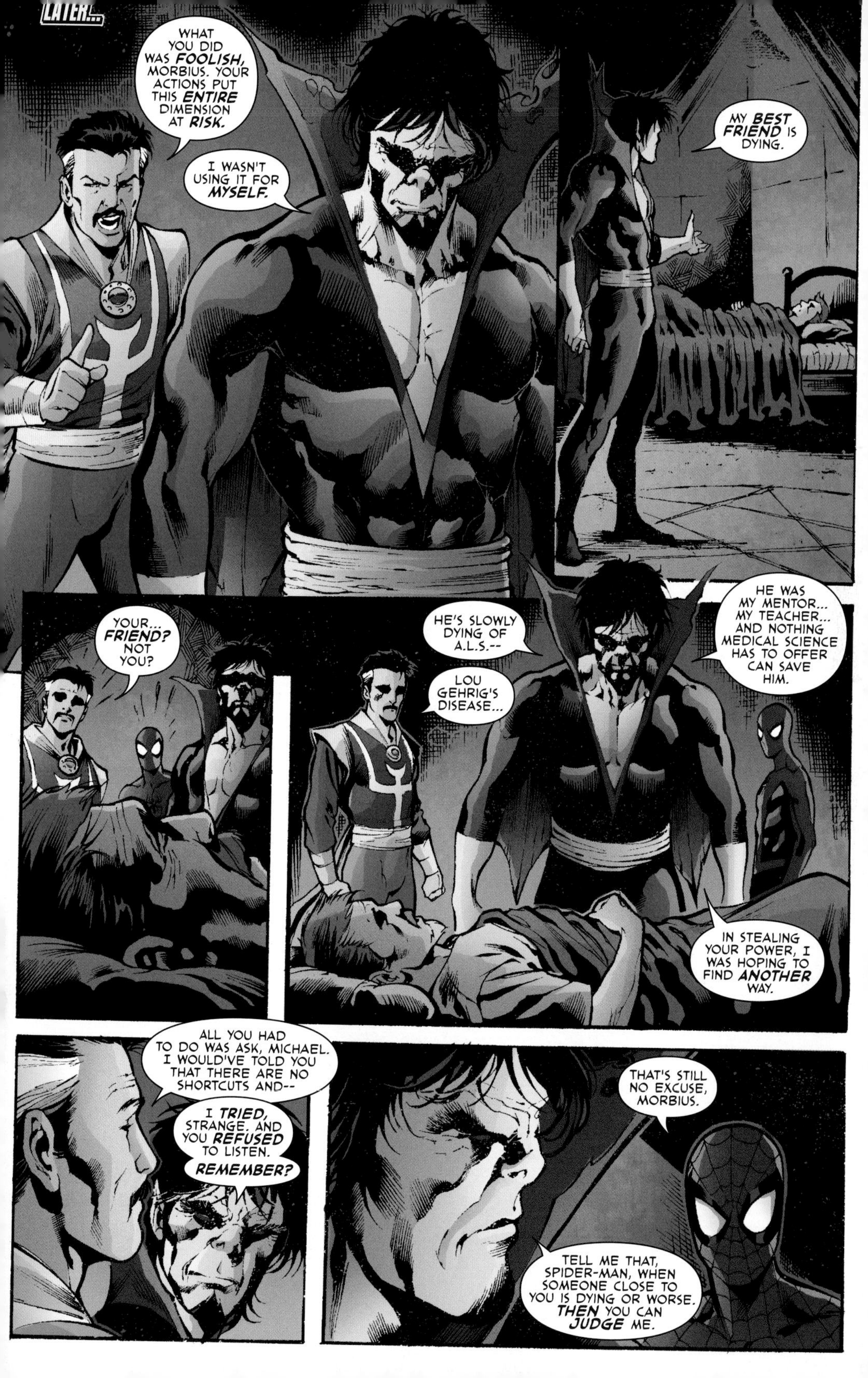
LATER...
WHAT YOU DID WAS FOOLISH, MORBIUS. YOUR ACTIONS PUT THIS ENTIRE DIMENSION AT RISK.
I WASN'T USING IT FOR MYSELF.
MY BEST FRIEND IS DYING.
YOUR... FRIEND? NOT YOU?
HE'S SLOWLY DYING OF A.L.S.--
LOU GEHRIG'S DISEASE...
HE WAS MY MENTOR... MY TEACHER... AND NOTHING MEDICAL SCIENCE HAS TO OFFER CAN SAVE HIM.
IN STEALING YOUR POWER, I WAS HOPING TO FIND ANOTHER WAY.
ALL YOU HAD TO DO WAS ASK, MICHAEL. I WOULD'VE TOLD YOU THAT THERE ARE NO SHORTCUTS AND--
I TRIED, STRANGE, AND YOU REFUSED TO LISTEN. REMEMBER?
THAT'S STILL NO EXCUSE, MORBIUS.
TELL ME THAT, SPIDER-MAN, WHEN SOMEONE CLOSE TO YOU IS DYING OR WORSE. THEN YOU CAN JUDGE ME.

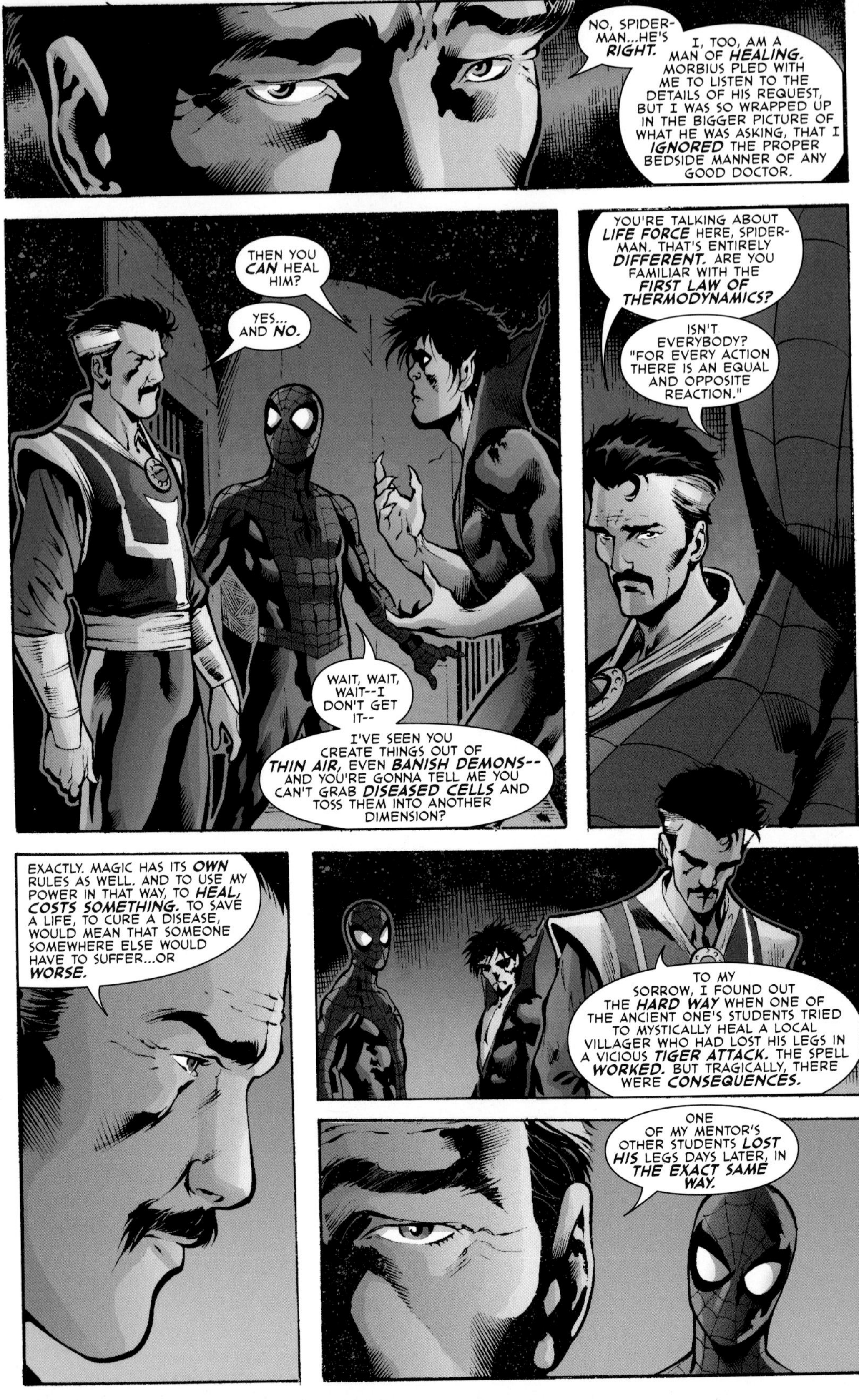

NO, SPIDER-MAN...HE'S RIGHT.
I, TOO, AM A MAN OF HEALING. MORBIUS PLED WITH ME TO LISTEN TO THE DETAILS OF HIS REQUEST, BUT I WAS SO WRAPPED UP IN THE BIGGER PICTURE OF WHAT HE WAS ASKING, THAT I IGNORED THE PROPER BEDSIDE MANNER OF ANY GOOD DOCTOR.
THEN YOU CAN HEAL HIM?
YES... AND NO.
WAIT, WAIT, WAIT--I DON'T GET IT--
I'VE SEEN YOU CREATE THINGS OUT OF THIN AIR, EVEN BANISH DEMONS--AND YOU'RE GONNA TELL ME YOU CAN'T GRAB DISEASED CELLS AND TOSS THEM INTO ANOTHER DIMENSION?
YOU'RE TALKING ABOUT LIFE FORCE HERE, SPIDER-MAN. THAT'S ENTIRELY DIFFERENT. ARE YOU FAMILIAR WITH THE FIRST LAW OF THERMODYNAMICS?
ISN'T EVERYBODY? "FOR EVERY ACTION THERE IS AN EQUAL AND OPPOSITE REACTION."
EXACTLY. MAGIC HAS ITS OWN RULES AS WELL. AND TO USE MY POWER IN THAT WAY, TO HEAL, COSTS SOMETHING. TO SAVE A LIFE, TO CURE A DISEASE, WOULD MEAN THAT SOMEONE SOMEWHERE ELSE WOULD HAVE TO SUFFER...OR WORSE.
TO MY SORROW, I FOUND OUT THE HARD WAY WHEN ONE OF THE ANCIENT ONE'S STUDENTS TRIED TO MYSTICALLY HEAL A LOCAL VILLAGER WHO HAD LOST HIS LEGS IN A VICIOUS TIGER ATTACK. THE SPELL WORKED. BUT TRAGICALLY, THERE WERE CONSEQUENCES.
ONE OF MY MENTOR'S OTHER STUDENTS LOST HIS LEGS DAYS LATER, IN THE EXACT SAME WAY.

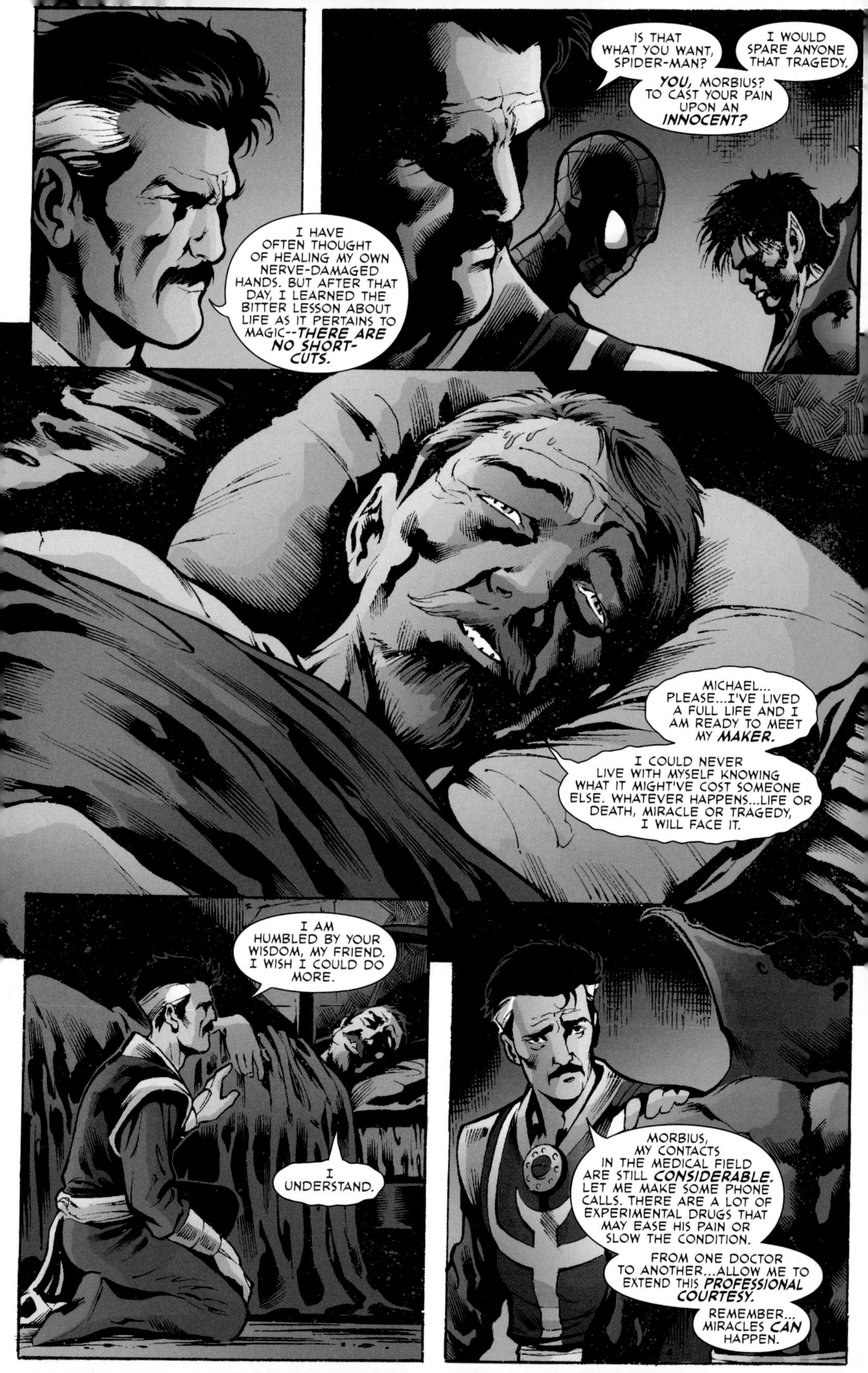
I HAVE OFTEN THOUGHT OF HEALING MY OWN NERVE-DAMAGED HANDS. BUT AFTER THAT DAY, I LEARNED THE BITTER LESSON ABOUT LIFE AS IT PERTAINS TO MAGIC--THERE ARE NO SHORT-CUTS.
IS THAT WHAT YOU WANT, SPIDER-MAN?
I WOULD SPARE ANYONE THAT TRAGEDY.
YOU, MORBIUS? TO CAST YOUR PAIN UPON AN INNOCENT?
MICHAEL... PLEASE...I'VE LIVED A FULL LIFE AND I AM READY TO MEET MY MAKER.
I COULD NEVER LIVE WITH MYSELF KNOWING WHAT IT MIGHT'VE COST SOMEONE ELSE. WHATEVER HAPPENS...LIFE OR DEATH, MIRACLE OR TRAGEDY, I WILL FACE IT.
I AM HUMBLED BY YOUR WISDOM, MY FRIEND. I WISH I COULD DO MORE.
I UNDERSTAND.
MORBIUS, MY CONTACTS IN THE MEDICAL FIELD ARE STILL CONSIDERABLE. LET ME MAKE SOME PHONE CALLS. THERE ARE A LOT OF EXPERIMENTAL DRUGS THAT MAY EASE HIS PAIN OR SLOW THE CONDITION.
FROM ONE DOCTOR TO ANOTHER...ALLOW ME TO EXTEND THIS PROFESSIONAL COURTESY.
REMEMBER... MIRACLES CAN HAPPEN.

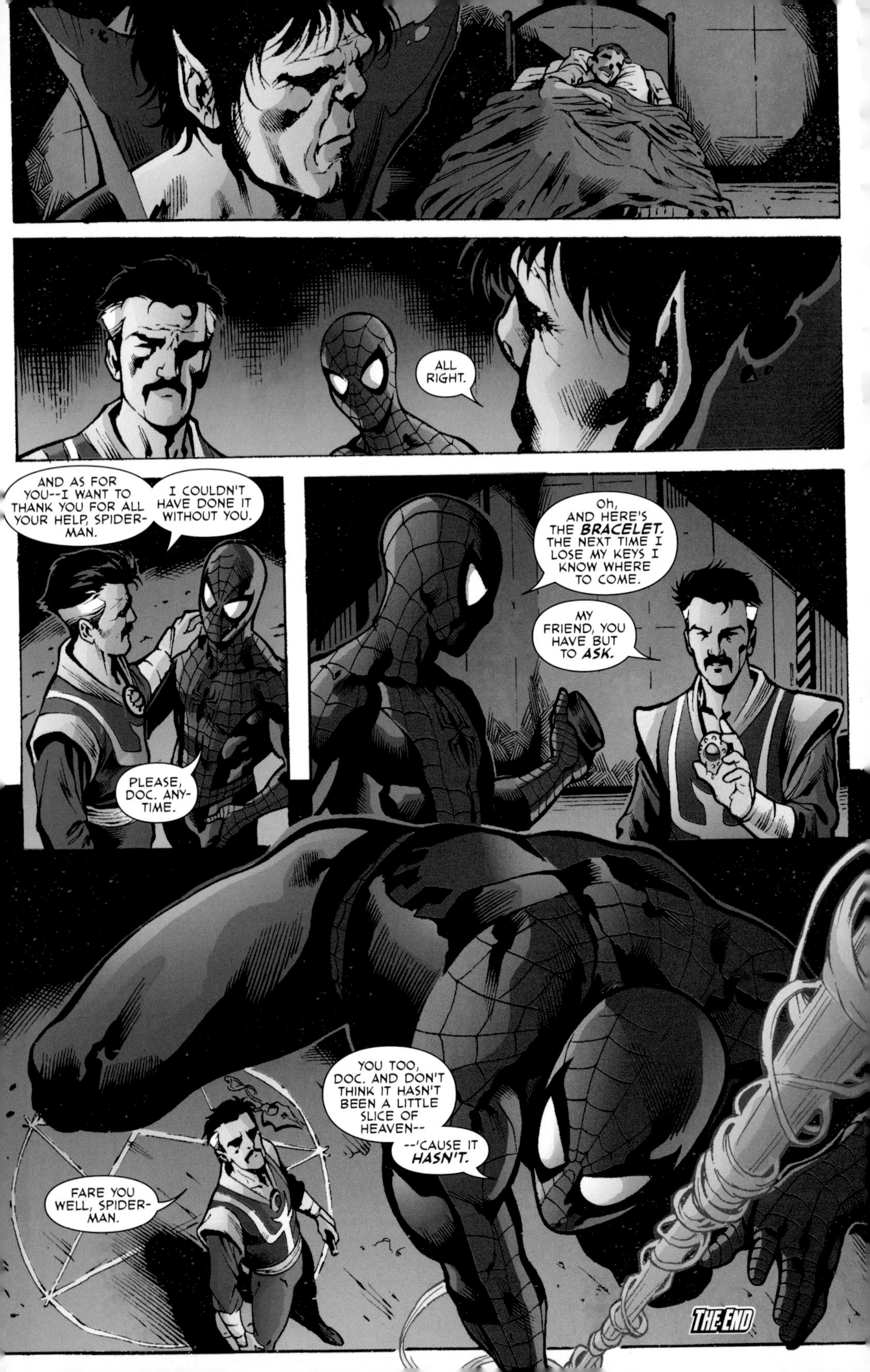

ALL RIGHT.
AND AS FOR YOU--I WANT TO THANK YOU FOR ALL YOUR HELP, SPIDER-MAN.
I COULDN'T HAVE DONE IT WITHOUT YOU.
PLEASE, DOC. ANY-TIME.
Oh, AND HERE'S THE BRACELET. THE NEXT TIME I LOSE MY KEYS I KNOW WHERE TO COME.
MY FRIEND, YOU HAVE BUT TO ASK.
YOU TOO, DOC. AND DON'T THINK IT HASN'T BEEN A LITTLE SLICE OF HEAVEN--
--'CAUSE IT HASN'T.
FARE YOU WELL, SPIDER-MAN.
THE END

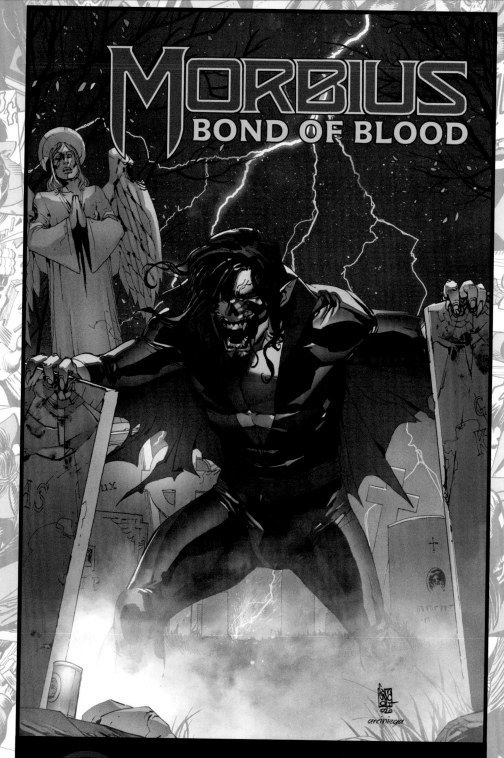

MORBIUS
BOND OF BLOOD

MORBIUS: BOND OF BLOOD

THE LIVING VAMPIRE FACES A GHOST FROM HIS PAST — AND
A TERRIFYING DECISION — WHEN MORBIUS LEARNS THAT HIS
FIRST VICTIM'S SON HAS DEVELOPED A RARE BLOOD DISEASE.

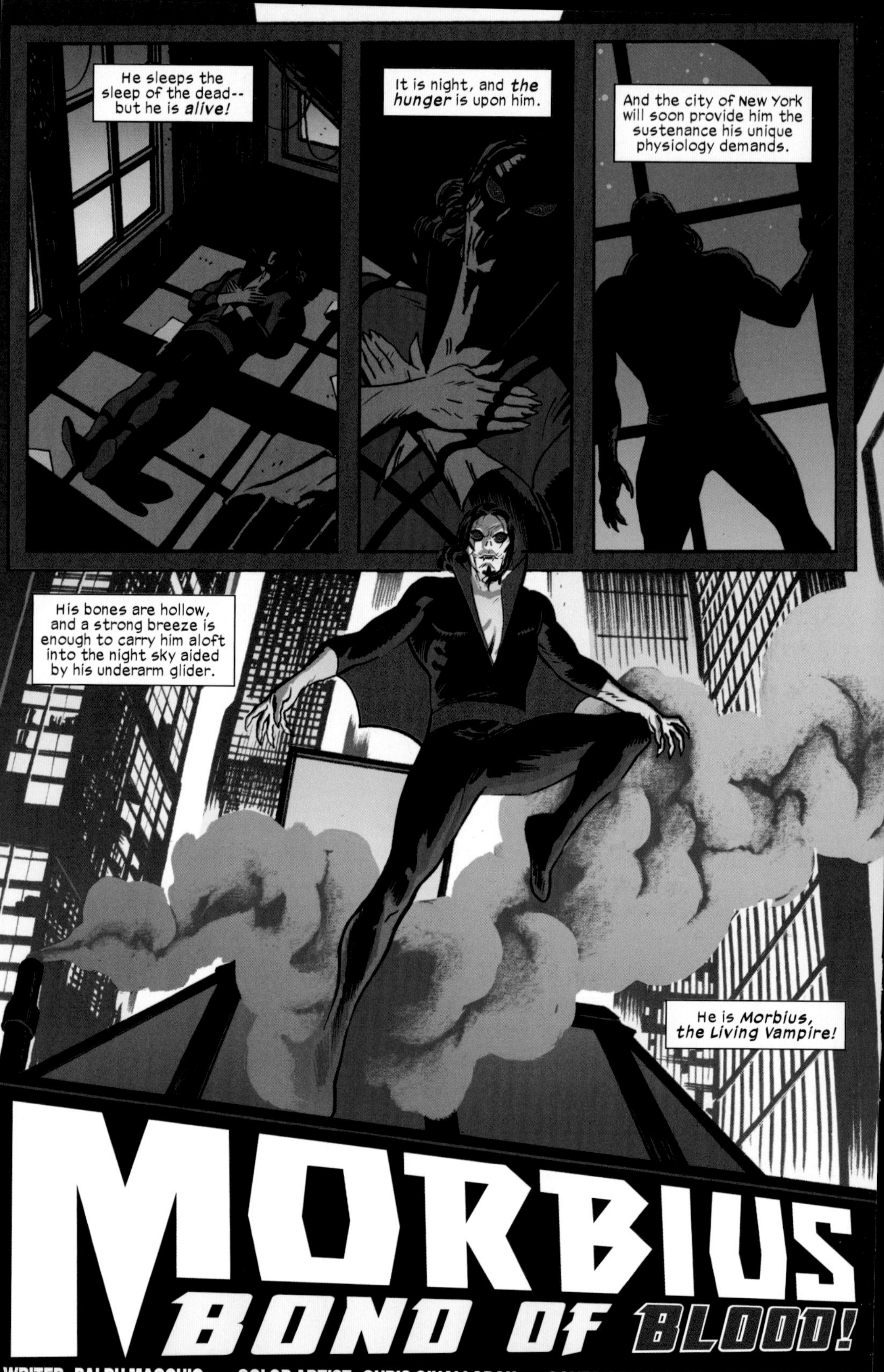
He sleeps the sleep of the dead-- but he is *alive!*
It is night, and *the hunger* is upon him.
And the city of New York will soon provide him the sustenance his unique physiology demands.
His bones are hollow, and a strong breeze is enough to carry him aloft into the night sky aided by his underarm glider.
He is *Morbius, the Living Vampire!*
MORBIUS
BOND OF BLOOD!

WRITER RALPH MACCHIO
ARTIST TOM REILLY
COLOR ARTIST CHRIS O'HALLORAN
LETTERER VC'S ARIANA MAHER
COVER ARTISTS GIUSEPPE CAMUNCOLI & ERICK ARCINIEGA

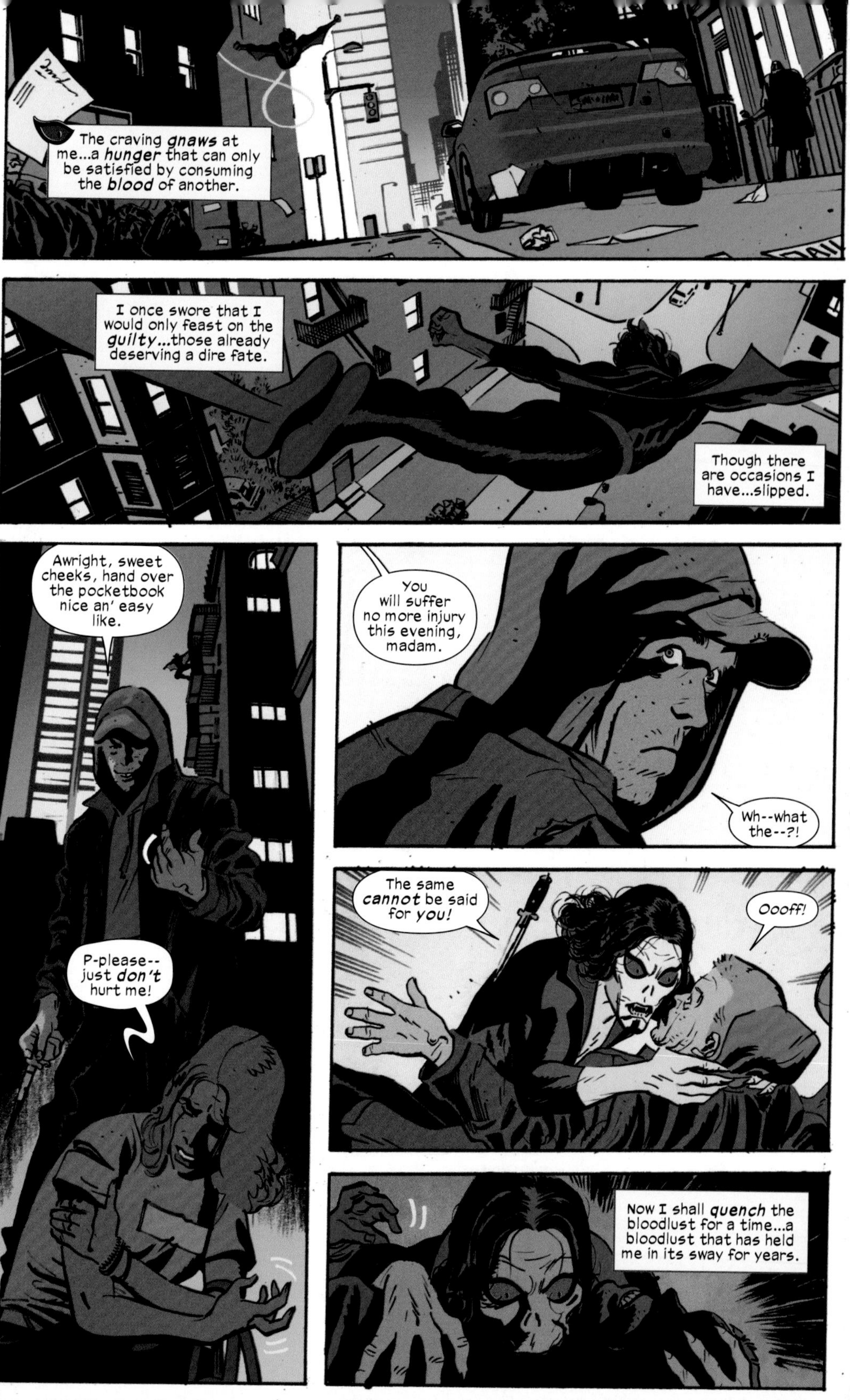
The craving gnaws at me...a hunger that can only be satisfied by consuming the blood of another.
I once swore that I would only feast on the guilty...those already deserving a dire fate.
Though there are occasions I have...slipped.
Awright, sweet cheeks, hand over the pocketbook nice an' easy like.
P-please-- just don't hurt me!
You will suffer no more injury this evening, madam.
Wh--what the--?!
The same cannot be said for you!
Oooff!
Now I shall quench the bloodlust for a time...a bloodlust that has held me in its sway for years.

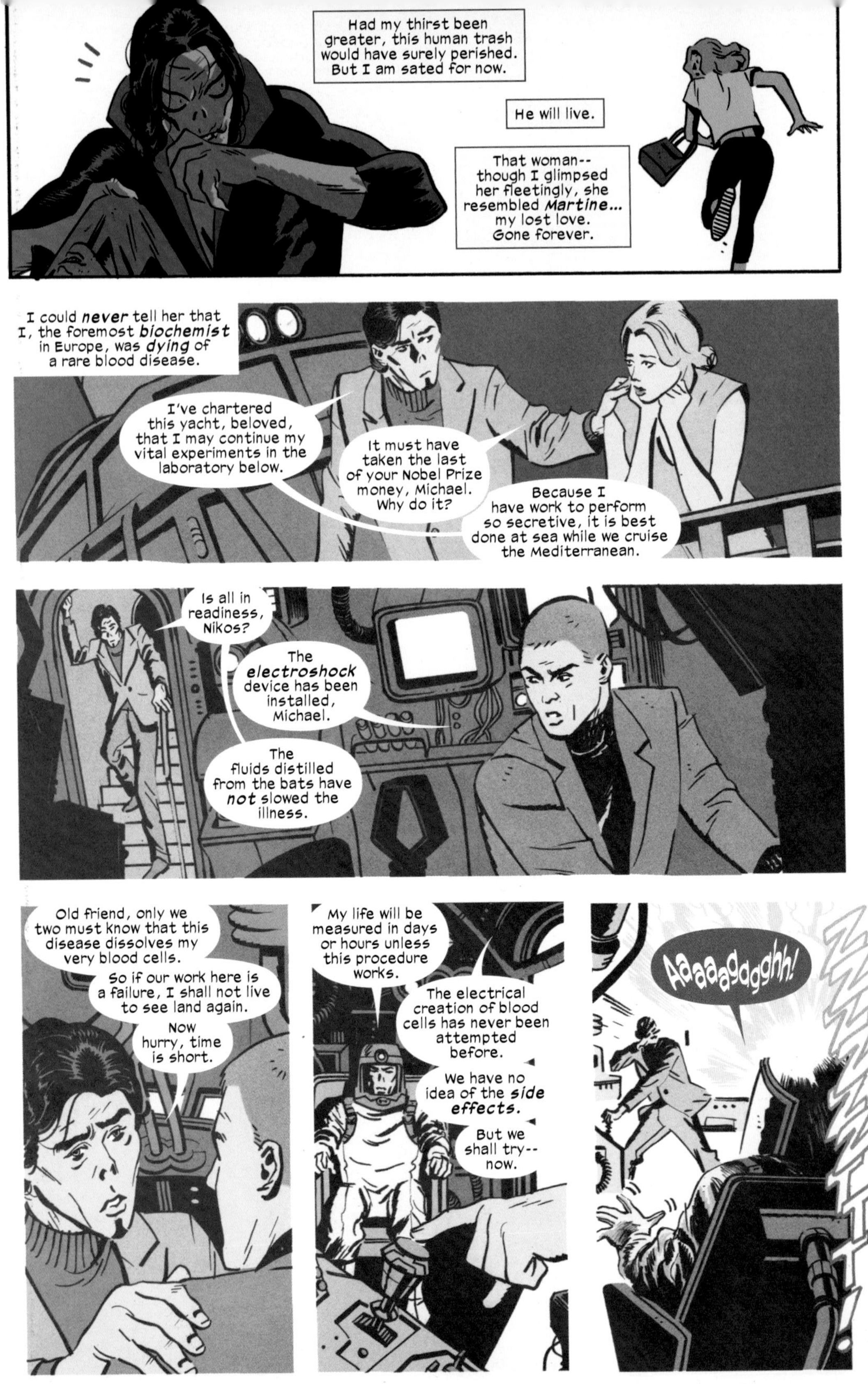
Had my thirst been greater, this human trash would have surely perished. But I am sated for now.
He will live.
That woman-- though I glimpsed her fleetingly, she resembled *Martine*... my lost love. Gone forever.
I could ***never*** tell her that I, the foremost ***biochemist*** in Europe, was ***dying*** of a rare blood disease.
I've chartered this yacht, beloved, that I may continue my vital experiments in the laboratory below.
It must have taken the last of your Nobel Prize money, Michael. Why do it?
Because I have work to perform so secretive, it is best done at sea while we cruise the Mediterranean.
Is all in readiness, Nikos?
The ***electroshock*** device has been installed, Michael.
The fluids distilled from the bats have ***not*** slowed the illness.
Old friend, only we two must know that this disease dissolves my very blood cells.
So if our work here is a failure, I shall not live to see land again.
Now hurry, time is short.
My life will be measured in days or hours unless this procedure works.
The electrical creation of blood cells has never been attempted before.
We have no idea of the ***side effects.***
But we shall try-- now.
Aaaaagggh!

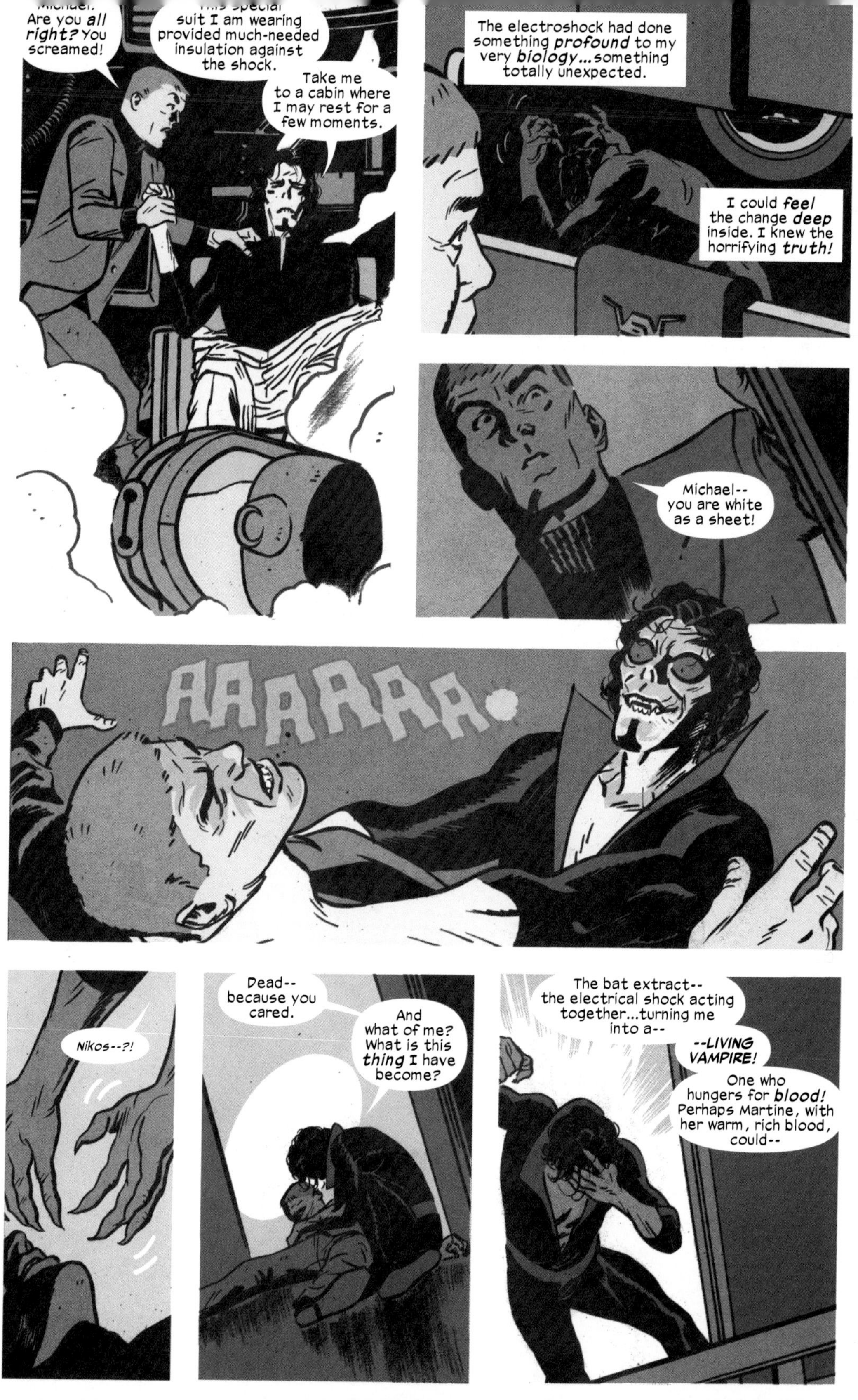
Michael! Are you all right? You screamed!
This special suit I am wearing provided much-needed insulation against the shock.
Take me to a cabin where I may rest for a few moments.
The electroshock had done something profound to my very biology...something totally unexpected.
I could feel the change deep inside. I knew the horrifying truth!
Michael--you are white as a sheet!
AAAAAA
Nikos--?!
Dead--because you cared.
And what of me? What is this thing I have become?
The bat extract--the electrical shock acting together...turning me into a--
--LIVING VAMPIRE!
One who hungers for blood! Perhaps Martine, with her warm, rich blood, could--

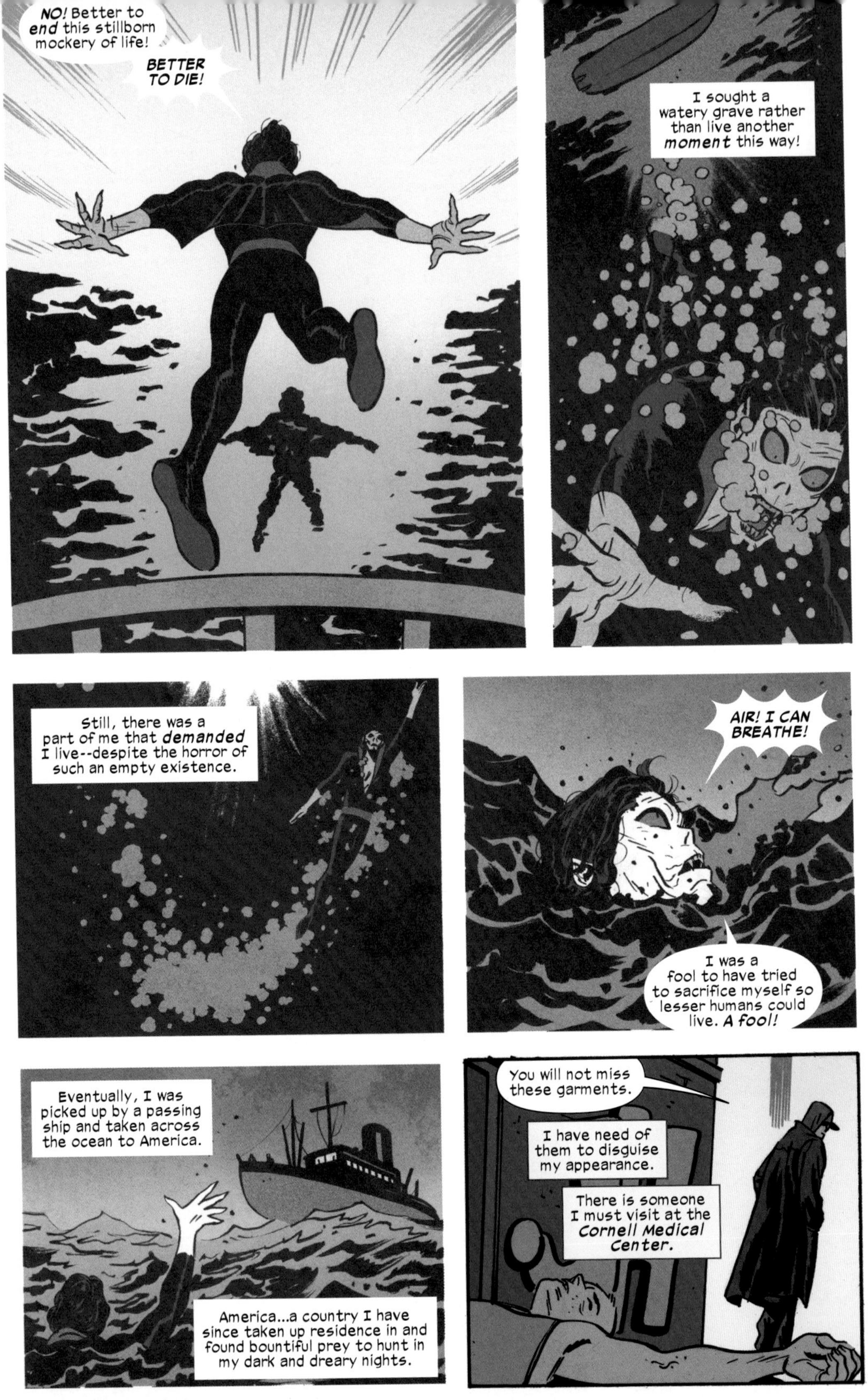

NO! Better to end this stillborn mockery of life!
BETTER TO DIE!
I sought a watery grave rather than live another moment this way!
Still, there was a part of me that demanded I live--despite the horror of such an empty existence.
AIR! I CAN BREATHE!
I was a fool to have tried to sacrifice myself so lesser humans could live. A fool!
Eventually, I was picked up by a passing ship and taken across the ocean to America.
America...a country I have since taken up residence in and found bountiful prey to hunt in my dark and dreary nights.
You will not miss these garments.
I have need of them to disguise my appearance.
There is someone I must visit at the Cornell Medical Center.

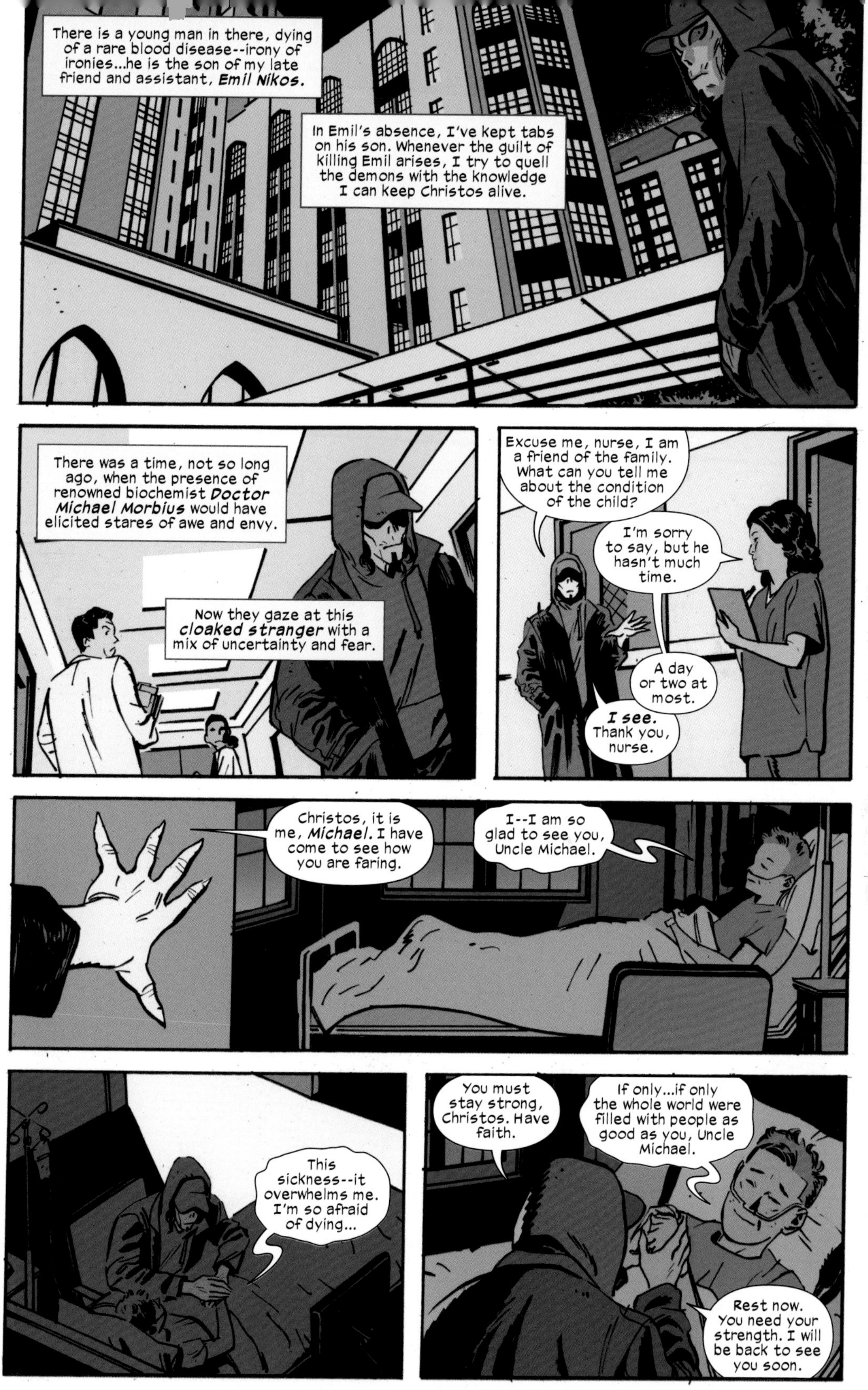

There is a young man in there, dying of a rare blood disease--irony of ironies...he is the son of my late friend and assistant, Emil Nikos.
In Emil's absence, I've kept tabs on his son. Whenever the guilt of killing Emil arises, I try to quell the demons with the knowledge I can keep Christos alive.
There was a time, not so long ago, when the presence of renowned biochemist Doctor Michael Morbius would have elicited stares of awe and envy.
Now they gaze at this cloaked stranger with a mix of uncertainty and fear.
Excuse me, nurse, I am a friend of the family. What can you tell me about the condition of the child?
I'm sorry to say, but he hasn't much time.
A day or two at most.
I see. Thank you, nurse.
Christos, it is me, Michael. I have come to see how you are faring.
I--I am so glad to see you, Uncle Michael.
This sickness--it overwhelms me. I'm so afraid of dying...
You must stay strong, Christos. Have faith.
If only...if only the whole world were filled with people as good as you, Uncle Michael.
Rest now. You need your strength. I will be back to see you soon.

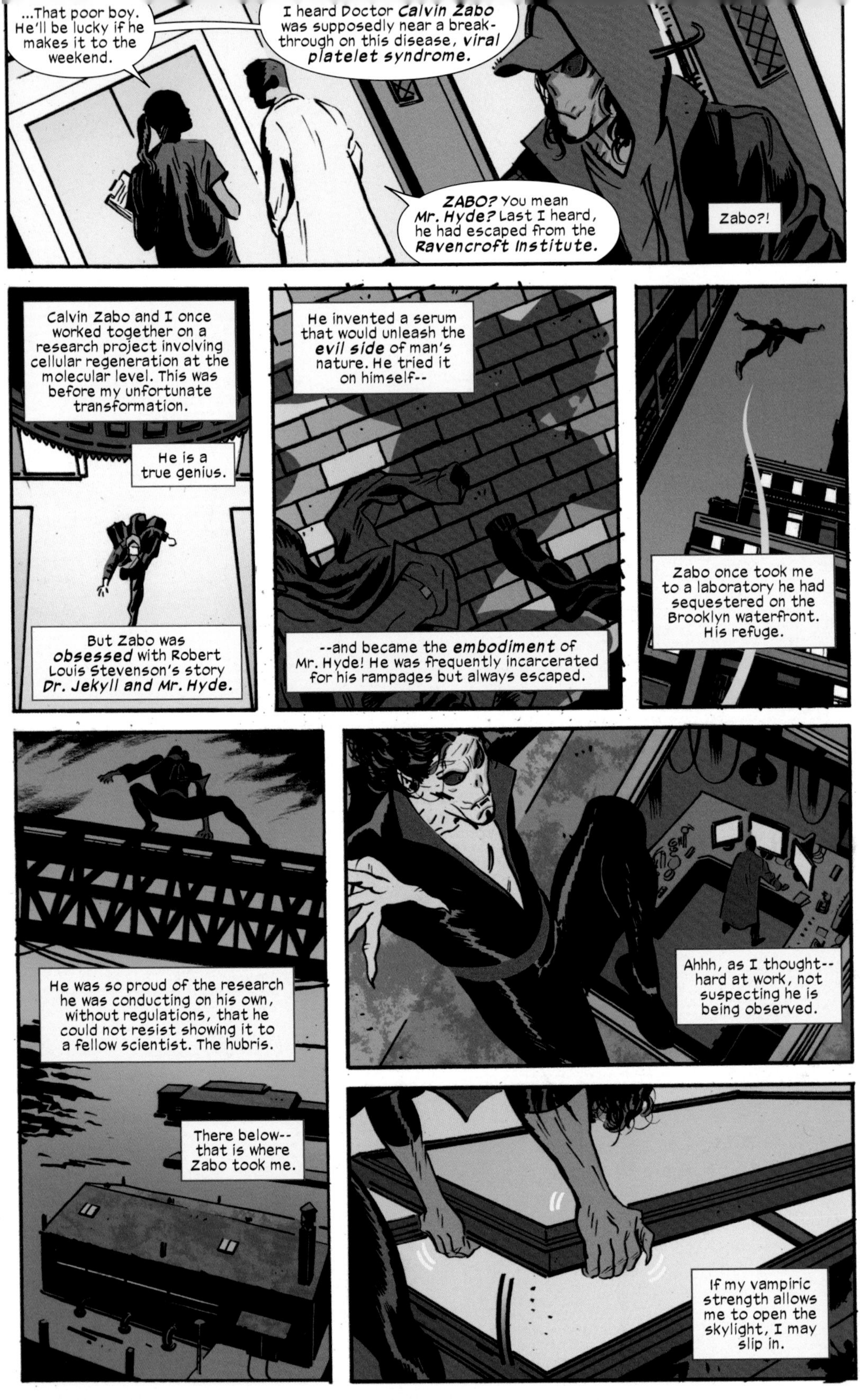
...That poor boy. He'll be lucky if he makes it to the weekend.
I heard Doctor Calvin Zabo was supposedly near a break-through on this disease, viral platelet syndrome.
ZABO? You mean Mr. Hyde? Last I heard, he had escaped from the Ravencroft Institute.
Zabo?!
Calvin Zabo and I once worked together on a research project involving cellular regeneration at the molecular level. This was before my unfortunate transformation.
He is a true genius.
But Zabo was obsessed with Robert Louis Stevenson's story Dr. Jekyll and Mr. Hyde.
He invented a serum that would unleash the evil side of man's nature. He tried it on himself--
--and became the embodiment of Mr. Hyde! He was frequently incarcerated for his rampages but always escaped.
Zabo once took me to a laboratory he had sequestered on the Brooklyn waterfront. His refuge.
He was so proud of the research he was conducting on his own, without regulations, that he could not resist showing it to a fellow scientist. The hubris.
There below--that is where Zabo took me.
Ahhh, as I thought--hard at work, not suspecting he is being observed.
If my vampiric strength allows me to open the skylight, I may slip in.

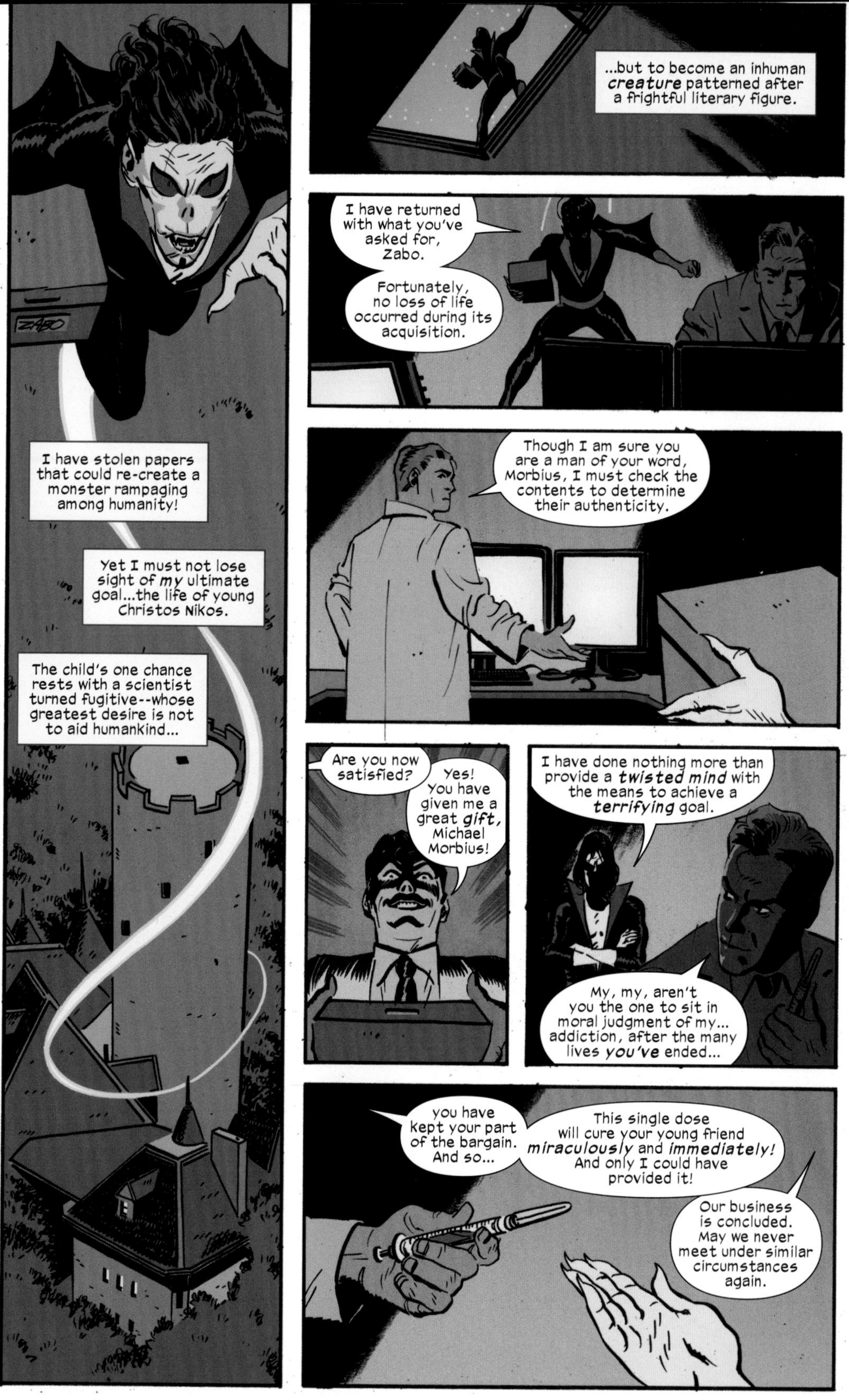
ZABO
I have stolen papers that could re-create a monster rampaging among humanity!
Yet I must not lose sight of *my* ultimate goal...the life of young Christos Nikos.
The child's one chance rests with a scientist turned fugitive--whose greatest desire is not to aid humankind...
...but to become an inhuman *creature* patterned after a frightful literary figure.
I have returned with what you've asked for, Zabo.
Fortunately, no loss of life occurred during its acquisition.
Though I am sure you are a man of your word, Morbius, I must check the contents to determine their authenticity.
Are you now satisfied?
Yes! You have given me a great *gift,* Michael Morbius!
I have done nothing more than provide a *twisted mind* with the means to achieve a *terrifying* goal.
My, my, aren't you the one to sit in moral judgment of my... addiction, after the many lives *you've* ended...
you have kept your part of the bargain. And so...
This single dose will cure your young friend *miraculously* and *immediately!* And only I could have provided it!
Our business is concluded. May we never meet under similar circumstances again.

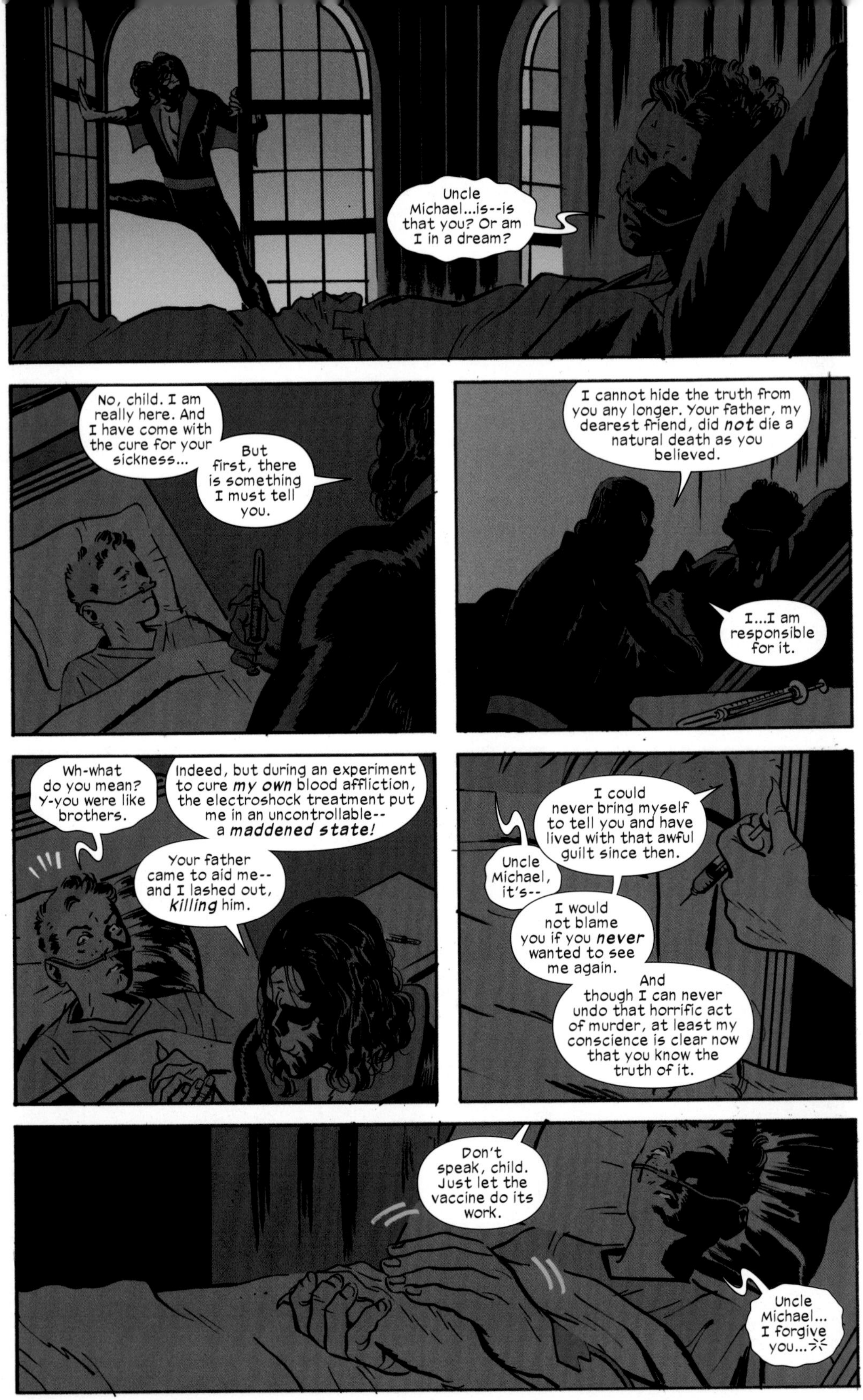
Uncle Michael...is--is that you? Or am I in a dream?
No, child. I am really here. And I have come with the cure for your sickness...
But first, there is something I must tell you.
I cannot hide the truth from you any longer. Your father, my dearest friend, did not die a natural death as you believed.
I...I am responsible for it.
Wh-what do you mean? Y-you were like brothers.
Indeed, but during an experiment to cure my own blood affliction, the electroshock treatment put me in an uncontrollable-- a maddened state!
Your father came to aid me-- and I lashed out, killing him.
I could never bring myself to tell you and have lived with that awful guilt since then.
Uncle Michael, it's--
I would not blame you if you never wanted to see me again.
And though I can never undo that horrific act of murder, at least my conscience is clear now that you know the truth of it.
Don't speak, child. Just let the vaccine do its work.
Uncle Michael... I forgive you...

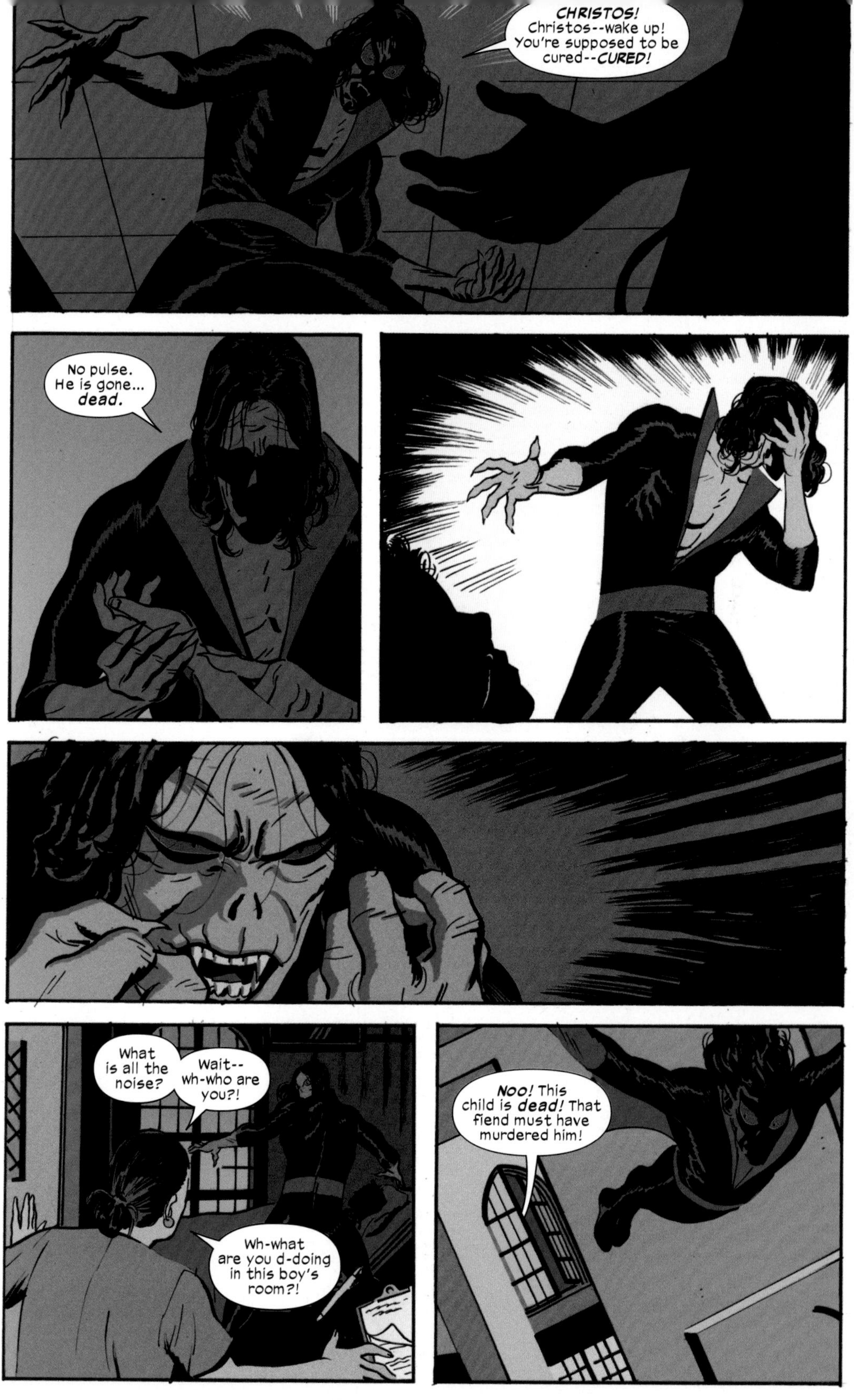
CHRISTOS! Christos--wake up! You're supposed to be cured--CURED!
No pulse. He is gone... dead.
What is all the noise?
Wait-- wh-who are you?!
Wh-what are you d-doing in this boy's room?!
NOO! This child is dead! That fiend must have murdered him!

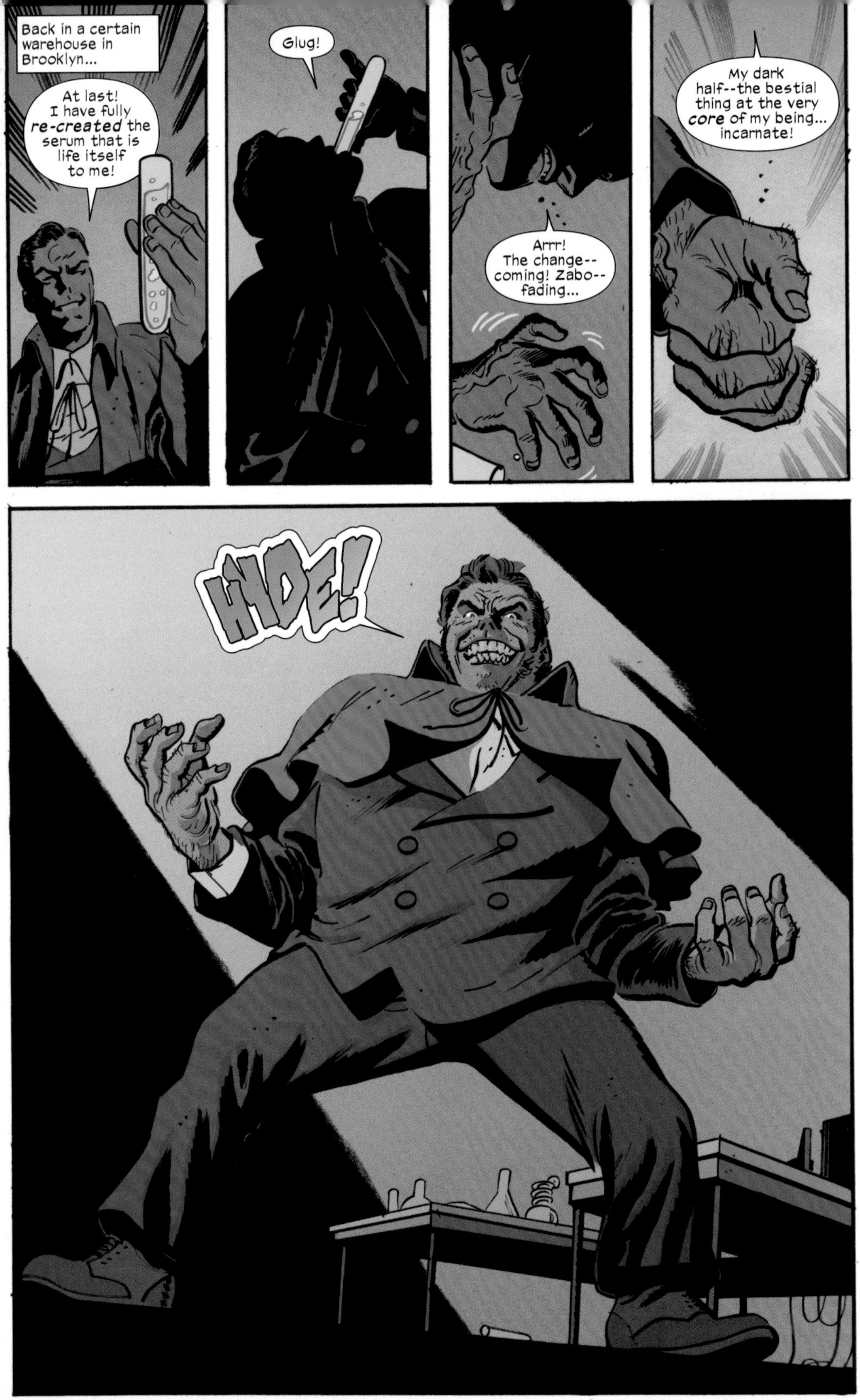

Back in a certain warehouse in Brooklyn...
At last! I have fully *re-created* the serum that is life itself to me!
Glug!
Arrr! The change--coming! Zabo--fading...
My dark half--the bestial thing at the very *core* of my being... incarnate!
HYDE!

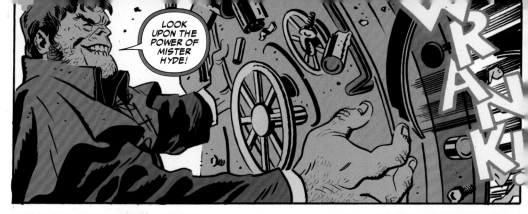

LOOK UPON THE POWER OF MISTER HYDE!

WRANK!

Empire State Bank on 57th St.

Ahh! The coin of the realm! What Zabo needs to keep playing with his test tubes and beakers for years to come.

I told you there would be *consequences* if you lied to me, Zabo--or Hyde--or whatever denizen of the pits you are now! Your cure was a *fake!* The boy *died!*

I care little about some tiny human meat bag who *perished* because of my other half! And I doubt Zabo does either!

So he *lied* to you to get the formula that brings me forth. All that matters is that *Hyde is here!*

Now remove yourself from my path, bloodsucker.

SSNVT

Not until I have my *revenge!*

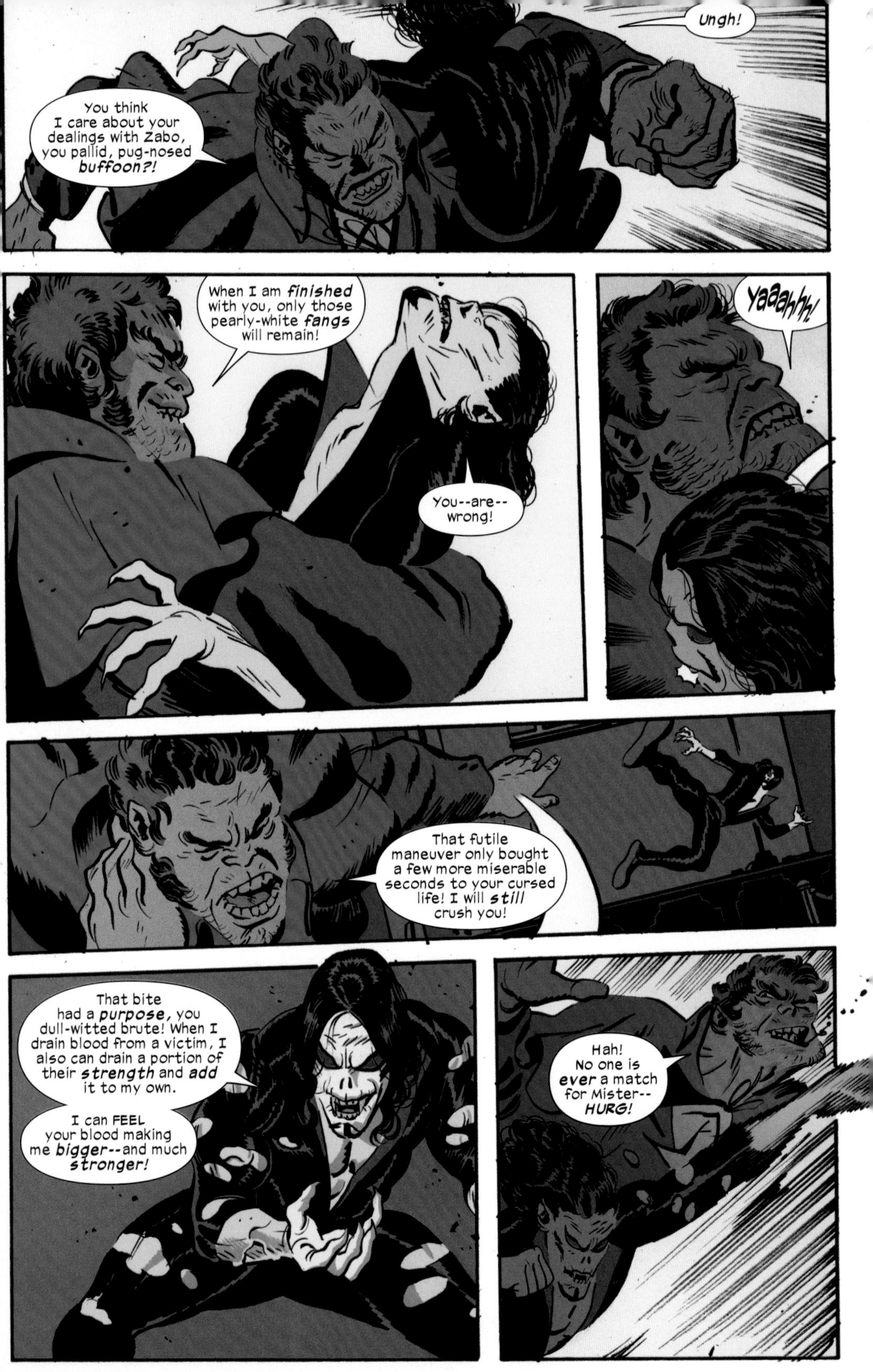
Ungh!
You think I care about your dealings with Zabo, you pallid, pug-nosed *buffoon?!*
When I am *finished* with you, only those pearly-white *fangs* will remain!
You--are--wrong!
Yaaahhh!
That futile maneuver only bought a few more miserable seconds to your cursed life! I will *still* crush you!
That bite had a *purpose,* you dull-witted brute! When I drain blood from a victim, I also can drain a portion of their *strength* and *add* it to my own.
I can FEEL your blood making me *bigger*--and much *stronger!*
Hah! No one is *ever* a match for Mister-- *HURG!*

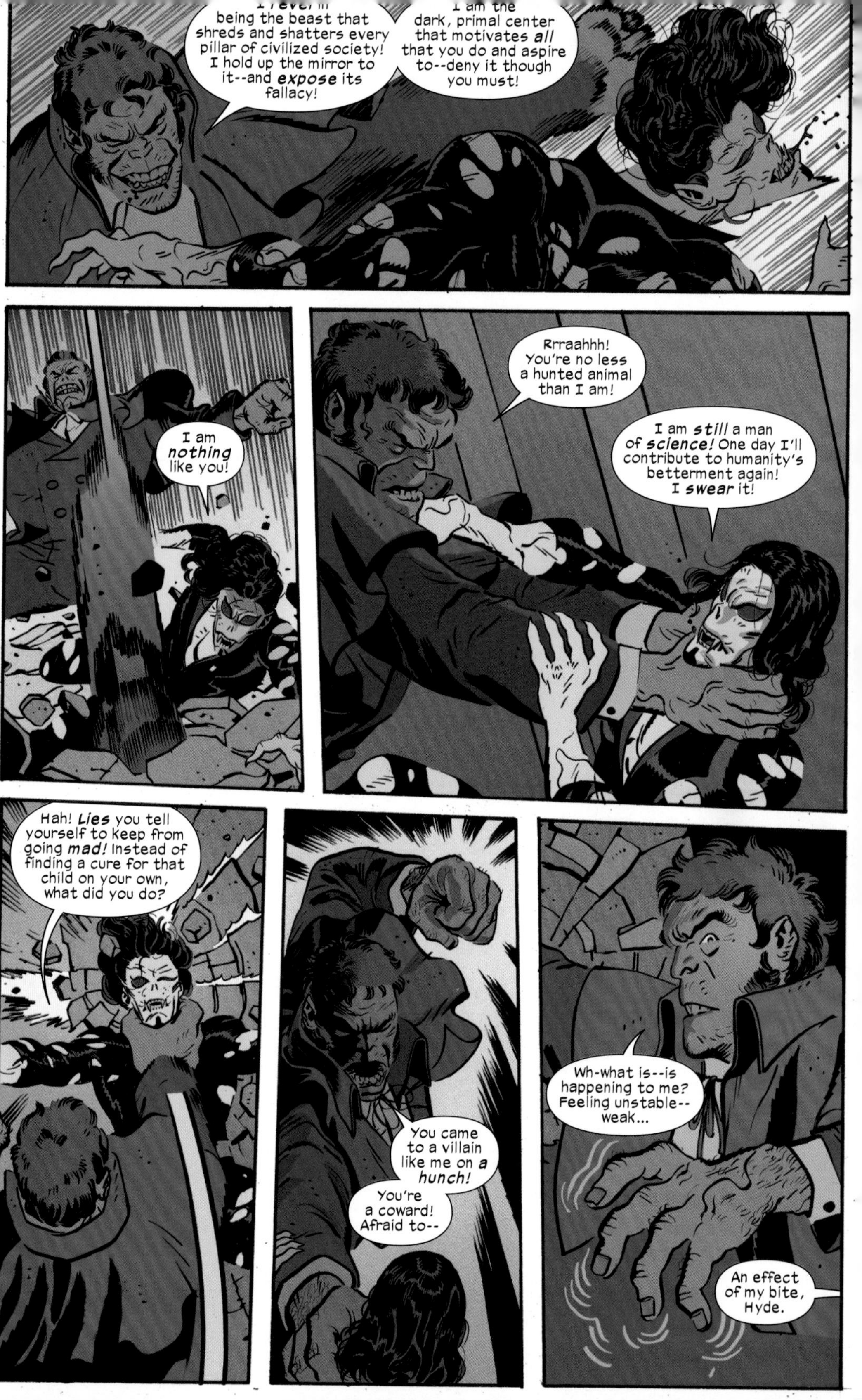
being the beast that shreds and shatters every pillar of civilized society! I hold up the mirror to it--and *expose* its fallacy!
I am the dark, primal center that motivates *all* that you do and aspire to--deny it though you must!
I am *nothing* like you!
Rrraahhh! You're no less a hunted animal than I am!
I am *still* a man of *science!* One day I'll contribute to humanity's betterment again! I *swear* it!
Hah! *Lies* you tell yourself to keep from going *mad!* Instead of finding a cure for that child on your own, what did you do?
You came to a villain like me on a *hunch!*
You're a coward! Afraid to--
Wh-what is--is happening to me? Feeling unstable--weak...
An effect of my bite, Hyde.

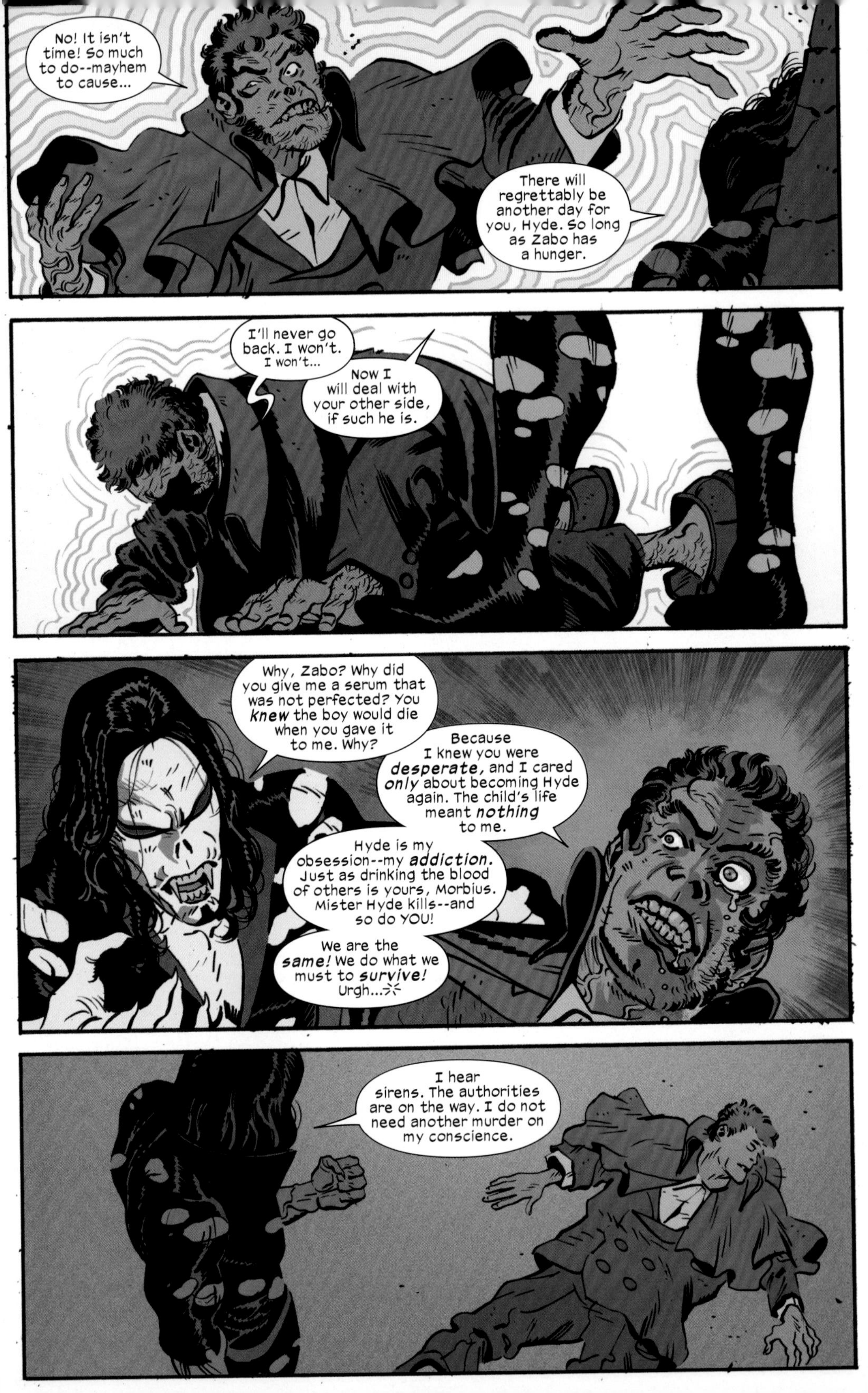
No! It isn't time! So much to do--mayhem to cause...
There will regrettably be another day for you, Hyde. So long as Zabo has a hunger.
I'll never go back. I won't. I won't...
Now I will deal with your other side, if such he is.
Why, Zabo? Why did you give me a serum that was not perfected? You *knew* the boy would die when you gave it to me. Why?
Because I knew you were *desperate,* and I cared *only* about becoming Hyde again. The child's life meant *nothing* to me.
Hyde is my obsession--my *addiction.* Just as drinking the blood of others is yours, Morbius. Mister Hyde kills--and so do YOU!
We are the *same!* We do what we must to *survive!* Urgh...
I hear sirens. The authorities are on the way. I do not need another murder on my conscience.

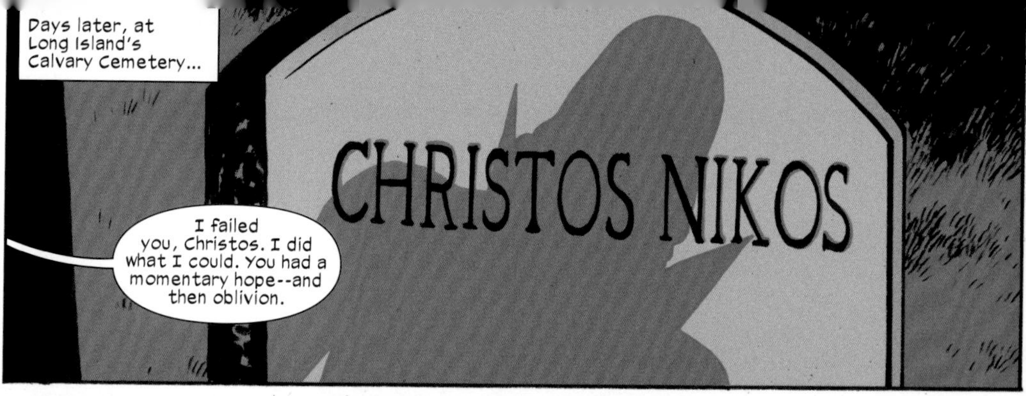
Days later, at Long Island's Calvary Cemetery...
CHRISTOS NIKOS
I failed you, Christos. I did what I could. You had a momentary hope--and then oblivion.

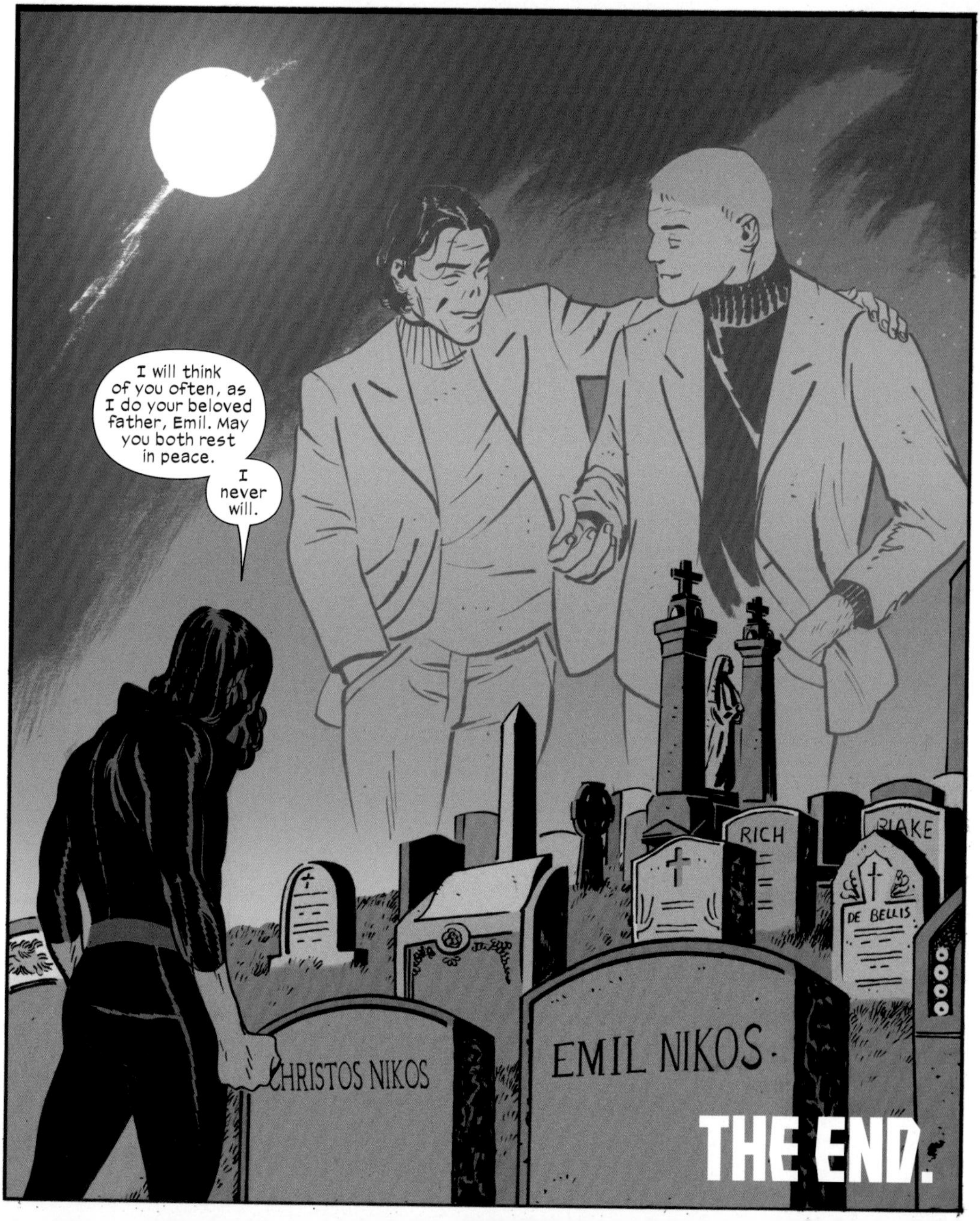
I will think of you often, as I do your beloved father, Emil. May you both rest in peace.
I never will.
RICH
DE BELLIS
CHRISTOS NIKOS
EMIL NIKOS
THE END.

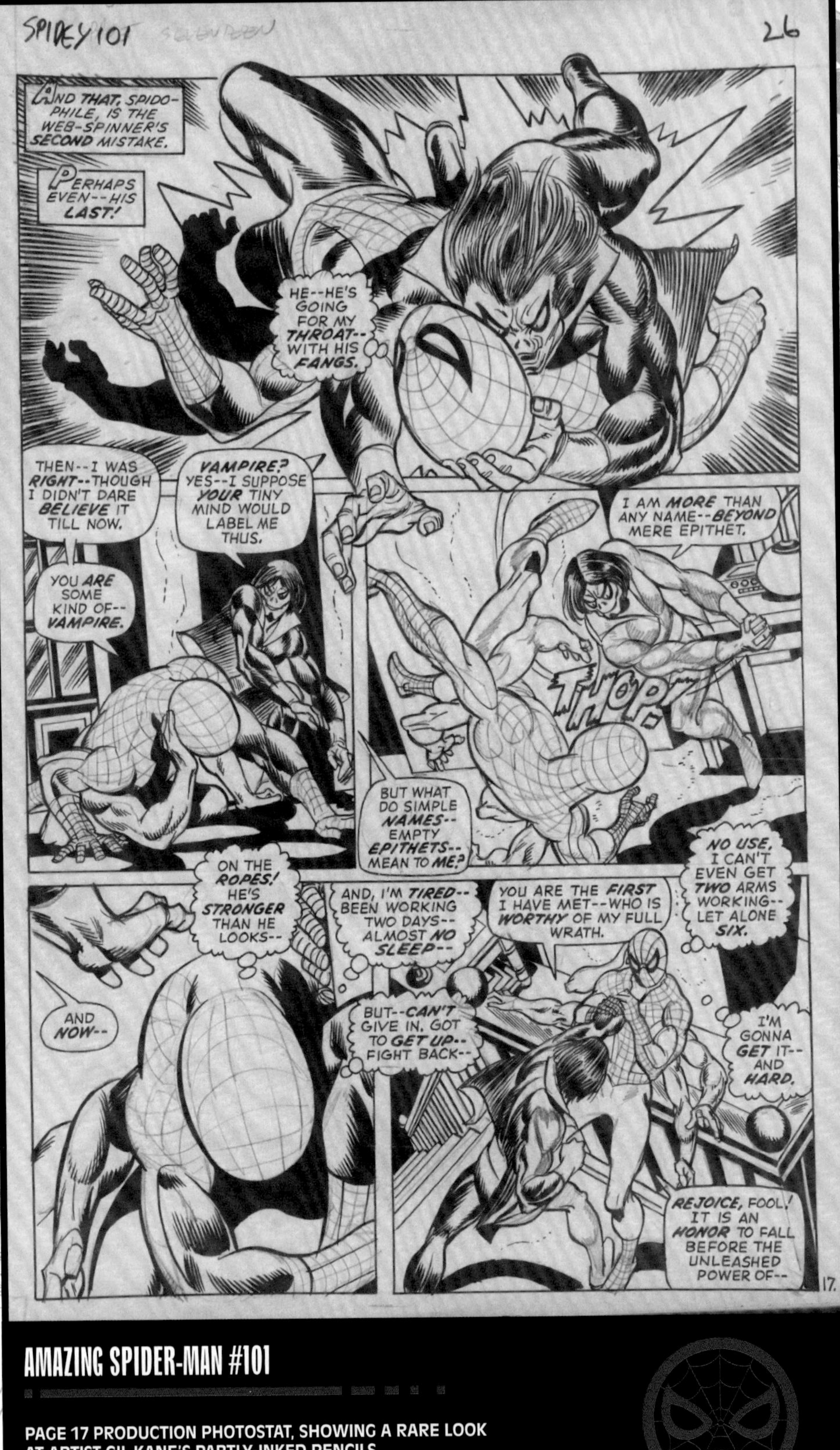
SPIDEY 101
26
AND THAT, SPIDOPHILE, IS THE WEB-SPINNER'S SECOND MISTAKE.
PERHAPS EVEN--HIS LAST!
HE--HE'S GOING FOR MY THROAT--WITH HIS FANGS.
THEN--I WAS RIGHT--THOUGH I DIDN'T DARE BELIEVE IT TILL NOW.
YOU ARE SOME KIND OF--VAMPIRE.
VAMPIRE? YES--I SUPPOSE YOUR TINY MIND WOULD LABEL ME THUS.
I AM MORE THAN ANY NAME--BEYOND MERE EPITHET.
THOP!
BUT WHAT DO SIMPLE NAMES--EMPTY EPITHETS--MEAN TO ME?
ON THE ROPES! HE'S STRONGER THAN HE LOOKS--
AND, I'M TIRED--BEEN WORKING TWO DAYS--ALMOST NO SLEEP--
AND NOW--
BUT--CAN'T GIVE IN. GOT TO GET UP--FIGHT BACK--
YOU ARE THE FIRST I HAVE MET--WHO IS WORTHY OF MY FULL WRATH.
NO USE. I CAN'T EVEN GET TWO ARMS WORKING--LET ALONE SIX.
I'M GONNA GET IT--AND HARD.
REJOICE, FOOL! IT IS AN HONOR TO FALL BEFORE THE UNLEASHED POWER OF--
17.

AMAZING SPIDER-MAN #101

PAGE 17 PRODUCTION PHOTOSTAT, SHOWING A RARE LOOK AT ARTIST GIL KANE'S PARTLY-INKED PENCILS

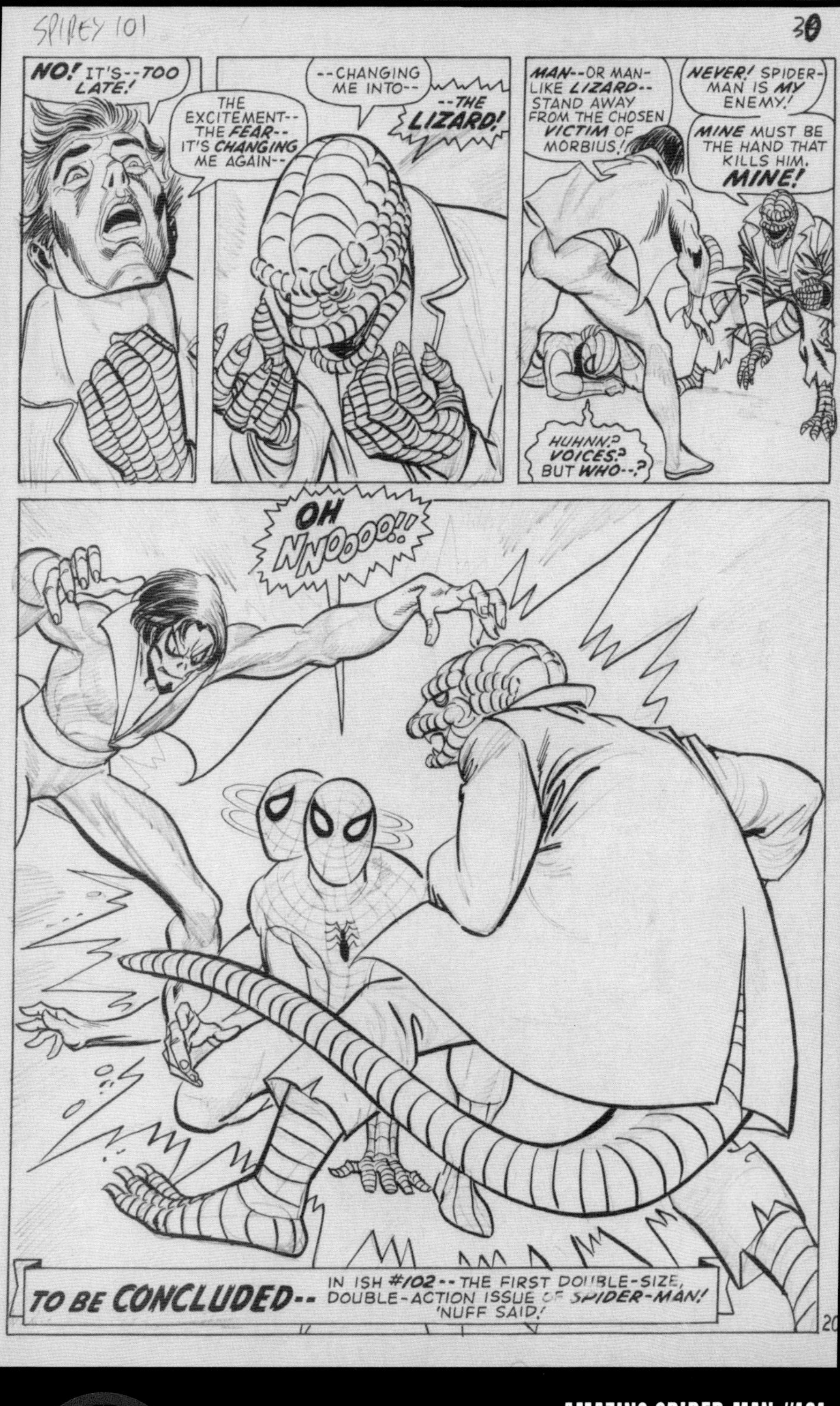
SPIDEY 101
30
NO! IT'S--TOO LATE!
THE EXCITEMENT--THE FEAR--IT'S CHANGING ME AGAIN--
--CHANGING ME INTO--
--THE LIZARD!
MAN--OR MAN-LIKE LIZARD--STAND AWAY FROM THE CHOSEN VICTIM OF MORBIUS!
NEVER! SPIDER-MAN IS MY ENEMY!
MINE MUST BE THE HAND THAT KILLS HIM. MINE!
HUHNN? VOICES? BUT WHO--?
OH NNOOOO!!
TO BE CONCLUDED-- IN ISH #102--THE FIRST DOUBLE-SIZE, DOUBLE-ACTION ISSUE OF SPIDER-MAN! 'NUFF SAID!
20

AMAZING SPIDER-MAN #101

PAGE 20 PRODUCTION PHOTOSTAT

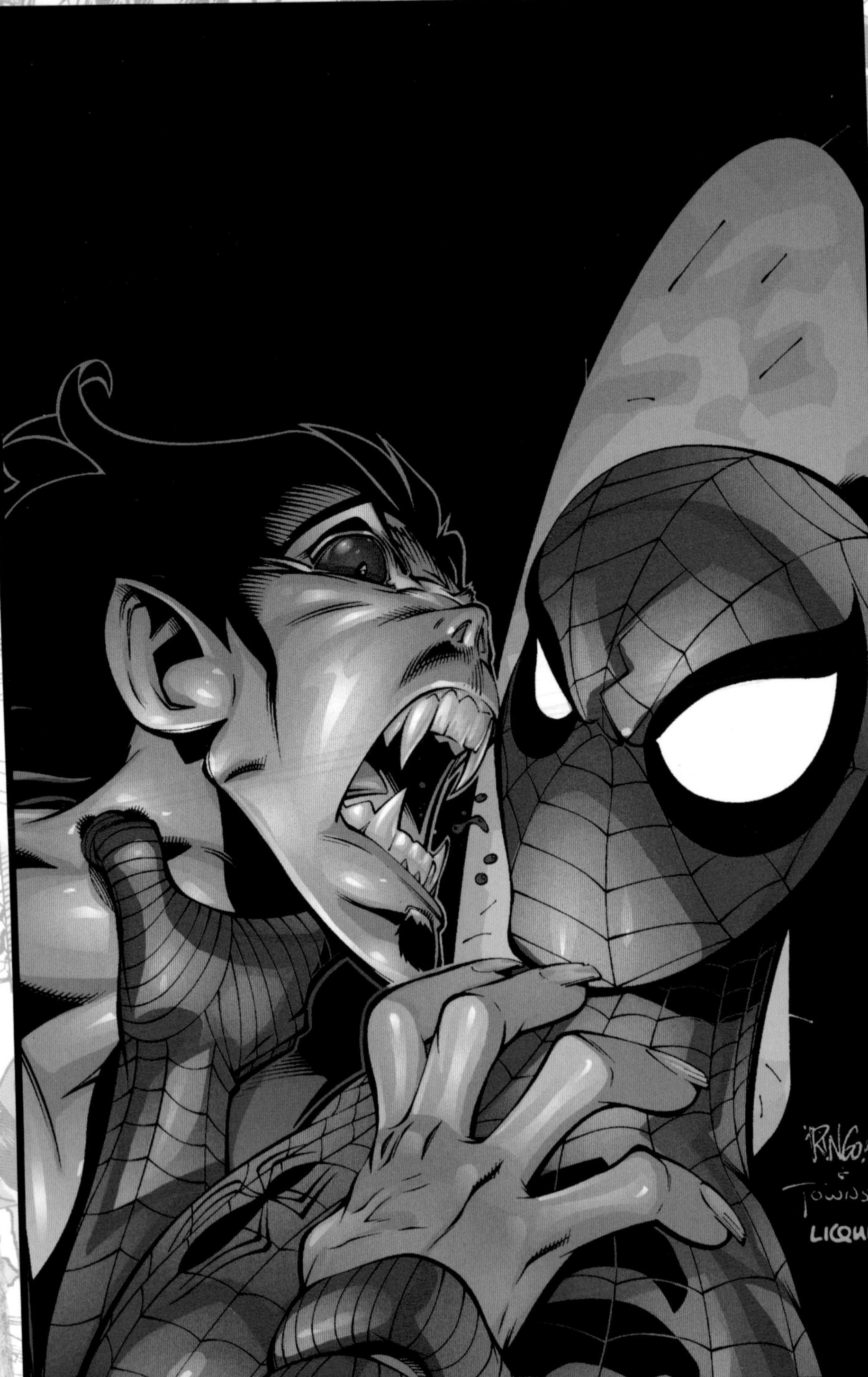
'RINGO!
&
TOWNSEND
LIQUID!

MARVEL SELECTS: SPIDER-MAN #2

REPRINTED *AMAZING SPIDER-MAN #101*. COVER BY MIKE WIERINGO, TIM TOWNSEND & LIQUID! GRAPHICS

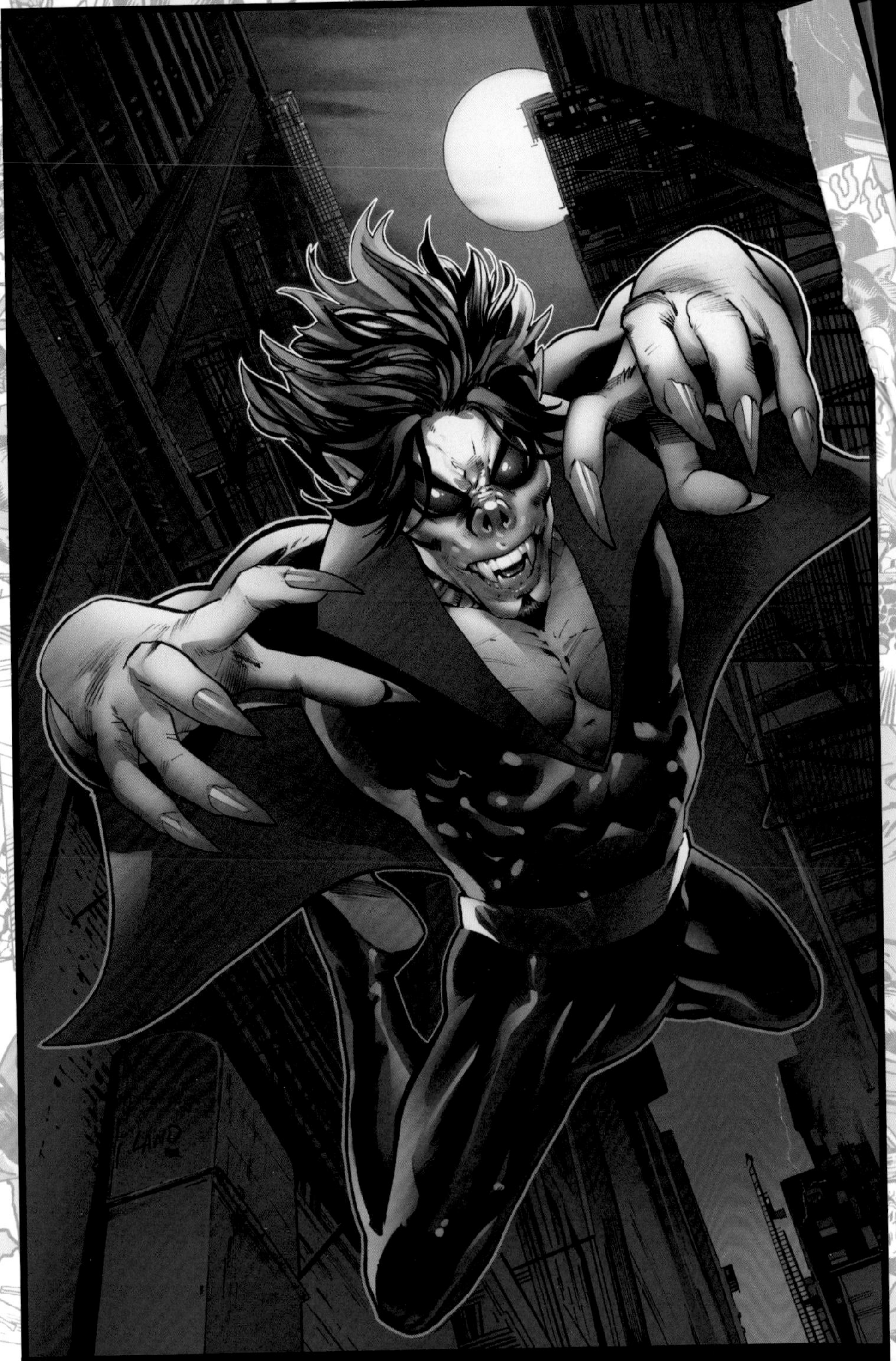

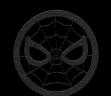

MORBIUS (2019) #1

VARIANT COVER BY GREG LAND & FRANK D'ARMATA

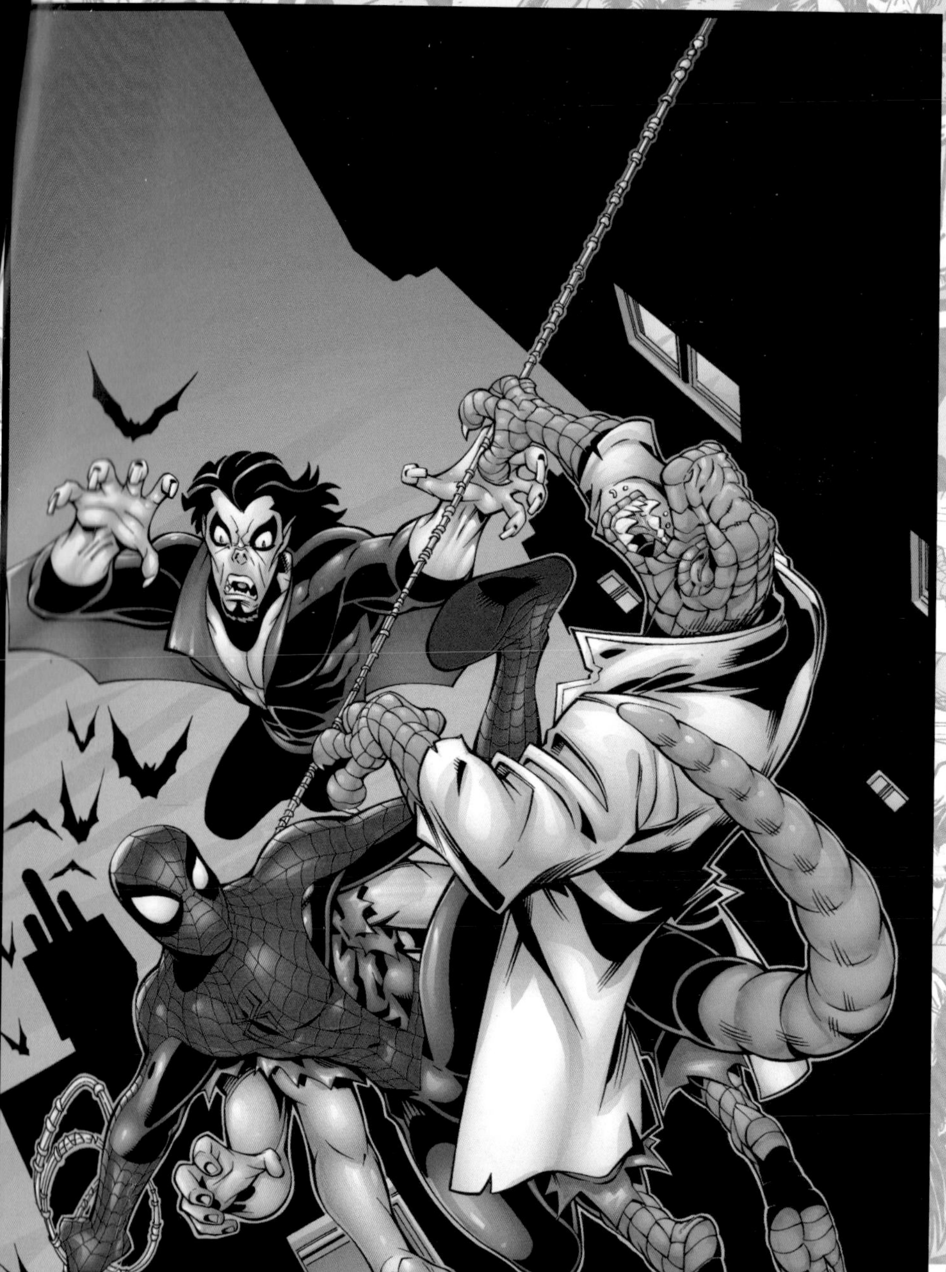

MARVEL SELECTS: SPIDER-MAN #3

REPRINTED *AMAZING SPIDER-MAN #102*. COVER BY MIKE WIERINGO, TIM TOWNSEND & LIQUID! GRAPHICS